in the mould of some of the classics.'

– Dorothy Koomson

'I highly recommend this moving, gripping story about a Nigerian family who starts a new life in England, only to find themselves cruelly torn apart.'

– Kitty Neale

'*Orphan Sisters* is wonderful, affecting and refreshing, with characters and a storyline that weave together flawlessly. An important slice of social history that I recommend without hesitation.'

– Alexandra Brown

Lola Jaye has penned four novels and a self-help book. Her work has been translated into several languages, included Korean, German and Serbian.

She grew up in South London, and has also lived in Nigeria and America. She admits to watching too much TV, but firmly believes it enhances her writing. She even taught a class on it!

Keep up to date with Lola via: her website, www.lolajaye.com, or on Twitter, Instagram and Facebook.

Wartime Sweethearts

LOLA JAYE

EBURY
PRESS

First published by Ebury Press in 2019

1 3 5 7 9 10 8 6 4 2

Ebury Press, an imprint of Ebury Publishing
20 Vauxhall Bridge Road,
London SW1V 2SA

Ebury Press is part of the Penguin Random House group of companies
whose addresses can be found at global.penguinrandomhouse.com

Penguin
Random House
UK

www.penguin.co.uk

A CIP catalogue record for this book is available from the British Library

ISBN 9781785036378

Typeset in 10.54/13.33 pt Times LT Std
by Integra Software Services Pvt. Ltd, Pondicherry

Printed and bound in Great Britain by Clays Ltd, Elcograf S.p.A.

Penguin Random House is committed to a sustainable future for
our business, our readers and our planet. This book is made from
Forest Stewardship Council® certified paper.

For Nanzo

BOOK ONE

Rose and Flora

Chapter One

1944

She had never experienced this type of pain before.

'Is the baby all right?' she said in between deepened breaths and a succession of quick pants. Wasn't the pain part supposed to be over by now? Why was she feeling as if she still needed to push something heavy out of her?

When she was little, she'd accidentally walked in on Mrs Bunting giving birth next door. Rose had been mesmerised at the aftermath of bright red blood splattered across the bed sheets and a fully formed, yet purple and reddened baby wailing in its mother's arms. The sight of something called the afterbirth, pooling out of her neighbour's nether regions a little while later, was not what she'd expected either because no one had actually mentioned that part. Perhaps this was what was next for her too – she just couldn't believe how much pain she'd endured so far, or that this beautifully formed, wailing infant now being tended to by her sister Flora, as Marigold, the oldest of the three, looked on, had actually come from her. In the blurred lines between pain and exhaustion, Rose was fighting pangs of envy at the time they'd already got to spend with the baby. Her first child. A little girl! She couldn't wait to be alone with her and stare into her perfect face. Absorb every single inch of this new person she'd got to know over the last eight months while safely cocooned in her stomach. She'd only managed a few seconds of a glimpse when Flora had placed her onto her chest right after she'd first entered this world. Their heartbeats had instantly connected and she felt an intoxication of love for this little being who had bombarded its way into her life at a time when the outside world had felt so uncertain.

'She is a beauty!' encouraged Marigold, standing at the end of Rose's bent legs, an uncharacteristic smile spread all over her wide face. The earlier embarrassment at her sisters viewing parts of her she herself had never seen, had long since disappeared. She'd never felt more grateful for their presence nor more at ease. Marigold had already birthed two of her own as well as taking in a couple of evacuees at the start of the war, while Flora was just a natural at being organised; the clever one of the family. 'Got a good pair of lungs on her too!' said Marigold.

'Time to give this beauty a nice clean and you can hold her,' said Flora in that voice adults seemed to have hidden most of the time, yet regularly pulled out for babies and little children. Perhaps Rose herself would talk that way to the little one from now on as she fed her, combed her hair (when she had some) and bathed her. Rose couldn't wait for these instances that would define her new role as a mother. At the age of thirty-one and already married for six years, she'd been waiting for this moment her entire life. This was her chance to do better as a wife and finally be able to prove to Pete, her husband, that she wasn't a bad wife for not giving him a child or whatever other reason he would come up with. He'd often remind her he could find better among the dead cows at the knackers yard where he worked.

He probably could.

She wasn't that much of a good wife. She sometimes burnt the food even though they were living on precious government rations and at times let the dust settle on the sideboards where their wedding photo and ornaments took pride of place. Pete hated dust, said it made him cough. When one day he placed both hands around her neck until she couldn't help but splutter in panic, he simply said, 'Now you know what it feels like,' before releasing her.

She was a bad wife, but this, motherhood, she could do. She'd lost her mother Lillian at a very young age and she and her sisters and brother had been raised by a succession of aunties and neighbours while her father, Albert, sat in a chair smoking a pipe and stroking his moustache, lamenting the loss of the only woman he'd ever loved. Just like he still did every single day of his miserable life. Out of a line-up of three girls and the much longed for son, Donald, who finally came along and, with him, a change that would affect their lives forever, Rose could admit she'd been the favoured one. Flora the middle girl was the forever spinster with 'too many big ideas' and 'just not ladylike enough', according to their father, with Marigold the plain and 'big' one. At least Rose was looked at as the one 'pretty enough' to secure a decent husband who would earn enough money to contribute to the family pot. Rose had wanted that too. Hoping at least for a husband who could be a better father than hers and perhaps be more like her little brother Donald who at least took an interest in her life. What she'd ended up with was a man who did odd jobs when he could, refused to contribute anything to the Baker family and stayed away at least three nights a week, showing up drunk and reeking of other women.

This baby was so important.

Five months ago, she'd stood between Pete and the wall, his hand tightened around her wrist, his thigh jammed in the space between her legs, his spittle landing on her cheek as he reeled off all the reasons why he should leave and never come back. Just like he usually did after a row. When, finally, she had landed him with the biggest reason of all – 'I'm having a baby, that's why!' – her eyes had stamped shut as she waited for what was next.

Instead, he'd gently pulled her into his arms, punching the air instead of her face and cheering with happiness. And for the next five months as the baby grew inside her, Pete began to behave differently; rubbing her swollen feet and letting her know almost every day that he had never loved her more. She thought – had believed – he would never hit her again and especially not with his baby inside her. So now it was only his words that stung and usually when he was too drunk to care. Marigold said this was good, an improvement, yet for Rose his words sometimes felt like punches.

Rose's new fear was that Pete would be upset the baby wasn't a boy. He may have said he didn't mind what she produced and wasn't fussed, but Pete said a lot of things. Having promised never to hit her again (many times but especially since she was pregnant), he'd recently succumbed with a sharp tug of her chestnut-coloured hair just after breakfast, the morning he left to work at the knackers yard four days ago.

'Look what you made me do!' he'd whined. Her hand had gently caressed the side of her head, she imagined would be a pinky red, as her other hand smoothed over her swollen belly. Thankfully, her baby was safe inside, moving around like normal. Seconds later, he was apologising as he pulled a pack of cigarettes and matches from his pocket. 'Anyway, you've got those meddling sisters of yours, you don't need me around. I don't know why you're moaning about me going away, anyway. Having a baby is a women's thing, so it's best I get back when it's all done and with a bit of cash in me pocket. You're both going to need feeding.' He lit the match and placed it to the tip of the cigarette. 'You've still got another month and I'll be back just before or on the dot. Don't you worry.'

He'd dragged on the cigarette as she imagined the instant joy she'd feel in stubbing it right into his cheek.

The sweet little mite was crying wildly now, a reassuring sound as Rose felt an enormous need to push again.

She screamed louder than she ever thought she could. Louder than when Pete had first struck her that second hour into their wedding. Louder than when he had 'accidentally' twisted her wrist when they had rowed about the woman at number twenty-three.

'Ahhhhhh!'

Marigold looked on, open-mouthed as Flora, always the most organised and sensible, placed the new baby into Marigold's arms.

'Please stop this pain – ahhhhhh!' Rose's screams were louder than when she'd been told her mother was never coming home after giving birth to Donald. What if a similar fate awaited her too? The thought had rushed through her mind many times and she was extremely angry with herself for not making it to the hospital on time for her own emergency. But as Marigold had pointed out helpfully or unhelpfully, their mother had died giving birth in a hospital anyway.

'Marigold, hold that baby tight over there,' said Flora with a warning tone to her voice. 'Something's happening here!'

Rose held her tears inside, the pain preventing such a luxury. This wasn't meant to be happening. This was it. She too was about to go the way of their mother and never see her child again.

'Oh my … No … This can't be!' shouted Flora, her hands now embedded between her sister's legs.

'What?' screamed Rose, in between each desperate pant. The pain kept coming at her like a huge tank, she imagined. Steamrolling over her entire body and then backing up to do it all over again.

'Keep pushing!' urged Flora, her own face red with concentration.

Marigold moved closer, still clutching the baby. 'I don't believe this!'

'Someone tell me what's going on? Ahhhhh!' The pain seared through her with an intensity she had never known. Every part of her enlarged with pain.

'It's another one!' said Flora.

'Another what?' yelled Rose.

'It's twins!!'

Those final pushes were the toughest. The screams were the most intense and even though her eyes were stamped shut, Rose knew it was enough. She'd done it. She'd released a second baby into the world and she couldn't have been more surprised … or happier. Her tears of joy, instant as she opened her eyes, but when she clocked the expression locked on each of her sister's faces, her smile dropped.

'What is it? Is my baby okay?' She could only hear the cries of the first baby.

'It's a girl. Another girl.' Gone was the joy in Flora's voice heard only moments earlier with the arrival of the first child. Even Marigold looked miserable, but then again, Marigold was regularly unable to keep a smile for long.

'Can … can I see her? Why isn't she crying?'

'I'm … Err … I'm just going to sort her out here … Clean her up …'

Something in Flora's tone didn't sit right with Rose. Of her three siblings, she and Flora were the closest. Although Rose was only just over a year younger, Flora was the one she looked up to. She'd been the first girl in their family to finish school with good marks and the first one to get a job long before women were expected to as part of the war effort. She even spoke proper too and Rose had always wanted to be like Flora. Not a spinster … No, not that, but to possess her strength and fearless attitude. Yet, the expression on Flora's face was that of fear.

'Flora, what's that face for? What's wrong with my baby?'

The loud and healthy cry from baby number two was reassuring and timely.

'Nothing is wrong. There you go, a healthy pair of lungs.'

'You sure about that, Flora?' added Marigold, rocking baby number one, Iris, in her arms. Pete and Rose had already decided to name their baby Iris if it was a girl – in keeping with the flower theme of their family. For a boy, they had decided on Donald after her brother who was currently fighting the Jerries and who they hoped would soon be home.

'Is there something wrong with my baby? Please tell me!'

'Once I give her a bath, everything will be okay. Marigold, give Rose the first baby.'

Marigold appeared to be dumbstruck, her eyes fixated on the baby in Flora's arms.

'Marigold, give her the baby!'

'Iris. Her name is Iris,' said Rose.

'Give little Iris to her. Go on!'

Rose's fears quickly floated away as she once again held baby Iris against her tired body. The smell of her, the uniqueness of this moment, overwhelming and eclipsing any joy she had previously felt during her thirty-one years of life. In her arms was her very own child and a combination of her and Pete. Although the marriage had been a bit rocky of late, Iris was proof that everything had happened to lead her to now. This beautiful human being wrapped safely in her arms; this moment; this love. And she had two of these little blessings. Pete would love her so much after this. Their love would be rock solid and never, ever become fractured again. The love of two babies binding them together, forever.

'Can I see my little Lily, now?' the name rolled off her tongue effortlessly. Lily, a shortened version of their mother's name, seemed so very fitting.

'Lily … That's a great choice,' said Flora uneasily.

There seemed to be a private conference going on between her sisters with Lily being at the centre of it. As Rose listened to the reassuring sound of her first daughter's breath, she also longed for the second one. She wanted to be close to her and to be reassured of her existence.

As Flora spoke, the expression on her face was grave. 'I thought when I washed her, it would come off …'

'What would come off?'

'Her colouring.'

'What?'

'Maybe in a few days. It's probably a birth thing ... you know because she's the second one?'

Flora moved closer to the bed, a white sheet covering the unexpected second baby, Lily. Rose handed Marigold (herself looking as white as the sheet) baby Iris and held out her arms for Lily. She felt an intense rush of warmth as Flora placed the baby into her arms. Were they identical? Would they have similar personalities or be totally different? Her sore and aching body managed to embrace a feeling of joy as she imagined the future, which now appeared amazing and full of sparkling possibilities. The country may have been at war, but in that moment Rose could not have asked for more as she settled Lily into her arms. She opened the sheet, excited about seeing her baby for the very first time.

Instead, her breath caught in her throat.

Her eyes widened, her breathing accelerated.

She couldn't speak. Not a word. If not for the presence of two babies, there would not have been a single sound in that room.

Then Marigold spoke. 'If I hadn't seen this myself I would have said the devil himself had come into the house this morning and did this. What. The. Hell. Is. That!?'

My Dearest Love,

I can still feel the harshness of the ground beneath my bare feet as I run towards my mama, as she calls us in to eat. I miss the smell of fresh cornbread and the sound of the birds chirping me awake in the morning. I also miss the sky as blue as the sea with the sunshine above the mammoth trees draped in Spanish moss as I trace the sweat dripping down to my cheek. Yes, this land of yours, Great Britain, has the birds, but it rarely has the sunlight.

Yet, one day, when I thought it was going to be just another grey day, the sun appeared in all its splendour. It was the day we arrived in the town of Alderberry and all those people were so welcoming to us. I couldn't be sure if I and the other seven guys were part of that welcome, but it appeared we were. To every one of the British who came to greet us, ask our names and thank us for 'helping get rid of the Jerries', I was just another American soldier walking the cobbled streets like they were reclaiming the land of their forefathers!

I admit it. I allowed the clapping and stares to go to my head. It wasn't something I was used to. The staring yes, but not the clapping. Not in America and not among my comrades either. It made me feel like a hero. Cornel told me to tone it down a little and put my chest back in. Maybe I should have. But for once I wasn't about to obey any orders.

'We ain't like them,' he said.

'Well, to these folks, we are!'

Cornel was my best friend in the army. We looked the same. And while we were stationed in areas far away from home and everything I had ever known we had a type of safety in numbers, strategy in defence of some of the other men, like Riker. Riker was from Augusta, Georgia and not too far from where I grew up in Savannah. And it's because of this that he hated me the most. The guys from the North weren't like Riker and his boys. They treated us well enough, didn't adhere to Jim Crow, but they sometimes called us spooks or Nigger. I didn't mind much ... well I did ... of course I did, but I was powerless in the face of it all. Just like I was when put on duties that really had nothing to do with fighting the Germans. I wanted to get in there and do what I had been sent to do – not clean out the bathrooms. But it wasn't worth a dime to say anything. Cornel was right and we were not the same in the eyes of Riker and his men or the law of our own country. So, if in Great Britain, it seemed like we were men – then I was going to enjoy that feeling for as long as I could.

Riker and the others truly believed they were movie stars. Big time operators stopping to hand out gifts to the ladies and kids. If the lady was pretty, she would get a little more than some cigarettes or candy. More like some nylons and a promise to 'see her later'. I'd never known of a man to get a date so easily! Back home, I'd had to patiently wait six weeks for just a kiss with sweet Augustine Jewson! How Riker and the other guys behaved was not my way and, even if it were, I and the other seven guys who looked like me would not be allowed to partake anyway. Instead, we simply 'minded our business' as Cornel would say. Content to enjoy the way you folks pronounced words like 'water' and to give out extra candy bars to anyone who even smiled our way.

As we stood in and among the last of the gathered crowds, my mouth dry with all the talking and laughing with the British folk, one of the seven said something about going to a bar or a 'pub', for lunch. It was called the Black Dog and I found this name a little unfortunate, but I was assured by one of the local men that the name referred to a real black dog that used to gather sheep in the area. As usual, Cornel was being negative, saying – 'Let's just all go back to base. I ain't going in no establishment called the Black Dog!' – five of the guys ignored him and carried on in the direction of the pub.

'You coming?' asked Cornel.

'This isn't home, we're in England now. The folks here have been nothing but cordial, nice and welcoming.'

'I don't know where you living but back at the base, ain't nothing changed.'

He was right about that. Men like Riker were still determined to keep up what they were used to back at home regardless of where we had landed – and drinking in the same area as them was not the done thing. Some drinking establishments had already agreed to rotating passes so that we Negro soldiers were never in on the same day as white soldiers. Not everyone in this village had agreed to that and this made me happy inside. It felt like England and its people were not going to be hostile towards us and that was great. But of course that made no difference to men like Riker. Of course, I was about to follow Cornel back to base …

But something or someone stopped me. I looked up again and there it was. A kind of vision that I hoped was real.

'You go on up ahead, and I'll meet you.' That was a lie.

Cornel was looking sour but I was not about to leave. Not at that moment. Maybe not ever, because I had just laid eyes on you, for the very first time.

Back home in Savannah, it wasn't hard for me to ignore the look of a woman – a white woman – because simply put, to look back could get me in serious trouble, even killed. Yet thousands of miles away, here in a British town called Alderberry, I tried once again to pretend that my way of life back home was far behind. I had to do that in combat anyway because I just couldn't afford to think about those I had left behind. Yet still, I, William Burrell, dared to look back at you. I dared to catch your pretty smile. A moment, which locked me into a time and space I never wanted to come out of. You were the first white woman I had ever looked at in that way before. Maybe even the first woman. Not even Augustine Jewson or Marie A. Rhodes or Viola Jackson had held my time in such a way. I knew that image of you would remain in my mind like a flower in a bed of concrete. I mean no disrespect when I say this, but you weren't Hollywood glamour like Gene Tierney, with your dressed-down flat shoes, your hair neatly styled, but with tendrils falling messily into your eyes, that to be honest did look a little tired. Yet, I could see they still sparkled with something.

And looking at you gave me a sense of peace within the chaos.

A calm I didn't know I had missed. A sense of acceptance in a world where I was risking my life for a country that failed to even see me as a man.

'Hello there,' you said. I adored that accent as well as your brazenness. I'd overheard Riker and the others talking a lot about British women being very forward and willing to 'give it up to a GI' on the first night if alcohol and 'fags' were involved. I knew you'd be different. I just knew.

'Why, hello. I'm William Burrell. How are you today, ma'am?'

'I'm fine, thank you, Mr Burrell.'

'You can call me Willie.'

'William will be fine.'

And there it was. Instant confirmation that what you already saw in me was more than what I had been used to. Men younger than I often referred to me, a grown man, as 'boy' while others just called me Willie. To me, Willie only ever sounded right coming from the lips of my mama and daddy and here stood you, beautiful sweet you, calling me by my full name and this just confirmed that everything I had felt in the ninety or so seconds we'd known one another was valid. It was real. You were not part of my wishful imagination.

'May I ask you your name?' I asked you.

A firm nudge almost knocked me off my feet.

'You should not be doing this,' whispered Cornel into my ear.

'I thought you were going back to base,' I said, momentarily out of my trance.

'I was until I saw you trying to commit a suicide.'

'Just being friendly to the lady.'

'Then be friendly to everyone, the same. Don't put trouble on yourself. It's not worth it. She ain't worth it.'

As Cornel moved away, I turned back and you were gone. Luckily, my gaze found you slowly moving away from the crowds, that smile and then your hand telling me to follow.

I stopped, remembering Cornell's words along with thirty years of my own memories locked away in my head and refusing to leave me. My heart beat fast. I was in another world. In England. They didn't do that here, did they?

14

I followed anyway and then you stopped and turned around, smiling at me once again, luring me further into your world and possibly a whole lot of trouble.

Soon, only a muddy ground and an abundance of trees surrounded us. Lush greenery and the absence of others. There was just you and I.

What if you screamed?

'My name is Rose.'

I walked closer to you, so slowly and giving you a chance to change your mind, tell me this had all been a mistake. I should have thought about the possibility that this could be a trap but I knew you wouldn't do that to me. I already trusted you. I already knew you. So, with my hand stretched out, I moved closer knowing as soon as our palms touched for the very first time, you'd become everything I never knew I needed.

Chapter Two

1943

'I don't usually go around dancing with strange men, you know.'

The small band was playing Glen Miller, she assumed, rather well. Rose had never been much of a one for music but when the Merryford Hall had advertised a tea dance and everyone was invited, she couldn't resist suggesting William come along and bring his friends. Surprisingly, he was the only soldier from his group to turn up.

'I'm not strange, Rose. We've been talking for weeks now. '

'Six days, actually.'

'Seems longer. I guess for me, anyway.'

'I know what you mean.' It was as if they had known one another for a lifetime. She had already felt comfortable in confiding so much, albeit not everything. William had a way about him that instantly put her at ease and this was something she was not used to. In his presence she need never look over her shoulder, but straight at him, sinking into those almond-shaped eyes.

'I can't quite believe I'm here dancing with you … in front of everyone,' he said.

'John here enjoys being a defiant old coot.' Rose smiled. 'All this about never bowing to the Yanks with this "coloureds on

Tuesday, whites on Monday" lark. He says, if you can't all dance together then bugger off!'

'I like the British spirit.'

'You're here helping us lot … the least we can do is treat you with a bit of respect. Besides …' She moved closer to his ear. 'You boys are so much more polite than the others … the white ones. You treat us like ladies.'

'It's nothing more than you deserve. I've watched my daddy treat my mama like a queen. Always said I'd do the same when I met the woman I could fall in love with.'

'Love?' she said quietly, a mixture of fear and excitement swirling around inside of her. They had known each other for a week and she already knew what type of man he was. Generous, clever, handsome, of course, and the exact opposite of *him*.

Every time they were together she sensed his need for her: the energy radiating from him despite the thickness of his uniform and regardless of the barrier he seemed to be more comfortable with when they were out in public.

She longed to be alone with William again. Like that first day they'd talked for hours away from prying eyes and among the trees and hilly terrain. They had remained locked into a world that included no one but themselves; no war, only peace. Just the two of them in an entity they had constructed and as far from reality – her reality – as could be. William was such a good listener too and surprisingly articulate. She really hadn't even expected him to speak English, let alone better English than anyone she knew! And with William behaving like such a gentleman, while the white GIs were rather loud and a bit showy, her assumptions had been rocked. Rose felt an unwelcome chill run through her body because something inside of her knew it wasn't right to have such ideas about people – especially those she had never even met.

But finally, she had met a man who had read more books than she could ever hope to and was far more educated than her entire family put together! Indeed, she had started to watch her Ps and Qs when she was around him, embarrassed at her casual use of quick slang while his American accent seemed to take time over the syllables. Indeed, she'd heard many of his close comrades speak and most sounded nothing like him. She never actually understood a word they said, which was fine as they never spoke to her anyway.

William was surely one of a kind, yet he never made her feel small like others in her life continued to do. A father who despite calling her his favourite had never forgiven her for marrying a man who didn't earn enough to support him and a husband who often saw her as less than human. William's presence in her life had the power to pull her away from it all, allowing for a brazenness she'd never known was possible.

It had been months since her loving husband had pawned her wedding ring for a booze-fuelled weekend she hadn't been invited to. He'd promised to return it, and over the months Rose began to care less and less whether she ever saw it again. The ring's disappearance had become the perfect comment on the state of the marriage. So the indent in her finger was now less noticeable. To the naked eye, she was a single woman, never married and free to see anyone she liked. Free to possibly fall in love with another man. Of course she'd planned none of this. Catching the eye of a dashing soldier who looked nothing like her. She'd never even spoken to a non-white person before in her life, had always been told by Pete not to mix with any if she saw them – not that she ever did. She'd simply been in Alderberry to support her dad and yet there she was, unable to get this man out of her mind.

She had thought about him every single day. Feeling not unlike a teenager embarking on a first love. Only this was much more serious and the stakes so much higher.

Now with each step on the dancefloor, she was running out of time. Soon she'd have to return home, back to her daily life and away from this fantasy. Her dad had been feeling better for days now and Marigold was able to cope with him alone. It would soon be time for Rose to go home back to Arkenwood – fifteen miles away from Alderberry.

'There's still a lot I don't know about you, William. What are you hiding from me?' she said as they moved away from the band.

'I should ask you the same thing. I mean, a stunningly beautiful woman like you should be married by now. Why hasn't anyone snapped you up?' He pulled out a wooden chair.

'Stunning, me?' She blushed, hoping she wasn't as crimson as she felt. He sat and faced her.

'Yes, you. Only you,' he said firmly, his beautifully shaped eyes drawing her further into his world.

'I'm just a girl from Alderberry, waiting on her prince,' she lied.

'Ah … I see …'

'There was a man once. But he died,' she said, her eyes to the floor so he would not see the truth.

'I'm so sorry—'

'No, don't be, I mean … I don't really like to talk about it …' It had been surprisingly easy to say the words, because in truth, her husband, the Pete she wanted, had died years ago.

That evening they sneaked away from the tea dance and to their 'spot'. William was first to leave, so as to dampen suspicion, with Rose following ten minutes behind. She leaned against the bark of a tree. Three of the buttons were missing from the yellow floral dress handed down from an aunt. She hoped William hadn't noticed. She wanted to look grand for him, because she knew that deep down she wasn't good enough for him.

William had brought a blanket, which he laid out for Rose to sit on. He threw a twig back onto the ground and began to speak once again about some book or other, which had influenced him. She leaned over and simply pressed her lips softly against his. With such softness came the weight of desire. A tingling that appeared up and down her body. A feeling she could not ever remember experiencing before. She felt beautiful, desirable … loved. And by a man she had known for a matter of days. Leaving her with a need to repeat the sensation even though it was most certainly wrong and went against everything she believed in.

'I wasn't expecting that,' he said with a smile.

'Neither was I really—'

Before she could finish, his full lips were on hers again, his hands squeezing her shoulders firmly, yet with a gentleness she was not used to. She felt from William a slight resistance that meant nothing to her because, in truth, she'd wanted him since the first day they had laid eyes on one another. The kiss, that glorious kiss, finally convincing her he felt the same way. None of what happened next was planned: Rose falling back onto the blanket, William lying on top of her, his lapel catching in her hair.

'Ouch!' she said, playfully.

He sprang back. 'I'm so sorry, Rose. Are you okay?'

'I'm only joking. I'm fine.' She had been momentarily touched by his concern. It meant more than he could ever know. 'Now kiss me, again, William Burrell,' she said. So, their lips locked, this time with more passion, more meaning, the words 'None of this was planned' swimming around guiltily in her head.

'Are you sure?' asked William, hoarsely, forever the gentleman.

'I want this,' she said. Indeed, Rose Katherine Jones, née Baker, had never felt more alive with passion in her entire life. She wanted this more than ever.

Then a sudden pull of rejection as he stood up abruptly. 'I can't, Rose … I just can't.'

She sat up. 'It's me, isn't it?'

He turned to her. 'No … of course it isn't you. You're beautiful. I just can't.'

Now, eight months later, and a day after she became a mother for the first time, she just wished she were dead.

Twenty-four hours ago she'd given birth to twins who looked as if they had originated from different countries let alone the same family. One had white skin like hers, the other, more a brown colour. One was bald, the other with a full head of shiny black curls. Perhaps Rose was simply floating within a dream, a nightmare, and none of this was actually real. Perhaps if she pinched herself she'd wake up and she'd still be pregnant, awaiting the birth of one white, perfect little girl. Just like the one she had been imagining over the last seven or so months. That little girl had a full head of blonde hair and beautiful blue eyes and despite what the government had advised about wearing hand-me-downs and utility clothing, she'd dressed her up in the prettiest of dresses, some of which she had already made. Beautiful bows tied at the back and in the brightest of colours.

Please wake up, Rose! Please wake up!

She'd pinched herself vigorously, just like the day they'd said her mother wasn't coming home from the hospital; just like the first time Pete had slapped her. Like those moments of complete and unending shock, this was real. She had given birth to two babies; one white, the other was not …

She gazed down at the beautiful, but brown-looking child in her arms. She had not held onto Iris much, choosing to give more of her affection to the already ostracised Lily – as if she felt that their time together would be limited. In what world would they be allowed to live together? Even within the confines of her bedroom there were already clues to what awaited this child on the outside. Marigold had refused to even touch Lily. Only Flora at times would give the little girl a cuddle, change her and hold her while Rose tended to Iris. Her sisters never pressed her for an explanation. She wasn't sure she even had one.

The toll of childbirth allowed her to drift in and out of sleep. If not for these two babies, she would have wished to fall asleep and never wake up. Rose had no idea of what to do or to say. She simply turned her back to her sisters, sobbing into her pillow.

Three days after giving birth, Flora sat on the edge of her bed.

'I don't know what to say to you, Rose,' she said.

'Can't none of your fancy books explain this?'

With the blank stare from Flora, Rose indeed knew she was doomed. Her sister knew everything and was usually the one to be able to fix what was broken. Whether it was her heart when she'd caught her first love kissing another girl at fifteen or when she twisted her ankle running after a chicken, Flora had fixed everything for her and if she didn't know what to do about this, then Rose was doomed.

One long week in and Rose had settled into a manageable routine with her babies. She tended to one as soon as she cried (which would usually be followed by the other crying). She enjoyed the closeness of breastfeeding, a feeling she could not describe, but a moment in which she felt powerful at being able to nourish her children. A feeling short-lived when she once again took notice of their stark differences.

Flora was able to purchase whatever provisions she needed, as the majority of the shopkeepers in the area knew the circumstances and accepted the ration book on Rose's behalf. Staying inside after the birth of a child was normal so no one, least of all her dad, had become suspicious. Marigold had been the same after the birth of her children, yet they all knew that the circumstances were different. Rose could never be seen with Lily. Not ever.

Pete was due home in less than three weeks. Thoughts of panic rose up in her mind, whenever she thought of him, preventing sleep even when Flora took the babies into the other room to give her a break. He could, of course, return home earlier than planned. Not that he ever would because she heavily suspected he was somewhere entertaining another woman. She'd once hoped the appearance of their own little family would have changed her husband's heart. Make him stop the hurt, make him realise what he had at home and finally give her the love she had yearned for her entire life. Now, staring down at this baby, with its dark skin and the type of hair she could not begin to fathom, she knew that Lily's inclusion in their lives would make that impossible. He may even kill her or kill them both and then Iris would be left motherless just like she had been.

Yet how could she convince him of what had happened if she herself didn't know? How was it possible to give birth to the children of two men? Even Iris didn't look much like Pete, her nose slightly broader than the rest of the family's noses, her piercing green eyes already noticeable and in the shape of almonds. Lily had the same shape eyes but hers were brown to go with her skin. Nothing about these babies made any sort of sense. Her children made no sense. Her shoulders began to heave with the weight of sobs as she picked up Lily and held her close, followed by a gentle cry from Iris in her wicker basket.

Flora appeared immediately.

'Rose, it's been a couple of weeks. When are you going to get out of bed?' She gently pulled Iris out from the basket and, as usual, Rose felt a surge of longing for her. 'At least go for a walk.'

'I've just given birth to two babies; I'm not about to start jumping all over the place. Maybe if you had some of your own—' She immediately caught the look on her beloved sister's face. 'I'm sorry, Flora.'

'If getting married and having kids brings all this hassle, you can keep it.'

'What happened to me, Flora? Tell me.'

'I have never read about anything like this. I should try and find some science books … Look …' She sat on the edge of the bed with baby Iris snug in her arms. 'Did you have relations with that GI I used to see you with? The handsome one?'

'You thought he was handsome?'

'I'm not Marigold, you know. Of course he was. Give you the sweet talk did he? Those GIs are good at that.'

'He wasn't like that, but yes, I did.' Hot tears ran down Rose's face as she nodded her head furiously. 'Am I being punished?'

'It must be some medical thing. I don't know, Rose. Maybe he's the father of one and Pete the other. Did you have relations with Pete around the same time?'

'Yes, sort of. Before and after he left. But he was gone for a month.'

'Then you fell for these babies around the same time give or take a month?'

'The babies were early I think. I don't know by how much and I can't work it out. Oh, Flora, what am I going to do?'

'Well, it's obvious this GI bloke is the father of one … maybe both.'

'How can it be both?'

'I don't know! I'm not a bloody expert!'

Rose had never seen Flora so exasperated and this scared her. Because if her level-headed and clever sister could lose her composure, what hope did she have of fixing this situation? This all needed to be sorted out before Pete came home and before anyone noticed she'd given birth to a darker hued baby and before she could no longer bear to be apart from either of her daughters. Although that was probably too late because when she looked down at the face of that little girl, all she could see was a man she had once known. The slant of his eyes, her skin tone closer to his than Rose's. All she saw was another life, another world. One where she could truly live, fearless and joyful.

Marigold appeared later that day. 'Are you still going to nurse it?' Her face crinkled in disgust.

'No, I'll let her starve, shall I?' Rose snapped at her. 'And her name is Lily.'

'I can't believe you would name her after Mum. What an insult!'

'She's my child. Whatever else you may be thinking, she came from me. You saw her come out of me, Marigold!'

'I still can't understand how you could do this?! Sleep with a—'

'Yes, I know what I have done. I know I committed adultery and I'm a bad person—'

'I'm not talking about that. I don't care about all that – because Pete had it coming. I'm just thinking that from all the Yanks you had to choose from, you chose that one. The ape!' Her accompanying laughter shocked Rose.

'Don't say that!'

'Why not? It's true! It's well known that they are close to animals and not very intelligent to boot!'

She tried to block out Marigold's hateful words. Longing for the warmth of her babies, especially Lily. But they were fast asleep in their basket, which thankfully was big enough for both.

Marigold continued. 'You can't make this up! He's halfway across the world fighting the Jerries or swinging from a tree with Tarzan, while you're lumbered with this thing, here in a town where everyone will be thinking just like me. You poor cow!'

'Not everyone thinks like you,' said Flora, walking into the room which had now become Rose's sanctuary from a world she

25

knew would be judging her and Lily just as much as Marigold was.

'Well, Dad will be thinking like me when he realises his little princess has been messing with a chimpanzee!'

'Oh, shut up, Marigold. If you can't say anything nice, try not to say anything at all!' said Flora. It was like they were kids again but this time with problems greater than whose turn it was to wash the dishes.

Rose was so grateful for Flora. In the mammoth mess she had made of her life, Flora offered an anchor, however weak, against the might of others.

'What are you going to do though, Rose?' whispered Flora.

'I'm going to feed my child.'

'You know what she means,' piped up Marigold. Rose wished Marigold would just leave them. All she wanted in that room were her babies and Flora. She needed to rest. Her exhausted body and mind just needed to rest.

'The doctor will be here soon,' said Flora. 'What do you want to do?'

Rose sprang up from the pillow, feeling more rested than she had in a long time. She had only recently opened her eyes and immediately checked on her sleeping babies in the basket beside the bed. 'How long have I been asleep?'

She stifled a yawn.

'About four hours.'

'What's all this about a doctor?' she asked, suddenly registering what Flora had just said.

'He'll be here in an hour.'

A shock of alarm. 'What?!'

'Calm down. Marigold took it upon herself to send for him and maybe she was right.'

'No! No doctors, I thought we agreed!'

'You have to get checked over. You gave birth to two babies. Plus they need a once-over too!'

'Why would she do that? Why would she send for him? Does she hate me that much?'

'She's concerned, Rose! Calm down, the doctor won't say anything. They're not allowed to.'

'How do we know? What if Pete finds out? The neighbours?'

Her mind was unable to produce anything she understood. She could only feel the acute fear associated with something precious being taken away from her. Flora suddenly looked concerned as if realising the enormity of what Marigold had done.

'Take Lily!' said Rose.

'What?'

'I don't want him to know about her, please!'

'But won't he be able to tell you've had two?'

'Not if we don't tell him. Just take her. I can't let anyone know. If Pete found out … I just need time to know what to do.'

'But—'

'Take her, Flora!'

'Okay, okay … I'll keep her in the other room. Blame the crying on Marigold's kids.'

'No, you take her, Flora. Take her for a little bit, get out of here! Come back when he's gone.'

'But—'

'Just take her before the doctor gets here! Look after her. She looks okay doesn't she? She doesn't need a check-up?'

'She's perfect,' said Flora. But they both knew that wasn't true.

'We may be able to hide her today but what about tomorrow and the next day? What are you going to do, Rose, because I don't want to be dragged into any of this?'

Flora knew that Pete could be a bit bad-tempered. That's all she knew. Only Marigold had guessed the truth.

'I don't know what I'm going to do in the long run. But for now, please just hide my baby!'

My Dearest Love,

Have you ever wondered why I sometimes begin your letters with 'My Dearest Love' and without your name? Firstly, you are my love. At the age of thirty, you are my very first love. I leave out your name because even now, I'm so fearful that someone here will find these letters and know that I am corresponding with you. Some fears just never leave you.

I still smile every time I think of you and our time together. I can't help but walk with my back straight with pride at knowing what we mean to one another, even though it was only for such a brief time. Didn't a philosopher say that sometimes the briefest of moments can be life-changing?

Life out here is hard. So hard that I will never talk about what I have seen or what I am expected to do. With each stroke of my pen, I prefer to pretend that none of it is happening. Cornel says all he has to do is lie down and think of his family, his wife and little girl, while I get to overthink. Then I have this need to either say my thoughts out loud or write them down.

My mama would call me the studious one as my head was always in a book when I was growing up. My father didn't like that side of me much. He has a farm that was handed down from his father and his father. Not a lot of cattle but enough to feed us and make a living out of it. Having only two sons meant we were both expected to take over once he passed. He never tired of telling me so, yet I was more interested in those storybooks my grandmother used to read to me. Let me tell you about her.

Gwendolyn Pamela Walker was her name. She was the smartest woman I knew and she attended Fisk University, a Negro-only college in Tennessee. She was so smart, I even believed her when she used to say to me, 'Your mama married beneath her, could have got herself a nice doctor or something. Ending up with a cattle farmer indeed!' I had always wanted to be like her and when she died, I was even more determined to make her proud, even if this meant turning my father against me. My little brother wasn't much into farming but enjoyed it better than I did. He refused to concentrate at school while I loved nothing more than setting off every morning. Placing my hand in the air whenever the kindly teacher asked a question. Miss Gloria took a shine to me, said I could be anything I wanted to be, and that shocked me. All my life my daddy had told me that I was a farmer. All my life, the white folks in town told me, without speaking, that I was worse than what came out of a swine's backside. Yet Miss Gloria said I could be who I wanted to be. Well, at that age I didn't really understand the statement but in my mind it literally meant I could be anything! So with that mind-set I believed it was possible to go to a college when I finished school and not have to work on the farm as my father wanted and like those before me had done.

I told my father one day, as we stood on the porch together in silence. We never spoke much to one another. He's the type of man who only speaks when he has something important to say.

'So, being a farmer not good enough for you now, Willie?'

'It's not that, Daddy, I just—'

'That woman's long dead, but she still influencing you from the other side?'

'Daddy, I just want to go to school.'

'You done been to school. Ain't that enough?'

'I want to learn so much more ...'

'There ain't nothing working on a farm can't teach you!'

'It can't teach me classics like Shakespeare and—'

'You disrespecting me?'

'No, sir.'

'Seems like you're ashamed to work the farm. Don't you know that my grandfather's family were owned? We may not

have been educated but we were free, do you understand that legacy?'

'Yes, sir.'

'Have you not been shown enough about the real world to know there's no place for you in it? That's why we stick together here on the farm, where no one can touch us!' His nose flared while I just couldn't understand why saying I wanted to go to college would make him so angry.

My mama came running outside. She moved closer to my father, her hand covering his. His demeanour instantly settling.

'This boy here having big ideas about going to some fancy school.'

'I was thinking of Fisk,' I said, sensing an ally. Mama was the only one my father ever listened to.

'Like my mama?' She smiled.

'Just like Grandma.'

She turned to my father. 'We can talk about it, can't we, baby?' she said looking up at him. I'm sure my mama was fluttering those eyelashes at my father. This strapping tall man with erect shoulders and proud ways was melting right there before me! It's then I knew the power a woman can have over a man. It's then I knew I wanted the same one day.

'We'll talk about it later. But I know where I stand.'

'I made your favourite,' she said as they walked back into the house hand in hand. 'Honey-backed ham.'

I don't know if this depiction is accurate, but it's how I remember it. My father was a harsh man, but with my mama he was different. As if fearful of losing her. Perhaps he always felt that my grandmother was right and she was too good for him. I think that's how I felt about you the first moment we met that, before I could truly get a chance to love you, I would be taken from you. Possibly by relocation, or death. I know everyone eventually dies but mine was probably a little more certain! As was the chance of being posted elsewhere. Both possibilities had almost equal power over my life and I was powerless to control the time I had with you. So from that first moment, I wanted to spend every piece of precious time I had, with you.

I had no idea it would be you who left me.

Chapter Three

Dr Pembleton was finally about to leave. He'd asked a number of questions, examined Rose briefly but was mainly interested in talking about his daughter-in-law who had recently given birth to twins. It took the remainder of Rose's strength not to blurt out: 'I had twins too! I have another baby and despite what anyone says, I love her! I already love her!'

'All is in order, Mrs Jones. Any problems, then just come and see me.'

Rose got up from the bed and escorted him to the front door. If she could have tipped him across the doorstep to make his departure that much quicker, she would have.

'Bye, now. I'll—' he said as she shut the door before he could finish. Her heart was beating furiously, the need to see her second baby increasing. Where had Flora taken her in such haste? Was she safe, uncomfortable or crying for her mother? Iris's cries instantly pulled her away from her thoughts and she bent to pick her up. She was hungry. Just like Lily would be if Flora didn't bring her home soon.

Half an hour later, with Iris newly fed and sleeping snugly in the basket, Rose finally heard the front door.

'Where have you been?' she said, pulling Lily from Flora's arms.

'You told me to take her so I did! What's wrong with you?'

'The doctor left ages ago.'

'I didn't want to come back early and have to explain why, me a spinster, I have a baby in my arms!'

Rose was in no mood for jokes.

'She's hungry!' she said, moving Lily onto her breast. Her heart rate was slowly returning to normal, her little girl safe in her arms.

'Rose, what are you going to do? I'll keep asking until you give me a decent answer. You're not going to be able to hide her away from Pete you know.'

'You think I don't know that?'

'So, what then?'

'I don't know, Flora. I really don't have a clue. I just don't want to lose her.'

It was clear to Rose that she was being punished for her adultery. She hadn't set out to be that type of woman. She had regularly raised her chin at the sight of the harlots in the village who seemed to throw themselves at GIs. Women who had married brave men who were risking their life overseas in combat and were perhaps dreaming of a time they'd be back in the arms of their wives. Instead, a few nylons, cigarettes and sweet talk with an American accent seemed to be all it took to pull down their girdles. But it had been different with William Burrell and the more she'd become intoxicated with him, the more her empathy for these women grew. It was often hard to articulate the loneliness and fear of wartime. The threat of a doodlebug landing on the town; German rockets shattering everyone and everything to pieces. Even though places like Arkenwood and Alderberry were deep in the countryside and were both deemed safer than the big cities, thoughts of death and carnage were still never far away. Her little brother Donald's absence a constant reminder that the country was still at war.

The uncertainty that conflict brings – whether it be with soldiers or in her own household – had been softened for Rose by those precious moments with William. If Pete had been the husband he'd promised, she'd never have looked at another man. Her father had once referred to Pete as 'the most useless man to have walked the earth', having lost any remaining respect for him the day they waved Donald off into battle. Pete had somehow got out of enlisting, blaming the limp he had acquired due to an injury caused after a night of drinking (a limp that would sometimes disappear on occasion). Spending most of what he earned on alcohol did not endear him to her father. Yet, Rose had been willing to live with the hope that her husband would one day change. A hope that diminished every time he silenced her with the back of his hand or a sharp pull of her hair, until she became hope-less.

Then William came along; the dashing American GI. To actually speak to someone resembling Paul Robeson, whom Flora had once pointed out in the newspaper, was something she'd never expected to do in her lifetime. Apparently there were plenty of people who looked like him in London, perhaps Bristol and Liverpool too according to Flora, but they were nowhere to be seen in any of the villages in which she'd ever lived.

Her instant attraction to William had been unexpected and something never experienced with anyone before, not even her husband. For years, she'd believed the love she felt for Pete was good enough; a nurturing love she hoped would cure him from the perpetual anger that seemed to live inside of him.

She had given up on that Hollywood type of love until the day William Burrell walked into her life.

'It's still here then?' said Marigold, lighting a match and placing it to the tip of the cigarette. Rose, as usual, was sitting up in bed.

'Where did you get those?' asked Flora.

'Our overfriendly GIs.'

'You can't smoke them here, they make me cough. Who knows what they can do to the babies?'

'They're harmless!'

'You don't know that.'

Rose, sensing a familiar stand-off between her sisters, piped up: 'Flora and I have been talking. About Lily.'

'There's really only one thing you can do,' said Marigold, just before placing the cigarette between her lips. There was a silence, as everything seemed to wait for an answer that differed to the one that had been lurking ever since Lily's birth. The one action that Rose could never bring herself to complete.

'All you can do is get rid of it.'

And there it was. The answer she knew was the only solution, but one she could never have said out loud.

'She's a baby, Marigold,' said Flora.

'If that's what you want to call it. Different name, same result.'

Rose blinked back a tear.

'Marigold, you're upsetting her.'

'Someone's got to. It's like you really think she can keep it. And if that's what you think then you're as stupid as you look. I suppose you didn't learn that much from all that reading, did you?'

Flora's silence served as conformation that, in their own jumbled ways, both sisters were in agreement. She would have to give Lily away.

Rose's heart beat rapidly again, her tummy fizzing with dread. She had known it the moment she had looked down at the beautiful little girl nestled in her arms moments after her birth. She had known what she'd have to do. Yet being prepared would never make it any easier. Bonding with her, loving her more each day, would only make the inevitable much worse.

If not for Iris, her other daughter, she would end her own life.

Flora placed her hand on Rose's arm. 'Look, I mean, if you wanted to keep her, I'd help.'

'What?' spat Marigold.

'People will look at you, of course – and Pete, he will most certainly leave. You'd have to do it with no money. Dad probably won't talk to you but no change there ...'

'Stop! Just stop giving her false hope. As usual, I'm the one who has to tell you what has to happen or else you will be left on the street with nothing and two kids to support. Listen here ...' Marigold said. 'My friend Caroline got up the duff with a sol-dier's kid and her old man was serving in the army. You should see the way she's getting treated and her kid's white.'

'Don't listen to Marigold, we have time to decide,' said Flora.

'Decide what? There is no choice!' added Marigold, furiously drawing on her cigarette. 'That thing has got to go.'

The fumes were entangling in Rose's lungs; she couldn't breathe. She wanted to scream. She couldn't do what Marigold was suggesting, not ever. The tickling on her throat became more urgent. Fits of coughs inevitable.

'Send it to one of those homes. I've heard of a couple and they take in kids like her. She'll be fed and clothed and no one need ever know what you did.'

A fit of coughs entwined with silent pleas engulfed her upper torso. 'You ... You mean no ... no one need ever know that ... that I got rid of my baby?'

'No, that you slept with a coloured man!'

My Dearest Love,

The most beautiful time of year for me is the season when the dogwood blossoms appear. My father would say flowers are not what a man should adore, but those pink and white blooms hanging off the edge of a tree branch if only for a short time each year are the most beautiful I have ever seen. They also remind me that beautiful things do not last very long. But then I'm reminded that they will be back the following year. And I look up to the sunshine, knowing it will be back even sooner.

I keep thinking about that first afternoon in Alderberry, the day we met. I never, ever wanted to let you go. I wanted to hold onto each and every one of your branches. I wanted to bloom with you and see out the rest of the seasons with you. Yet, just like the dogwood tree, I knew our season would soon be over and this made me sad, even angry at times.

The memory of your laughter is what sometimes gets me through the darkest moments out here. It's making me smile, right now. I am smiling for the first time in a whole week. It is a weak smile, but a smile nevertheless.

All because of you, my love.

Chapter Four

Pete was due back in seven days.

Rose's tummy refused to settle and she was unable to sleep even while the babies slept.

She was petrified.

It was round about this week that her baby was meant to have been born but instead she would be sending Lily away. Today.

It would only be temporary, she kept telling herself, over and over again. Until she could work out what to do, she needed her daughter to be safe because even now, a part of her still believed she could keep both babies, raise both her daughters. Marigold remarked more than once that she was 'wrong in the head' to even consider it – and she was right. Deep down, Rose knew there was no way to actually keep Lily. Instead she should be thankful for being able to at least keep one and that perhaps she wasn't being punished after all. No – of course she was being punished and because of this, her penance had to be losing Lily. That made sense to her troubled and sleep-deprived mind, while nothing else did.

When not fighting the endless sense of loss she already felt for Lily, Rose was questioning how she'd even got here.

The day Lily was conceived, she had almost told William the truth. About her life. Everything. They'd been meeting for just under two weeks. Their time spent talking about books she had never read,

English life, the blandness of English food (that was William!) – nothing and everything was off limits. She owed him the truth.

She sat on a cold, hard step as he stood before her, tall and gangly and the most handsome man she had ever set eyes on.

'William, I have something to tell you.'

'Yes, my love?' the way he spoke – his almond-shaped eyes widened with an innocence she was not ready to break. She couldn't do it. She couldn't reveal to this man her true self. She couldn't bear for him to look at her in a way that defied how he had been making her feel. So as usual, she deflected the associated emotions right back to him.

'Why the face, William Burrell? Something on your mind. Anything you want to tell me?'

'Just drinking you in. Your beauty.'

'I'm not beautiful. Not like the women you're probably used to in Hollywood.'

'Well, for one, I have never been to Hollywood. I'd liken your beauty to a dogwood.'

'You're saying I look like a dog?'

His laugh was intoxicating, his eyes intense. 'They're beautiful trees with flowers, stunning pink flowers.'

'As you may have already guessed, my family like flowers. Well, my mum did.'

'You must miss her.'

'All the time.'

'I'm like that with my grandmother. Losing someone reminds us how short life is. That we shouldn't waste a minute.'

'I agree.'

'Just like this war … a constant reminder.'

'You're so wise, William.'

'Why, because I state the obvious?'

She stood, the top of her head reaching his nose. 'You just are. And I like it, I really do. Not exactly what I'm used to around here. I think Flora's the only clever one in my family.'

'Wisdom, I feel, comes from experience. I look at you and I see plenty of that.'

'I don't want to talk about the past. I'm just glad you're here with me now. We don't know what tomorrow's going to bring, do we?'

'You understand. See, you're as wise as I am!'

Of course she understood. She understood that the sympathy her family had poured onto one of the neighbours whose son was killed in action was indeed peppered with a relief that it wasn't Donald. She knew the frailty of life and how it could change in a heartbeat. Just like her hopes and dreams would shatter into tiny pieces with every strike across her face from Pete.

'I want to kiss you,' she said. 'But I'm afraid after the other day that you won't want me to.'

'Of course I do. I guess I was too focused on the consequences … What people would do if they found us out.'

'But aren't you just letting things that happened in the past affect us now? I know some people wouldn't be all right about us knocking about together but—'

'You don't understand, it's worse where I'm from.'

'You're not in Savannah now, you're here in England and no one's going to kill you for talking to me.'

They both knew it would be more than talking. There was an emotional pull she could not explain to anyone, even if she wanted too.

'I don't want to get you into trouble,' he said, the tip of his finger touching her lips.

'Don't worry about me, William Burrell. I want this.' It was like her voice belonged to another person. She stepped away from him slowly. He followed her, a few seconds behind, as he usually did. Weaving through streets, bushes and finally to their spot overlooking a beautifully lush landscape, the innocence of woodland that would never reveal their secret.

This time there were no sweet words, just her back to him and the feel of his hands against her skin as he pressed his lips firmly against her neck. She turned around to face his lips, feeling every fear, every excitement and every shard of sadness.

'The Jerries could bomb us all now and we're gone. We have to live for now, William. For now,' she said breathlessly.

'No harm will come to you while I'm around,' he said confidently. That familiar swell of protection engulfed her as she felt his arms tighten around her. This time she knew she would let him have his way with her. She wanted it too and would think about the consequences later. She needed to live in this moment. She needed to feel alive. She needed to feel loved.

'Are you sure?' he asked in that gentlemanly way he had, one of the many things she loved about him. She unhooked her brassiere and placed it wantonly (like she imagined Rita Hayworth would) onto the ground.

'I'm sure.'

Sometime later, unconcerned about the time, they lay on the grass, entwined within one another, unable to decipher where she ended or he began.

'I love you, William, and I'm not ashamed. I could never be ashamed of you.'

'I love you too, you know that and to hear you say it ...'

'It's so soon and—'

'It doesn't matter. Days, weeks, months. All that matters is that I love you too. More than life itself.'

She moved in closer to him.

He stroked her cheek. 'I just wish you lived closer to Alderberry. How far can it really be? I can come and spend some time with you on my days off.'

'No ... I ...'

'I thought you said you weren't ashamed of me, Rose.'

'I'm not ... I ... Please don't spoil this moment. Remember what we said ... Life is short ...' She was scrambling for words, so she could escape his suggestion, her mouth further silencing him with kisses.

Rose was convinced they had conceived at least one of the twins that day. Her darling Lily, whom she would now be sending away.

'The home for wayward girls is about four miles from here,' said Flora. As usual these days, Rose lay on the bed but this time she was dressed with Lily asleep in her arms and Iris in the basket beside the bed. 'There's nothing to stop you visiting her. You can pretend you knew her mother—'

'Don't be silly, you ninny!' said Marigold. 'It wouldn't take someone long to work it out. You need to leave her there and never go back! Didn't you say there was one a little further away, towards Willow on the Grange?'

'That's too far!' said Rose. The baby stirred.

Marigold clenched each fist. 'She doesn't need to be any closer; what's wrong with you? Do you want to lose everything?'

'No.'

'Flora, you'll have to take her to the home for the feeble-minded.'

'But she isn't feeble-minded, Marigold.'

'She's one of them … things! They'll know what to do with her.'

The reality of what they were about to do enveloped Rose's entire being once more. Her hands shook. She really should hand Lily over to Flora before she dropped her, yet couldn't bear to be apart from her, knowing what they were about to do.

'I can't … Not yet …'

'You must!' insisted Marigold.

'Wait,' said Rose. She handed Lily to Flora and pulled out a pair of sky-blue knitted baby booties from her pocket. 'I knitted these before they were born. Keep one with her things.'

'What is she going to do with one bootie?' asked Marigold.

'Flora, keep it with Lily at all times. I'll keep one with Iris.'

'Why? It doesn't—'

'Please. Just take it.' She placed the bootie into Flora's hand.

'M-make sure they look after her ... please.'

'I will. You can trust me, Rose,' said Flora.

Flora

The little girl, her niece, gurgled contently in Flora's arms in the threadbare white blanket she'd wrapped her in on the day she was born. The poor little mite didn't own much, like many of them thanks to this war, just a change of clothes and one blue bootie. A misguided gift from a mother who was sending her child away.

The journey to the home for wayward girls hadn't been a smooth one. Two bus rides and then a long walk to where she now stood in front of an imposing building that made her feel as small as Lily. Lily was fast asleep in her arms. Earlier on the bus, a greying woman had sat beside them, insisting on taking a look at the baby, possibly armed with clichés that would undoubtedly include, 'What a bobby dazzler!' and 'Isn't she lovely?', instead a look of absolute horror crossed her face when she caught sight of her.

'I found her,' she'd almost said, yet said nothing.

Flora looked up at the imposing building, at first unable to move from where she stood. None of this felt remotely right. When she finally walked to the front entrance, the grandness promised by the size soon gave way to a tatty entrance with a handwritten sign: 'The Home for Wayward Girls. Welcome'. Flora hadn't realised until that moment that it was actually called 'The Home for Wayward Girls'. She nodded her head in disbelief and with her one free hand pulled on the stubborn handle attached to an iron door. The corridor was bleak, the stench of bleach and faeces colliding in her nostrils. A threat of nausea. The sound of multiple crying babies doing nothing to reassure her that this was the right place for baby Lily.

A thin woman with a pinched nose and dressed in a soiled nurse's uniform, appeared.

'Yes, may I help you?'

'I've come to … to look around.'

'Well, this is not a market place. You come here because you have made a mistake. You come here so that you don't have to live in shame. Or you can just look around and see if we are the ones good enough for you. Which is it?'

A young girl, no more than a teenager and in need of a good bath and a brush, appeared – a toddler waddling innocently behind her, naked except for a soiled nappy.

'Petronella, go back to your room please, it's late. And do keep the boy under control.'

The girl looked on suspiciously and Flora briefly wondered about her story.

'I … I'm not sure if I can do this. How do I know she'll be looked after?' said Flora.

The nurse raised an eyebrow. 'She?'

'Yes, Lily.'

'Well at least she has a name. It will make our job much easier. Are you staying or just dropping her off?'

'What do you mean?'

'Some of the girls leave them here with us or some stay for a while. We don't encourage it if you have no intention of keeping the child, as we don't really have the resources for your upkeep. We are in the middle of a war in case you have forgotten. People seem to forget that. The irony being that more illegitimate babies are born because of it! I don't know why girls have to be so … wanton. It isn't the men's fault when women do not care who they open their legs to.'

'I see.'

Flora had not come for a debate, but what with the state of the hallway, the little girl with the baby and this nurse's attitude, she was feeling less and less inclined to leave her niece at the Home for Wayward Girls or whatever it was called.

'If you are still unsure, I suggest you take a seat here and think about what you have done and what would be best from now on. I would expect a woman of your years to have known better. Now, if you'll excuse me, I have more than a dozen babies to tend to.'

Flora was alarmed at her coldness. Even Marigold showed some type of motherly love towards her children and she was the most miserable person she'd ever known. How could she leave her niece in such a place?

Suddenly, the nurse reappeared.

'I forgot to add. If this is a brown baby, which I suspect from what you have allowed me to see, she is – we won't accept her. We are currently overrun with children and must give priority to English babies. Besides, there are special places for the likes of them ... I can give you an address?'

The nurse had clearly been toying with her. What a cruel harsh world this already was for Lily and she was not yet three weeks old.

Lily sounded hungry. Flora hadn't planned on her niece still being in her care and now she'd no choice but to take her back to her own home before the whimpers turned to fully fledged cries. Flora was evidently good at delivering babies, but after that she'd never had much interest in them.

'Let's get you inside,' she said, turning the key in the lock. How women managed to open doors while carrying a child was a mystery. The door opened and the chill was immediately noticeable.

When the effects of the coal fire set in, Lily stopped whimpering as Flora held her close for extra warmth, reminded of the criticism she'd faced in living in such a big house that would 'cost a fortune to heat'. Her family thought it strange that she had opted to live by herself rather than stay with their father or find a man to marry. The handful of times her sisters had visited, they had offered many matters of opinion, including, 'It's a bit big for one isn't it?' But Flora enjoyed the space and could certainly afford the rent with her wages as a bookkeeper at the candle factory. Yet even with so much space, it still felt peculiar bringing a child into her home, her sanctuary that allowed her to shut out the world and just be Flora Baker.

Lily's whimpering grew again. Flora's pantry contained just a few items and nothing a new-born baby could eat. She was even out of powdered milk and would not be allowed any more for at least three days. She checked the windows, grateful for the blackout curtains compulsory for every home, to stop the Germans from targeting individual areas. Even though the 'blackout' rules were becoming a bit more relaxed now, she had no intention of bringing any attention to her or to Lily.

She placed Lily onto her bed and hesitated. She could easily roll off; what was she thinking? Panic rose in her body. She had not thought any of this through.

Lily's whimpering calmed a little but it would only be a matter of time until the cries returned yet again. She placed the baby onto the floor, apologising profusely under her breath as she left the house.

Outside her neighbour's house, she exhaled and banged on the door.

'Oh, hello?' said Elsie, wrapping a robe around her waist. As neighbours they hardly spoke, which was just how Flora liked things, but Elsie had been the one to 'keep an eye' on the house while she'd gone to look after Rose.

'Sorry to call around so late, but I was wondering if I could swap some food with you?'

'What do you need?'

'Some dried milk or something.'

'What you need that for? Fancy a cup of tea?'

'Something like that. So ... do you have it?'

'Yes, that's fine, hang on.'

Elsie returned with the item.

'What would you like as a swap? Some lard? A bit of jam?'

'Don't worry about all that, you just go and have your cup of tea. You can owe me.'

Flora raced back home, relieved to find Lily where she had left her – on the cold, hard floor.

'I'm so sorry, my love,' she said, burying herself into Lily's glorious scent. She never realised babies could smell so sweet, equating them with dirty nappies, no sleep and a permanently angered expression – or maybe that was just Marigold!

Luckily, Rose had packed a bottle. She could only hope that Lily didn't fuss once she realised this wasn't her mother's milk.

Luckily, Lily accepted the bottle easily and as she slept off her dinner, Flora lay beside her, aware she herself would not be sleeping that night because of the fear of Lily rolling off the bed. She used the time to think about the current predicament and her own life.

Much to her family's disbelief, Flora had never needed much more than what her life currently gave her. She had an education, a skill and was earning a good wage. She also volunteered where she could for the war effort and would go hop picking in the summer with a number of women who, like her, had yet to acquire a husband. She had initially blamed the shortage of exceptional men on the war, but Flora's interest in the opposite sex could never match Marigold's and Rose's. Indeed, Marigold's much older husband seemed to lead a separate life from his wife while Pete and Rose ... well, everyone knew he liked to be around other women. That was not a secret. More than once she'd urged her sister to leave him, with Rose insisting she 'loved him'. Well, if that was love, then Flora wanted no part of it. Flora had also seen from an early age what falling in love had done to their mother, Lillian. Sent to an early grave after having four children and catering to a man's every need. That would not be Flora's future. She needed to satisfy the lust to work hard and be compensated. Attain all the things she never saw her mother do before dying at such a young age. For the most part, she had earned an excellent wage before the war reduced the capacity to continue doing so. But Flora had been shrewd enough to put money away each month, so that in essence, she would never need a man to take care of her financially. Sometimes, just sometimes and usually in the middle of the night, she would lean over to the side of her bed and reach for someone who wasn't there. Just sometimes.

When Lily woke up again, it was a tiny baby that Flora leaned over to touch. Whimpering quickly turning into wails.

Flora felt an unexpected pleasure in watching Lily feed, as in some small way she was contributing to her niece's wellbeing, releasing inside her a satisfaction she hadn't really felt before. Perhaps she would like children one day but knowing that came with a husband and marriage effectively vetoed that idea!

She rubbed the tiny back of her niece, completing the feeding process. Such a beautiful little girl and one half of a twin, the half no one wanted.

'Oh, Lily, darling. What will become of you?'

A new day began, yet Flora was still unable to come up with any firm answers on what to do next. All she did know was that she would not be going to any home for the feeble-minded. Their mother's sister Aunt Maud had resided in such a place for many years and Flora could still remember lots of stories recounted over time, until no one ever talked about Aunt Maud again.

'We're not taking you there,' she whispered into Lily's tiny ear. 'Never! That I promise you.'

Flora made a crib out of the bottom drawer of her dressing table and placed Lily inside.

'Now, you be good, young lady. No crying and I won't be long,' she promised. Again, a feeling of dread grew inside of her as she wondered if being a parent was just one long wave of anxiety. 'Just you stay asleep and no crying,' she sang quietly. It probably wasn't wise to leave a new-born baby alone for such an extended time, but she'd no choice. She could hardly ask one of the neighbours to watch over her.

She made it to Rose's in record time, her mind constantly on Lily and what would happen if one of the neighbours heard a crying baby and went in to investigate.

She banged on the door and immediately heard his voice.

'Hang on, hang on! Keep your hair on!'

'Hello, Pete.' She exhaled as the realisation that Pete had missed Lily by a matter of hours quickly set in.

'My favourite old maid sister-in-law!'

'Long time, no see.'

'Not really long enough, if you ask me.'

She felt the venom oozing from his pores as he stepped aside with a bow and let her in. Pete had never been a fan of most of the women in her family except, perhaps, Marigold. But this never concerned Flora.

Rose was sitting on the settee, nursing Iris. 'Flora!' she said with a bit too much surprise in her voice.

Pete thankfully left the room and Flora sat beside her sister.

'Did you do it?' whispered Rose. Her anxious voice and the hateful words so at odds with how she held onto Iris; the beautiful little girl suckling innocently at her mother's breast.

'No, yes. Sort of.'

'What do you mean, sort of? Did they not want to take her, you know, because—?'

'I couldn't do it, Rose. I couldn't leave her in that place.'

Suddenly, Rose's face turned to crimson. 'Are you mad?'

'No, I—'

'Pete's back now. He came back early, so one more day here and he would have seen her and it would have been over for me!'

'I know, I just . . .'

'You've got to take her away. Please. He'll kill me if . . .'

'What's going on here?' asked Pete, appearing at the doorway.

'Just women's talk, love,' said Rose in a high-pitched tone.

'Always cooking up something, you women.'

'You know what we're like,' replied Rose, pulling Iris away from her breast.

'She's a beauty isn't she? My daughter!' said Pete in a show of pride that Flora had never seen in him before.

'She's just like her dad,' added Rose. 'You should see Pete giving her a kiss when she's asleep. A sight for sore eyes!'

'Turning me into a right softie, ain't ya!'

'We're so happy now . . .' said Rose, looking directly at Flora. She wasn't sure if she had lip-read her sister correctly but she thought what followed silently were the words: 'Don't spoil this.'

With no opportunity to talk to Rose in private, Flora made it back home just before Lily's whimpering descended into wails. She picked her up, apologised once again for leaving her and held her close, her own tears wetting the baby's soft curls. Lily's cries now sounded reminiscent of her birth cries, which perhaps made sense because today would be a type of rebirth. She could never be taken back to Rose and she now officially had no parents.

From now on, and at the age of two and a half weeks, Lily Baker had a new life, although Flora still wasn't quite sure what that would entail.

'What are we going to do with you, Bub?'

As her own tears continued to fall, so did Lily's loud accompanying wails. Flora didn't care who heard them because this child had a right to wail and complain at the injustice that had befallen her life.

'I'm so sorry, little one,' cried Flora. 'So very, very sorry.'

Chapter Five

Rose

It had been three sickening, gut-wrenching weeks since she'd last seen her baby. She needed to stop referring to her as that because Rose was a mother of one. Had always been. Lily had been a blip. Sweet little Lily. Her own flesh and blood, Lily.

'Here we are. All fresh and clean!' said Pete, walking into the living room, clutching a freshly bathed Iris in his arms. At seven weeks old, she was changing every day. Pete swore she smiled only for him as Rose joked that this usually happened after a good meal! Her husband was also beyond recognition. Only last night changing his first ever nappy and insisting on looking after her as Rose took some much-needed sleep. She'd never, in all her life, seen a man behave this way towards a child. Her own father and most men were of the 'it's women's work' mind-set, but Pete had shocked her with his insistence on helping with Iris. It was more than she could ever have asked for. It was more than she deserved.

The erasure of Lily did not mean she didn't often think of William. Especially in the still of the night, with Pete snoring beside her, and the reassuring sound of Iris's contentment as she lay in the basket beside the bed. As a light sleeper, she wished for sleep to clear away the thoughts of him. The way he'd look at her with those almond-shaped eyes; his smile only for her. The way her skin tingled at his slightest touch. Sometimes she feared Pete waking up, as if her treacherous thoughts were loud enough to be heard outside her own head. But the regular grunting and at times shifting round to hold her, told Rose she had got away with everything. Well, that's what Marigold liked to say, when all Rose could think of was the punishment of her little baby being sent away like a criminal. The child she was no longer allowed to think about. Yet to think of William meant to also think of Lily. It was like her youngest daughter was dead, but with no graveyard to visit and with no one allowed to even mention her name. So perhaps it was somewhat easier to think of William instead of Lily during those early hours. Less pain, yet painful.

Rose's legs were draped over Pete's on the settee as they held hands, a scene reminiscent of their courting days.

'I love being a dad,' said Pete. Iris lay in the cot he had restored. The same wooden one she'd slept in as a baby, with Marigold having held onto it for long enough. It was hers now, just as their father had promised.

'I know you do, love. I can see that!'

'One thing though …' he said.

She squeezed his hand.

'She doesn't look like me at all.'

Rose was sure he could feel just how sweaty her palms had suddenly become. 'Oh?'

'Just as well, I'm an ugly bugger. Better she takes after you lot!'

'Yes … she … she does look more like my side of the family …'

She was glad he couldn't see her face or he might have been able to notice the lies etched in every corner, the betrayal in every expression.

'We should have all the family over. I want to show off my little girl,' he said. 'She's almost a couple of months old now. Let's get everyone over!'

'The place isn't big enough. Everyone who needs to see her, already has.'

'We can have it at your dad's. Old Albert needs to see what a beauty the little 'un is. Yeah, let's do that. I haven't seen much of your sisters lately, either. They usually can't wait to meddle in our business!'

'Marigold comes when she can, but what with the kids ...'

'What about Flora? She should be here every day, helping you out. It's not as if she has anything taking up her time. Frigid cow!'

'Don't say that.'

'Why not? It's true. Thought she wouldn't be able to stay away. Hasn't she always wanted what you had? Your looks ... Me.' He stuck out his tongue playfully.

'Ha ha!' said Rose, herself having noted that Flora had stayed away. Rose was aware she blamed her for getting rid of Lily so it was better she stay away, if judgement was all she had for her.

'I don't need anyone, anyway. I have you and Iris. You're all I need.'

'Finally, you get it. Took you a while,' he said, holding her tightly against his chest.

'She's bonny,' her father enthused. A rare smile on Albert Baker's face as he sat in his large brown chair nicknamed 'Dad's chair' by their mother. Refusing to hold his new granddaughter, instead choosing to enthusiastically pat her bald head decorated with a white ribbon, as Rose sat with her on the edge of the chair. Marigold, her husband and kids, John and Tommy, were there as well as a scattering of family members Rose couldn't care if she never saw again. Of course, this was all about the arrival of Iris – the newest member of the Baker family – even if she was officially a Jones, and she would smile, be sweet and get through the day.

What with rationing, there wasn't much to serve, but there was an abundance of Spam sandwiches and enough tea for at least one cup each if they reused the teabags. However, the huge chocolate cake Marigold arrived with brought questions Rose had no intention of asking. Rose had defiantly worn the floral dress she'd had on the first day she met William, now with the missing buttons replaced. Her way of including Lily. Her way of fighting back when all she could feel was powerless. Especially after this morning.

'You could have at least called her after your mum,' complained her dad, right on cue. 'Marigold has all boys and there's no chance with Flora!'

Upon hearing her name, Marigold walked in from the kitchen, clutching a piece of bread. 'You were talking about me!'

'Dad was just saying I could have named Iris Lillian.'

'Or at least Lily. That would have been nice.'

A thousand expressions caught in one gaze between two sisters.

'Dad, you want a nice cup of tea?' asked Marigold, breaking the gaze.

'Yes, get me a cuppa and some more of that cake.'

She hoped there would be enough food for everyone, even though every guest had brought a small item of food along with them. She really just wanted the day to end.

'Don't eat too much of that cake, Marigold, you're already a big girl!' said their father. Rose felt a pang of sadness for Marigold, especially as her eyes clouded over, and her lips pursed in a weakened show of defiance.

'What, you want me to be a skinny rake like our Rose and Flora, Dad?'

'She's not skinny, she's perfect,' said Pete, moving his arms over her and almost causing her to topple over. She froze.

'Pete, careful,' she whispered. 'The baby.'

'Sorry, my darling,' he said in exaggerated tones. She would keep up the pretence of this sudden change in her husband because once again, that was all this was.

'Where is your Flora, anyway?' he said.

'Said she couldn't make it. Probably working or something. You know what she's like!' said Marigold.

'Behaves just like a man, that one. Living by herself ... I don't know what I did to deserve a child like that. Lillian would be turning in her grave!'

'We'll name the next one Lily, how about that?' said Pete, taking Iris from her hands, clearly keen to impress everyone with this new improved version of himself. The man who now changed nappies, soothed his baby into the night and had been nothing more than loving since Iris's birth.

At least until that morning.

'Are you seeing someone else?' he'd spat.

Rose had been cocooned snugly in bed, peacefully drifting into sleep before the sound of her husband's voice jolted her into a reality she never wanted.

'Admit it!' he hissed, poking his finger into her shoulder.

A line of dread descended into her stomach as her eyes began to focus. His eyes were bloodshot, his face almost matching their tone.

'You'll wake Iris up! I only just got her to sleep,' she'd said, knowing what was next, how this would end, how it always ended.

'Answer the question, Rose.'

'We were just asleep. Did you have a bad dream?'

'Answer the question, Rose!'

'Why would you ask me that?' She dreaded answering. He was friendly with Marigold and perhaps she'd told him. No, Marigold hated everyone but she wouldn't do that to her. Especially when the disgrace would surely impact her also. No. This was something else.

She sat up and tenderly cupped his face in her hands. 'It's you I love. Only you, Pete.'

Shrugging her away, she instantly felt the rejection.

'Then why won't you let me lie with you like a man has the right to with his own wife?'

'I've just had two kids!'

'What?'

She shook her head rapidly. Why had she said that? 'I mean, I've just had a baby and ... and ... that child of yours was a whopper. Took me hours to get her out, just ask the girls.'

'It's been almost two months, Rose.'

'I know, but I need more time. At least another few weeks.'

'Who told you that?'

'The doctor did.'

'Since when can we afford one of those?'

'Flora paid for one to come just after the birth.'

'Another way to try and take over eh? Paying for stuff that should be for me to sort out.'

'You weren't here, Pete.'

His expression switched. 'So that gives you and that bitch the right to do what you want? Her job was to deliver my kid safely, not throw money about and make me look useless!'

'She wasn't trying to do that, I promise.' She swallowed. She knew this look. In a moment, he would no longer be able to hear her. No longer able to understand the simplest of things. The man she had married six years ago was now morphing into that stranger he had introduced her to many times before.

She placed her hand on his arm, and he shrugged it away.

'I'm sick of this, Rose! You wonder why I spend so much time away.'

'I—' she began, just as his hand was around her neck, his weight pushing her back onto their bed. His grip weak enough to allow her breath, but strong enough to hold her captive against the pillow.

'Why do you make me do this, Rose? Why?' he said over and over again, as he ripped off her undergarments and pushed his weight onto her. Her body stiffened and no words left her mouth. Her eyes wide open but levelled up at the ceiling where she saw her daughters playing together on a freshly cut lawn, both wearing crisp white dresses that flared above their knees. Iris wore an orange bow in her long, flowing hair and Lily a pink one in between soft curls. They held onto each other's hands, skipping in a circle, as the glow of a beautiful bright sun sparkled upon them.

When Pete released his grip, she opened her eyes as a single tear travelled down her cheek.

She was unsure of how long she remained like that, on the bed and motionless, but it was the sound of her baby that forced her to sit up.

'No!' she said, quickly, rushing from the bed and to the cot where Pete stood. 'Don't hurt her!'

Pete looked behind himself, then back at Rose, his features softening.

'How could you think—?'

'Just don't hurt her, Pete. Never hurt her, please.'

'You're doolally if you think I would.'

Her tears were plentiful now, as she glanced over at the soiled bed.

'That? That was just a husband getting what is his right.'

She held the baby close.

'That's what married people do,' explained Pete.

'Y-yes …' She hadn't noticed her hands trembling, her chest moving rapidly up and down. Perhaps Iris had noticed because she let out a wail she had never heard before in her daughter. It spoke of pain, betrayal, hurt and, worst of all, utter despair.

Now, just hours later as her family gathered to welcome Iris, Pete was a different man. The doting father swaying to the wireless with Iris in his arms; telling jokes to her nephews as they looked up with admiration. It was her father who chose to stare at Pete with narrowed eyes. He'd disliked Pete from the start but more so from the moment he'd found out he'd 'got out of enlisting' and repeating just how much he hated 'cowards' whenever Pete was in earshot. She wished she could run to her dad and tell him everything. Instead she looked on at the supposedly happy family scene and remained mute, alone in a room full of people.

My Dearest Love,

What are you doing right now? Are you thinking of me? Missing me as much as I miss you? You are the only light in my darkness now. I never want to pull you down no matter how I'm feeling. I never want to do that.

To know you are happy, simply keeps me happy on the days that I am unable to be.

Be happy. Please be happy.

Chapter Six

Flora

Reginald House was a large stately home she assumed once housed a bunch of aristocrats. Surrounded by lush grounds and that smell of the countryside she'd never tire of, Flora hoped this would be a better home for Lily.

She walked up the gravel path, cradling her baby niece. The door was opened by a kindly looking lady, a bit younger than Flora, this time not in a nurse's uniform, but in a pleasant brown dress.

'I saw you through the window. I'm Beryl and who is this then?'

'I'm Flora and this is Lily.' So used to keeping her concealed, Flora had forgotten there was no need, because Lily would no longer be in the minority.

'Isn't she beautiful?' said Flora, having never been able to say this to anyone before.

'Such a shame.'

'She's ... fine ...' said Flora, already on the defensive.

'This war I mean. It's brought so much misery to these beautiful brown babies. Here, let me show you.'

Flora followed Beryl into a large room filled with about a dozen 'brown' babies, some lying on the floor on blankets, some asleep, some looking up at the ceiling, chubby legs kicking in the air, others asleep in tiny cots.

'There are so many children ...' said Flora, her eyes darting to each and every child in the room.

'Oh, those coloured soldiers really left their mark.'

Again, a need to defend. 'What about the white soldiers? I know of a few girls—'

'No one is excusing them, but at least with those babies, they have a chance of a dad when the men return home, none the wiser. Or if they are unmarried, have a chance of finding a husband. These girls should have thought of the consequences, don't you think?'

'Anyway,' said Flora, feeling mildly uncomfortable.

'Let's get this little brown baby registered and take it from there.'

'Lily. Her name is Lily.'

Thankfully, Lily was asleep by the time Flora was about to leave. 'So I can visit when I want ... with my sister, her mother ...'

'I don't see any of them being adopted any time soon. To be honest, we don't know what to do with them. We seem to be getting a new baby here every week. The American government will have to chip in and do something because this can't go on.'

'What do you mean?'

'All this talk about them being collateral damage of the war is not helping anyone. We need money to feed these children. The authorities will only be sympathetic for so long.'

'I will send what I can.'

'That will help. But what about all the other poor mites? We are filled to the rafters.'

Once the paperwork had been signed, a rush of emotion caught in her throat at the thought of leaving Lily behind.

'I'll leave you to say your goodbyes,' said the woman, whose name Flora had already forgotten, as a blinding grief took over her body.

'Goodbye, little one,' she whispered. Flora clocked what she thought was a smile on Lily's face. She placed a soft kiss onto her forehead, reassuring herself this wouldn't be the last time. She would visit whenever she could, but how often she couldn't tell. There was a war on and she had a job and Lily would have to remain a secret forever. All these variables, colossal and necessary, and yet the thought of never seeing her again made her feel sick inside.

As she walked away from the imposing building of Reginald House, Flora told herself she had done the right thing. Indeed, the burden of this should really have fallen on Rose because none of this had anything to do with Flora. Lily had nothing to do with her.

She woke up with a start, her heartbeat racing as she felt the side of her bed for the baby. During the night she'd heard a baby crying, her heart heavy as soon as she remembered. Flora lay back down on the pillow with the weight of loss, tears flooding her eyes and then the sides of her pillow. She missed that little baby, the smell of her, even her incessant crying when all she wanted was something to eat. She'd been at the birth of both Marigold's kids and had felt nothing more than a mild relief when she'd handed the child over to its red-faced mother so she could go home and resume her own life. Never bitten by any sort of maternal bug, she had assumed herself immune to such things. Then came Lily. There was something about Lily that she hadn't even felt for Iris. Lily was the abandoned one. The outcast nobody wanted. Perhaps that's how she'd always seen herself – as that tiny baby with no mother and a father who had no interest in who she was.

Now she had gone away, living in Reginald House while the majority of her blood family knew nothing of her existence. The tragedy being that even if they knew, they still wouldn't care.

The sobs that followed surprised her. Flora rarely cried, if at all. The only time she remembered crying before today was the day they said her mother was never coming home. She would never forget the confusion of welcoming a new brother, yet no mummy. None of it had made sense and for a while she had blamed Donald for their mother's death. Now, she would do anything to just have him return safely, if only to give him a big hug and tell him just how sorry she was for being such a horrible sister. That morning, she not only cried for Lily, but also for her brother Donald.

'I missed you at the party the other day,' Rose had the audacity to say. She'd once loved Rose the most, but at that moment knew it wouldn't be hard to actually hate her.

'What, did you want me to bring Lily along and show everyone?'

'Shush!' she hissed, grabbing Flora's hand and leading her out into the back yard.

Flora shrugged her arm away, wondering where her sister had learned such a hard grip.

'I only meant I wanted to talk to you ...' said Rose.

'About what?'

'Just ... just something that happened that morning.'

'What happened? What could be more important than—?'

'Something happened with Pete.'

'Another woman? Spare me the details. You have more important things to think about – remember your other daughter, Lily? The one I was looking after on that day? Sorry I couldn't come and stand between you and your husband, but I was a bit busy!'

'I thought you had taken her to that place we talked about.'

Flora felt a heat rise within her. She guessed that Pete could be cruel, but had her sister suddenly taken on some of his characteristics? 'You mean the place Marigold suggested? It was terrible. I really should have known that, though, coming from Marigold. So I took her to Reginald House.'

'Okay.'

'A place for brown babies, if you're interested.'

'Oh course I'm interested.' Rose placed her middle finger into her mouth, chewing her nail. 'She's in a good place then.'

'That's all you can say? Don't you even want to know where it is?'

'You know where it is so I can just ask you, if I ever need to go and see her.'

'If?' The casual cruelty of her sister's words blinded her senses. Of all the people in her family, Rose had been there for her the most. Her staunch if not timid supporter. The one sister she could rely on and vice versa, and yet the woman in front of her was hard to recognise.

Flora made a decision that night to keep her distance. She hated Pete and couldn't really look at Iris without thinking of Lily so it wouldn't be too difficult. She would immerse herself in work duties and just get on with her life. She missed Lily with all her being, bursting into tears whenever she brought out the sky-blue bootie she kept in the drawer. She would try and visit once a month or at least every six weeks. Her relationship with Rose was beyond repair for now, but she probably wouldn't even notice. All Rose seemed to care about was Pete and Iris anyway.

It was six weeks before Flora managed to visit Reginald House to see Lily again and was astonished at how much she had grown. As the woman she'd met on that first day, Beryl, had predicted, the number of babies had since doubled.

'It really does surprise me how many girls had relations with those types of men. It just wasn't the done thing in my day. Must be something in the water,' Beryl said.

Flora had no interest in probing this line of questioning any further. 'How has her development been?'

'Development?' said Beryl. 'She's a baby – she eats, fills her nappy and then goes to sleep.'

Flora had to remind herself that not everyone was as well read as she, although she had hoped that Beryl and the other staff at Reginald House would be clued up on some things.

'Your sister not coming then?'

'No.'

'Not a surprise. So many of the mothers won't or can't even look at their kiddies. Such a shame.'

'How's my little angel?' Flora cooed as she smoothed her hand over Lily's head of curls and immediately felt a small bump on her forehead.

'What's this?' she asked.

'She probably rolled off somewhere.'

'Off what?'

'I don't know,'

'Is no one looking after these children?'

'I beg your pardon? We do our best here. If you don't like it, perhaps you'd better not come here any more.'

'I'm ... sorry.' Flora was instantly reminded of when she herself had had to leave Lily alone, the guilt that came with the knowledge that it could only take a minute for an accident to occur – she had been lucky.

'Look, you're clearly a little bit more educated than most of the people who bring children here and, frankly, they are not in the habit of visiting so there is something different about you. But please, never question what we do here. There aren't a lot of places who will take in coloured children and we do our best under very trying circumstances.'

'Of course.' She smoothed her hand over the bump on Lily's head again. Accidents happened. Once, Marigold and Flora were simply having a cup of tea, and in a moment Marigold's eldest, John, had bumped his head on the edge of the table. Accidents happened.

My Dearest Love,

As you can only imagine, I have had to do a lot in the name of being a soldier. For my country. For survival. But nothing could prepare me for the bloodstained shirt, the broken bones and bruised-up face of a man I had started to call my friend. When I discovered Cornel's broken body, just outside our room, I was just glad he was breathing. I asked him who did this and he mouthed, 'Riker.'

Cornel was the quiet one, kept himself to himself and I couldn't imagine why Riker or his men – because Riker would not have struck alone – would have done this to him.

'I been seeing me a sweetheart from the village,' he said hoarsely. I for one had never seen nothing but English women in these parts.

'An English lady?' I asked. As he nodded slowly, I hope I was able to conceal my surprise at Cornel. He was not only married, but after everything he had said about not mixing with 'them', toeing the line and staying out of trouble ...

Cornel refused to report it to the military police but I was angry. I did something I maybe should have thought about first – I squared up to Riker, a heat rising in my body as my fists clenched.

'What did you do?'

'You really can't be talking to me this way, boy.' The way he said 'boy', long and drawn out, the way I had heard it so many times before. But this time I wasn't ready to back down. He and his men had beaten my friend, a good man, to a pulp and he'd done nothing to deserve it.

'Unless you also want a trip to the military hospital, I suggest you change your tone,' said Riker.

Some of Riker's stooges stood beside him, ready to hand out to me whatever they had given to Cornel. But I didn't care. All I could see was years of accepting things I hadn't asked for, keeping quiet and carrying on until the next time.

'*As long as you boys stay in your place and leave them nice English girls alone, everything gonna be all right around here.*'

'*Will, leave it!*' *called one of my friends.* '*Please, Will!*' *His voice had turned into my mama's and I could see her in my mind's eye, pleading with me to stop this. And then I saw a vision of you.*

I unclenched my fists. More of the men had gathered, some of whom were also southern boys who stuck together in their quest to keep the defenceless English girls from the clutches of us beastly Negro soldiers.

The divisions only got worse after Cornel's beating. I and the other six soldiers were now even more wary and angry, a strange combination that could only leave me feeling powerless. Do you know what that feels like, my love? To know that something is wrong, yet be unable to do anything about it because to do so would mean the end of your life?

Chapter Seven

1945 – post war

She hadn't planned on asking Joyce, affectionately known to everyone as 'our Joycey', to drive her to Reginald House but she knew she could be trusted – and had a car. Flora hadn't made many friends at the factory office where she volunteered, because as soon as they got married or had a baby, they were gone. But, like her, Joycey didn't seem as interested in landing a sweetheart among the handful of men returning home from war. With her flaming auburn hair and buxom figure now dressed in trousers and a checked shirt rolled into a knot at the front, she could have her pick of men, but as she'd often complained, 'Those blokes coming back from the war aren't used to a woman like me.' So with Joycey, Flora never had to explain her lack of a husband or even suitors as they sat in the staff canteen or took a walk in the fields. With Joycey, Flora had found someone almost like her.

Joycey also asked no questions as she stayed put in the car and Flora made her way up the gravelled path. It had been three whole months since her last visit, not because she couldn't be bothered but because it had become increasingly hard to make time for the journey. She only hoped her niece could still remember her.

Her knock remained unanswered, so she moved to a window and peered inside. A low light hovered over a number of small babies lying on an unwashed floor as toddlers aimlessly hobbled around. A young girl, no more than eighteen, was sitting on the floor, a look of exhaustion on her face. Flora searched the room for Lily.

She was about to tap on the window when she saw the door to the room fly open and Beryl appear, holding Lily by her legs with the child upside down.

Flora swallowed, her body rooted to the spot and not expecting what happened next – her little niece to be shoved onto the floor headfirst. Flora began to shake, unable to believe what she was witnessing. The other children looked on without flinching. Even as Lily began to bawl, no one appeared to notice. The younger woman simply produced a comb from her pocket and started pulling at the hair of one of the little girls now on her lap. That child began to cry with the force of each tug – the flimsy comb clearly inadequate for the textured hair.

Both Lily's and the other little girl's cries were piercing. Flora, now able to focus her mind, pounded her fists onto the window.

'It's okay, Lily, I'm coming.'

She ran to the door and pounded her fists yet again, this time onto the strong wood.

As the door opened, Flora rushed past Beryl and into the room where Lily and a couple of the other babies were now wailing at the top of their lungs. She feared for each and every child in that place and wished she could grab them all, but she had to stay focused on Lily and Lily alone.

'Come here, little baby,' she soothed as Lily held out her two chubby little arms. Flora felt an instant rush of love mixed in with guilt as she scooped Lily up from the floor. Her own cheeks against her niece's wet tears. Without saying a word and with Lily moulded onto her chest, Flora turned and walked through the open door and onto the gravel path. Joycey had fallen asleep but sprang awake as soon as she heard the bang on the window.

'I'm sorry, Joycey!'

'What's all this?'

'Change of plan!'

'Blimey!'

'I had to take her!'

'Get in!' said Joycey. 'And you can explain on the way!'

As they drove towards home, the car filled with streams of sunlight as the little baby called Lily let out gurgles of pleasure as Flora smiled away. She'd really no idea what faced them, but, for the first time in months, she felt like what she was doing was right.

'You won't find rent as cheap as mine anywhere else around here, you know,' said the landlord as she stood in the kitchen where she had cooked ever since moving out of home at the age of twenty-one. Her dad had been most distraught about that, often commenting that if she wasn't leaving home to be with a husband, she could at least stay and take care of him. Yet now, someone more vulnerable needed her, which meant she would have to leave a home once again.

'You also won't find anyone else accepting of these types of shenanigans,' he added, pointing to the sleeping baby resting in the cot she had borrowed from a neighbour. The same neighbour who couldn't wait to meet Flora's new 'houseguest' and another reason why she had to leave. The landlord had been disapproving enough of the appearance of a baby without a husband, but after studying the child's obvious features, he'd almost fallen where he stood. Flora had dealt with judgements for what felt like her entire life and it had to stop.

'Perhaps we'll end up someplace more tolerant?'

'Good luck with that. All that fancy education still hasn't taught you that once you've been tarnished at the hands of …

Anyway, imagine what an insult that must be to our boys. To return home and find out their girl had had relations with …'

'I didn't ask for a lecture.'

'Don't you care that our boys won the war for us? For you!'

'Of course I care, don't you dare say I don't. You know nothing about me or my family! Nothing!' His words had wobbled a nerve, but not for the reasons he perhaps thought.

The landlord widened his eyes, nostrils flared. 'Post the keys through the letterbox and good day to you.'

She bent to pick up Lily. 'Not long to go and we'll be off on our little adventure. You'll like that, won't you?' As Marigold's kids had been able to say one or two little words by the same age, Flora hoped that Lily would have followed suit. 'Yes?' said Flora, encouragingly.

The little girl shook her head. Flora would need to be patient.

Flora had been very prudent over the years, living on a shoestring while earning more a year than her sisters had earned in a lifetime combined. The mind-set was always that of never knowing when the war would end or if it ever would. Now it had, and Flora could finally look forward to a future and one that involved Lily. The money would be enough for a good deposit on a house to rent far enough away from all the family and old friends. If she, if they, were to start again it would have to be away from everything and everyone she knew. Flora would miss her family to an extent, yet would be glad not to have to see the constant disappointment in their eyes as they downplayed her achievements while pitting her against the women in her family who had married and borne children. She was doing this for Lily, so that she'd never have to grow up feeling alone and neglected. Or perhaps she was doing this for herself. She hadn't suddenly been overcome by an overwhelming surge of maternal urges; or maybe just a bit. But it was more to do with decency and what was right. Flora had to do what was right.

*

With Joycey's help, it took three days and, finally, they were packed up and ready for this new adventure. She sent Joycey to return the cot so as to avoid any questions as she loaded the large Bedford automobile with the last of their things. They were to embark on a new life together in a lovely village called Willow on the Grange. It was far enough away so that no member of the Baker family would ever think of dropping in and quiet enough to live a life that would never place Lily in the spotlight.

When she'd informed Marigold about taking Lily, her sister had laughed so hard, her pinny had come undone. She had not been able to face Rose so trusted Marigold to pass on the message. She suspected Rose would be relieved, because her secret would be even further away, albeit still not far enough.

As promised, Joycey had asked no more questions surrounding the situation with Lily. Flora had been vague with the truth anyway, simply explaining that she had always wanted a child and with no husband had turned to adoption. When she had seen how ill-treated Lily had been at the children's home, she was the obvious choice. Lily needed her. Of course, there was no need for Flora to include the family connection and Joycey seemed satisfied with the explanation as she placed the last of the cases into the automobile while Lily slept soundly in Flora's arms. Joycey didn't say much about where the van had come from, but Flora could only guess that she had 'borrowed' it from work like she usually did. Joycey would only be dropping them halfway and then they'd get a bus. Joycey had done so much for her and she hoped she could repay her someday.

As the van pulled up to the bus station, Flora felt overcome with emotion. Joycey had been a good friend and she really hoped she would see her again.

Joycey reached into her trouser pocket. 'Look here, I've written down my address with the office number. I suspect you remember that anyway. Give me a ring and let me know you're both all right.'

As Flora stood by the suitcases, Lily in her arms, she watched as the van moved off with Joycey driving. Already, she missed her one and only friend. Flora's introverted ways had prevented her from making any more. She had always assumed people judged her so decided to cut herself off. She'd better snap out of that thinking, because wherever she and Lily were about to end up, judgements were about to be made in abundance.

My Dearest Love,

I can only hope you feel as happy as I do right now.

I'm going home! I am finally going home! The news hasn't truly sunk into my soul as of yet. I'm still expecting to feel some more excitement. I guess it's hard to believe it's actually going to happen. I have seen so many things change in a heartbeat. One minute a man talking about the date set for his wedding only for him to not live to see the rest of the day.

I know I have to remain positive. To believe in this possibility that, once again, I will get to see my family. How I long to hold my mama close again. I've even missed my father's less than smiling face. I don't know whether my brother will be home at the same time. I hope so. We have so many stories to share.

My flower – I don't even know if you get these letters. In my heart I know you do, I just don't have any concrete evidence. That's the thing about faith, it doesn't work on anything that is seen. I just know they will make their way round to you one day. Of course, the real dream would be to reunite with you once more. Then insecurity sets in. Does she even want me? Does she even want to be with me? If you do, I will do everything in my power to bring us together. Of course we can't live here in Savannah, but there are places in the North. We could maybe go to Philadelphia or New York City. You once told me you'd love to visit there. I don't desire riches or admiration, I just want to become an honourable man and when people say 'William Burrell is a good man', for it to be true.

I'd be lying if I said this war hasn't changed me. I have seen and done things that shook my beliefs about myself, right down to their foundations. But still I try to be the person I have always wanted to be and I simply want a good woman by my side, a wife and a room full of children. I believe I would make a good father. Better than my own but, like him, be a good provider. I will play ball with my boys and read with my girls. When I picture my life as a husband and father, you are by my side. I just want to be with you – but you have to want it too because achieving this would be the hardest thing either of us would ever do. Let's not pretend – our love is illegal in the place I was born and both our families would probably want nothing to do with us, but I'm willing to take that risk if you are. I helped fight a war, surely I can do what is necessary to keep you with me.

If I do make it back home, I'll write down my mama and father's address. That farm has stood for a very long time and will be there for years to come, no matter where I end up. You can always find me there or be led to where I am. So, if you get a letter with my folks' address, you'll know I've made it back. But if I don't hear from you within three months of that letter, I will assume you never want to hear from me again and I'll accept that.

I have to move on. I have to start living.

If this war has taught me anything it's that life is for the living. And I am tired of waiting to live.

Chapter Eight

'Things are going to get so much better for us now. The war's over and our little 'un is one!' said Pete.

Iris lay asleep in her cot, still wearing the floral print dress with a silky blue bow tied at the back, which Rose had made for her.

'Pretty as a picture she is. My beautiful girl,' said Pete, proudly gazing over at Iris. Her chubby limbs were forming a length that hinted she would one day stand tall like her uncle Donald. Her full head of summery curls reminded Rose of a cherub she had seen in the stained-glass windows of the village church.

'I can't help but think about Donald and everything ...'

'He'll be all right! Stop fussing. As I said, everything's going to get better from now on. You'll see!'

If you say so, she thought. She massaged the gap where her tooth had once been, grateful it was out of sight. If she didn't smile too widely, no one except her and Pete need ever know what he had done. Her only reason to smile was Iris anyway. Her sole reason to live. She thought about Lily sometimes, her thoughts usually peppered with envy that Flora got to be with her – but she dared not think of her often. If only for the simple reason that if Pete ever found out, he would probably kill the little baby and herself.

This was her life now. She'd only ever had one chance to escape it. Just one.

It had been the day before William was to leave.

'I don't know what I'm going to do without you, William Burrell.' They lay together on the wet grass, surrounded by the luscious trees she hoped would keep their secret. Their own little part of the world that involved nothing but two people desperate to drink in the scent of one another, absorb the sound of each other's voice and remain secluded for as long as possible.

William sat up. 'Then don't, my love.'

'What do you mean?' asked Rose, sitting up beside him and flicking a tiny twig from his hair. 'Are … are you saying you want me to travel to America with you?'

'Maybe that's exactly what I'm saying.'

'I thought you said our love would be against the law there.' She allowed a glimmer of hope to pierce through.

'It is. But I could come here. We don't know when the war will end but I think it will be soon. When things calm down—'

'No … You can't …' said Rose, any hope, however small, however unrealistic, having quickly disappeared.

'Are you saying you don't want to wait for me, Rose?'

She turned her gaze away, so he couldn't see the tears she was unable to prevent from running down her cheeks.

'Would you be ashamed of me if I came back to claim you? Is that it?'

She turned to him, an abundance of tears flowing. 'Never!' she said passionately.

William's expression softened. 'Oh, my love, don't cry. Please don't cry.'

'We'd have no peace here. It's probably not as bad as what you've told me about Savannah, but we'd get no peace.'

'I understand that. I understand it all.'

75

She hated the lying. Even the address she had given him was Marigold's, confident her sister wouldn't judge her for 'playing away' as she herself had done worse over the years to her long-suffering husband. As long as she never found out William was not a white man. The uproar from both the Baker and Jones family would be catastrophic when added to the fact that she was an adulteress. Clearly this … this romance had been doomed the very moment it had been born.

'So, this is really it then,' said William, not for the first time. Because their parting was all they had ever talked about ever since William had got news of his new posting. In between kisses, they had discussed their limited options and felt weighed down with the inevitability of their reality. The thought of never being with one another again, so outlandish, so unfair. This may not have been the first time they had discussed their limited future but now they were only twenty-four hours from saying goodbye forever.

Now, as she thought back on it, losing William and then Lily had been the only way things could have played out and as long as Rose continued to suppress any longing for them, she could continue in this life, bringing up Iris and trying her hardest to be a good wife to a man she'd wronged by being with another. No longer would she allow any more thoughts of William Burrell to form in her mind. He was a bit player in a past she had no business thinking about. She had seen a couple of his early letters, which Marigold had slapped into her hand with disgust. She had only glanced at them, her reading not being up to par – another secret she had kept from him. Besides, his words scared her, because they had the power to make her think about things she should never, ever be thinking about. So she had instructed her sister to throw them away. Then she'd changed her mind.

'No, don't chuck them all away. Keep some.'

'What for?'

She wanted to say 'for Lily', but her little baby was never coming back and did not exist to her any more. She also wanted to say 'for Iris', because each new month brought with it a different gesture or sound, a subtle shift in her baby features in which she could see William's eyes. She also noted characteristics she was sure were his, real or imagined. For reasons she never wanted to think about, she had given birth to two different-coloured children, which now she had come to think of it, had to be from one man. She wasn't as educated as Flora, but she knew in her heart that both girls had to be William's. She wanted them both to be his, because the thought of any part of Pete living within her children only made her fearful.

And now both girls were a year old.

'What are you thinking about?' asked Pete, leaning over the chair. He began to gently nibble on her ear in a way she used to enjoy when they first started courting. She grabbed the edge of the armchair.

'Stop it. You know I'm ticklish.' Her laugh was faint, false.

'Sorry, love. You just look so nice today.'

'Thanks, Pete.'

The sense of euphoria at the end of the war was far reaching and long lasting. Pete had behaved lovingly for weeks now. Throwing compliments her way and promising their lives could only get better. He'd even found a job closer to home, continued to do things for Iris without her asking, washed the dishes from time to time and as far as she'd noticed, hadn't got drunk in at least a month. His devotion to Iris was something that never seemed to falter.

'What would you like for tea?' asked Rose.

'Whatever's left. Although I may be able to get us a nice bit of beef, no questions asked.'

'I really thought rationing would be over by now.'

'Will take a while for this country to get back to normal, but it will.'

He sat down beside her as she moved backwards towards the edge of the settee.

'Little princess still asleep, I see,' he said.

'Yes.'

He placed his hand on her thigh. 'You sure you're all right?'

Her body tensed. She hadn't meant that to happen. 'Yes.'

His hand moved up her thigh and along the hem of her dress. His fingers slipping inside her underwear.

'Not now, Pete. '

He moved his hand away. 'So when then? Seems like you never want me near you these days.'

'I do, I just—'

'You're my wife, you know?'

'I know I should. I just need a bit if time. Maybe tomorrow.'

'I don't even know if I want to. It's not as if you even smile much these days unless it's something to do with Iris.'

Her mind recorded his words. 'What?'

'Everything seems to be about her ...'

'She's our daughter!' Rose wasn't one to raise her voice at anyone, let alone Pete, but his whining about their daughter had awakened an anger in her borne out of the need to always protect her little girl.

'Calm down,' he said quietly. 'You'll wake her up. I'm just saying, if you won't lie with me, there are plenty of women who want to.'

She wanted to openly scoff, yet felt she would never have a right to. Her own transgressions had put paid to that. But these days she hated sharing the same bed as Pete, let alone allowing him to touch her. He was now staying out at least once a week and when he returned smelling of perfume, it was fine with her, because at least it meant his urges were satisfied.

He patted her knee and Rose was overcome with a wave of revulsion and fear. For this to work, she would have to dispense with any feeling. She had loved him once and had desired him, but each slap or shove or unkind word had eroded whatever feelings she had ever had. Then when he had forced himself on her the morning of Iris's party, not only had any residual affection for him died that day, so had a part of her.

But Iris needed a last name and a home and frankly Rose needed a husband to look after them. She needed Pete, however unsuitable, if only to atone for what she had done. So when his hand crept steadily inside her brassiere, she squeezed her eyes tightly shut as usual, and focused on the beautiful image of her little girls, the sounds of the Glen Miller band playing as her daughters, older than they were now, dressed in pink silk dresses, their hair tied in velvet bows, danced on the grass.

'Dad's heard from Flora,' whispered Marigold. Pete was in the other room talking to their dad as Iris sat on her grandfather's lap.

'What did she say?'

'Just that she's all right. Nothing much and no address. We hardly hear from her. What about you?'

'I think I heard from her once last year – a Christmas card.'

'I still can't believe she has … it …'

'She's a child, Marigold.' *My daughter*, she wanted to say.

'One you didn't want, remember? So don't get all sanctimonious with me!'

Rose wasn't aware that Marigold knew such a big word.

'What's all this whispering?' said their father's voice as he hobbled into the kitchen, familiar cap on his head. The walking stick, the only new addition, was a stark reminder he was getting older.

'Nothing, Dad,' said Marigold.

'Always whispering you lot. Even as kids. My three girls and my boy. When Donald came home I was looking forward to having you all together. But now he's gone off again and so has that sister of yours. Always had big ideas that one. Never knew her place!'

They all knew where Donald was. Everyone in the immediate family knew but wasn't allowed to say where. 'At least Flora has the good sense to send me some money from time to time.'

'That's good news, Dad!' said Rose.

'I can't afford to give you any!' said Marigold.

'I wasn't asking,' he said. This news had brought an unexpected ray of sunshine into Rose's world. Because, to know that wherever she was, Flora was doing okay, meant by default that Lily was too.

My Dearest Love,

It has been a while since my last letter to you. A lot has happened, including the end of this war, as you know and I needed to readjust to this new life that has been thrust upon us all. This is another change that is out of my control, only this time it's one that is positive. My head just needed time to adjust to the new physical location of my body.

I needed to believe and accept that the war was truly over, even though it has been for six months.

My first month at home, I kept myself holed up in my old room. The one I used to rest my head in as a child, where I would read the classics with a glass of sweet iced tea by my side. I was a different man, then. A boy. Now, I have participated in things that warranted me a man. Things a boy had no business doing.

I walked through the door of my childhood home and my mama sank to her knees, wailing in happiness. My father stood beside the wooden table where we had eaten as a family so many times, his hand steadying himself.

'Mama, Daddy, I'm home,' I whispered. I don't think they heard me, but I heard myself. I finally rushed over to my mama and held onto her as she crumpled towards the floor, her face flooded in tears. She'd never been one to be so emotional, but I assumed she was just overcome with happiness to see me.

It wasn't until she stopped sobbing and my father stood above us and said, 'Your brother didn't make it,' that I realised.

When my father told my mama to stop babying me and that four weeks holed up at home was enough, I didn't agree. I wanted to stay cocooned in the house. I also wanted to get up before the cockerel, get to preparing the breakfast for my men. I missed that life. But how could I? How could I miss cooking and herding cattle instead of doing what I had signed up for? They said it was because of my farm experience, but we all knew the truth – me and the other negro soldiers 'forced' to work in the kitchens instead of where we really wanted to be. And how could I miss not being allowed to use the same bathroom as my men yet be expected to save their lives in battle while trusting them to save mine? Men like Riker, who never looked me in the eye but cheered on the likes of Joe Louis and proclaimed Ethel Waters as the greatest singer he'd ever heard. Yet was happy to beat Cornel and me to a near pulp.

I had unrealistically hoped that things had changed in Savannah during my absence but they hadn't. So, at least when I was holed up in my childhood bedroom I didn't have to acknowledge any of it. I was safer in my bed. I didn't have to participate in the larger world any more.

'You got to get up, Willie. Earn your keep, like a man should,' my father kept saying. Like I hadn't heard him the first or second time.

I had a beautiful dream of you and me walking hand in hand, stopping only to taste each other's lips and to talk. Maybe take a sip of iced tea that would suddenly appear. Now my father was standing over my bed with that baritone voice I used to fear as a child.

'Willie, get up! How long you going to do this? Your mama is worried, everyone is worried. You needs to start working.'

'I will look for something, I will,' I promised, but not really meaning any of my words. I pulled the quilt away from my face

out of respect, when all I wanted was to stay under that warm cover that my grandmother had made.

'There's plenty of work around here. Especially as your brother ...'

As he'd constantly done since I'd arrived, my father never said his name. The brother born two years before me. The brother who I would chase around the yard and scuffle with. The brother I had loved more than myself. My father refused to say his name and maybe that was a good thing, because then I could pretend too. I could pretend that none of it had happened.

If it wasn't for Mama crying almost every day, while cutting up a vegetable or gazing at something he'd made – like the tiny wooden house he'd carved in a week – it would have been easier to forget. I thought about going back to the army – in an admin role now that it was clear my leg was permanently injured, but couldn't do that to my mama. I didn't tell you about that did I? I wish I could say my gait was a badge of honour, a battle scar, but it was a result of a piece of machinery falling on me 'accidentally'. I don't think some of the men appreciated my involvement in Cornel's defence after his beating. This was no accident.

'Daddy, I will help out at the farm. Just give me some time.'

'How much more time you need? Now your brother's gone, this will be all yours one day and then your son's,' said my father, who had not taken the hint to leave my room. I needed peace. I just wanted peace. Something the world now enjoyed yet was something that still eluded my thoughts and my senses.

'Now you're here we can make the farm yield more,' he continued.

I didn't have the courage to tell my father I wanted nothing to do with the farm. That my dream to escape the South had never diminished. I was heading to the North where there were plenty of opportunities. Besides, there was no reason my first cousin and her husband couldn't take over the farm when the time came. Why was she deemed less so because she was a woman, anyway? I think about the women I met in England who kept the country going without their men. I noticed them all, even though I only had eyes for one.

My father didn't need to know of my plans to visit the home of the writer Langston Hughes in New York City, where I planned to live in a huge brownstone writing stories, even poems. I would read until my heart's content and on nights off go to the Cotton Club I've heard so much about. I would walk the streets not fearing the Klan, dressed in their white sheets, coming on up behind me. I just wanted to feel like a free man. Yet every day I wake up in my old bedroom and dare to read a little bit of My Bondage and My Freedom *by Frederick Douglass, I know I'm not free. I'm still there, institutionalised in my mind. I'm still in the South where I will never, ever be free.*

I'm still very much trapped.

Chapter Nine

1947

After two years, Flora finally allowed herself to believe she and Lily were settled. Willow on the Grange, a village in the Home Counties, offered seclusion in the form of a pretty little cottage with no immediate neighbours, which Flora could afford to rent thanks to the generous savings she had accrued before and during the war. A spiral of roses framed the doorway and inside was a good-sized living room with two bedrooms upstairs, which meant Lily had a corner where she could play. Ironically, they spent most of their time in the kitchen, especially in the winter thanks to the powerful wood-burning oven, which kept the room warm. The house was fully furnished with second-hand furniture, although if not for the war and the shortage of such things, Flora would have ensured everything was brand new. She could afford it. Flora vowed that as soon as the country dusted off the residue of war, she would finally be able to raise Lily in the surroundings she fully deserved. Her family would call such thinking foolish and 'not for the likes of them', but Flora simply wanted the best for Lily. Besides, it was no one's business what she did with her money. None of her family had ever filled her pantry with food so, therefore, they had no say in how she ran her life. She often grew angry at the thought of the

Baker family, but the rush of warmth she felt whenever this little girl simply smiled at her made everything worthwhile.

At three years old, Lily was already becoming a 'little madam', who had short tantrums, as well as being a kind, warm-hearted child with a hidden strength and determination Flora had already noticed. She would need it one day, too, when she left the safety of their home to venture outside into the unknown – something that filled Flora with utter dread anytime she allowed herself to think about it. Thankfully, for now, it was still a long way off and Lily could remain under her careful and watchful eye.

Soon after their arrival, Flora had been able to secure private work for a number of local firms by cold calling as Lily slept in her pram outside the office or shop, a soft blanket covering most of her face. They would set off early in the morning and before the village fully came to life. Her efforts paid off as she was now able to work from home and look after Lily. As a woman, she'd had to undercut most of their current providers, but that was the price she was prepared to pay for the freedom to keep Lily away from the outside world. It was Joycey who commented once during a visit: 'You can't keep her locked away forever.' Flora had smiled, while the only thought running through her mind was how she was prepared to do just that.

Joycey, fuelled by the simplicity of life in Willow on the Grange, announced that she and her new family were moving to live half a mile away! Flora was elated. Joycey was the only person she would ever trust Lily with and there were times when she needed to go out on errands and had left Lily asleep at home. Flora was also grateful to have another adult to speak to and had missed her one and only friend dearly. However, she felt their friendship had diminished slightly when Joycey announced she'd fallen for someone and got married almost immediately. Joycey had incorrectly assumed that Flora's irritation was to do with not getting an invite, but it was so much more than that.

'You're the last person I thought would do that – get married – that's all,' said Flora sheepishly. She was keen not to alienate her only friend, but she couldn't brush off the feeling of being let down. That Joycey had gone and done what every other woman she knew eventually did.

'I got up the duff. I was already months gone so I had to get the wedding over with quickly. We only had two guests and only then so they could sign the register!'

'I see.'

'What else was I supposed to do?' said Joycey in a rare show of defensiveness. Kenneth appeared to be a decent man, though. Like Joycey, he never judged and never asked questions. Which was why, on the day Joycey, Kenneth and baby Walter moved into their new home, Flora, for the first time, felt a strong urge to confide the entire story surrounding the birth of Lily.

Kenneth only once mentioned Lily's skin colour. 'I don't care what anyone looks like. With what I've seen over the past few years, I know what's important. Brave men come in all shades. We had black and brown men fighting the same war with us and they all bled the same. They all bled the same.'

Such sentiments were why Flora felt so at ease with the couple. Yet, despite her strong urge to do so, she could not bring herself to tell Joycey and Kenneth the whole truth surrounding Lily's birth and the involvement of her sister Rose. The less people knew, the less chance of the truth filtering through to those who could harm Lily ... and Rose. Although at present she didn't care if she never saw Rose again, she wanted no harm to come to her.

Lily's parentage was a secret that Flora was prepared to take to the grave.

Whenever Lily and Walter played together, it was a reminder of what could be. That the world could be a safe place for Lily after all.

'Let anyone say a word and I'll have 'em,' Joycey often said, her hand curled into a fist shape. Although she was being playful, Joycey had to be one of the toughest women she knew. Yet she doubted Joycey would ever need to defend them in Willow on the Grange. Since their arrival over two years ago, the looks had stopped after Flora had shrewdly 'confessed' that after losing her husband she'd adopted the poor unfortunate child of a young girl who could not afford to keep the unlucky little mite. Flora had hated herself for using such language to describe her beautiful and clever little girl, but it was the only way to reel in the self-appointed village gossip who sat behind the till of the only shop for four miles. This woman inadvertently put a stop to the pointing and overlong stares of curiosity, with Lily and Flora now an accepted, albeit curious part of the community.

Now that Joycey could take care of Lily, Flora had been able to regularly embark on a twenty-mile trip to visit a place she could never have taken a young child.

'I'll be back tonight,' she assured Joycey as four-year-old Lily held onto her legs. 'Mummy Flora, where go?' Lily's speech had finally began to improve over the last year what with Flora's tutition and Lily's interaction with Walter. She still had a way to go though.

Flora extracted herself from Lily's slight grip. 'Just once in a while I have to go and make a visit.'

'But where?' These days, Lily was full of questions and Flora liked to answer them all truthfully and in detail so that the child could learn. But this time she would lie.

'I have to work,' she said.

'Lily, do you want to see some ladybirds? Would you like that?' Joycey shrewdly interrupted as she shooed Flora out of the front door. Lily would be occupied within seconds. No tears or questions.

*

The building reminded her of Reginald House but was bigger and well maintained. A freshly cut lawn with well-trimmed rose bushes was in front of the vast doorway which had a familiar figure standing in the middle of it.

'Hello, Ruth,' said Flora.

'It's nice to see you again.'

Ruth had aged since Flora's last visit. This was perhaps not surprising as she was here a lot more times in the month than Flora. They had talked at length once. A sweet tale of a real-life love affair, which still refused to end despite the circumstances. Ruth's husband had returned from the war unable to even recognise her. And yet, she still visited him regularly. Never giving up hope. Her love as strong as ever.

Flora felt a rush of shame.

'I'm just taking a break,' said Ruth as Flora patted her arm, before opening the door. Inside, was the total antithesis to the brightness captured outside. The walls were grey, perhaps more with age than through choice, the atmosphere reeking of a bleach-like substance. She headed towards the ward and one row of beds facing a second row. Her shoes made a click-clack sound as she walked to the end of the room.

The plastic curtains were closed. 'Hello, are you decent?' she asked pointlessly, because if he were indeed semi-clad, he wouldn't be the one to tell her. She slowly opened the curtain to silence. Donald was sitting facing the window, his eyes apparently not focused on anything in particular. He was dressed in striped pyjamas and a brown dressing grown. She leaned in, planting a kiss on his cold cheek. His eyes shut and then opened.

'I didn't bring you anything today. I was told not to bother because you didn't eat the fruit I brought last time and it took us three hours to queue up for those oranges.'

The silence she was now used to, but during that first visit, it had been hard. There were no words to explain the disappearance of the vibrant and sometimes loud little brother who had terrorised them playfully as kids and protected them as soon as he had grown into his role as the only boy in the Baker family. The first time he'd donned his army uniform, Flora knew he would take his role seriously and serve his country with pride. Now, the man who sat with his back to her was not known to anyone anymore, perhaps not even himself. The war had taken out what was left of him and dumped a shell of a man back into a society that simply didn't know what to do with him. This made her angry – as did this feeling of powerlessness. With all she had learned over the years, reading books, educating herself on conditions such as shell shock, she still couldn't find a way to reach her little brother. She couldn't even persuade her family he was worth visiting and was more than just an embarrassing little secret. All she could do was visit with him once in a while and tell him he was loved.

Flora read the telegram and a flood of emotion almost left her gasping for air.

She scrunched the telegram into her pocket and pulled out her hand for Lily to hold onto. Now at the age of five, her huge coils of hair that Flora found difficult to manage framed her beautiful, oval-shaped face. She no longer ran away for the sheer joy of childishness, but liked to keep close to Flora, to feel her touch. Now, Flora would have to leave Lily for a longer length of time because something was wrong. The telegram of course was brief and simply told her to get home – back to the Baker house – immediately. She knew this had something to do with her father because the last time she'd seen him, a year before, Albert Baker, wearing his trademark cap, had remained as cantankerous as always, but had certainly slowed down. Though visibly aged and sitting in his chair more frequently than ever, when he did move about, his back remained stooped over a walking stick and his hands shook. But by still managing to criticise her life choices and question why she wasn't married to a nice man, this had eased her fears. If he was still criticising her, he must be okay!

She wasn't going to cry, not in front of Lily, but heavy guilt and fear began to follow her. She had never really had a good relationship with her father and they had possibly never really understood one another. But the thought of him dying and her not being there was something that filled her with sorrow.

Being back in the street in Alderberry, where she had grown up, made her feel uneasy. The odd times she'd visited since taking in Lily were always laced with anxiety. First for leaving Lily with Joycey, whom she would drop off on the way, and then tuning into those feelings associated with seeing her immediate family again.

Whether imagined or real, Marigold seemed to constantly gawp at her with a permanent look of distaste. Of course, Marigold was like this with most people, but with Flora there appeared to be added venom. As for Rose, Flora hadn't seen her during the last two visits. Even their father had expressed concern over hardly seeing her any more, lamenting the fact that he had to be stuck with 'fat arsed' Marigold for company.

As Flora walked towards the half-opened door that led to her childhood home, she was filled with a blast of dread. Regardless of her relationship with him, if anything happened to her father she'd be devastated. He was the final part of the couple who were once Albert and Lillian Baker. Two people who met, fell in love and sired three girls and a baby boy that would ultimately lead to the end of Lillian's life. Flora would be heartbroken if her father died before she'd had a chance to tell him she actually did love him; before she had a chance to look into his eyes and receive the love she never realised she'd craved for so very long. He did love her, didn't he? Weren't parents supposed to love their children, no matter what? Did Rose love Lily? Flora, with every fibre of her being, loved little Lily without condition, regardless of what shade her skin was or how 'different' her hair felt. She loved that little girl with a love she'd never experienced before and yet she hadn't even given birth to her. Of course Albert loved her. Of course he did!

As she walked through each doorway, ignoring the faces around her, she instinctively headed to her father's bedroom, longing to touch his hand once more. Inside his room were a group of ashen-faced family members and, immediately, she knew her father was dead.

It wasn't until after the funeral service, outside the church, that she saw Rose again. Like the rest of them, her body was stooped as she walked with the slow gait of those who mourned, the hat tipped to the side like Betty Grable's doing nothing to hide a healing bruise under her eye. The last time Flora had seen her father alive, Marigold had hinted, with a wink, that Rose's absence was due to Pete and their incessant 'rowing' and the odd backhander. Flora hadn't wanted to believe there was violence involved, hoping Marigold was just being hateful as always.

'Did he do that to you?' challenged Flora, no longer in any doubt at how Pete treated her sister. She was thankful that Lily was not a part of that household, yet fearful for her other niece.

'Don't start,' said Rose. 'This is Dad's day.'

'And he'd want you to be with a man like that, would he? Someone who would harm his daughter and granddaughter?'

'He'd never touch Iris!'

'But it's all right to touch *you*?'

'You don't know what you're talking about. Anyway, Dad loved Pete and Pete loved him back!'

'So much that he didn't even let you go and see him.'

'That isn't what happened. I fell and—'

'It actually took me leaving to really understand what was going on with you two.'

'Don't—'

'Why do you stay?'

'You wouldn't understand.'

'No, I don't.'

Rose pulled a tissue from her jacket pocket. 'Are you going back to the house? Marigold's laid on a spread.'

'No. I'm going back. To *your* daughter.'

Rose dabbed at her eyes as the tears refused to appear. 'H ... how is she?'

'Do you care?' Anger had risen within her. Flora was angry ... at Rose, Pete, even her dad.

'Of course I care.'

'When I first told you I took her you said I should have left her at that place!'

'I was just ... shocked, that's all.'

'Frightened you mean. Scared I would let out your secret. Or, as Marigold would say, your dirty little secret.'

'Don't ...' Now the tears.

'Well, Lily isn't anyone's dirty little secret. She is a beautiful five-year-old girl who reads and writes beyond her years, is never without the little rag doll my friend Joycey gave her and she calls me Mummy in the sweetest voice you have ever heard. She is everything a mother would want. She is my love.'

'She ... she calls you Mummy?'

'Yes!' lied Flora, wanting the word to pierce Rose's heart and make it bleed just as hers did. She was totally unconcerned that Rose was now crying incessantly into an impossibly small handkerchief. She just hoped the pain was fresh, raw, because she deserved it. She did not deserve the physical bruises, but she deserved this moment.

'Rose?' Pete's voice cut short the longest conversation Rose and Flora had had in years.

'Rose, there you are. Come on, don't upset yourself.' He placed his arm protectively over her shoulder, glancing at Flora.

'We'll see you back at the house,' said Pete.

'No you won't. I'm going home. I have a long journey back,' said Flora.

'Charming. Can't wait to get away, eh? Shouldn't be a surprise; you hardly saw your dad when he was alive.'

'Same as you two, I hear.'

'Flora!' said Rose, her eyebrows arched.

'I'm going home because my life is there now, not here,' she said, turning to leave. Her breathing accelerated with each step, as her anger increased. When she was sure she was out of sight, along came her own hot tears. At first mingling beneath her eyelids, before sprinkling down like water from a dripping tap. She was crying once again for the death of her father but also the diminished relationship with the sister she now pitied and disliked. With their dad gone, she no longer needed to be tied to the Bakers any more. Lily had been her world for four years now and that little girl was all Flora would ever need. She would keep her close, protect her from everything that was bitter, twisted and hateful. She would make sure that Lily never felt the pain of disappointment, loss, of not being good enough, like she had. Lily meant everything to her. Lily *was* everything to her.

My Dearest Love,

I am unable to recall the very day I began to feel better but the sky was blue and the sun was glazing its majestic beauty over the landscape I loved. I was smiling as I paid for some bread at the store, walked out with my walking stick and there she was: Augustine Jewson, in a fine summer dress and straw hat. Apart from you, I'd never seen a woman look so pretty.

'Good to see you,' she said. 'I heard you were back.' I noted her voice. The same tone my mama would have when me or my brother was sent home from school for fighting. A love mixed in with disappointment at our wayward behaviour.

'I been busy.'

'You could have come by and said hello, William. My family have known you a long time.'

'*You're right.*'

'*My condolences for the loss of your brother.*'

'*Thank you.*'

'*He was a good man.*'

'*Yes, yes, he was.*' *I wanted to stop this talk of my brother. Like my father, I preferred it this way. Every mention of him brought out questions leading to feelings I thought were better kept inside. We had both gone into the same battle and yet only one of us had returned home.*

'*There's a dance tonight at the Century. Will you be attending?*' *asked Augustine in such a way that once upon a time would have got me fired up. By now though I was less fire, more tepid water. I had only recently started to feel 'happy' again.*

'*I'd love to come to the dance ... if you would permit me to have a dance with you.*'

'*Even with your leg?*'

'*Nothing will stop me. I may not be able to do the jitterbug, but I can still lead you around that dance floor, Miss Jewson.*'

'*That sounds wonderful,*' *she said with that smile. Augustine Jewson will never be you, no one could, but it was time for me to get out from under my grandmother's quilt and start living my life!*

I'll spare you the details, my love, but the night I accompanied Augustine Jewson to the dance, we moved as one across the dance floor like two people in love. I had to move slow because of my leg, while everyone moved quickly around us – but it didn't matter. It was like Augustine and I were the only two people there anyway!

The band was lively, the drinks were flowing and for two solid hours I was able to forget about the army, my brother, you. When I accompanied her to her doorstep, I knew I wouldn't get more than a kiss – and it was everything I needed it to be.

'*That was real nice. And unexpected,*' *I said.*

'*You've been away for a very long time.*'

I gently flicked my finger under her chin. 'But I'm home now.'

I placed my lips on hers, feeling a stir. I apologise, but I'm a man and it had been so very long since you and I even touched. I craved the feel of a woman even if it was just one sweet kiss. We sat on the swing chairs, outside of her family home, holding hands like sweethearts and that was enough for me. It felt like magic!

'Do you remember when we were kids, we used to sit here?' she said.

'Of course. We were best friends. I used to get teased about having a girl as my friend.'

'That was until we became more than just good friends.'

'That was your fault!' I laughed, remembering the innocence of our youth. We talked about what she'd been doing since I had 'left' and of course I asked why she'd never married. Her answer was clear, concise and confident. 'Because I was waiting for you.'

That evening became the promise of something, anything. A future. I had always believed that Augustine Jewson would make a good wife and here she was reinforcing my belief. We were laughing together, becoming more aquatinted and then the door opened.

I recognised her mother Harriet Jewson immediately.

'I heard you were back. Good to see you. Condolences for your loss.'

I stood. 'Thank you, ma'am.'

'It is very late, could you come in now, Augustine?'

Not that I would ever be disrespectful, but I wanted to tell Augustine's mother that this woman was almost thirty years old!

As if reading my mind, she said, 'She got a baby to feed. Now, Augustine, will you please come and do that?'

The door slammed in her wake and I turned to Augustine.

'A baby?'

'He's not a baby, he's three.'

'Okay, but that's not the point, is it?'

'Of course I was going to tell you the truth. We just met after all these years and I wanted to stay fourteen again, just for another hour.'

'You're still not making any sense.' I was angry, pride a little dented.

'What do you want me to tell you? I got married and he died. I'm a widow. What, did you really expect me to sit tight and wait for you? I was already twenty-six and soon no one would want me. My husband was a good man. He didn't make me go weak like you do when you smile or look towards the sky when you are thinking, but he was good. A provider too and my mama liked him.'

I exhaled, as the quick dreams I had for us both just disappeared. I never liked a liar. Anything but that.

I sat back down on the swing, my feet anchoring me.

'You weren't around, William, and you never wrote to me or nothing. What was I supposed to do?' Her tears told me she was genuine.

'How did your husband die?'

'Not in war. He was knocked down and killed by Mr Brewster's son.'

'Mr Brewster who runs the mill?'

'Yes. The day after they had words.'

'What did the police say about it?' I knew as soon as I spoke them, my words were pointless.

'Nothing.'

I beckoned for her to come beside me once more. My earlier surprise and disappointment replaced by a shared understanding of how it was to lose someone and the sheer injustice of the world Augustine and I shared.

Chapter Ten

1952

'Mummy, can't we have something else for breakfast?'

Eight-year-old Iris had yet to understand that just because the war had been over for seven years now, it didn't mean the end of food rationing. For the first time in many years, tea had been taken off the ration list and Pete seemed confident a lot more could follow. Although over the years Rose had tried not to let her daughter go without, it was hard, especially when she'd find precious cuts of meat missing from the meat safe. Clearly, Pete's promise to stay away from other women was long since forgotten and Rose no longer cared. But taking the family's food to feed his women was a step too far and she would be having words with him about it. For the most part, Rose relied on whatever cooking tips she could get from Grandma Buggins on the wireless. She knew how to make a simple pie go a long way!

Rose smoothed her hands down her daughter's shoulder-length curls. Iris often complained about them, asking why she didn't have straight and easy hair like her mummy.

'You look like a princess with all that hair. You don't want to be like me.' Her daughter's skin tone remained a bright, pale hue framing a beautiful smile thanks to a pair of lips that seemed to spread from ear to ear. Rose would do anything to keep that smile on her face.

'Don't worry, I'll get us some more corned beef in a couple of days. I know that's your favourite,' said Rose.

'On toast?'

'On toast.'

'When's Daddy coming back?' asked Iris, which she often did when Pete disappeared for long stretches. He was rumoured to be visiting a woman in Latchford and, just last week, Iris had spotted him with a blonde woman as she walked home from school with her two best friends. Rose had brushed it off with 'Oh that's just a lady he works with.' Yet from the corner of her eye she could see her daughter's confusion. This was the last thing she wanted for her daughter. She wanted Iris living in a happy and conflict-free household.

She wanted the sacrifice to have been worth it.

As mother and daughter sat at the kitchen table, the air felt thick with disappointment.

'You better hope the wind doesn't change or your face will stay like that!'

Iris's frown quickly turned into that huge smile. 'You're silly, Mummy!'

'I'm serious. You don't want to look that miserable for long!'

'Okay!'

'Why don't we play a game? How about ... I Spy?'

'That's boring!'

'I spy with my little eye, something beginning with O.'

'That's easy, oven!'

'Good girl. Your turn.'

She rolled her eyes. 'I spy ...' She looked up to the ceiling, something she always did when deep in thought.

'Okay, ermm ... I spy with my little eye' – her eyes rolled and her frown returned – 'something beginning with D!'

'Dishes?'

'Daddy!'

'What, where?'

She stood up and turned around to see Pete standing in front of her.

'You spoiled it!' he said as Iris walked tentatively towards her father and into his arms, After kissing his daughter's cheek, he leaned into Rose, reeking of another women's perfume.

She flinched.

'What's wrong?' he asked, voice filled with innocence. She had hated him a little bit more each day, especially after bringing Iris into his sordid little life. This was beyond anything he had ever done and there was no way she could hate him any more than she did at that very moment.

'Are you going to tell me what's wrong?' he reiterated.

'Nothing,' she mumbled.

'No, I'm not having that. There's something obviously going on. Iris, what's wrong with your mum?'

'You leave her out of it!' screamed Rose, unable to lower the volume on a voice that didn't even sound like her.

Iris's eyes widened.

'You think it's okay to talk to me like that? And in front of our kid?'

'You weren't thinking about all of that when you were parading that tart in front of her, were you?'

His eyes fixated on Iris.

'Mummy, don't shout!'

'Listen to her,' warned Pete.

'It's okay, my love. No one's shouting any more.'

'You always shout. You and Daddy are always shouting!'

At that moment Rose realised she too had failed to keep Iris out of the mess. She was no better than Pete.

'Iris, go to your room,' said Pete.

Iris, her mounting sobs suppressed, looked to her mother for confirmation.

'I said go to your room!' shouted Pete.

'Don't you shout at her!' said Rose, squaring up to her husband. Iris looked on with an expression of confusion, her parents locked in their own private stand-off.

'No one tells me what to do. I pay the bills around here and you'd do well to remember that!'

Turning her back on him, she pulled a sobbing Iris into her embrace.

'Don't you turn your back on me!' he hissed as Rose held tightly onto her daughter.

'Mummy!' screamed Iris. The fear in her voice tore Rose apart and weakened her resolve against Pete. Her little girl was frightened.

'Look at me!' Pete hissed but Rose would not and could not, choosing to bury her head in her daughter's quivering chest, comforted by the feel of her hair. He would stop soon, leave her alone and maybe go back to the blonde woman's house. Instead, they remained in a strange tug of war as Pete attempted to extract his wife from their daughter's tightened grip.

'I said, don't turn your back on me!' He gripped her shoulder and in a flash her teeth had sunk into his hand.

'Ow!' he cried, swiping the back of his hand across her face. Rose fell to the ground with Iris in her arms, her body protecting the little girl from harm.

'You all right?' Rose asked as Iris stood up immediately, bursting into a fit of even louder tears.

'Shut up!' roared Pete, moving towards her. Rose on the ground, her mind hazy with shock, watched him move towards her child, her baby, his face red with an anger she had seen too many times before.

She no longer heard a sound. Her eyes darted to his clenched fists. She had to get up, she needed to save her daughter.

All she could hear were the loud, intense screams.

Her own.

*

At the age of eight, Lily was thriving academically. Flora's home schooling had surpassed anything she could have learned at the only school in the village. Once he realised that Lily was a 'brown' child, the headmaster had more or less questioned the point of Lily even attending the school. He hadn't said it in so many words, but Flora had felt it during their exchange. As if he was saying, 'What's the point? There's no way she'll find a job when she grows up anyway.' Imagined or real, Flora was clear on one thing; only she could provide the best for Lily. So thanks to her exemplary teaching skills, Lily was now excellent at maths and English, and Flora had even thrown in a bit of science. Lily was a willing and eager student, more than capable of retaining vast amounts of information without complaint. It was clear that the studies Flora had read, like those of Samuel George Morton, were incorrect. Black people were no more or less intelligent than white people. It was clear that those scientists clearly had the same views as the local headmaster!

'Come on, Lil, you know your seven times table!'

Lily rested her chin in her hands as they both sat at the kitchen table. Flora had promised a treat if she got full marks.

'Erm ...' She looked up to the ceiling in that way she always did when deep in thought.

'I forgot! Can't I just have the treat?'

'You can have the treat.'

'Where is it?' She jumped with excitement in the way that always made Flora's heart sing. It didn't matter what type of day she'd had, buried under an avalanche of paperwork for her clients, or how gloomy the sky was, just seeing the excitement on Lily's face was enough to erase every low thought.

'Over in the bottom cupboard,' she said.

Lily ran over to the cupboard beside the new white gas cooker Flora had purchased just a week before. Flora was proud of the mod cons she had accumulated over the past year.

'Open the bag then!' encouraged Flora. Lily carefully pulled out a soft-clothed doll with stringy pigtails and red circles for cheeks.

'This is for me?'

'Who else is it for?'

'Thank you, Mummy Flora!' she said, flinging herself into Flora's arms and squeezing her tightly. This was to replace the one that Joycey had given her many years ago. Flora liked her to have new things and now clothes rationing had ended, enjoyed buying Lily the prettiest of dresses and little bows to tie in her hair. She wasn't very good at styling Lily's beautiful and tight coils and the noise she'd make any time Flora attempted to run the inadequate comb through it was enough to make her give up and simply place a ribbon around her head. A ribbon always made a difference. Lily never wanted for anything, though, least of all food. Sharing a couple of hens with Joycey meant a regular supply of eggs with Flora able to swap her coupons for something else. Something that Lily desired, of course. Luckily, corned beef hash on toast was her favourite. Indeed, everything she had was for Lily, who had quickly become a child who'd never known what it felt like to go without and never would. Flora would make sure of that.

'Thank you!' enthused Lily. With the doll firmly between them, Flora and Lily held onto one another in a warm hug and when Lily looked up at her with those beautiful almond-shaped eyes, Flora sensed a question.

'What is it?'

'I was wondering.'

'What were you wondering?'

Lily spoke so much better than even Joycey's kids. Not that she would ever comment on this fact.

'I have been wondering whether what Walter said was correct.'

'And what did Walter say?'

'That you are not my real mummy because you adopted me.'

Flora gently extracted herself from Lily and faced her. 'What do you think?'

'That my first mummy carried me here.' She pointed to her own tiny rounded stomach, recounting a conversation they had had when Lily was six. 'But because you don't have any children, you became my second mummy. My Mummy Flora!'

'That's right.'

'Is it all right if I told everyone you were my first mummy. Even if you didn't carry me in your tummy?'

'Of course!' Flora was afraid her heart would burst. 'I ... I don't see anything wrong with that.'

She pulled the little girl, her daughter, into a tight yet loving embrace. All the love she could no longer receive from her mother and father, her sisters and a brother who didn't even know who she was, no longer left a void. Indeed it hadn't since the moment this little girl had been born.

'Are you sure it's all right?' asked Lily with such tenderness in her voice.

'Of course I'm sure, you silly billy!'

'So then, Mummy Flora, why are you crying?'

BOOK TWO

Lily and Iris

Chapter Eleven

1958

She awoke with a start.

Strands of damp, curly chestnut hair clamped to her head, her nightdress like a second skin. She'd just had another one: a dream of vivid images and feelings associated with being left alone and feeling helpless.

Once every few months they would come at her without warning and with more frequency around her birthday. As she would be fifteen years old in a matter of weeks, its onset made perfect sense. The first set had started around the time of her eleventh birthday. She hated having to think about that time – sleeping alone in her parents' bed as the rest of the house filled with people she hardly knew. Family apparently. During those first few weeks she had seen Aunt Marigold more times than she had in her whole life. Aunt Flora hadn't even bothered to come.

The door to her bedroom opened.

'You all right there, love?' her father said, his unshaven face instantly reminding her of where he'd been the night before.

'Yeah, I'm okay.'

'Good girl. You got breakfast in hand then?'

'Yes, Dad.' She dutifully pulled herself out of bed, rubbing at her eyes gently, but not before glancing at herself in the oblong mirror, which stood against the bedroom wall and had once belonged to her grandmother Lillian. As usual, she was disappointed to see her red lips had not disappeared overnight. Some of the girls at school said they envied them as she 'didn't have to buy any lipstick', while Iris had simply placed them into the part of life she deemed abnormal and annoying. Like the size of her lips in comparison to others and that huge head of curly hair no one in her family (as far as she knew) had the misfortune of having to deal with. Dad had never known his own dad. Perhaps her paternal grandfather also had a curly head like a mop.

'Make sure you make plenty. I'm half starved!' called her father predictably. She had stopped wondering what he got up to during his nights away from the house. Indeed, she was often grateful for it as she wouldn't have to worry about making sure he was fed or if he choked on his own vomit during the night. For those few hours, he was someone else's problem. She sometimes enjoyed going to school simply for the break, even though she hated the place. She wasn't as bright as some of the girls and, as her dad often said, there really wasn't any point in school for a girl anyway. The rest of her life would be spent at home. And he was right. Looking after him was her role until she found a nice chap to marry and then it would start all over again.

For Iris, that didn't sound all that bad. She'd love to meet someone, if only to escape life with her father. She'd make a good wife, too. She was good at cleaning and her mother had taught her how to cook vast meals from next to nothing. She could only hope her future husband turned out to be more like the blokes in those American movies she watched at Maureen's house (the only person she knew with a television set). Beautiful movie stars like Doris Day always ended up in the arms of a handsome man and lived happily ever after. Although Iris was as 'thick as two planks' according to one of her teachers, she was clever enough to work out that a lot of those films were fantasy and for girls who looked a bit odd like she did, there were even fewer men like Cary Grant around. Most were probably like her dad; demanding and needing her to look after them, make them happy.

She missed her mum.

Not as much as she used to though, and this switch in emotion frightened her, infusing her at times with a gut-wrenching guilt, tied with not wanting ever to forget her. She was pleased she had the same colour hair and slim hands – she remembered her mum's hands most of all. Everything else would have faded if not for the few black-and-white pictures in a small photo album and a framed photo on the sideboard, which sat beside one taken on her parents' wedding day. It was of the entire Baker family: Grandad Albert in his cap with Granny Lil and their four young children, including her mum and Aunty Rose holding hands and wearing what looked like matching dresses.

Iris pulled one of her mum's floral dresses out of the wardrobe. A faded yellow one. There was never enough money to buy any new clothes so she was grateful she was now the same size her mum had once been.

Breakfast was prepared within minutes. She'd never be able to cook as well as her mum used to and her father would often remind her: 'If your mum was here when they got rid of rationing she would have made us a banquet. She could make something out of nothing. Not just with food!' She wasn't quite sure what the latter end of that sentence meant but she was able to smile at the memory of being taught to make a pancake without eggs.

'Now you flip it over like this!' she had said, her hand over Iris's wrist.

'Mum, I can't. It'll break or it will fall on the floor!'

'No it won't. Try it!'

Her father had walked in all smiles. 'All this for me, eh?'

'Your girl's not exactly a dab hand at this!'

'I'm trying, Mum!' said Iris, the tears welling up in her eyes. With a final burst of energy and a turn of her wrist, the hardened mixture turned perfectly in the pan.

'There you go, love! All done!'

The elation she felt began to stem the tears as the food, which had required so much effort, was consumed by the three of them within minutes.

'You didn't like that!' joked her mum.

'That was lovely. Great first effort for my little 'un,' said her father as she perched herself on his knee, her mum looking on with a smile. Oh, how she missed that smile. She missed her presence, her smell. She missed everything about her. It was just Iris and her father now and sometimes, just sometimes, she wished she could see more of her aunties, but Aunt Marigold had her boys and Aunt Flora had never married but stayed away from the entire family. According to her father, her uncle Donald was locked away in a loony bin. But she longed to see them all. Perhaps talk about her mum and find out what she was like as a little girl. She longed to feel a part of the Baker family in some way, however small, but as she was always reminded by her father, 'None of them give a hoot about you, so why should you about them?' Her father, however much booze he downed or however long he stayed away each week, was the only person she could rely on.

Turning fifteen meant Iris was finally old enough to leave school and make decisions about the rest of her life. School was a waste of time anyway, and she still found it hard to read complete sentences without struggling. She was a growing girl, as her father would always say and boys like Gary Moorgate had noticed. They had necked one night after he'd walked her home from the shops. It was the first time a boy had ever kissed her and she hadn't been prepared for what came next.

'Gary!' she'd said, brushing his hands away from her bosom.

His blond hair blew slightly in the weak wind. 'Sorry,' he said, his eyes staring at the floor. 'I didn't mean to ...'

Iris was torn. Her mum had always shown her it was better to keep a man happy, just like she had with her own husband. Well, most of the time, anyway. And Iris wanted Gary to be happy, even if she wasn't really liking what he'd just done.

'Do you still want to walk with me?' she asked, fearful of the answer.

'Of course I do. I only did that because my older brother said it's what girls like. I'm really sorry, Iris. I hope I didn't upset you.'

'I'm okay, really. It was my fault, anyway.' She wasn't quite sure why she felt it was her fault; it just felt like the right thing to say. She hated to see Gary look so sad and to know she had caused that sadness.

'I'll meet you every day after school, if you like. When I earn enough dosh I can even take you out, maybe for some fish and chips or the pictures?'

'I'd love that,' she said. Her heart began to dance. Her palms felt a bit sweaty.

'I like you, Iris, I mean really like you. I have for ages.'

She noticed how deeply imbedded his freckles were, too. He was so handsome. Not Carey Grant handsome, but really nice. She wondered what her mum would think of him. She wondered what he saw in her.

'Well?' he questioned.

Her cheeks blushed a slight pink.

'I like you too, I s'pose.'

'You suppose?' They both fell into giggles and she began to relax. She could already imagine marrying Gary and getting out of the house she had lived in her entire life. Her father would understand – she hoped. Indeed, he was never home enough to notice.

A week later, her smile was still intact. True to his word, Gary had walked her home from school almost every day and they had even held hands during the last two trips. Iris wondered if this was what it meant to fall in love as she bent to pull out a hot dish from the oven.

'What's for tea?' asked her father.

'Toad in the hole.'

'My favourite. What you buttering me up for?'

'Nothing!' she laughed.

They sat at the table and ate in silence. They never really talked much and, as she had grown older, they appeared to have less and less in common. The one person who had truly united them was gone. But she knew her father loved her. Most men would have palmed her off on a female relative by now, but not him. That was love.

That night as she lay in bed, she thought about Gary as she now did every night, followed by a delightful swoosh in her tummy. She was definitely looking forward to him walking her home tomorrow and the next day and the next!

The day of Iris's fifteenth birthday, Gary was waiting for her outside the gates with a yellow rose in his hand. His mere presence would allow the day to pass without the usual sadness this time of year would usually bring.

'Can I carry anything for you?' he asked. 'You know, so you can hold your rose properly.' She handed over her satchel and immediately began to giggle.

'What's so funny?' he asked, just as he himself began to guffaw.

'I don't know!' she said. There was something so light and free about being with Gary and he seemed to make everything feel okay. Since the age of eleven, every birthday had felt like a reliving of a nightmare and yet here she was laughing, actually laughing! Once upon a time, the mere sight of a rose, especially on this day, would send her into floods of tears. Not today, thanks to Gary. The early misunderstanding regarding her bosoms seemed like a distant memory. They talked so much (in between kisses of course) about their hopes and dreams. Gary wanted to be a mechanic because he loved automobiles and now she could finally leave school, Iris wanted to get married and have a house full of noisy kids. They spoke to one another like the players in each of their dreams were each other, which made her feel both nervous and ecstatic.

Their route home forked into an area unfamiliar to their usual journey.

'Where are we going?'

'I just thought it would be nice to have a chat, away from everyone. I thought we'd go to the green near my house. I like being around nature and that ...'

'That's a bit girly. That's what I like too!'

'Is it?' He smiled. Iris was pleased she hadn't offended him. It was hard to believe that not all men possessed her father's temper. She'd once seen her father lay into a man who'd accidentally brushed his shoulder in the pub. She'd only gone there to look for him because a man had knocked on the door demanding money.

They sat on the grass, their hands entwined. 'We've been going together for a few weeks now and I still don't know that much about you, Iris Jones.'

She gently fell back onto the grass, her eyes clouding over as she looked up to the sky. 'Well, I live with my dad because my—'

'I know about that. I'm so sorry.'

'It happened when I was eleven. Ages ago!'

'That ain't that long. She was your mum.'

She appreciated that one line. Oh how she appreciated it, because ever since her mum had gone, she was hardly ever mentioned in the house. Her father was seeing another woman and Iris had found no place to go with her grief. With the extended Baker family no longer a part of their lives, her pain had never been acknowledged ... until now. She wanted to thank this boy she'd admired from afar but had only known for a matter of weeks. She wanted him to take her in his arms and kiss her, maybe do a bit more. He deserved more, especially because of the kindness he had just shown her.

Iris's disappointment was palpable when he leaned down towards her, planted his lips onto her forehead and held her close.

'Don't you like me?' she asked.

'I really, really do. I like everything about you. Your beautiful hair, your—'

'So if you like me, why …?'

'That's why.'

Mixed with the confusion as to why Gary had not wanted to go further with her, she was also pleased because really, she simply enjoyed holding hands with him and those kisses and in all honesty wasn't ready to go 'all the way'.

'As it's your birthday, I'm walking you to your front door. No arguments,' insisted Gary as he pulled her gently up from the grass.

She should have refused the offer. She should have thought better, because fifteen minutes later, everything changed.

'GET AWAY FROM HER, YOU COW SON!!'

Her father's voice was loud and earth-shattering.

By the time she looked down, Gary was already on the floor with her father delivering another kick to his abdomen.

'Stop it! Please!' She held onto her father's shoulders as he pulled Gary up off the floor by his lapels. Iris could not believe what was happening. Not again. Not on her birthday.

'Stay away from my daughter!' he hissed, before pushing him away and grabbing her arm. She twisted her body to catch a glimpse of Gary doubled over as her dad marched her inside, feeling the searing pain of his fingers as they dug into her arm.

After slamming the door behind them, he released her.

'Why did you do that?' she screamed.

'I don't want anyone around here thinking you're easy!'

'We were just talking!'

'I don't care!'

Anger she had never felt before rose in her body.

'I know what boys like him are like!' he spat.

'Like you, you mean?'

'What's that supposed to mean?'

She ran to the front door.

'You're not going out there!' he said, blocking her path.

'I need to see if he's okay.'

'I hardly touched him.'

'What, like you "hardly touched" Mum?'

'Shut your mouth!'

'If you weren't holed up with some tart, you were laying into her, every chance you got. I saw it. I saw it all!'

'Shut it!' he roared, moving closer to her, fists clenched. She ran into the living room, her eyes immediately connecting with the three glass ducks on the wall, and below them, the sideboard containing ornaments and picture frames. She stopped, couldn't move. An image popped into her head.

She had been little. Not even at big school yet. She had been lying in bed with her hands clamped over her ears, desperately trying to block out the sound of her parents fighting.

INAUDIBLE

'Maybe I should wake her, so she can see what a tart her mother is!'

INAUDIBLE

'I warned you, Rose. You could do anything, but not that, never that! I warned you!'

INAUDIBLE

'YOU BROKE MY HEART ROSE!'

Then the sound of crockery hitting the ground.

'Shut it, all right? Just shut it!'

Rubbing at her eyes, Iris had stepped out of the bed and moved to the door of the living room. Her father's hands were around her mum's neck. It was not the first time she had seen this, but the only time he'd stopped only to burst into tears. He began to apologise profusely as her mum held him, assuring him she'd never make him angry again. A big red mark would usually form on her neck, but this time, he'd moved his hands away quicker.

'Why do you make me do this?' he said. 'Pretending you did stuff with someone else, just to get my goat! You know how to press my buttons, eh!'

Her mum looked up at him, with gratitude, Iris believed and this was enough for her to believe the fight was over. So she went to bed.

The following morning her mum was on the floor in the living room, beside the sideboard, with a glistening wound on the side of her head. She was dead.

That was Iris's eleventh birthday.

Now, she backed away from her father who had uncurled his fists.

'You made her life a misery when she was alive. I used to see you hurt her and I saw her bruises afterwards. You thought I didn't know but I did!'

She watched her father's face turn an even angrier crimson, yet still she continued. 'I hate you for what you put her through and how you treat me like a slave. I hate you!'

The swipe across her face was swift and with the power to knock her to the ground. Then the image of the sideboard again, her mum on the floor beside it, where Iris had found her the next morning. Eleven-year-old Iris, sleeping while her mum lay dying. She'd hated herself for not being there for her mum, or calling a doctor, or at least holding her in her arms until the very end.

Over the years, Iris so fixated on her own guilt, that she had never bothered to work out how her mum had ended up on the floor dead. She had seemed to be satisfied with the explanation her dad offered to anyone who would listen; that his wife had 'taken a funny turn, hit her head on the edge of the sideboard and died'.

'Iris, Iris, look I'm sorry, okay? Here, get up!' he proffered his hand. She looked at it. That image of her mum again. And then clarity.

'It was you.'

'What?'

'You hurt her.'

'What are you talking about?'

'That day. You really hurt her. You carried on hurting her after I went to bed. IT WAS YOU!'

'What are you talking about?'

Iris was on her knees now, her body heaving with sobs. 'YOU KILLED MY MUMMY!' Her body weakened in the moment and her eyes closed. She cried out for the mum she would never see again because this man, who called himself her father, had taken her away.

'It was an accident ... She fell ...' he said.

She opened her eyes and saw guilt in its purest form reflected in his eyes.

'H ... how could you?'

His words offered no confession, his expression enough.

She stood with precision, wiping the tears from her reddened face. 'I ... I have to get away.' Suddenly, the world had changed and she did not belong anywhere in it.

'I said I'm sorry.' His voice echoed in her wake as she ran to her room and shut the door, grateful for the lock her mum had insisted on, although at the time Iris had not questioned why.

She threw her body onto the bed and cried for what seemed like an eternity. Along with the tears, an outpouring of memories she had carefully locked away and refused to acknowledge. She had never cried like this for her mum before ... and vowed never to again.

Chapter Twelve

1959

'Aren't you the prettiest girl I've ever seen?' said Mummy Flora. Just like she had done for the last fifteen years, only this time her words were the faintest whisper, her usual smile requiring a strength she could no longer muster.

When Lily was younger, these were the words she heard regularly but mostly just before they ventured out of the house to go shopping or something, which wasn't very often. Mummy Flora said the world could be a cruel place and it was better to stay at home – not that Lily would ever have become bored. Over the years, she had owned a succession of toys including a plastic doll dressed in a pink dress and a wooden rocking horse delivered on her eleventh birthday. Even though she was far too old for it now, that horse remained in the corner of her room with all the other things she had not gifted to Joycey's children. Indeed, a few years ago and because of her growing number of clothes, books and toys, Mummy Flora had swapped rooms with Lily, allowing her to have the master bedroom. Aunty Joycey and Uncle Kenneth had helped decorate it into what Mummy Flora called a 'girl's palace' with crisp white net curtains overlooking the comfiest pink bedspread that indeed made her feel like a princess.

Ironically it was in Mummy Flora's room where Lily had spent the last two nights.

'Get some rest,' encouraged Lily. Once Mummy Flora had fallen asleep, she tiptoed into her own bedroom and sat on the cushioned chair in front of her dressing table adorned with many items including a sweet-smelling perfume in a beautiful pink crystal atomiser, a musical jewellery box and a fan decorated with roses. Lily loved anything floral and guessed this may have had something to do with her and Mummy Flora's name. She had been told many times about the history of the Baker family and that all the girls had been named after flowers. She was proud to have also been named after one at birth. A coincidence, considering she wasn't even blood according to Mummy Flora. Not that she even knew any of them – just Uncle Donald – whom she was never allowed to visit with Mummy Flora.

'Aren't you the prettiest girl I have ever seen?' The words echoed in her mind as she peered towards the dressing table mirror, pondering if fifteen years of hearing this had in some way filtered into her psyche. Some of it had. She was a fine figure of a girl, as she had once heard Uncle Kenneth say to Aunty Joycey – the only people she and Mummy Flora ever mixed with. She also believed she was clever. Very clever. She'd overheard Aunty Joycey and Mummy Flora discuss this on many occasions. She also believed Mummy Flora when she said, 'You can be anything you want in life. Don't let anybody hold you back.' Such words held up well until one day just after Lily turned eleven.

Mummy Flora had been talking to the greengrocer for far too long. Bored and seeking distraction, Lily did something she'd always been warned not to do. She broke away from Mummy Flora and quickly found herself outside and face to face with a little girl not much younger than herself.

'Look ...' said the girl, pointing in Lily's direction. Mummy Flora had come rushing out, pulling Lily into her arms, just as the mother of the little pulled her own daughter away, her eyes widening.

'Please don't run off like that, Lily. You scared the life out of me!'

'I didn't run off and I was bored.'

Mummy Flora had pulled her back inside, but Lily never forgot that girl pointing at her and the way her mother had stared at her, as if she was a rotten fruit.

When she had broached the subject again, Mummy Flora had simply said, 'Some people are just frightened of difference ... but don't you worry, because you have just as much right to be here as anyone else.'

Even though she was a clever little girl, that explanation had simply confused her. Why wouldn't she have a right to be anywhere? She had never really felt different up until that moment. Of course, she knew she wasn't from the same family as Mummy Flora. She wasn't an idiot! She'd been put in a home for brown babies during the war and her father had been a brave GI from America! Yet from that moment at the greengrocer's, she began to think about her origins more, her mind refusing to focus on who had given birth to her because she didn't want to betray Mummy Flora, but allowing for thoughts of her father and whether he looked at all like Sidney Poitier or if indeed he *was* Sidney Poitier. She'd been fascinated with this movie star ever since she had seen him on the television set she and Mummy Flora watched almost every day. She never saw men or anyone with such skin colour living in their village. Not ever. Perhaps if she went to a normal school, she would, but Mummy Flora had refused that request more than once.

'I can teach you all you need to learn right here. Why do you need to go to school?'

'To make friends. What about when you go to work? I could go then.'

'I thought you liked spending time at Joycey's. You're never complained before. Besides, you have friends. What about Walter and Lucy, they love you!' Indeed, Joycey and Kenneth's kids were good fun, but she wanted to make friends who lived a bit further away from their street and were her own age … Perhaps even looked a bit like her. It was just so hard to understand how she was able to almost get anything she wanted except what she truly wanted – a bit more freedom. As always, Lily had stopped badgering the moment she'd clocked the hurt in Mummy Flora's eyes.

'I just want to keep you safe, Lily.'

'I know,' she'd said.

'Lily!' Her name was faint and said with so much effort. A stab of guilt followed her as she ran next door to Mummy Flora's room where she lay in bed, her face ashen, her eyelids drooped.

'There you are. My pretty girl.'

She held Mummy Flora's hand, now birdlike and devoid of life. Just skin and bone.

She moved her head closer to Mummy Flora's.

'My sweet little girl.'

'Try not to speak so much.' She leaned over to retrieve the untouched glass of water and moved it towards Mummy Flora's mouth. Lily had tried to ignore the rapid weight loss; her usually neatly styled hair a dull, ruffled mess on top of her head. The colour was literally draining from her skin, as if she had aged at least twenty years overnight. Something was terribly wrong with Mummy Flora. The doctor and Aunty Joycey had been vague, their talk ceasing as soon as she entered the room. She was fifteen years old now and not a baby. Why wouldn't they trust her with whatever was wrong with Mummy Flora? Perhaps she could help. She needed to help, to give back to the woman who had done everything for her for most of her life.

'You have to eat something,' she said, as Mummy Flora shook her head at the tiny piece of bread she offered her. She'd only taken a sip of water in twenty-four hours and the knowledge of what this could lead to felt all-consuming. She knew from her science books that not eating food would be okay for the time being as long as liquids were consumed.

'How about some more water? Please, Mummy, just a sip.'

She obliged. A token gesture. It was something.

A knock at the bedroom door startled them both.

'Only me!' said Aunty Joycey, her pregnant belly protruding in the spotted smock dress.

'How is she?' she asked.

'She just drank a bit of water!' said Lily hopefully. She wasn't sure why this didn't thrill Aunty Joycey as much as it did her.

Aunty Joycey sat on the other end of the bed and Mummy Flora, with much effort, placed a hand on her best friend's swollen belly.

Aunty Joycey spoke with sadness in her voice. 'What are we going to do with you, eh?' She gripped her friend's hand and, at that moment, Lily felt a lump rise in her own throat.

'I . . . I can't wait to see this one,' said Mummy Flora, her lips pursed, eyes closing and widening.

'You will. But this time, you might not get to deliver it like the last one!'

'Maybe the next one,' she replied, ever so quietly.

'You've got to be joking! As much as I love my Kenneth, he ain't knocking me up again. Three is enough and I'm in my forties. No more! This shop is closed!'

Lily was pleased to see Mummy Flora smile, however brief, however much it was clearly laced with pain.

'Don't you worry, you'll be around to see her or him, okay?' said Aunty Joycey. Lily scrunched her eyebrows in confusion. What did she mean by that? Of course Mummy Flora would be around to see the baby.

As she walked Aunty Joycey to the door, she asked the question that had been burning in her mouth throughout the hour-long visit.

'What did you mean earlier about Mummy Flora being around to see the baby?'

'Nothing ... I—'

'Please, Aunty Joycey. Please tell me.'

The way her eyelids closed and then slowly reopened, forced Lily into a state of sudden panic. 'What's going on?'

'She told me not to say.'

'Say what?'

Aunty Joycey softly gripped Lily's shoulders and at first she assumed it was to stop herself from toppling over. Her belly was huge after all.

'Not here,' said Aunty Joycey, as they headed towards the kitchen.

They both sat down at the table.

'She's going,' she began.

'Going where?'

'She's dying, my sweet love. And she hasn't got long.'

It had been four whole days since Aunty Joycey had revealed the news. At first Lily had simply stood over Mummy Flora's bed as she slept, searching for anything 'deathlike'. She looked different, yes, and the change had been rapid, but she'd been sick before and recovered with the aid of medicines and a doctor's visit.

When one of the men Mummy Flora did bookkeeping for came to sit with her, Lily saw this as a chance to set off on her quest to find out more.

'Take as long as you like, poor love. I'll be here for another hour and Patricia from the office will take over.'

Lily looked at the man's face for longer than necessary, noticing the pity in his eyes.

At Doctor Pike's surgery, she was asked to wait by Barbara the nurse whom she recognised from previous visits to their home. Barbara who told her everything was going to be all right when she had a bellyache after getting food poisoning. Who also told her that Mummy Flora simply had a bug after Doctor Pike's last visit.

'Won't be a minute,' said Barbara.

It had been quite a thrill walking the short distance to the doctor's, alone. Especially as she'd never really been allowed further than Aunty Joycey's when walking by herself. A woman dressed in a smart grey suit and white hat walked into the waiting area and headed towards the reception desk – but not without giving her a once-over.

Lily could have asked why she was staring but Mummy Flora had told her to always be polite and if you didn't have anything nice to say, don't say anything!

Lily sat with her hands resting on her knees and was relieved to hear Dr Pike's voice as he called her in.

'Lily Baker. How may I help you today?' He sat behind the large desk, a stethoscope around his neck.

'It's about Mummy Flora.'

His face relaxed. 'What has happened?'

'Oh nothing! It's just that ... well ... Aunty Joycey said ...'

'What did she say?'

'She said that Mummy Flora didn't have ...' her words refused to complete the clearly incorrect statement.

'Lily, what do you need me to tell you here today?'

'Well ... You're a doctor.'

'Yes, indeed, I am.'

'What's wrong with my mummy?'

He swallowed. 'She is my patient and I am really not allowed to discuss her case. You will have to speak with her.'

She wasn't sure what it was, but something in his tone didn't feel right, his demeanour constantly switching from confident doctor to a man with something to hide.

'I have a right to know!' she said with unfamiliar conviction.

'That you do. Go home and speak to your mother. Ask her.'

She had to wonder why she hadn't just done that first. Perhaps she was scared of the response or had just wanted someone medically qualified to tell her exactly what was wrong with her and what they could do to fix it.

She left the doctor's surgery shrouded in disappointment, with each footstep back to the house filling her with the fear of what would happen next.

Patricia was sitting by the bed, her voice lowering as soon as Lily entered the room.

'I was just telling your mum what a lovely young woman you have turned out to be.'

'Thank you,' she replied automatically. When Patricia finally left, Lily took Mummy Flora's hand.

'You're smiling!' enthused Lily. It would appear the visits had energised her. Her voice even sounded stronger.

'It was good to see them but I'm even happier to see you. Where did you go?'

'Just for a walk.'

'You probably needed to clear your head, poor love. I'm sorry to put you through all this, you don't deserve it.'

'Don't be silly! You're ill. And once you get better …' She searched Mummy Flora's expression.'

'Lily,' she began. 'I—'

'You are going to get better, aren't you? You're even talking better now!'

Mummy Flora turned away and looked straight ahead.

'Oh, my darling little girl. I need you to listen and to do so carefully, promise?'

'Yes, I promise,' said Lily.

One of the things Lily enjoyed most was learning about science. According to the books Mummy Flora insisted she read, it was changing daily. So regardless of what she said about 'there being nothing the doctors could do', that actually wasn't correct because Mummy Flora was on the mend.

It had started at 6am on the Wednesday, with Lily believing she was in the midst of a dream. The noises were actually coming from the kitchen and she at first thought that Aunty Joycey had wandered inside with her own key and begun cooking as she sometimes did. But she was on bed rest after complications with her pregnancy so it couldn't be her. Lily put her head around the kitchen doorway and was amazed at what she saw.

'Mummy Flora?' She rubbed her eyes, shocked at the sight of her, still in her nightdress, cooking at the stove. This had to be the most delightful scene she had ever witnessed. Better than when she received the rocking horse for her birthday or the smell of corned beef hash on toast. 'You're out of bed!'

The accompanying cough was the only real evidence of the last two weeks because she looked brighter and Lily was sure that Mummy Flora had gained some weight during the night!

'I want to make my little girl a breakfast, is that all right?' She smiled warmly as Lily grabbed hold of her from behind. She tried to suppress alarm at her bony frame, and just be glad to see Mummy Flora standing up and cooking for her again. This had to be the best day of her life.

'Now, you go and get dressed young lady and by the time you come back, the eggs will be cooked and a fresh mug of tea will be waiting for you.'

'Scrambled eggs?'

'Yes, scrambled eggs.'

'The way I like them?'

'Yes, all yellow and fluffy! Gosh you are a spoiled child. Good job you didn't have to survive for long on powered egg like we did during the war!'

Lily was astonished in this sudden change in Mummy Flora. She skipped back to her bedroom and fell back happily onto her

126

bed. Everything was going to be all right because Mummy Flora was back and at last their lives could get back to normal.

After breakfast, Mummy Flora read to her, just like they used to in the old days. She read four pages of the book *Five Get into a Fix* by Enid Blyton and Lily promised to carry on reading the rest.

By noon, it was obvious she was tired out, with Lily happy to tuck her into bed, just as Mummy Flora had done for her countless times over the years.

'Sleep tight,' said Lily, resting her lips on her warm forehead. Lily felt confident enough to not have to sleep with Mummy Flora that night. For the first time in weeks, she would sleep in her own bed without any fear.

The following morning, as normal, she entered Mummy Flora's bedroom where she was surely asleep, clearly exhausted from the day before.

Lily placed her hand gently onto Mummy Flora's shoulder hoping not to wake her, but just wanting to feel her. It was only at that moment she knew that Mummy Flora was dead.

My Dearest Love,

It has been so long since I have written to you. So very, very long.

So much has occurred during this 'absence' I'm not even sure I recognise my own life!

My love, I can only hope that you are happy and living the life you deserve.

Well, in the United States here, we are now allowed to attend the same school as whites. This is a big change but meaningless because as you can guess, not everyone is happy about this change and they do everything in their power to stop it from going ahead, even now. Some of our children, even little ones, were spat at as they tried to go to class. There's a school in Mississippi where the white students who dared to attend school with black students faced being thrown in jail! So nothing much has really changed around here, although I'm really excited about a young man who is making some great waves. You've probably never heard of him. His name is Dr Martin Luther King and he may just be the man to save us all.

So as we approach a new decade – wow the nineteen sixties will soon be upon us – I'm pleased to say I'm doing well as can be.

My life with Augustine is good. Really good. She's a great mother to our boy who I couldn't love more if he were my own. She would like to give me a child but I'm okay with how things are. If the good Lord sees fit to give us a daughter that would be fine. If not, that's okay too. Working on the farm that's been in my family for generations isn't a passion of mine, but it has paid for the ring I presented to Augustine on our wedding anniversary because the first one wasn't that fancy. It also helps me take care of my responsibilities, and if there's one thing the army teaches you, it's that you never run away from those. When Clyde looks up at me with those big brown eyes, I never want to disappoint him. I want to be the father he deserves. I have been in his life for more than I have been out of it and I vow to take care of that boy and his mother for the rest of our natural lives. It's what a real man does.

I do have a secret, though.

Over the years I've been saving a portion of the money I earn for a trip to New York City. Yes, I still hope to do that trip one day. It's my dream. I can only get up at 4am to start work on the farm if, in the back of my mind, I'm also working towards my dream. If I thought that my life began and ended in Savannah, fearful that one day I would be looking down the barrel of a white man's gun, fearful that I would end up like my father, bitter and devoid of joy apart from when he looked into his woman's eyes, I would probably not be able to get out of bed each morning.

We all need our dreams.

Cornel is not much of a writer, but he did let me know he's moved to Philadelphia with his family and is living a wonderful life. He works as a janitor, doesn't make much money 'but I feel

free', he said. Again, he is not a man of many words, but I under-
stood. Hearing from him keeps my dream alive. No one I know in
this town has ever been any further than Atlanta.

I often speak to Augustine about moving. She has her mama
here, her whole family. But she will always end the discussion
with 'Well, if I had a proper ring.' Now she does.

One of the reasons I didn't think it was honourable to write
to you during that time was out of respect to my wife-to-be, and
besides, I needed to get over you first.

When I was about to present the first ring to Augustine, I
finally felt this sense of purpose at becoming a husband and
father all at once. I patted the ring box in the pocket of my pants,
nervous, as I'd never proposed to a woman before. There was
that one moment in time, back in 1943, when I imagined what it
would feel like to get down on one knee and propose to you, but
that seems like another lifetime ago now. And besides, even now
in 1959 it would still be deemed illegal over here. Our love in no
way would have been recognised.

The day I did propose, I passed by Mr Preston's general
store, and that alone reminded me that when we moved to New
York, I'd never have to be faced with THAT reminder again. I
turned into the 'coloureds only' bathroom at the gas station and
saw an old face from the past, pumping gas into his automobile.
When I came out, he was still there so I smiled, just hoping to get
on my merry way.

'How you doing there, Willie? Been a long time.'

'Sure has.' I just wanted to get to Augustine, propose and
begin the rest of our lives.

'You don't remember me do you? I'm Brett. Not seen you for
a long time.'

'I remember. How you doing?'

'Good, good. Me and the family live in Tennessee now.
Sometimes drive back these parts to see my folks. You back here
now?'

'Yes. I am.'

'Did my duty, it's good to be out.'

'As did I.'

The defence was in my voice and I didn't care if he heard it. Many have been struck for less, but at that moment I didn't care for his small talk and I resented Brett's presence on the day I was about to propose to my lady. When Augustine agreed to marry me, the first thing I did was lift her high up into the air, even with my leg the way it is. I was happy she'd no longer have to bear the sniggers from neighbors who pitied a single woman or the lustful gazes from men who thought it was okay to look just because she didn't have a man at home. I was happy for me, for Clyde, happy for my entire family because we needed this. We needed something good to happen. I insisted on a long engagement because I had things to seek and hopefully find in the meantime. I wanted to go into this new phase of my life with no thoughts of the previous one. No what-ifs. I needed to be sure of a few things. So I took a huge chunk of the New York fund and did what I needed to do, confiding in no one, not even my intended, Augustine. This was part of a dream that I wasn't ready to let go of just yet.

Not yet.

Chapter Thirteen

1959

Lily

Joycey and Kenneth sorted everything. Even the food served at the wake. Apparently, Mummy Flora had sat down with Aunty Joycey and planned the entire day. It was as if she'd known all along that she wasn't going to make it out alive. Meticulous in her organisation, calm in the face of her reality.

Lily had experienced a myriad of emotions. Sadness mixed with an anger that refused to subside; why hadn't Mummy Flora been honest with her before the end? At the age of fifteen she was old enough to take it. She'd heard Aunty Joycey on more than one occasion say to her husband, 'She shields that girl way too much. How is she supposed to ever learn? I was working at her age!'

As Mummy Flora's work colleagues and neighbours ate and drank in the living room, Lily found it difficult to leave Mummy Flora's room where her empty bed stood. This was where she had spent many a night recently holding onto her frail body. Almost every night in fact. And yet the moment she had died, Lily had decided to go back to her own room – a decision she would surely regret for the rest of her life.

'You mustn't feel guilty about that. Sometimes, people wait till you leave before they go ...' Aunty Joycey hadn't made any sense when she had said this. Why hadn't Mummy Flora slipped away in her arms like in the film they had both watched on the television set? That would have been better than seeing her like ... that.

Lily's peace was disturbed by a faint knock on the door.

'Hello, love. Just checking on you. Everyone's leaving now. Do you want to say goodbye?' asked Aunty Joycey.

'I don't know anyone. They were all Mummy Flora's work people,' she said without thinking. Because if she had been thinking she'd have realised that everyone leaving meant she'd now be totally alone in that house. There'd be no more appearances at the front door of visitors armed with a casserole or hollow words of condolence. Although she resented it all at the time, in some small way they had prevented her from remaining transfixed on the ongoing horror of the situation – a life without Mummy Flora in it.

'You're coming home with us tonight. I can't have you stay here by yourself.'

'You're only a few yards away, I can stay here and call out if I need anything.'

Aunty Joycey manoeuvred her rounded body onto Mummy Flora's bed. An act that felt so hurtful and an invasion of her space.

'I don't think you understand, love. The rent is only paid until the end of the month. You will have to leave the property really soon.'

'Where will I go?'

'You can come live with us. It's what your mum wanted and it's what we want. Me and Ken.'

Something in her tone left Lily feeling unconvinced of this, but she was just relieved to have a place to stay not too far from the house in which she grew up. Not too far away from memories of Mummy Flora.

'Your mum was such a clever woman and frugal too – except when it came to you.'

'She said her biggest joy was getting me whatever I wanted,' said Lily fondly. Her eyes quickly filled with tears. 'But all I want is her. I want her back, Aunty Joycey.'

'I know you do, love. So do I. She was the best friend I ever had.'

They both composed themselves before continuing.

'Flora left quite a bit of money for you. Enough to keep you going until you can get a job and support yourself.'

'A job?'

'Don't worry, that won't be for a while. She wants you to get a good education first. Go to college and all of that.'

'I'd like that. I want to be a scientist.'

'So she said. For now, though, maybe set your sights on something useful like secretarial school?'

'Why?'

'Don't get me wrong, I'm the last person to think you can't do anything as good as a man and it doesn't mean you can't become a scientist later. I just think you should learn a trade first, you know, as a back-up.'

Lily crinkled her forehead and looked upwards, Mummy Flora's voice echoing in her mind: 'You can do anything you set your mind to, you hear?'

'Yes, Mummy Flora.'

'Don't let anyone tell you any different. There will be loads who will. Just because you're a woman and also because you're ...'

'I'm what?'

'Special. Because you're a special and beautiful and unique young woman.'

'Unique?'

'Yes, around these parts anyway.'

'Where am I not unique, Mummy?'

'In countries far away like Africa or the Caribbean ... Even in places like London. There are more special people like you. Just not around here!'

'Maybe we should go to London then so I can say hello to them. Can we?'

That night, Lily slept on a rather comfortable mattress in an already overcrowded room belonging to Walter and Lucy. With five human beings and one on the way in a tiny house, it would be tighter than she was used to, but at least she wasn't alone.

It had taken longer than she had realised to pack up the home she'd shared with Mummy Flora. Uncle Kenneth was more ruthless in grabbing items which meant nothing to him but everything to Lily. Like the copper kettle Mummy Flora had loved so much and the refrigerator she said they were very lucky to own.

'We never had stuff like this growing up; I want you to experience everything I never had. All the mod cons,' she'd say.

'Maybe we can find use for the kettle even though we already have two,' said Kenneth with a hint of sensitivity in his voice.

'That would be nice. What about the refrigerator?'

'Joycey would love that.'

Uncle Kenneth was less charitable about the clothes Joycey had bagged up. Some still smelled of Mummy Flora and Lily wasn't ready to part with them.

'I have to take them, Lily.'

'Where to?' she asked.

'To the church. They can find good homes for these clothes,' he insisted.

'They belong to Mummy Flora!'

'Lily!' said Uncle Kenneth, with a look of impatience perhaps because at fifteen Lily was no longer a child. Yet, she still felt like one. She also felt lost, alone and not yet ready to live a life without the protection and guidance of Mummy Flora.

She bent to pick up the tiny sky-blue bootie, which had fallen from one of the bags.

'What's that?' asked Uncle Kenneth, his voice intruding on the moment. Mummy Flora had kept her baby bootie! 'You want to stick that in the bag too? Maybe there's another one.'

Supplies had been scarce during the war and blue wool – which just happened to be Lily's favourite colour – was all they had at that time according to one of the stories Mummy Flora had shared with her. Lily fell to her knees, the knitted bootie clasped to her chest, which began to heave with the weight of her sobs. The tears were a surprise and they were plentiful. They drowned out her vision as well as Uncle Kenneth's voice. The simplicity of a blue baby bootie drawing out every emotion she had kept stored away until that moment. Mummy Flora, the only person who had truly loved her. The only person who would ever love her was gone.

It felt just too painful to visit the house again, even though it wasn't that far away. Soon, new tenants would occupy the space that was once hers so she decided to say goodbye to her home before fully committing to a life with Aunty Joycey, Uncle Kenneth and the kids.

Each empty room echoed with the sound of Mummy Flora's voice; reading to her about science or explaining the nuances of a classic novel. Sweet tales of her brother and sisters when they were younger or reliving a meeting with her colleagues, a joke or a story they had told. In the kitchen, she could still smell the aroma of toad in the hole, pease pudding and soda bread. Recipes passed down from her mother and grandmother before her. Recipes she could never replicate because Mummy Flora had never taught her how to cook. If only they'd had more time. The tears came again, but this time she refused to let them linger. She now had a new life with a family who would look after her forever.

She closed the door to her former home, caressed a flower that curled over the door knocker, trying not to hang onto a feeling of hopelessness.

When Lily sat with Aunty Joycey who was now on complete bed rest, and they shared their fondest memories, she was able to place the pain to one side and truly revel in the moment.

'Do you remember that time when that tractor drove past and spread muck onto her trousers?'

'Oh yes. Flora was never one for clothes, but drew the line at being covered in muck!'

Lily and Aunty Joycey burst into laughter – the older woman clutching her tummy.

'You're going to put me into labour, you are!'

'How long to go now?'

'Just a month we think.'

'I thought about my real mum the other day.'

There – she'd said it. She had found an opening and voiced a fear that had plagued her ever since Mummy Flora's funeral. It wasn't that she wanted to find her real mum or anything, she just had questions.

'It's not surprising you've thought about her, especially as we've just buried Flora.'

'I do wonder why she didn't want me. I couldn't speak to Mummy Flora about it much because … Well, I didn't want to upset her.'

'Oh I know, love. That must have been hard for you. I know that with each of my kids I couldn't imagine being away from any of them. Never.'

This admission wasn't helping as it just reinforced the fact she had been unwanted.

'I think your real mum must have had a big reason to leave you at the home. It may have had something to do with …'

Joycey's face crinkled. 'You know … It wasn't accepted back then. It still isn't in most parts.'

'You mean coloureds and whites?'

'It may be better in London, or it might be worse.'

There it was again, that word: London. The place where more people who looked like her could be living. A magical place where she longed to one day visit, if she could. Perhaps she and Aunty Joycey could take a trip there once the baby was old enough to be left at home.

'I'll do right by you as best as I can. Flora was my best friend. I'd never met anyone like her and I doubt I will again.'

'That's funny. She used to say that about you!'

Joycey reached out her hand and Lily grabbed hold of it hungrily, her head resting on the swollen belly. A place of comfort.

Iris

It was a lot to expect of Gary. To put her up just because she'd stuffed a few items of clothing into a tiny suitcase and ended up on his doorstep. Especially after the beating, of which he still bore the bruises. Yet for the last two weeks he had been smuggling her into his room every day after school, sleeping on the floor while she took the bed.

Iris had left home in such haste she hadn't even packed an extra pair of shoes and at some point would need to sneak back for the only other pair she owned as well as raiding the housekeeping tin – that's if her father hadn't taken the money for drink and cigarettes.

'I don't think I've even thanked you … for letting me stay.'

'Don't thank me yet. If my mum finds you in my room, she'll have my guts for garters!'

After uncovering the truth about her father and what he'd done to her mum, Iris wondered if she could ever truly know someone, yet was willing to believe that Gary was one of the good ones. At least for now.

He switched off the light that night as, once again, Iris would attempt to get to sleep. She missed her mum greatly, even more so since finding out the truth. The guilt at not being able to save her and of sleeping comfortably in her bed while her mum lay dead on a cold hard floor, was all too much and now it felt like she would never sleep again.

She sat up and looked over at the floor. Gary was asleep if his slight snores were anything to go by. She lay back on the bed, thinking about the colour of her mum's hair that had been chestnut brown and just a bit darker than hers. She was tall or maybe not. Perhaps her mum just appeared tall to an eleven-year-old Iris. Now, without her father censoring what she felt or said about her mum, she had the freedom to talk about her freely. She just needed to find someone to do that with.

The next morning, she woke with the sun. As he'd been doing for two weeks, Gary smuggled two hunks of bread and a steaming cup of tea into the room.

'Mum won't miss these,' he said as she tore hungrily at the bread. The smell and texture of the bread reminded her of those days spent with her mum in the kitchen. Reeling off old recipes handed down from Grandma Lillian. If only she could retrieve them from the house – not that she could even read them properly anyway. Her reading hadn't improved much since the age of eleven.

'I need to run some errands for my mum. You'll have to make yourself scarce until I get back.'

'I need to go back home anyway.'

'Back to your dad?'

'Never!' she said with passion. She would sooner die herself than live in that house one moment with a murderer. 'I need to get a few things, like my other pair of shoes and some recipes.'

'Recipes? Will you be safe?'

'He'll be at work or with some tart.'

As she suspected, her father wasn't home. She retrieved her shoes from the bedroom, which was just as she'd left it. She'd somehow imagined her father turning the room upside down in a rage, when in reality he probably hadn't even noticed she'd gone.

She reached above the kitchen cupboard. The housekeeping tin was still full of the money left for her to get the week's shopping. She stuffed the cash into her pocket, picked up the bag containing her shoes and recipes and headed for the door.

Halfway down the street, she remembered.

The photo album. She needed to go back for the photo album and the photo of her mum and family. It was all she had left of her.

She turned back in the direction of the house and then she saw him. Her father, struggling to place the key in the lock, clearly drunk and perhaps not in the right frame of mind to be charitable.

She took another step forward and then stopped. She felt a heat rise up in her body, her fist curled as she thought about what her father had done.

And then she turned on her heel and headed in the opposite direction.

No, she could never go back.

It was surprisingly easy to sneak out of Gary's room each morning and back inside after he finished school or sometimes later when he went to work. It became a ritual she was comfortable with while being aware that it couldn't go on forever.

'Maybe one day ... soon ... we can get a place together. I'm earning a bit at the garage at weekends and after school and I can save up for a place. I'll be able to go full-time when I leave school too.'

'Do you mean that?' she said excitedly.

'You're my girl, aren't you?'

'Yes,' she whispered, resting her head in the crook of his shoulders. Warmth radiated from him, mixed in with the scent of soap. She exhaled slowly having not felt this safe in a very long time. She looked up at him and she knew that he would kiss her. She wanted him to kiss her as he hadn't done so for a long time. And as they approached one another's lips, the door of the bedroom flew open.

'I knew it!'

'Mum!' Gary stood up, his face flushed.

'I'll give you Mum! You've got ten seconds to tell me what she's doing in my house. One, two, three ...'

When my brother and I were young, my daddy was strict with how far we should roam and I never understood why. As long as we stayed in the Negro part of town and were back by curfew, we couldn't work out why it mattered where we went! He'd say, 'You boys need to be mighty careful what you go looking for. You may not like what you find.'

Now, as a grown man, I finally knew what he meant.

Nevertheless, I still wanted to leave Augustine, Clyde and my entire family behind in Savannah to seek what could have remained inside of my head because I had to know.

My grandaddy had the ability to tell days in advance when a storm was about to hit. I never inherited this gift until now but in a different way. I could now work out the moment a 'cloud' arrived and the storm inside of me was about to wreak havoc on my being. The cloud could lead to the simple act of staying in bed longer than necessary or replaying in my mind the pain my brother must have felt right before he died. Then the blame would set in. 'Why wasn't it me instead of him?' He wanted the farm and enjoyed working there, while I was the fanciful son who thought he was better than all of this and wanted more. I was the one who wanted New York City and to read novels and hang with authors, poets and trumpeters. On and on the thoughts would go until it left me burdened with so much guilt that I would no longer have the strength to go on. This could last days, weeks and sometimes even months.

So when in 1959 I received a letter, my entire world came crashing down around me. Every emotion I have ever felt – all the bad ones – mingled inside my head and took me hostage.

I had learned to put a firm hold on these thoughts by doing other things, like taking a long walk among the huge trees covered in Spanish moss or simply lying on the ground to stare up at the beautiful clear sky or by cutting off a piece of a dogwood tree and placing it beside my bed. I would also have to remind myself more of what I did have, like my physical health, my family, the love of a good woman, a farm which fed us all. I was lucky. I was blessed. I felt that way on the day Augustine and I had jumped the broom, convincing myself I was totally satisfied that all roads leading to Rose Baker could never be travelled. I was ready to move on with my life. Augustine looking pretty as a picture and Clyde calling me his daddy gave me the best feeling in the world. My mama now the happiest I had seen her for so long. Even as she would ask 'Where are my grandbabies?' she couldn't know the pain she ignited with her words. I'd never blame her for saying them. The death of my brother had left a gaping hole in all our lives and perhaps only a baby could fill it. For her, for all of us.

So, how could I now tell her that just before that huge hurricane of '59 went off in my mind, my body, my very being, just the day before, I had received a letter.

One letter from England that changed everything.

To William Burrell,

Please stop sending these lettas to Rose becus she is dead. She died 4 years ago in 1955 no fanks to the misery you put her through when you got her pregnant with a couple of kids. You must have known what that did to her. She was married!

Don't bother coming or getting in touch, the twin girls were adopted out and better off without you, just like Rose would have been if she neva met you.

Marigold

Chapter Fourteen

Living in a house with five other people did not mean she was never alone.

With Joycey on bed rest and sleeping for most of the day, Lily spent her days pottering around the house while the kids were at school and Uncle Kenneth at work. The house came alive in the early evening with the sound of the children playing and Uncle Kenneth attempting to cook. Lily had wanted to feel useful so had tried to cook the family tea on more than one occasion, every time failing miserably and almost burning the kitchen down on her fourth and final attempt.

'We won't have any food left if you try and cook any more!' joked Aunty Joycey, but Lily could see the disappointment in her eyes. Helping the kids clean the house was something she knew she could do, until the youngest daughter slipped on the floor that Lily had flooded with too much soap.

'I'm so sorry, Uncle Kenneth!' she cried.

'Hey, that's okay. My Lucy is as tough as her mum, so no harm done.'

'I can't get anything right and you've both been so kind to me.'

'We loved your mum and you. It's the least we could do and we love having you here.'

'And I like being here, I just … I just miss her that's all.'

'Of course you do.'

'I wish I could give her a hug.'

'Oh you poor love. Well, our Joycey's good at those.'

She smiled. 'She is. But she's always asleep these days!'

They both shared a much needed giggle.

'I was never much for cuddles until I met our Joycey and she landed me with all these kids. I realise that little girls love their cuddles … so … if I'll do … I can give you a cuddle.'

She didn't have to think. 'Yes, please, Uncle Kenneth!'

He moved closer to her, arms outstretched. 'Oh, you poor love. Come here.'

She sank into his embrace and imagined him to be Mummy Flora. She could smell her, sense the smile on her face that had appeared simply because she had passed a maths test or looked pretty in yet another dress she'd bought. Lily lost herself in that embrace, her eyes closed, as warm hands ran up and down her back, comforting her. Soothing her.

'Thank you,' she said.

'Any time, my lovely. You just ask. Any time.'

Each morning, Lily would greet Aunty Joycey with tea and toast, a meal she could prepare without drama. They'd have a quick chat and then Aunty Joycey would go back to sleep. The loneliness didn't feel as acute any more because Uncle Kenneth was happy to cuddle her when she asked and had done so on numerous occasions. All she had to do was ask.

As she packed the crockery away – something else she could do without drama – she heard the front door go.

'Uncle Kenneth, why aren't you at work?'

'Finished early today. Now the baby's due, I get worried about our Joycey.'

'She's fine. I gave her some breakfast and she's sound asleep.'

'Oh good. How about you? Need any more cuddling?'

'I'm okay today thanks. Aunty Joycey let me cuddle her belly and I felt the baby move. It was very sweet and strange!'

'Oh right,' he said. Lily sensed something was wrong.

'What is it, Uncle Kenneth?'

'Nothing much. Just a hard day at work. I could do with an ear.'

'Can I help?'

'Come and sit with me on the sofa. Maybe you can give me some advice.'

Lily was both surprised and excited that Uncle Kenneth was seeking her advice about anything. Then again, she was clever and well advanced for her age group, so perhaps she could be of help to him after all.

He scooted up to her on the sofa. 'The lads at work are not pulling their weight and as I'm the foreman, it reflects really badly on me.'

She thought for a moment, looking to the ceiling. The problem had a simple solution. 'You're going to have to call a meeting with each and every one of them and tell them. Bad performance affects everybody, not just one.'

'You are such a clever girl.'

'Thanks!'

'And pretty too. The prettiest,' he said. She smiled at the familiar words she was used to hearing from Mummy Flora. Her mind drifted to her former life, almost missing Uncle Kenneth's hand placed firmly on her thigh. Her mind blank and her body tense as he squeezed her knee while looking her straight in the eyes. It was as if his face and hands were not connected.

'Uncle Kenneth ...' Her mind had turned into a mixture of white and fuzzy grey. What was this? She felt waves of confusion. She knew this was wrong, yet Uncle Kenneth was her uncle ... or as good as and would never do anything that was wrong.

'It's okay. You'll be okay,' he kept saying. She'd not been prepared for his other hand to move onto her chest, her body tensing even more. He closed his eyes and exhaled. She felt bile rise up in her throat.

'No.'

'It's okay.'

'I don't know what you are doing, Uncle Kenneth.'

'We both like to feel better, don't we? That's why we cuddle.'

'Not like this ...'

He removed his hands. 'Why would you say that? I thought you liked me, Lily? I thought we were friends.'

'We are ... I mean ...'

'Look, I'm sorry, okay. I misread things. Please don't tell our Joycey, she doesn't have relations with me any more and I forgot myself. Please don't say a word. It could hurt the baby and you wouldn't want that.'

That afternoon, Uncle Kenneth suddenly had to go back into work while Lily spent the rest of the afternoon sitting on the floor of the kitchen, sobbing ever so quietly into her hands, so that Aunty Joycey couldn't hear.

The next morning, they must have believed she was out of earshot, but Lily could hear everything the husband and wife were saying.

'It's not as if she does anything to earn her keep does she, Joycey?'

'We promised Flora! And she did leave enough money for Lily to live on, Ken.'

'I know but how long will that last? She doesn't have any skills that will get her work. Can't even clean up after herself! You're laid up and I can't do everything.'

'Flora did shelter her a bit. It's not her fault. I'll have a word.'

'You don't need the stress, Joycey. You're delivering this baby any day now plus your mum is coming to help out. We simply don't have the room.'

'You were all right about this before, Ken. Why all this now?'

'Joycey, ever since we got married I let you dictate everything. My friends tell me how soft I am with you and that's okay because I love you. But let me decide this one thing. For once, let me be the man of the house!'

'I'm too tired to argue, Ken. But I can't turf her out on the street. I won't do that!'

'Of course not. We'll find her aunt, Flora's sister. I know one's dead and the brother's doolally, but didn't she say she had another one living?'

'Yes, Marigold. She never spoke much about them but I know they sent a couple of letters from time to time, not much though.'

'Let's see if she can take over. We need the help, love. We can't bury our heads in the sand any longer.'

The realisation that Uncle Kenneth might be trying to get rid of her because of what had happened on the sofa floated in her mind. Surely not? She'd promised not to tell, after all. She did feel a smidgen of excitement at the mention of her Aunty Marigold's name though. She was a Baker, that was her family, and as much as she loved Aunty Joycey and the kids, she no longer felt the same way about Uncle Kenneth and perhaps going to live with her real aunty was the solution.

Iris

Iris ran her hand over the smooth fabric of the dressing grown Gary's mum said she could keep. She also insisted she call her Sal instead of Mrs Moorgate and had agreed to Iris staying, this time with no deception and in the front room on the settee. This arrangement saw her accompany Sal to the hop-picking fields where Iris was able to earn a wage and at least contribute to the household.

'Thank you so much for allowing me to stay,' she said, not for the first time over the past month.

Sal was undertaking a complicated knitting conundrum with her fingers, the blue wool moving incessantly between her fingers.

'No need to thank me. My Gary has clearly taken a shine to you and I can see why. Pretty as a picture.'

Iris felt anything but. 'Thank you, Sal.'

'It's a lot better when everything's out in the open, isn't it? It's not that I mind you being here, I just don't want my boy lying to me.'

'I'm so sorry about that,' she replied sheepishly.

'Nice to have another girl around anyway.' She smiled. Gary's dad had never returned from the war and Gary and his mum were very close. Iris hated the thought of coming between them.

'So your dad …' began Sal. Over the past month, Iris had lived in fear of her father banging the door down and demanding she return home. But apart from accosting her in the street once and begging her to come home, she hadn't seen or heard from him. 'What's he like?'

'Not very nice,' replied Iris truthfully. 'His name's Pete and I know it's disrespectful to say, but I really don't miss him.'

'Sounds like a right one!'

'Oh he is. You don't know the half of it, Sal. Pete Jones is a right piece of work.'

'Jones? I thought you said your name was Baker?'

'Baker is my mum's maiden name. I don't want to be a Jones any more.'

'Oh right. So, is your dad … is he a dark fella then?'

'Yes, he has dark brown hair if that's what you mean.'

When Sal didn't answer that, Iris couldn't help noticing how uncomfortable she looked. Iris was good at picking up on energy and changes in mood, something she'd had to do with her father on many occasions.

'Sal?'

'Yes, that's what I meant by dark. Handsome, is he?'

'Not really.'

'Then I bet your mum was a beauty.'

Iris filled up with light at the mention of her mum, yet still couldn't shake off the feeling that something was wrong. 'Of what I can remember, she was.'

'No pictures, then?'

Iris felt certain that Sal was pumping her for information about her parents and she wanted to know why.

'There are a few but I had to leave them at the house.'

'That's a shame.'

Sal's demeanour had changed and Iris decided to park her fears to one side until she had cause for alarm.

That day came sooner than she hoped.

'IRIS!'

She had just taken the soda bread out of the oven, almost dropping the baking dish at the sound of her name.

'I'll sort it out!' said Gary, running into the kitchen, Sal not far behind him.

'No! Stay away from him. Especially after what he did to you before!'

'What did he do?' asked Sal.

'He gave me a bit of a belting ...' began Gary.

'That was him? The rotten bastard. No one touches my son!'

'No, Mum!' said Gary. 'I'll handle it. Iris is my girl and I will look after her and you.'

'Be careful!' said Iris. Her hands began to shake. This man had killed her mum and now he was about to be let loose on her boyfriend again – another person who cared about her.

Sal followed hotly behind Gary as Iris watched from behind the window. Her father had been drinking, that much she could tell from his gait, and she could only imagine the hateful words spewing from his lips.

She opened the window so she could hear them properly.

'I just wanna talk, Iris. You're my little 'un, stop behaving like this. I just wanna talk!'

'Leave us alone!' she screamed from the window.

'Close the window!' instructed Sal. 'It's all under control.'

'Oh shut it, Sal!' said her father. Gary's mum's full name was Sally and only those who knew her intimately were allowed to call her Sal. She'd said so on many occasions. So, Iris wondered, why was her father calling her Sal?

'Pete, get out of here now. Don't cause a scene,' said Sal. It was then that Iris noticed it. That flash of recognition between two people.

Iris closed the window and headed outside.

'That true? You'd rather stay here with a woman your mum hated?' said Pete to Iris.

'What are you talking about?' said Iris.

'Don't listen to him, he's a drunkard,' said Sal.

'We were at it for months and your mum knew!'

'Is this true, Mum?' asked Gary.

'Sal?' said Iris, fearing she already knew the answer. The way Sal avoided eye contact, told Iris all she needed to know.

'Iris' began Sal.

But Iris was already stepping away, turning back into the house. Now an expert at packing everything she owned into a small suitcase within the space of a few minutes.

'Slow down, slow down!' said Gary, pulling her into his arms. She could smell the scent of soap again, safety.

'Please don't leave. I almost have enough money saved and we can get a place together.'

'I have to go now. You don't know what he did!'

'Tell me!'

'I have to go, Gary!'

'Where to?'

She couldn't even see Gary's face any more, and could only just about hear his voice. She needed to get out of that house and away from everyone. She had to leave the village, it was the only way.

'I don't know, but I can't stay here,' she said. She'd miss him, but this was so much bigger than Gary. She could not be anywhere near the woman who had contributed to her mum's misery over the very last months, weeks or even days of her life. And, sadly, she now had no desire to be near her son.

'I love you, Iris!'

The world stopped for a moment. No one, not even her mum, had ever told her they loved her.

'You love ... me?'

'Yes. So stay, and in about six months I'll have enough for us to move out.'

'I just ... can't.'

My mum's sorry she really is.

'You're amazing. The best chap I have ever met. But I have to go Gary.'

His voice sounded defeated. 'I need to know you'll be safe.'

'I'll be safe because I'll be with my mum's sister. Her name's Marigold.'

Chapter Fifteen

Lily

The reality hadn't dawned on her. That in a matter of hours she would be in the home of Mummy Flora's sister Marigold. Away from Willow on the Grange and all that she had known for most of her life. And away from Aunty Joycey, Walter, Lucy and Uncle Kenneth.

'I'll be back to visit,' said Lily, releasing herself from Aunty Joycey's warm embrace. She wore one of her favourite outfits – a blue A-line dress with pretty white shoes.

'You better!' said Joycey, weakly squeezing her hand. Lily felt a swell of emotion at what this wonderful woman had meant to Mummy Flora and to her.

'Take care, my lovely,' said Joycey as Uncle Kenneth gently ushered her into a car weighed down with three suitcases. Waving goodbye to Joycey and the kids felt harder than she could have imagined because it was like she was saying farewell to Mummy Flora all over again. Everything that had happened between them, the love they shared, the bond, had taken place in that little village and as Kenneth drove further and further away, more tears followed.

'If there could have been any other way,' he kept saying. Lily remained silent, wiping her eyes and staring blankly through the car window.

They were nearing their destination. Her view no longer green countryside, but replaced with an abundance of houses and people. Children playing by the roadside, raggedy dogs and washing hanging on lines.

'Joycey said to give you half the money your mum left and I'll give the other half to Marigold for your keep. Clever one your mum was. To make sure you were looked after. Should last a good couple of years if you're frugal.'

Lily smiled at that description of Mummy Flora. She had always promised to look after her and was even doing so after her death.

'Why don't you just give all of the money to my aunty? That way she can look after me properly.' She stared at the black drawstring purse, containing the money.

'No, don't do that. Don't tell anyone you have it, all right?'

'Why?'

'It's for you in case of an emergency.'

She wasn't quite sure why Uncle Kenneth was behaving so dramatically and after how he'd been with her recently, Lily was finding it hard to believe anything he said anyway.

They stopped outside a row of houses. Lily had never seen so many stuck together like this before. She could tell that whoever lived here didn't care much about keeping the front yard tidy. Washing hung from a line that extended from one window to the next. Battered shoes were strewn across the small patch of grass and a couple of children with dirty faces kicked a deflated football in the road.

'There you go,' said Kenneth, attempting to put some joviality in the announcement. 'Your Aunty Marigold's.'

Lily stepped out of the car and immediately the front door of the house opened to reveal a large-set lady grinning in Kenneth's direction. When her gaze turned to Lily standing behind him, her smile immediately dropped.

'You'd better come in then,' she said.

Inside was not as bad as outside but Lily couldn't help comparing it to what she'd been used to. They walked into the kitchen first. A pile of dirty dishes littered the sink with a stench to go along with it. The living room reeked of cigarette smoke.

'You just missed my eldest boy, John. They hardly stay here any more. Got their own lives now … which is why I really didn't want to take in any more kids.'

'Oh …' said Uncle Kenneth.

'But for some reason, kids seem to like it here. Everyone knows I never turn a kid away. I got quite the reputation.'

'As my wife said in the letter, your sister left a bit of cash for her keep. It should be enough until she gets a job.'

'I knew my sister wouldn't have let her go without. Still can't believe she's gone.'

'I'm surprised you weren't notified.'

'Must have got lost in the post.'

'Telegrams are reliable.'

'Not this one.'

'Poor Lily here has been beside herself. We all have. She's lucky she has you.'

It was strange to listen to people talk about her as if she wasn't in the room, but Lily used this time to study her aunt's features. She looked nothing much like Mummy Flora and this disappointed her. And just as she was about to give up hope of connecting with anything to do with Mummy Flora, she spotted something.

'Is that …?' Lily moved over to the sideboard.

'That's a picture of me, Flora, Rose, Donald and Mum and Dad. We all got one of those. Rose as well. Didn't Flora have one then?'

'Yes, I have the picture in my suitcase!' replied Lily excitedly.

'Good for you,' she said uninterestedly. 'Now how about that cash? I can't feed her on fresh air and windy pudding, can I?' she said, turning to Uncle Kenneth with her palm open. Her eyes widened as he handed over a brown paper bag.

'Ta,' she said as it disappeared into Aunty Marigold's shirt and possibly into her brassiere. Lily had never seen such shameful behaviour. She could also see that even Uncle Kenneth was temporarily taken aback.

'Will you be all right then?' he asked hastily. A question that could only require once response.

'Yes,' she said. He brushed her shoulder, and she flinched.

'I'll bring her stuff from the car and be on my way.'

'You got a lot of stuff there,' said Aunty Marigold. 'Did Flora leave a will then?'

'Aunty Joycey and Uncle Kenneth dealt with all of that.'

'I bet they did,' she said with a smirk. As Uncle Kenneth reappeared, she was all smiles again. 'How much more stuff?'

'That's the last of them,' he said.

Lily didn't want to mention they had given a lot of her stuff away and that these three cases simply contained the things she could not part with.

After Uncle Kenneth had left it was just Lily and Aunty Marigold standing in a room smelling of cigarette smoke, the sound of children playing with their ball outside.

'Well, well. This is a turn-up for the book,' said Aunty Marigold surveying Lily with a look of curiosity.

'Can you help me take my cases to my room?'

'Room? What room?'

'Where I'm going to sleep?'

'We haven't got a spare room for you here.'

'I thought you said your children had left home—'

'You get to sleep in here,' she said, walking towards the kitchen. Lily followed behind. 'We'll have to look at what you

155

can keep and what you should sell. I haven't got the space for even more junk.'

She at first assumed that Aunty Marigold might have been joking. Surely she didn't actually expect Lily to sleep on the floor like an animal! Then she noticed a stained pillow on the kitchen table.

'Aunty Marigold, I think there's been some mistake.'

'What mistake?' She pulled out a cigarette, which had been hidden by her hair, from behind her ear.

'I thought there was room here for me.'

Aunty Marigold appeared to ignore the question because she simply switched off the kitchen light and told Lily not to make any noise.

Disbelief turned to worry.

Lily hadn't gone to the toilet in hours and desperately wanted to wash herself. Mummy Flora always insisted she wash before bed, but Aunty Marigold hadn't even shown her the washing faculties in the back yard yet. There was no bedding to even go with the pillow, which stank faintly of mould, but she rested her tired head on it anyway, just grateful for the much needed barrier against the sticky floor.

She squeezed her eyes shut but sleep wouldn't come. It was inconceivable to think that just a few hours ago, she was living with Aunty Joycey in a packed home yet slept on a real mattress even if it was on the floor beside the children's bed. It was unbelievable that just a few months ago, she and Mummy Flora lived in a large house, just the two of them – happy. Believing that life would be this good forever and that nothing would ever change.

Chapter Sixteen

That first morning, Aunty Marigold hardly spoke to Lily or even looked in her direction – even when informing her she'd better start washing up the dirty dishes or else. And to not take too long before making a start on the floor.

'And you can stop calling me aunty.'

'It's respectful. Mummy Flora always said—'

'I don't care what she said! You just call me Marigold. I don't need the poxy backchat!'

'Yes, Aun—I mean, Marigold.'

'You'll find the carbolic soap next to the brush that's under the sink. Oh and you can use that brush to scrub the floor with.'

Lily thought for a moment. She had so many things to ask Marigold about the sleeping arrangements. Last night had felt very uncomfortable. The harshness of the kitchen floor was bad enough, but the sound of what she feared was a mouse just a few feet away meant she had to do something to prevent another identical night.

'I have to insist on a bed,' she said.

Marigold placed a hand on each of her wide hips. 'You do, do you?'

'Yes … please?' Suddenly she was losing her resolve.

'I'll repeat myself shall I? You will be sleeping on the floor and maybe that will make you clean it better. Now get on with it,' she said.

'There's a mouse … I don't like mice …' she managed.

'A mouse isn't going to hurt anyone. Aren't people like you used to animals anyway?'

Lily didn't quite understand what Marigold meant but the tone of her voice had risen and Lily wasn't about to disobey her.

Four hours later, the dishes were clean and the floor no longer felt sticky. Her knees hurt from kneeling down as she scrubbed every inch of that floor. She couldn't quite believe it when Marigold dumped a pile of washing onto the newly cleaned floor and told her to get on with that too.

She'd never washed an item of clothing in her life.

'Do you have any soap powder?' she asked.

'The carbolic soap works fine,' said Marigold.

Lily feared the answer to her next question. 'Where do you keep the twin tub and mangle? I don't see it—'

'Are you kidding?'

Three hours later and after stooping in the back yard to hand wash every single garment at least three times, Lily's entire body ached.

'Aunt – erm, Marigold?'

'What?' Lying on the settee, she stubbed a cigarette into a glass ashtray.

'Can we buy me a small mattress I could sleep on? I don't mind pulling it into the kitchen every night.'

'Mattresses ain't cheap.'

'We can use the money.'

'What money?'

'The money Uncle Kenneth gave you?'

'That money's spoken for. The sooner you get a job and earn your keep, the better. Then we can think about buying you a poxy bed.'

It probably wasn't the time to mention Mummy Flora's insistence she get an education. She would leave that for another day.

That night and the night after that, Lily slept on the kitchen floor, willing herself not to cry. Her attempts to block out the sounds of the mouse had not been successful and it was only exhaustion that pushed her into any sort of sleep. Marigold would awaken her with a shove, immediately placing a broom into her hand, or a bag of clothes to wash, or a duster. Whatever needed doing around the house was Lily's task for that day. Luckily, she was a fast learner and was getting better at each job as Marigold's booming voice was never far behind: 'If you don't do it right the first time, I'll just make you do it again!'

Lily had been at Marigold's for almost a month and had hardly left the house. People would sometimes drop by and Lily would be banished to the narrow and freezing toilet cubicle in the back yard. She didn't mind those moments, because at least she could doze off for a few minutes, sitting on top of the closed toilet pan – that's if she remembered to smuggle the blanket inside.

She wasn't sure why Marigold insisted she remain a secret until one of her sons came home for the weekend. Lily was headed for the toilet cubicle once more, but stopped at the back door, and listened in on a conversation that would change everything.

'So she's my cousin, then?' said Tommy with amused fascination.

'Yes. No … No, not at all, look at her! Does she look like we could be related? Behave!'

Laughter.

'Then what is she then?'

'A freak of nature. Not one or the other!'

A freak of nature? Lily knew why Marigold could be confused. Lily being adopted meant they were not actually blood related but to call her a freak of nature was both hurtful, confusing and basically incorrect. The more she got to know Marigold, the less she wanted them to be related anyway.

She listened on.

'I blame Flora for all of this. Should have left her in that home. At least she was among her own sort.'

'Yeah, it's not natural.'

'Now she's dead, I'm lumbered with her.'

'Kick 'er out then, Mum. You can't let her stay here too long, cos people are gonna find out and then what?'

'I know, I know, son. I have to keep Flora's meddling neighbours happy or they'll want the cash back. She won't be here too much longer. Once I make it hard for her here, she'll probably run off.'

'That's what you want ain't it, Mum?'

'How did you guess? At least then they can't say I turfed her out.'

A tear ran down Lily's face as the pieces finally fell into place. She'd arrived at Marigold's hoping to find a family that would at least try to love her as Mummy Flora had, but this wasn't going to happen.

Now, with absolutely nowhere to go to and no family she knew of, Lily had no idea of what to do next. She opened the door to the toilet, wrapping the blanket around her. She closed her eyes and an image of Mummy Flora flooded her head.

'Don't let anyone tell you you're different. You're the same as anyone else and don't you forget that.'

Lily had been full of questions. 'What do you mean?'

'When I was growing up, everyone wanted to make me into something they thought I should be. They called me names. But I'm my own woman, aren't I? Just as you will be. Don't let anyone try and tell you you're something you're not – especially if it's derogatory, which it will be.'

'What is dog ... dogrotory?' asked Lily.

Mummy Flora had simply smiled and burrowed her head onto Lily's tummy, something that always made her fall into a fit of giggles.

Now, sitting in that cold toilet, Mummy Flora's words had finally begun to make sense. Yet, where was she now to explain all of this? What was Lily actually supposed to do without her? She had always been there to help her, advise her and now she simply felt lost at sea without any sort of anchor. Just a rope that could pull her further back into misery.

Lily wiped her eyes, tears brought on by grief for Mummy Flora but also anger at not being told the truth. She was different – at least to everyone here. The colour of her skin was so much more than what Mummy Flora had ever told her. Although Lily now realised that being so different was why Marigold had kept her away from the neighbours, and it also explained why Mummy Flora, in her love and wisdom, had also done the same.

My Dearest Love,

I don't know why I'm telling you this. I guess I want you to under-stand me a bit more. You see, we look different you and I due to the colour we happened to be born into. But the real difference is in how we get to see the world because of those differences.

Am I making sense? Or am I just confusing you?

When I was around seven or eight years old, my father and I were on an errand. The man who ran the gas station, Mr Preston, would always tip his hat when he saw us. It was quite a surprise, as many white folk didn't do that. I went to a segregated school so this was the only white man I had any contact with. So, one day a small truck with some men sitting at the rear pulled up. They stared at us in a way that was the opposite of Mr Preston. I wasn't scared though. They were just men after all and my father could take down each of them with his bare hands. One of them said, 'What you doing around these parts? Shouldn't you be elsewhere?' I opened my mouth to answer, but it was my father who did that.

'I'm just passing hereby to see about some cattle.'

'Cattle huh. You sure you ain't looking to make some trouble for yo'self, boy?'

'No, I am not.'

'No, SIR!' he instructed.

'No, sir,' replied my father.

At first I thought this had to be a joke. I looked up at my daddy and his face was bowed. He looked smaller than usual. This was not the father I had grown to fear throughout my life. This was a stranger. A cowardly stranger.

'Well, you run along, get that child home now, yer hear?'

'Yes, sir,' he replied, eyes resting on the floor. The other men were laughing. Or maybe they weren't. I really can't remember, but I do believe that if they weren't laughing at him outwardly, they were doing so inwardly.

We walked the long way back home, without any words.

'Daddy, what was that about?' I asked.

'Stop talking. We are not to talk about that again!' he roared, while all I could think of was why he hadn't raised his voice to those men.

Back at home that night, as my mama put me to bed, I told her about the men and how mean they had sounded.

'Your daddy told me what happened.'

'Why didn't he tell them to go away, Mama?'

'You go to sleep now, baby, and don't worry yourself about it.'

'I want to know!' I was a stubborn kid, even then.

'Please let this rest!'

She kissed me on my forehead. 'Go to sleep, baby.'

It wasn't until I turned sixteen years old and had experienced countless similar encounters of my own, did I fully begin to understand my father. Like the time in middle school when I was sitting on the grass near the store, and a boy named Brett came up to me and, without so much as a sentence, cleared the entire contents of his throat onto my face. His spittle landed directly on my nose and trickled down to my chin. I recall curling my fists and my instinct was to strike him, but my sensible and brave brother, who appeared out of nowhere, pulled my fists away before I could change all our lives. Brett simply walked away, oblivious to what I had wanted to do to him. My brother said, 'It's not worth it. You know what they will do to us, if you hurt him.'

I remember unclenching my fist that day and realising, even at such a young age, that my need to be a man would always be hampered by people like Brett. That kid had walked off as casual as anything, knowing that because of the colour of his skin he had the upper hand. He would always have the upper hand when it came to me, and people like me.

Chapter Seventeen

Iris

Iris couldn't be certain whether Marigold still lived at the address because so much time had passed.

'Marigold Baker?' asked Iris as the door slowly opened.

'It's Marigold Smith actually. Who wants … to know …?' Slowly a look of recognition formed on Marigold's face.

'It's me, Rose's kid!' Iris felt a pang of excitement despite herself. She'd no real interest in Marigold and simply needed a place to stay for a few nights.

'Iris?'

She shook her head enthusiastically as she leaned down to pick up her suitcase.

'Wait there for a bit …' The door closed and Iris hoped she hadn't called around at a bad time. A moment later, Marigold reappeared, inviting her inside.

'What brings you here then?'

'A catch-up. I haven't seen Mum's family in a few years. Not since the funeral anyway.'

'Not my fault.' She shrugged.

'It would have been nice to hear from one of you.' She hadn't meant to be combative but Marigold's couldn't care less attitude had already infected her. 'Actually, where were any of you even before she died? I only saw you once or twice—'

'You really don't know what you're talking about so I'd stop right there.'

Iris exhaled slowly.

'Your dad was the one who kept you away. Even when Rose was alive. Didn't like us being around you both so we stopped trying. At least I did.'

'I didn't come here for a fight.'

'Why are you here?'

Marigold was turning out to be worse than she'd imagined. Perhaps this had all been a waste of time.

'Do you have Flora's address? Maybe I'll pay her a visit. She'll probably be a bit more welcoming.'

Marigold's laughter that followed was not expected. Nor was the way she suddenly stopped as she stared into her face. 'Flora died.'

'What?'

'I guess you lot were in the dark too. I only recently found out, though she was dead to me a long time ago.'

Iris closed her eyes and exhaled. Not to grieve for a person she didn't know, but because Marigold seemed to be the only chance she'd have of a bed for the night.

'So there you have it. All you have is little old me and that's really bad luck on your part.'

'Why is that?'

'Because, unless you have some cold hard cash to give me, I am not interested in another mouth to feed around here.'

'I don't—'

'Thought so. Looks like you'll have to take your chances out there like the rest of us have to.'

Iris headed for the door. 'Why do you hate me so much, Marigold?'

'Don't flatter yourself, love. I don't hate you, I just don't care. That any better?'

She would wonder what had made Marigold so bitter, later. For now, it was getting dark and she needed a bed for the night. She contemplated going back to Gary and Sal's as guilt would surely afford her a couple of free nights at least. But Iris would rather die than spend another minute under the roof of a woman who had caused her mum so much pain. She already missed Gary immensely, but like Sal, her father and Marigold, he was now part of a past she had no intention of reliving.

The only person she could rely on was herself.

Hours later, clutching her small suitcase, she headed up the steps of a large bus, relieved it was almost empty. A man helped her place the case in the overhead locker and she sat by the window. Iris was on her way to London, the most glamorous city in the world (probably after New York) and far enough away from the demons of her past. Although slightly nervous at the prospect of starting over in a big city, she simply couldn't wait to get away and begin again. She had no idea how she would achieve such a goal, but if living with her parents had taught her anything, it was that she could survive anything.

Lily

As well as disappearing into the outside toilet whenever there was a knock at the door, another of Marigold's strict instructions was to never go into her room. Luckily, Marigold was out and wouldn't be back for a while.

The bedroom was just as Lily had imagined, with a messy bed and a dressing table containing an assortment of random items from lighters to empty cigarette boxes. Lily opened each drawer and quickly noticed two small paper bags. The first one contained a number of letters held together by string. She placed them back inside the bag and opened the second one she knew had once housed the money Uncle Kenneth had handed over for her keep, but now only contained a few pounds. She sat on Marigold's bed and exhaled. The mattress felt so soft, her body still not used to the harshness of the kitchen floor. She allowed her sore back to connect with the mattress, happily sinking into its softness, and she closed her eyes and simply drifted.

Lily awakened some time later to the sound of profanity before being roughly shoved off the bed and onto the hard floor.

'What are you doing on my bed?' spat Marigold.

'I'm sorry, I—'

'I told you not to come in here! Looking to steal from me, eh?'

'No. Not at all.'

'Don't you dare answer back to me, you little cow. After all I've done for you, taking you in and you want to steal from me? What would Flora say, eh? Is this the thanks I get for taking the likes of you under my wing? Is it?'

'I am grateful—' she said, just as Marigold's hand landed firmly across her cheek.

Lily let out a loud scream. She had never been struck before, not by anyone and the shock and the sting rendered her into complete shock.

'Get up and get out of my sight!' roared Marigold. As her mind came back to the present, Lily managed to scramble to her feet as Marigold's voice boomed behind her. 'This is above a joke this is! This time, you've gone too far!'

Something extraordinary happened. There was a knock at the door and as Lily leapt to take her place in the outside toilet, Marigold stopped her.

'You don't have to go. Not this time.'

Lily greeted the thin man who walked in and nodded his head in her direction.

'This is Ralph, one of my boy's mates,' said Marigold. Lily didn't bother to offer her hand. It would appear her manners were becoming as bad as Marigold's.

'Nice to meet you, Lily. Nice indeed,' said Ralph. The centre of his head was bald with strands of hair circling the outer edges. He rocked on the balls of his feet, hands in his pockets. 'How old are you then?'

'I'll be sixteen soon.'

Ralph nodded his head enthusiastically. 'Still okay. Still okay.'

'How's that son of mine? Keeping his nose clean?' asked Marigold.

'Well of course!' replied Ralph with what sounded like insincerity. 'John's doing well in the big smoke. Told me to give you this.' He slid his hand into his pocket and produced another one of those small brown paper bags Marigold seemed to love receiving.

'I won't need to count it. My boy always sees me right.' She slid the wad of money into her brassiere.

'Looks like Lily here will be perfect for the job,' said Ralph.

Lily tried to hide her excitement. She was ready to get out of this house and join the real world and work in a job. Perhaps become a bookkeeper like Mummy Flora. At least until she could go to college. And she could save up for a mattress!

'You'll be meeting and greeting,' replied Ralph without looking at her.

'I've never done that before.'

'You'll be able to pick it up. Don't you worry about that,' added Marigold. 'You're no good at cleaning so this will probably suit you better.'

'When do I start?'

'In a week, so you better go and get your things together. Best not to keep Ralph here waiting.'

'I don't understand ...'

'Doesn't she understand English?' said Ralph with a snigger, while Lily wanted to remind him that her English was better than anyone she had heard in this house.

'The job's in a hotel, so it's best you stay there. Your money's run out here so I can't keep you. And I'm sick of telling people they can't use the toilet when they come over.'

Lily wasn't sad about leaving, but she had hoped for some notice to pack her things. However, the idea of sleeping in a real bed overtook any lingering trepidation.

'You can only pack one suitcase, so take what you need.'

'But my clothes—'

'I will send them along when I'm ready.'

Since her arrival at Marigold's she had only worn two outfits. Party dresses and fancy shoes had not been needed. As long as she packed the black drawstring sack containing the last of the money, the Baker family photo and the sky-blue knitted bootie, she really didn't need anything else for now.

'You'd better take some bread from the kitchen. You've got a long journey ahead,' said Marigold in a rare show of concern.

'Why, where are we going?'

'London.'

London. Lily wanted to scream with joy. She was off to the glamorous streets of London where Mummy Flora had promised to take her but, of course, had never got round to, but instead they had watched countless films together that gave the impression London was certainly the place to be.

An hour later and filled with excitement, she followed Ralph outside and Marigold simply shut the door before Lily could say goodbye. As the car pulled away from that scruffy-looking front yard and down the street, Lily was reminded that in all the time she had spent here, she'd only seen past the front door once – and that was the day she had arrived.

Lily had been hidden her entire life and now she was on her way to London where she would no longer be tucked away. Lily was more than ready to finally see the real world and for the world to see her.

And she'd never felt more frightened.

Chapter Eighteen

Iris

She sat in a café nursing a hot mug of tea and a bacon sandwich, waiting for the outside fog to clear. Iris relished the challenge of finding both a place to stay and a job in one day, as there was no way she was going back to her old life.

She sipped the last of the tea and stepped outside into a sunshine that covered up the fact it was indeed a cold day. Each 'no' she encountered – at a bakery, a greengrocer's and a fishmonger's – only fuelled her determination. On her second attempt she managed to read the 'Help Wanted' sign and the accompanying instructions on the front of a hotel called the Shangri La. Iris had never been in a hotel before, let alone one with such an unusually foreign name, but she was willing to do anything; make the beds, cook. She was good at all forms of housekeeping.

'Can I help you?' said the give behind the wooden counter.

'I'm asking about the Help Wanted sign.'

'Oh … well. I don't think they're looking for someone like you.'

'What does that mean?'

'Just what I said.'

'Can I at least speak to the person in charge, please?'

171

If this was going to be another no, she'd rather hear it from the person who counted. She'd come too far to just be fobbed off by anyone. Besides, she was becoming desperate.

'Very well,' said the girl, who reappeared moments later with an older man, dressed in a silver-coloured three-piece suit that actually shone. Iris had once seen a circus act come to the village and he reminded her of one of the animal tamers, minus the tall hat.

'I'm sorry, my sweet,' he spoke loudly too, as if announcing something to a crowd of people. 'The position has been filled. In fact she's on her way now.'

'Bad timing then?'

'Not really – Pam, take the sign down – we were looking for someone quite specific and you wouldn't have fit the bill anyway.'

'Someone prettier?' she said before she could stop herself.

'No, you look okay … Nice bosoms, lovely shape you got there. You are just missing one vital ingredient and there's no way you'd be able to get that in time for tea!'

She wouldn't cry. Iris had done enough of that over the years, but she was tired. So very tired of remaining strong.

'Oh, you poor thing. Pam, get some water!'

'I'm okay, really.' She placed her fingers to her cheek. It was wet. How she hated herself for such weakness.

He placed an arm around her shoulders. 'I don't usually do this … I have a friend who's abroad right now, Robbie his name his. His mum has a big house. I think they're always looking for staff. A right battleaxe she is though, so they don't last long. Think you can stick it out?'

Iris looked to the ceiling, and tried to ignore an image of her father forming in her head. 'I'm sure I can.'

'The job comes with board I think.'

'Even better.'

'Thought that would help, judging by the tatty case. Sorry, but it *is* tatty, my sweet.'

Pam sniggered.

'I'll write the address down. Tell them Mickey Roux sent you. I can't promise she'll remember me. As I said my dealings were mostly with the son and she doesn't know half of what he gets up to, to be honest! Those posh types are always the worst!'

'I don't think anyone could forget you,' said Iris, hoping she didn't offend him.

'I think you're right!' he said proudly.

Less than an hour later, Iris was standing at the top of the steps outside an imposing three-storey house. She knocked again, this time gazing around her surroundings. A neat street with identical three-storey homes, this was like nothing she had ever seen in real life before. Her first impressions of London had been of crowds, shops and hordes of people. This quieter side suited her a lot more.

The large door opened to a much older, sour-faced woman with her hair pulled into a severe chignon. 'Yes,' she said, appraising her appearance and clearly not liking what she saw.

'I'm Iris ...'

'Iris?' she shook her head impatiently. 'Iris who?'

'I'm a friend of Mickey Roux.' She felt ridiculous, as she had only met the man once and for less than ten minutes.

'Who?'

'I've come about the job.'

The woman's eyes widened in what looked to be terror. 'All employment queries are dealt with downstairs. Off you go.' She closed the door before Iris could respond.

The same woman opened the door downstairs and led her into a small and dark room. 'Shall we start again?' Her accent had changed and was no longer laced with haughtiness. 'Sit down and I'll take your particulars.'

Iris sat on a wooden chair, her back to the window that looked out onto concrete. The kitchen could do with more light, perhaps a casualty of being so low down, and a faint smell of bleach permeated the air. The woman had no idea who Mickey Roux was, but agreed that Iris had arrived at a good time if she needed work.

The woman reappeared holding out what looked like a set of black-and-white garments.

'This will be your uniform, the pay is as agreed and you can start on Monday.'

'I'd prefer to start now.'

'Now?'

'Or in the morning, please ... If that's okay.' Iris had nowhere to sleep, but wasn't about to tell this woman, this stranger who hadn't even offered her name yet.

'A little urchin, are we?'

Iris scrunched her eyebrows.

'On the streets?'

'I have a home, but it's a way away. I'm no urchin.'

'If you say so,' she said, turned on her heel and left, the clickety-clack of her shoes leading up the stairs and into, as of yet, an unknown world.

'That hair looks like a wig!'

Regina talked non-stop and was the girl who shared the room along with two beds and a wardrobe. At first Iris had thought it good luck to be paired up with a girl close to her age, but now she craved some peace and Regina had no intention of granting her that wish.

'It's not a wig. All my own hair, Regina.'

'I should have said, people around here call me Reg.'

'You said a lot of things, but not that.'

'I know, silly me!'

Even though Iris had stifled a fake yawn just so Reg would leave her alone, there really wasn't any need as she was soon able to produce real ones as Reg explained the rules of the big house. And there were many.

'Long day?'

'Something like that. I really should get to bed. It's my first day tomorrow.'

The bed should have afforded her a comfortable night's sleep. Reg was a surprisingly quiet sleeper and until about five o'clock there were no sounds entering the small, dark room. Instead, Iris had done her usual act of staying awake, her mind racing with an abundance of thoughts. The one that stood out the most was: why hadn't she moved away much sooner?

Lily

Lily had fallen in and out of sleep in Ralph's car and by the time they arrived in London, it was already dark.

'Wakey, wakey,' said Ralph. She wasn't sure what the hotel looked like or if it was as grand as the one in the many films she had watched with Mummy Flora.

She held onto her suitcase handle and walked under a stretched-out awning leading to the main entrance of the hotel. There wasn't much lighting and if not for Ralph by her side, Lily would have felt quite frightened.

Inside, the Shangri La was probably in need of some decoration but it wasn't bad. Certainly nicer than Marigold's house.

'Hello,' said a kind-faced lady behind the counter.

'I'm Lily,' she said.

'Indeed you are. It's great to have you here.'

A man dressed in a sparkling silver jacket and matching trousers greeted her with a warm hello.

'Hello there, my sweet!'

The familiarity didn't shock her; indeed she was glad for the warmth.

'Hello ...' she replied. He took her hand and brought it to his lips. She flinched slightly.

'Not to worry. I'm harmless, me. I'm Mickey Roux and it's a pleasure to have you here. When Ralphy here told me about you I couldn't wait to meet you!'

'Oh, that's lovely, thanks.' It had been so long since anyone had been pleased to see her and Lily had forgotten how good that felt.

'Anyone told you how pretty you are? Gosh, you are stunning!'

'They have, but thanks,' she replied truthfully. They didn't have to know it was a long time ago and it was Mummy Flora who constantly said it. Hearing such words again just reinforced how true it was and that all these doubts she'd been having lately were unfounded. Marigold was just a bitter woman.

'This is Pam who works the front desk. You won't be seeing much of her as you'll be on nights and she works days.'

'Nights is good!' said Lily.

He turned to Pam. 'Oooh I love this girl already. So accommodating.'

Ralph seemed to have disappeared but Lily was unconcerned as Mickey was making her feel so welcome.

'This is where you'll sleep. Hope it isn't too poky,' said Mickey as they stood inside a medium-sized room with a bed and a side table. Lily had almost got used to Marigold's kitchen floor, so a real bed excited her more than this trip to London!

'I'll leave you to unpack, get some rest.'

Suddenly the thought of being in London wasn't that exciting after all, in fact it was a bit scary. 'Are you coming back?'

'I'm always around, my sweet. If you need anything at all, just let me know!'

Reassured, Lily didn't bother to unpack before throwing herself onto the soft and inviting bed and was asleep within minutes, a huge smile across her face.

Lily was grateful for the comfortable bed and a room she didn't even have to share with anyone. In the daylight, the room was basic, functional. As time went on she would certainly be able to buy a dressing table like the one she had in Willow on the Grange, maybe even a jewellery box like the one she'd had to leave behind.

There was a knock at the door and in walked a girl rubbing her eyes. Her hair was blonde and dishevelled, make-up smeared on her face. Mummy Flora said Lily was never allowed to wear make-up until she was at least eighteen.

'I'm Audrey. I sleep in the room next door with another girl. How come you get to have a room all to yourself?'

I guess I'm special, Lily wanted to say, because for the first time since Mummy Flora had died, that's how she felt.

'Maybe it's because I'm new?'

She sat on the bed uninvited. 'I don't remember getting that type of treatment when I was new.' Lily detected an accent. Northern maybe.

'Are you a chambermaid?' asked Lily.

'What?'

'I mean, what do you do here? I see there are lots of positions.'

'Lots of those!' A snort of laughter followed and Lily wasn't sure why this statement would be funny. Lily felt awkward. Engaging with someone her own age wasn't something she was used to. Should she be asking questions? Listening? The only person close to her age she had ever engaged with was Walter and he was a boy!

'Is this a nice place to work?' asked Lily.

'It's okay,' said Audrey, now lying flat on Lily's precious bed.

'I think I'm going to like it here.'

'Whatever you say,' said Audrey.

'How far are we from Trafalgar Square?'

'Not that far I suppose, if you take a bus.'

'Maybe you can show me around one day. On our day off.'

'I doubt you'll get many of those to start off with. I reckon you'll be really busy.'

'You think so?'

'Definitely. And when you do have a day off it won't be the same as mine. If I were you I'd just go alone as soon as you can and explore.'

'On my own?'

'Why not?'

'No reason …' Her heart rate increased at the thought of walking the streets of London, of anywhere, totally alone.

'So, what brings you here?'

'My mummy died,' she said out of nowhere. She hadn't heard herself say those words to anyone and here she now was, saying them to a stranger.

'I'm sorry,' said Audrey and Lily was glad of the compassion. 'You got any brothers and sisters?'

'No, just me.'

'Me too.'

'I have wondered what it would have been like to have siblings – even a brother. But it was just me and Mummy Flora.'

'At least you had her. I have no idea who my mum is!'

'I don't know who my dad is. Just that he was a brave soldier.'

'That's something to be proud of!'

The more they spoke, the more she felt warmly towards her new friend, Audrey.

'I left quite a good home in Leeds to travel to London to make it as a singer three long years ago.'

'I did wonder about your accent. So why aren't you singing?'

'Got stuck here, didn't I?'

'There's still time. Mummy Flora used to say it was never too late to follow your dreams.'

'Your mum sounds like a wise one.'

'She was.'

'Look, Lily … are you sure you want to work here? You seem a bit young.'

'I'm sixteen now.'

'That's still young and you even come across as a bit younger, even with your fancy words, no offence. I just don't think this place is what you're used to. You seem really educated. I'm sure someone around these parts would give you a job.'

'I'm okay here for now. I'm quite happy to be meeting and greeting after staying at Marigold's.'

'Meeting and greeting?'

'Yes.'

'Right, that's what you'll be doing here?'

'It is and I really can't wait to start. It's such a nice hotel and I get to make friends with you.'

'Just be careful, okay?'

Lily was grateful for these crumbs of concern. She already liked Mickey Roux and now Audrey. Pamela wasn't bad either, even when she handed her a paper bag filled with clothes that looked nothing like what she had been expecting.

She showed the outfit to Audrey some time later.

'Looks a bit like fancy dress,' said Audrey, pulling out a slim, tiger-print dress. Lily peered into the bag and pulled out a string of plastic fruit.

'Looks like the hotel's having a theme night,' said Audrey.

'I can't meet anyone in this!'

'Sure you can. I just wouldn't advise you to bend over or it might split at the seams!'

'Is this the kind of thing they wear in London?'

'Not really ... but if it's a theme night then ... well, anything goes. Especially during the gentlemen's nights.'

'What are those?'

'Exactly what it says. Gentlemen come to drink and have a good time. It can get a bit rowdy but the tips are good.'

Minutes later, Lily emerged wearing the animal-print dress, her hair gathered into a full-feathered headdress and a golden snake wrapped around her ankle.

'I must say I do feel rather scantily clad in this.'

Audrey stifled a giggle. 'You don't look very comfy. And where is the fruit?'

'I left that out.'

'Wise.'

'I must say, I'm a little cold and I still don't see how I can move about wearing this.'

'These fell out of the bag,' said Audrey, handing over a set of bone-style earrings.

'Do you think they're real bones?'

'No! Well, I hope not.'

When she appeared to Pam at reception, loitering guests stopped to stare.

'Pamela, may I speak with Mickey?'

Pam glared at her quizzically, before moving from her base.

'You look great, my sweet! Fabulous! Good girl!' enthused Mickey, clapping his hands with enthusiasm. 'Now, is there a problem?'

'I was just wondering if I could get a looser dress because there's no way I'd be able to get around in this, Mickey. I'm terribly sorry.'

'Oh, you poor sweet thing. You will be fine it's just serving drinks and tending to the bar. A bit of hosting. You would make a great hostess and there's good money in it.'

'That sounds okay but I have to be honest and say I have never done anything like that before. I don't want to let you down.'

'Oh how thoughtful, my sweet, but don't you worry, you'll get the hang of it in no time.'

'I feel a bit silly in this ...'

'No way! You look great. Like, what do they call it, an exotic Negress?'

'A what?'

'Never mind. You just go and relax. You'll enjoy it – you'll see.'

The shift began very well. All she had to do was meet and greet a succession of gentlemen guests and keep them entertained with stories of what it was like to grow up in Africa. Lily had never been to Africa and as far as she knew was the offspring of an American GI! She knew nothing past that, but, apparently, it was all part of the 'show' and she was fine to play along – especially when she saw the size of some of the tips.

'What are your favourite foods, bananas?'

'Do you all run around naked?'

'Have you met Tarzan?'

The questions were quite strange, but as Mickey had said when he popped in earlier, she was to make up stories from her head. 'An intelligent and special girl like you should be great at that.'

However, their questions made her feel like she should be insulted. And a part of her was, mixed in with a gratitude that she actually had a real, paying job and a comfortable bed to sleep in.

The following morning, Lily awoke to the realisation that she'd made two whole pounds that night. Money she was allowed to take and keep for herself. She sat up in bed, the excitement of the night before still brimming in her head. She'd never been one for showmanship, preferring to read a good maths or science-based book. But this experience had felt highly exhilarating and she was keen to try more of it. In the space of one evening, she had met more new people than she had in a whole year stuck in Willow on the Grange.

Audrey wasn't as pleased for her though.

'Why aren't you happy for me? I thought you were my friend,' she said to Audrey.

'I didn't say I wasn't pleased for you. I just want you to be careful, that's all. Not everyone's as nice as you think.'

'Everyone was jolly well nice to me last night.'

'Just be careful, okay? You're a nice kid.'

Mummy Flora had warned her about people like Audrey.

That evening as Lily got ready for work, she couldn't hold the excitement building up inside. She used to love wearing the pretty dresses Mummy Flora would buy for her and, now she'd left most of them behind, she rather enjoyed dressing up. She was like an actress. She just wished she didn't have to wear her hair out. Mickey said she should wear it 'wild' and if wild meant unkempt then that wasn't a good thing, but for two pounds a night she was okay with that!

This time, she was to make an entrance to the sound of African bongo music. She'd never heard of that before but was confident she would soon get used to it. The lights remained low, the beats pulsating the air along with thick cigarette smoke as she walked into the room. She had been told to dance, but apart from dancing along to the wireless with Mummy Flora she hadn't ever danced in front of anyone else, let alone a crowd! Luckily the group of gentleman was smaller this time – about eight to ten – with silvery hair and happy expressions. The drums seemed to get louder, and the room looked as if it was spinning as she moved her hips from side to side, sure she was out of time to the music. She only hoped no one had noticed. She moved her fingers into the air, the way she'd seen a lady do in a film set in a place called Hawaii. Yes, she would be that girl. Moving her hips and fingers in time to a pulsating beat. The music stopped, accompanied by a round of applause. Feeling a heat of embarrassment as she realised that all eyes were on her.

'Bravo!' shouted a stranger.

'Our very own Josephine Baker!'

'More!' shouted another. Lily suddenly felt disrobed and vulnerable, even though the animal-print dress was indeed intact, bone earrings swaying in her ears. This just didn't feel right.

'Good girl,' said Mickey, appearing from nowhere and ushering her out of the room.

'You did really well tonight.'

'Mickey, I don't want to go back in there tonight.'

'And you don't have to. Take the rest of the night off, you've earned it. Okay, my sweet?'

A mass of confusion buzzed around in her head as she headed towards her room. Just as she reached her floor, Lily was astounded by what she saw. A girl walking towards her. A girl. Who. Looked. Like. Her.

Exactly like her.

Lily's arms fell limp at her side. She felt weak, shocked to her very core.

Chapter Nineteen

Iris

The sound of the door being banged lifted her up and out of bed just as it had the very first morning in her new surroundings.

Then, everything had been new and had to be explained at least twice before it could penetrate her memory.

'It's 5.30 and time to start the day!' Mrs Ambers, the sour-looking woman with the severe chignon, had said.

Reg was up and changed into her uniform within minutes as Iris trailed behind, noticing that her new uniform was a bit loose around the middle.

'Better get someone to take that in for you,' said Reg. 'The last girl was a lot plumper than you. Especially towards the end if you know what I mean.'

'Mrs Taylor is the lady of the house and a stickler for everything to be clean. Even a speck of dust and she goes loopy,' said Reg as they toured the vast kitchen. Iris had never seen any-thing like it. From the beautifully tiled black-and-white floor to the curved drawers she longed to open one by one, just to see what was inside. There was a vibrant green work surface that Reg told her was Formica, whatever that meant. A pristine double sink that looked as if it had never contained any dishes. She'd never seen so much aluminium, having been used to the wooden kitchen at home where she had spent most of her time.

'The delivery boys come every other day to deliver the veg and the coal man is due later today but don't worry about him as I will sort him out, if you know what I mean,' she'd said with a wink.

'Today's washing day,' said Reg as she led Iris to a large oblong and stationary machine.

'It's called a twin tub and is very fancy. Have you seen one before?'

'No.'

'One side's a washing machine and the other is what you call a spin dryer! The clothes wash and you lift them out with these wooden things.' She lifted up a pair of tongs. 'Then you put them in the mangle to squeeze out the water.'

Iris had always hand washed everything – even her father's dirty underwear.

'Then you put it in the spin drier. You have to be careful 'cos the kitchen can get all steamy and Mrs Taylor hates that. Not that's she's ever in here. So we try to do the washing when she's taking a kip or something. Tell a lie, she doesn't really moan about it that much, only Mrs Ambers likes to do that and it's not even her 'ouse!'

Iris's head had spun with information. Names she had to remember, instructions on fancy machines. It had all felt too much, the huge kitchen with all its mod cons and Reg spouting off about something.

'I know it's a lot,' Reg had said. 'But you'll soon get the hang of everything, I promise. We'll leave it at that, but there's still so much more to show you.'

'There is?'

'This house is huge! But you'll be okay with just seeing the place you'll be working today. Tomorrow, I'll show you a bit more, like the bedrooms. Oh wait till you see those! The housekeeper tends to those so you won't have to be there much, unless ...'

'Unless what?' Iris hadn't liked the way Reg's eyes had widened as her lips remained pursed – as if she knew a secret.

'It's nice to have a new friend. In a place as large as this, you'll be surprised how lonely it gets.'

Now, on her third morning, she had finally managed a few hours of sleep and woke up before anyone else and brought in the milk from the doorstep.

Mrs Ambers appeared, looking less than pristine, her earlier chignon slightly collapsed to the side, dark circles around her watery eyes. Iris placed the last of the milk bottles onto the green work surface.

'Getting up early won't curry favour you know.'

'I was up anyway.'

'Report to the pantry in fifteen minutes.'

'Yes, Mrs Ambers.'

With the help of an ever so chatty Reg, they stockpiled the pantry with more food than Iris had seen in her whole life. With posh stuff like actual sugar cubes.

'Here!' said Reg, handing her a packet of crisps.

'I can't, it's stealing.'

'No it isn't. The delivery boys smuggle them in for me. Go on.'

Iris opened the bag and retrieved the small packet of salt and shook it over the contents of the bag. 'You get on well with all the boys, don't you?'

She hadn't meant to sound offensive and watched tentatively to see if she had indeed caused offence.

Reg simply shrugged her shoulders and popped a crisp into her mouth. 'You'll find that making friends is the best way to survive around here.'

Iris didn't need any friends she thought and placed the remainder of the bag of crisps into her pocket. She had work to do.

The fresh food delivered every few days was sometimes stored in a refrigerator, a large white contraption that Iris had been constantly fascinated with since her arrival. Indeed, everything she'd encountered in the last three days had unearthed something new and she hadn't even seen the main part of the house yet. That began to change when she followed Reg into one of the guest bedrooms. The huge double four-poster bed was draped in what could only be described as silk (Iris wasn't sure as she'd never touched anything remotely silk in her life). She ran her fingers over the surface, eyes closed, with only an amused Reg able to jolt her out of her daydreams.

'Lovely, ain't it?'

'Yes, it is.'

'We'll have to strip it and put on some clean bedding.'

'It's not even been slept in!'

'Doesn't matter. Mrs Taylor insists.'

Iris had long decided that Mrs Taylor, whoever she was, sounded like a wasteful woman.

When Iris finally met Mrs Taylor, there were no formal introductions, just a nod of the head from her new boss to acknowledge her existence. She was just as Iris had imagined; short, with neatly styled hair and pursed lips. Basically a smaller version of Mrs Ambers but evidently with much more power, especially as a widow armed with her husband's money. Mrs Taylor did not scare Iris though. She'd lived with a brute of a man her entire life and, compared to him, Mrs Taylor would be as soft as the bedding she had just changed.

Of that she was sure.

Lily

It had been several days since Lily had first laid eyes on that girl who looked exactly like her. She had wanted to touch her to make sure she was real. She'd wanted to smooth her own fingers over the girl's shiny arms and gently tug at the tufts of hair that framed her beautiful face. But the girl had scuttled away before Lily had found the words to even say hello.

Of course, they didn't look exactly alike and the only similarity she shared with this girl she now knew was called Nina, was skin tone. Nina's skin was a lot darker than hers but was the closest she'd ever come to seeing someone who looked like her. So when she saw her for a second time, Lily was not about to waste an opportunity.

'Why do you keep staring at me?' said Nina.

'Sorry.'

'You're worse than the white people here.'

'I just ... I like your ... your dress,' she said, unable to think of anything else to say. Nina was dressed in an ankle-length blue dress, her mass of hair held back by a white hair band. She was smoking a cigarette.

'It's 1960. I try. Makes a change from what I have to wear for these shows.'

'They're not that bad.'

'Really? You like the style of the savagely uncivilised, do you?'

Lily scrunched her eyebrows, unsure of if she was being made fun of or not.

'Never mind.' She pulled out a box of cigarettes. 'Want one?'

'No thanks. I don't smoke.'

'Then you should do. Especially if you want to stay here. Actually, ignore that. You will need something stronger. A lot stronger ...'

Lily had no real interest in appearing sophisticated like Nina by smoking a cigarette. She'd read in one of her books what smoke inhalation could do to the body and it didn't take a genius to apply that to cigarette smoking.

'I was surprised to see you here too, you know,' said Nina, moving her lips over the cigarette. 'I was a bit put out to be honest. I was what you call a niche market here. They weren't quite sure how I'd pan out but clearly I've been doing well because here you are.'

'I'm just Lily Baker ...'

The laughter that followed was exaggerated, insulting and went on for way too long. 'You have a lot to learn, princess. Sheltered in a small, cosy village were you?'

'No!' she said unconvincingly.

'They're usually worse in those small places, so your naivety surprises me.'

The friendship Lily had imagined in her head was slowly ebbing away.

'You don't know me!' she spat.

'Quite. But it also seems like you don't actually know yourself.' She turned away with a smirk. Lily opened her mouth to speak, before realising she had nothing profound enough to say.

'See you around. Unfortunately,' said Nina as she stepped onto the cigarette stub and made her way back inside.

'I wouldn't pay any mind to Nina,' said Audrey later. 'Always had a chip on her shoulder, that one. Hardly ever smiles, always angry and aggressive-looking. I'd stay away from her if I were you. You're obviously well liked here and she's just jealous.'

'That's what I thought.'

Pamela came into the room an hour before Lily's shift was to start and handed Lily a small package.

'These are for you to put on for the show tonight. We have a select client who demands more classy clothes. It was going to be Nina, but Mickey says you've been going down a treat.'

Unsure if she wanted to make an enemy of Nina, she unfurled the package. The outfit, a zebra print, was cut into a style even more revealing than the leopard-patterned one, especially around the bosom area.

'I'm not sure I should wear this.'

'Take it up with Mickey,' Pamela said, before leaving the room.

'Don't do what you don't want to do,' said Audrey.

'They've been good to me here ... I don't want to disappoint anyone.'

'At least see what it feels like when you put the frock on. If you don't like it, speak to Mickey. He seems to have a soft spot for you.'

'Do you think so?'

'Even Nina, like us, had to pay her dues with cleaning and washing before she got that spot and you walked right into it. I'd say he likes you a lot!'

That night, dressed in the zebra-print dress that just seemed to skim her cleavage, Lily walked into the room. A small number of gentlemen were present and this time the music was slower than usual. The air was thick with smoke and laughter, yet everything seemed to stop and focus on her. Her swaying hips, the way her breasts swung uneasily in the top half of the bodice. One man beckoned her over and she felt a gentle shove moving her closer to him. She wasn't sure who had done that, but she followed the path to where he stood and he beckoned her to sit on his lap.

'I don't bite,' he said. 'Just you sit on my lap, you sweet little Negress.'

There was that word again; Negress. She scrunched her eyebrows in confusion and even though it felt like the worst thing in the world to do, she contemplated sitting on this man's lap. Then she thought of Uncle Kenneth and how he had made her feel. She felt the bile rise in her throat and she wanted to retch, to vomit, to run away. But what would become of her if she did? As he gently pulled her down and onto his lap, she jumped up. 'I have to ... I have to dance.'

'No problem. I'll be here,' he said. Her dance was clumsy and rushed, not that anyone appeared to notice, judging by the exaggerated applause. It was when the music started up again and she realised she would have to do another number, that she decided enough was enough.

'Hey, where are you going?'

'I have a headache,' she said, rushing out of the room.

Audrey was still up.

'I don't want to do another number, Audrey. I don't want to do this dancing thing any more.'

'Why? You get to make tons of money and you don't have to have your hand down a toilet.'

'It doesn't feel right. It feels horrible. I can't put my finger on it but—'

'Were there just a few men in there this time?'

'Yes.'

'Did they touch you?'

'One asked me to sit on his lap.'

The way Audrey widened her eyes.

'What?' said Lily.

'Gosh you are a bit naive, aren't you?'

'I wish people would stop calling me that!'

Audrey moved closer to her. 'You said your aunt sent you here.'

'Marigold, yes.'

'What did she say you'd be doing?'

'She said I'd be working at a hotel and I assumed at the front desk or something. But when I saw it was entertaining I wasn't too put out. I mean, I prefer reading and numbers—'

'This is not a hotel!'

'Then what is it?'

'It's a gentleman's club. A whorehouse!'

'What … What's that?'

'You really don't know, do you? It's a place where women are paid to entertain men.'

'I know that. I'm being paid to dance.'

As Audrey fell back onto the bed with an exaggerated growl, Pamela appeared. 'You can't just walk out like that. Get yourself together, they haven't got all day.'

'I just need another minute or two.'

'That's it, I'm getting Mickey.'

'Yes, do that, he'll understand.'

Moments later, Mickey Roux appeared, dressed in a gold jacket and royal blue cufflinks. The familiarity of his outrageous clothing soothed her.

'Mickey. I really don't want to dance tonight.'

'On your monthlies, are you my sweet?'

'No, I just don't ... It just doesn't feel right.'

'And that's it?'

'Yes ... sorry.'

'Oh, you poor thing. I tell you what, have a good dance tonight and you have the entire morning to sleep it off.'

'I said I can't, Mickey. Please.'

'What do I tell all those lovely gentleman who have paid good money to see you tonight? Not Nina, but our very own Lily. What do I tell them? Do you want me to get into trouble?'

'No, of course not ...' As if sensing trouble, Audrey left the room and it was just Mickey and Lily.

He exhaled slowly. 'Lily, I'm going to need you to dance tonight.'

'But ...'

'What?'

When Lily didn't answer, he gently held onto her wrist. 'Look here, I paid a good price for you and I intend to get my money's worth. So you get your little arse out there, and dance until you can no longer move. And if anyone wants a bit extra with you, you let them. You hear?'

His grip tightened on her wrist and she was in no doubt that the real Mickey Roux had now appeared.

He released her arm, exhaled again and patted down his chest. 'Pamela will accompany you back to the room.'

Pam's grip was a lot harder than Mickey's as she shoved Lily in front of the wide-eyed audience. The music started up again, this time a rapid type of drum music along with flashing lights. A large-bellied man got up from his chair, grabbed her by the shoulders and began swaying with her out of time to the music. His tongue swept across her neck and into her ear. She wanted to gag, she wanted this moment or her life to end. He grabbed her behind, pulling her closer to him and when she felt his hardness against her thigh she was instantly filled with the strength to break free as the side of her dress ripped, exposing her flesh. The rest of the men in the room thought this to be hysterical and as the music came to a stop, she ran to the door, attempting to hide her modesty with one hand.

Another man pulled her back as she opened her mouth to scream but absolutely nothing came out.

'Don't be scared. We're all friends,' said one. Her body tensed, her eyes widening as she found herself inside a circle of men. There was no way out. Nowhere to turn. They were staring, laughing, expecting. She was running out of options. Then she heard a voice.

A female voice. 'Let her go and I'll give you what you want. It's not for free though. I want double the usual. I'm of quality African stock remember. Just let her go.'

Nina grabbed Lily by the shoulder and whispered, 'Get the heck out of here before I change my mind.'

Without looking back, Lily turned and headed for her bedroom where Audrey was waiting for her.

'Are you okay?' asked Audrey as Lily threw herself onto the bed. She wished Audrey wasn't here because she wanted to be alone. Needed to shut out the world around her. It wasn't the world she had been born into, it wasn't the world she was used to.

'It's usually all right after the first time,' said Audrey. 'Next time just down some booze, that will help.'

The tears were plentiful, mixed in with anger at Mickey, Pamela, Marigold, Audrey and even Mummy Flora. She hated her life and everything in it.

The sound of the door being flung open and hitting the wall made her jump.

Mickey stood at the end of her bed. 'What was that?' His voice sounded deeper.

She sat up uneasily. 'I didn't want anyone touching me.'

'And what do you think they pay good money for? To watch a nigger dance?'

That word crawled against her skin like an insect, fighting to pierce her skin, but she wouldn't let it. It was a bad word. A very bad word.

'Your aunt said you were a good worker, but tonight, Nina had to fill in for you. You owe her a lot. Next time I won't be so forgiving. So get yourself together, Lily. I really like you. Don't disappoint me. I paid good money for you.'

Her head began to spin. She couldn't keep up with the words being thrown at her. Threats. And the knowledge she'd been sold by her own aunty?

'Marigold sold me ... to you?'

'To this establishment and you owe us what we paid. You should be grateful we allow you to keep the tips. Now, I'll let this slip tonight but tomorrow, you will do whatever is asked of you or there will be consequences.'

Everyone, including Audrey, had been implicit in this disgusting deception. The only person who had been upfront with her had been Nina. The very person she'd assumed was against her.

'What do you want?' Just like before, Nina dragged heavily on a cigarette.

'I need to talk to you.'

'What about?'

'First I'd like to thank you for what you did in there. Did they ... Did they hurt you?'

'I only had one this time. The rest just like to watch. It was fine, I've done a lot worse.'

'Like what? What have you done in the past?'

'Never mind. Some things you don't need to hear, princess.'

'Why did you do that for me? You don't even like me.'

'Being here for six years hasn't turned me into a complete monster. You shouldn't be here. You need to get out. And fast.'

'I will. I can't do what Mickey wants. Do you want to come with me?'

'No, I absolutely don't. Look, Lily, I'm not sure what you want from me.'

'Don't you want to be free of this horrible place?'

She threw the cigarette on the floor and rubbed it out with her foot. 'I don't need you to judge me, I do enough of that for myself every single night.'

'I didn't mean to offend you.'

'I'm nothing like you, Lily. We're not the same. We may look similar but that's where it ends. Let me guess, you're the pampered princess of a nice white lady in the country. You've grown up with everything you've ever wanted or needed. My grandfather was born in Africa and brought over as a plaything for some rich aristocrat when he was ten years old. Not sure how I came about, but as you can see, I have carried on the family tradition.

'Just take this chance now and run. Get out of here and never look back. And be prepared to keep running because if Mickey and his lot find you ... well it won't be pretty. They make a lot of money out of this place and novelties like you and I ... well ... We bring in the sickos who like a bit extra on their menu, if you know what I mean.'

'I don't ...'

Nina's eye roll and sigh signalled to Lily that she only had a few minutes with her.

'Dressing up in jungle outfits, walking around on all fours and making monkey noises.'

'I thought that I was just acting.'

'Have you even done it before?'

'Done what?'

'Had relations with a man.'

'No.'

'Then they're probably collecting bids as we speak.'

The matter-of-fact way in which Nina spoke did nothing to diminish the unfurling horror of what she was being told or what was to become of her if she stayed at the Shangri La.

'Leave tonight, Lily.'

Lily closed her eyes and opened them again. Her body suddenly bereft of strength, yet spiked with a determination not to end up like Nina, whatever the cost.

'If you're going to run away, it's probably best to travel light,' said Audrey an hour later.

'You won't tell, will you?' asked Lily, still finding it hard to trust anyone.

'Of course not! Good luck to you, you're going to need it.'

'Thanks,' Lily said sarcastically.

'It's best you leave a lot of your clothes behind; you don't want to get weighed down.'

Lily was learning quickly. If her newly acquired instincts were correct, Audrey was blackmailing her for clothes. 'You're right. Is there anything you'd like?'

Audrey almost jumped out of her bed. 'Yes, there's quite a few bits here that will suit me,' she said, rummaging through the open case.

Even after Audrey had taken a few items, she was still too overloaded. Nina agreed to keep some of the less 'prissy' items and she would probably have to just leave the rest. Many of the clothes had sentimental value but would only weigh her down. She refused to ever part with the precious photograph of the Baker family in which Mummy Flora and Aunty Rose were holding hands, or the blue knitted bootie. These were precious and all she really had left of Mummy Flora.

The plan was to leave when everyone was asleep, between the hours of five and seven in the morning.

Nina was waiting for her just outside the hotel. 'Make sure they never find you.' She stuffed a piece of paper into Lily's hands. 'Here's the address and all the details. As I said, Ron knows me as Curly and just say you know me from somewhere but do not mention this place. I don't want this getting back to me.'

'I won't.'

'Do you have some cash on you?'

'Yes, I have my tips in my pocket and some money in my case from my mummy.'

'Your mother?'

'Before she died, she left me some money.'

Nina's eye roll was hard to understand. 'Of course she did.'

'It should be enough in case I don't find anything.'

'You will get something. You can put that money towards something else.'

'My education. I want to go to university some day.'

'And I have no doubt you will. Now get out of here, princess.'

She wanted to throw her arms around Nina, but felt this wouldn't be welcome.

The stillness of that moment suited the atmosphere. When night meets morning. The immediate surroundings asleep while the rest of the world was about to begin its day.

'Thank you, Nina,' she said.

'Not a problem, princess.'

Lily smiled warmly. Nina had touched a part of her in the very short time they had known one another. She had also taught her

197

a lot. Made her look at herself in the mirror and what she'd seen was a naive little girl who, as a matter of life or death, needed to grow up. She needed to stop looking for connections because Lily Baker was alone in this world – with only herself to rely on.

To my Beautiful Twin Daughters,

Not a day goes by when I don't think about you both. There's a desperation to see you and to tell you I am here and you are NOT alone. I am here for you, thinking about you every single day of my life.

But you will never see this letter.

I no longer ask myself how or why our lives have turned out this way. That I am thousands of miles apart from you both with no way of finding you. Like the death of my brother and my experiences in the war, I choose not to dwell on that part too long because I do not want that cloud and subsequent storm to pay me an extended visit.

Yet, how when I see a new flower bloom in my mama's little garden can I not think of how many inches you would have grown? How, when the seasons change from fall to winter can I not think of what changes you face in your life? How, when Daddy died could I not see what he has left behind and wonder what my legacy will be.

I was at peace with not having any children with Augustine. Because however much we wanted it to happen, it just hasn't. I was content with a son and a wife who seemed to love me no matter how many times I fell into what my wife called 'dem moods'. Outside of my stormy days, I was content and happy. But since finding out the truth, I can't get you both out of the happy section of my mind. Thinking of you did not contribute to a storm – trying not to think of you did that! But as I can't talk to you or touch you, writing these letters helps. Just like it did with your dearly departed mother.

I still can't believe it. I have two children, two girls! You are here, there, you exist. Two people who look alike and possibly like me. It's funny but there haven't been any baby girls in the Burrell family for many, many years.

If you were here you would most certainly be adored by us all. But you are not and I don't even have anywhere I can send this letter. Regardless, I WILL continue to write to you because I have to. I need to.

So, let me tell you about your family.

You'd love your grandmother. She's the most kindest, patient and loving woman I have ever known. Whatever happens you won't get to meet your grandfather now. He left us recently and it hit me hard. Harder than I thought it would. We didn't have the same relationship he had with my brother, but I loved him and, in his own way, he loved me too. He was born free in 1890. A proud man who worked the land to support his family. He always treated my mama well which was important, but when it came to us boys, he never saw it necessary to smile. He'd wink at our mama but smirk at us. I sometimes asked why he never wanted to play catch with us and he said, 'My job is to make sure your mama puts food on the table and is able to clothe you.' I think it's then I knew that when I had children, I'd be a different type of father. I was already different anyway. I was into the arts, liked to look at fancy paintings and I enjoyed writing so much I knew I wanted to make it a career. Joining the army was something that was not in question as it was in the Burrell blood. Like my grandaddy – born into slavery yet he escaped and joined the US navy. He wasn't about to remain in bondage and made sure he did something about it. It's a little ironic that by joining the army myself and forgoing my dreams of becoming a writer, I had unwittingly entered a form of bondage.

Then there's Clyde – your big brother. We have a good relationship and he comes to me if he needs advice or just a shoulder. We have what me and my father never did. That said, I know that if you girls were here, I would be like a plate of grits – all mushy. I don't know what's it's like to have daughters, but I suspect it would be different than having a son. In fact, I'm sure of it. I'm laughing right now.

I married a good woman in Augustine and she came complete with the best son a man could want. She knows how to cook my favourite – southern biscuit – and we talk well into the night, about anything and everything. She doesn't think I'm too soft for her. She once told me she admires my strength.

I work the farm but some days I have enough time to write, just as I am doing now. It's the creative outlet I have always needed. The one thing to keep me sane in and among the madness that can be life. When I think about the injustices that my family, my ancestors, my father and my brother endured, writing helps me to release. Now I know my two daughters are out there, I have even more of a reason to leave a legacy. You see, this farm may have been in my family for some years now but what I really want is to leave you these letters. So I am going to keep writing them for as long as I am able to.

I don't know your names. I have no idea who you look like. Do you have your mother's beautiful smile or my broad nose? I don't know if you hate orange juice like me and adore raisins. I don't know what the sound of your voice is like but can imagine it sounds not unlike the way honey looks like when it is being poured onto a warm cup. That's how your mother sounded to me.

I never believed you could fall in love at first sight until I met your mom. I never knew it was possible to love another human being having never set eyes on them before, yet here I am loving my two beautiful daughters I have never met.

My family keep asking me 'What's wrong?' but are scared to push me. They still remember what I was like not that long ago, what I am still like. The hurricane of '59 has left its mark and lingers. It still lingers.

I'm bursting to tell them about you and I will. I just can't bring myself to reveal this news only to accompany it with nothing more than a 'I don't have any more information'. It would be too heart-breaking for my mama who has already lost a son and a husband. To then lose two grandchildren would be a burden I refuse to place on her. Then there's Augustine.

What are your names? I think I would have called you Annie after my mama and Wilhelmina after me. That does reek of a narcissistic nature that I am not familiar with, but knowing I will never have another son would in some way justify that indulgence, don't you think?

Are you happy? Do you have people in your life you can rely on and who love you unconditionally? Are you well fed and looked after? Do you laugh every single day of your life despite the fact that your blood parents are not in your life? I could not love my stepson any more if he were my own and I hope you too have found someone just like that.

Chapter Twenty

1961

Iris

It was during those moments when Iris ran the vacuum cleaner over the floor, or when she paused while wiping inside the cupboards. It's then she would think about the fact she'd swapped one life as a maid for another life as a maid. 'At least I'm getting paid for it this time,' she'd mumble, before continuing with her tasks. Her duties never included cooking, which she missed simply because it allowed her to feel closer to her mum. She managed to tolerate Reg on most days, although found it hard to take her seriously. However, Reg at times provided much needed relief to a life that mostly felt mundane, although at other times Iris found her very irritating.

Iris's routine rarely changed. She would rise at four-thirty every morning, receive the food from the delivery boy and sometimes help prepare breakfast and dinner for the house by cutting vegetables but never actually cooking. She would clean, make the beds (whether they needed changing or not) and do it all over again the next day. She enjoyed her one day off a month which she used wisely with solitary trips to the park. She enjoyed being surrounded by the summer flowers she and her family had been named after.

'Why were you and your family named after flowers?' asked Reg.

'I dunno. I think my grandmother Lillian just liked flowers.'

'Lillian, so none of her kids were called Lily then?'

'No.' She smiled.

'That's the first time I've seen you smile!' said Reg as if this was some personal triumph. 'So, what about your uncle Donald, he's the odd one out, isn't he?'

In more ways than one, she wanted to say. She'd been too young to remember actual conversations about Donald. The 'your uncle's a loony' remarks courtesy of her father were much more vivid. But the black-and-white picture she had forgotten to pack into her suitcase was one of the only reminders she'd had of a family that should have been hers. Now, any links with them were gone forever. She was simply Iris, a live-in maid to the Taylor family and living in a posh part of London.

'Happy seventeenth birthday! The old prune has a heart after all,' sang Reg.

'Since when?' asked Iris, not that enthused about her birthday and hoping the day would pass quickly.

'Mrs Ambers has given permission for you to cook up a nice toad in the 'ole and suet pudding for our lunch. I'll help you of course. I know you said that was what you used to cook with your mum, God rest her soul.'

Her face dropped.

'You don't want to?' asked Reg.

'No, no ... I mean I do. I can follow the recipes I took ...' She swallowed. 'Thanks, Reg. That's really ... nice of you.'

'I know what it's like to miss a mother. Let's get the rooms done then we can make a start on those toads!'

The toad in the hole was in the oven and it was time to make a start on the suet pudding.

'I must admit, I've never liked the stuff,' admitted Reg as they rolled the soft dough into the pudding cloth. Iris rolled up the cloth and tied it at both ends.

'Is the water boiled?' she asked. Her mum would never let her place the pudding into the water when she was little, said it was too dangerous.

The entire meal turned out perfectly thanks to Grandma Lillian's recipe that Reg helped with by reading it out to her while she prepped. The staff were complimentary and appreciative of Iris's efforts.

'I can't eat another piece!' said Iris as Mrs Ambers walked in.

'Did you enjoy your birthday treat, Iris?' said Mrs Ambers. Only she could see cooking for others as a treat – although to Iris it actually was. Until recently, she had not been able to enjoy a birthday without soaking her pillow with tears. Until today.

'Yes I did, very much!'

Something huge was happening in the Taylor household.

Every inch of furniture was to be wiped and dusted until it shone like the sun. Bulky items had to be moved into other rooms for temporary storage. The food order was thrice the size and no staff were permitted to take a day off.

'What's going on?' asked Iris.

'The prodigal son,' said Reg. 'Master Robert is his name. Although the last time I saw him, he was less a little boy, more a fine-looking man.'

'Reg, is there any bloke you don't fancy?'

'Not really,' she laughed.

The imminent arrival of Mrs Taylor's son had turned the predictability of her day on its head, with the entire household buzzing at this new development.

'Why is Mrs Taylor having a big party for him anyway?'

'It's like a homecoming, right? After he left university, he travelled to all over what's left of the British colonies. He has been back for short trips but he's mainly been away.'

'What's a colonies?'

'Don't know much do you?'

Iris ignored that comment.

'Well, you know we own half the world right? Well we did, but now they're getting independent and all that. That's as far as I know! I'm no swot!'

Of course Iris had known about Africa and India. Her dad had spoken enough about it in the past. 'These wogs need us. See how long they last without our help! We gave them English and clothes to wear to cover their arses.'

'My dad knew a lot about it. He told me all I need to know.'

'You don't mention your dad much.'

'There's no need.'

'So who's coming tonight?' asked Iris moments later as she tucked a sheet into the side of a huge mattress.

'Friends of the Taylors I s'pose. You wait till you see Master Robert.'

'I'm sure he's just another man ... they're all the same, aren't they?'

When Robert Taylor accompanied his mother to greet the staff, Iris could not believe her eyes. Much taller than Mrs Taylor's tiny stature, his skin glowed like he'd been out in the sun all day, his smile laced with the privilege only this amount of wealth could give him.

'Mummy, aren't you going to tell me the name of the new girl?' he said. It took seconds for Iris to realise he was talking about her.

'Whatever for? She's just the help.'

'Now, now, Mummy, that's not a very nice thing to say.' He walked up towards her and she hated the fact that the skin of her cheeks began to feel clammy.

'I'm Robert,' he said, proffering his hand to her. She wished her nails weren't so untidy and laced with brown specs of dirt.

'I'm Iris ...'

'A pleasure to finally meet you, Iris.' His right eyebrow rose. 'Such amazing hair. Unable to be tamed, much like its owner perhaps?'

'What do you mean by finally?'

'You've clearly been in my dreams up until now.'

She stifled a giggle. The shine in his eyes was as unmistakable as the fizz running between them via his touch.

'I'll see you later,' he said, upon finally releasing her hand but clearly not her attention.

As he turned and walked away, Iris was nudged out of her trance by Reg.

'What was all *that* about, lady?' she said.

'Nothing.'

'I thought you had a boyfriend back home. Gary, didn't you say?'

'He's not my boyfriend. I'll never see him again. Also, I'm not stupid enough to think that a man like that would be interested in the likes of me.'

'He wouldn't. Not for anything serious ... but you never know ...'

'I'm not that type of girl, Reg. You know that.'

Now when she was on her knees on the floor, scrubbing at a stain on the tiles, she'd sense him watching her. When she ran a duster over the tops of the cupboards, he'd be standing feet away, observing. She enjoyed the tiny bit of power it afforded her, something she wasn't used to.

'Men really shouldn't be in the kitchen.'

'You sound like my mother.'

'She's right.'

'I like looking at you ... but if it's making you feel uncomfortable, I'll offer my apologies and stop.'

'I didn't say that, Mr Taylor.'

'I told you, call me Robert.'

If she ever did feel any level of discomfort it was only if she worried that her hair was slightly out of place or she had an impossibly unladylike sweat patch under her arm.

'I'd stare at you all day if it was permitted. But it's not befitting of a gentleman so I'll stop this instant. You're just so beautiful.'

She stopped scrubbing, stood up and smoothed down the front of her uniform. No one had ever called her beautiful before.

'You must be having a laugh with me.'

'That, I am not.'

'You could have your pick of girls.'

'I'm not sure that's true. Besides, there's something profoundly different about you, Iris Baker.'

'I'm the same as anyone else who works here. No airs and graces.'

'Unlike my people, you mean?'

'Sorry ... I didn't mean ...'

'It doesn't matter, you're probably right. And that's a good thing. You're just you, natural and real. I met a lot of people like that during my travels. Real people who weren't bound by their trappings. I got on well with them.'

'That's nice for you.'

'I didn't mean to sound patronising. I'm explaining this all wrong. I'm just trying to let you know that I'm not like the rest of the Taylors, so please, whatever you do, don't judge me.'

Iris began to wake up each morning with a smile. Just the thought of seeing Robert each day held the promise of a pleasant morning, afternoon and evening. Her heart was alive in ways that felt more than just an incessant beat. If she could sing she'd do so like Doris Day.

Robert would make countless excuses to enter the kitchen for 'a quick glass of water', as she chopped vegetables, their eyes meeting perhaps only for a moment. It was simply the thought of him, infusing her with happiness and, above all, something she was not familiar with: hope.

What was it about Robert Taylor that had captured her so much? It had never been this way with Gary. She'd felt like only a child then but now she was practically a woman and she knew her own mind.

And right now, she wanted Robert Taylor.

'I saw you,' said Reg as they settled down for the night. Iris couldn't wait to fall asleep, if only to dream about Robert and what his arms would feel like around her. 'You and Robert talking.'

'We were just being friendly.'

'Be careful,' said Reg as she plumped her pillow.

'Just because he's not looking at you!' She wasn't sure why she'd said it but it was too late to take back.

'You might find this hard to believe but I do care about you and I don't want you getting hurt. Men like Robert don't marry girls like us. We are just their playthings.'

'Speak for yourself,' she said and turned her back to Reg and her tales of doom. She enjoyed her dreams surrounding Robert Taylor, even though she knew deep down that she wasn't good enough for the likes of him. But she had her dreams and no one could take them away from her.

On her day off, she sat in the park as usual and was shocked to find Robert Taylor standing in front of her.

She had to make sure she was not dreaming this time. 'Robert?'

'Iris. A flower among the flowers.'

Her cheeks felt a rush of heat. She could wish he didn't have such power over her, but now she felt comfortable with the inevitability.

He sat down beside her on the bench.

'How did you know I was here?'

'I followed you.'

Her eyes widened.

'I'm sorry, that sounds utterly wrong and probably quite frightening. No, I was out walking myself one day, saw you were heading into the park. It was your day off so I didn't want to disturb you.'

'Yet, here you are.'

'Oh no, that was a couple of months ago. I decided I couldn't stay away any longer.'

She didn't have a chance to answer, because he felt for her hand and held onto it. Her heart rate accelerated.

'I should be getting back,' she said.

'Why? It's your day off.'

Indeed she had nothing much else to say. Here she was on her day off, holding hands with Mr Taylor's son. If Reg could see her now!

'Come on,' he said, pulling her to her feet. 'Let's go and explore.'

She hoped that weaving in and out of clothes shops was as exciting to Robert as game expeditions in Africa. Or that pointing at paintings in the museum was as thrilling to him as seeing a place called the Taj Mahal in India. He expressed more than once that he wanted her to experience the brilliance of this artist and that. 'Broaden your horizons. A good education is more useful than a hot plate of food.' But all she could really think about was Robert. Hoping he was enjoying this trip and not feeling short-changed because of her lack of sophistication and education. She hoped the day was as pleasurable for him as it was for her.

She was relieved when they sat down in a little teashop. She tried to ignore the prices for one cup of tea and a sandwich before reminding herself that Robert could afford it.

'Would you like some cake too? A scone perhaps?'

'I'd really like a scone, please.'

She looked around her, clocking various ladies dressed smartly in sky-blue suits and white gloves. She had seen a picture of Jackie Kennedy and decided that all of the women in that little teashop looked just like her. Iris could not remember her own mum taking time out of the house to have tea and cake. Indeed, she never remembered anywhere like this even existing where she grew up. Just the odd café that needed a thorough once-over with a mop.

She bit into a deliciously warm scone.

'Don't you want to add any jam to that?'

'It's perfect like this.'

'Just like you.'

She rolled her eyes, secretly liking the compliment.

'Sorry!' he laughed.

'It reminds me of my mum's, the scone,' she said out of nowhere.

'Where is your mother?' he asked before taking an elegant sip of tea.

'She's dead.'

'Oh, I'm so sorry. I suppose we have that in common.'

'Your dad?'

'Yes.'

More scones arrived along with a fresh pot of tea. This was all rather proper for her and she felt like a princess.

'I hope you enjoyed my little tour of London today.'

'It was lovely, thank you,'

'Spending the day with me can feel a bit overwhelming sometimes. I can be a bit of a show-off just because I've travelled.' His eyes narrowed. 'But what about you? Tell me more about you.'

Her resistance was weak and that was okay. There wasn't much to tell anyway! She missed out the violent dad, murdered mum and 'loony' uncle and invented a story that was palatable and wouldn't invite any questions.

Then he said something that had the power to shock her to the core.

'Are you fully white?'

She almost spat out her tea.

'What?'

'Being mulatto is nothing to be ashamed of. I saw lots of them during my travels. White men and native women, it's—'

'I don't know what a mula … mula—'

'Mulatto,' he corrected.

'I don't know what one of them is, but I know what I am and that's English. I'm English, thank you very much!'

'I didn't mean to offend you.'

'My mum and dad are white. What do you think this is?' She stood up abruptly and the table shook. In all her life she had never been more insulted. Perhaps all that travelling had done something to his head!

'I can see this is very upsetting for you and I'm sorry.'

'How do you expect me to react? Saying I'm not white and I've got something mixed in with me.'

She thought about what her dad would say to this – after punching this 'toffee-nosed' bastard's lights out.

'I said I'm sorry,' he said firmly.

She recoiled into her seat.

'Forget I said anything, Iris. I am a fool.'

Despite one huge, uncomfortable moment, the day continued into late afternoon. The pair giggled over a myriad of very funny jokes about Mrs Taylor; holding hands as they sneaked back into the house through the front door; and folding into his arms the minute his lips touched hers. When she woke up, still in his arms an hour later, she realised it had not all been a dream.

She looked down at the sleeping Robert in that huge four-poster bed. It was as comfortable as she'd imagined.

'Hello?' he said as one eye sprang open.

'I'll go, shall I?' she said, hoping he would stop her. He did.

'Noooo, Mummy won't be back for hours. Stay with me. No one will miss you as it's your day off.'

'That … that was my first time …' She felt it important to tell him, so he didn't assume she was loose.

'I gathered that. And I'm honoured you chose me.' He kissed her forehead. She wasn't sure he'd had any choice in the matter really because from the moment he'd entered her life it had almost felt inevitable that this moment would come. She was already in love with him and had dared herself to think of a life with him as her husband and she his wife. He wasn't like other posh people. He went against the grain, had cavorted with wild animals in the jungle. He knew things she would never hope to know.

'I love you,' she whispered into his neck, hoping he hadn't heard her but also hoping he had.

Lily

Lily had never seen anything like this. The address Nina had given her was in the famous area of Soho and from the moment she stepped off the bus, she had become intoxicated with the blaring music wafting from shop doorways adorned with multi-coloured cloths and beads, and the smell of unfamiliar food like Chinese. An actual restaurant that sold Chinese food! Women wearing skirts at least eight inches above their knees, their hair packed into a long cone shaped on their heads, heels as high as a building. Most importantly she had seen at least five people in the last two hours who looked like her!

Soho was the place she wanted to be and could see why Nina had sent her here. Her plan was to find lodgings, freshen up, dump her things and then go to the address on the piece of paper. So far, the first part of her plan had proved futile.

'Sorry, no rooms.'

'Booked up.'

'No vacancies, sorry.'

Lily was aware that at least two of the establishments had the 'Vacancies' sign lit up when she had gone inside. Lily was no longer naive enough to believe that all was fair in this world so she waited until someone with a kindly face walked past.

'Excuse me, miss?'

The woman was wearing long white boots and a matching dress with a black patent belt. To Lily she was the most beautiful woman she had ever seen and looked just like one of the dollies she used to own. 'Sorry to bother you, miss, but I'd like to purchase a room for the night at this establishment. However, they refuse to rent a room to someone like me, so I was hoping you could go inside, pretend the room's for you and just hand me the key? I will give you some money on top. I just really need a place to stay tonight.'

Throughout her story, the woman's expression switched from shock to sympathy. 'I'll do it.'

Ten minutes later the woman handed Lily the key. 'Better make sure they don't see you.'

'I'll just say I'm visiting. Thank you so much.'

'Pleasure.'

Lily reached into her pocket. 'No, you keep the money. I did it because it was the right thing to do. Good luck.'

Lily watched the woman, whose name she hadn't even asked, move away and warmth filled her heart. She was surrounded by good people; she just had to make better judgements because, clearly, not everyone was good.

The club called Flamingos had yet to open for the night, and this was the perfect time to speak to the manager according to Nina.

Lily rapped on the front door to no avail but after walking towards the side of the building, she noticed a door was ajar.

'Hello?' she called. A man with skin darker than hers appeared, eyes scrunched, hand patting his portly belly. 'To what do I owe this visit?' His voice, a harsh baritone, made her jolt.

'I'm sorry, the front entrance was locked.'

'That's because we're closed, love.'

'I'm looking for Ron.'

His eyes narrowed.

'I'm a friend of someone he knows. She said there may be some work for me here.'

'Wait here,' he said.

His voice boomed from inside the building. 'I thought I told you to get rid of the chipped glasses! Has anyone seen to the blocked toilet yet?'

A number of people passed by, each carrying crates of drink. She felt in the way as she shifted her weight onto each foot, biting the top of her lip. She moved out of the way as a woman balancing bottles of wine or champagne almost collided with her.

The man reappeared. 'It's a bit busy as you can see. Who did you say sent you?'

'Nina ... Curly?'

'Curly, yes! How is she?'

'She's ... err ... okay.'

'Come in, come in. We'll go and talk in my office.'

The girl with the champagne was back, now eyeing her suspiciously.

'Curly was one of my best barmaids, but kept complaining she wasn't getting paid enough. I hope she's gone onto better things?'

'Sort of,' said Lily.

She followed him into a small office. Black-and-white pictures of people she did not recognise, but assumed might have been famous, adorned the walls. Men with saxophones, glamorous women with slick hair singing into microphones. The most alarming thing to Lily was that this man, this man who looked like her, owned an office and appeared to answer to no one. This was a revelation.

She sat down as he took a seat behind the cluttered desk.

'Excuse the mess. I'm Ron,' he said, proffering his hand. He shuffled a few pieces of paper on the desk and repositioned a couple of stray pens, yet still this made no difference to the state of it.

'We always need good bar staff around here. We get really busy especially Thursday to Sunday. Have you ever pulled a pint before?'

Mummy Flora had told her never to lie, because 'You'll get found out eventually'.

'No.'

However if he asked her age, she'd probably have to lie about that.

'Never mind, we always need glass collectors and the like. Although a posh bird like you would probably be good at greeting the guests.'

'Front of house?'

'If that's what you like to call it.'

'But I'm coloured.

'Well I run the joint and what I say goes.'

'This is your place?'

'Well, part-owned with a mate of mine who looks nothing like me. But that's how you beat the system. Attach yourself to people who can help you get where you wanna be. That's my motto and now I run a club in one of the most sought-after areas in London. Not bad for a soldier's kid from East London.'

'Your father was in the army?' she asked.

'Sure was.' He leaned over to a side shelf and retrieved a photograph, which had curled with age.

'My dad was part of the British West Indies Regiment during the First World War. Here's a picture of him and some of the lads.'

He pointed to the darkest of the three men in the picture, with his hand resting on the shoulder of his comrade. Lily swallowed and forced herself to hold back her emotion. That simple gesture ... of belonging. She hoped her dad had felt the same way in the American army. She hoped to one day feel that way again too.

'You all right, love?'

'Your dad ... he looks so brave.'

'They all were. People don't know that people from the colonies helped fight both world wars. I wouldn't bloody know if it weren't for my dad.'

'My dad was in the army too!' It felt odd to speak about a man she had never met.

'That's great! What regiment?'

'I don't know. He was an American GI. That's all I know.'

'Ah, love. You never met him then?'

'No.'

'I heard a lot of stories about the GIs. Had a couple of their kids working here. They didn't know their fathers too.'

'Are they still here?' Lily suddenly felt a desperation to speak to more people who could also relate to the losses she had endured. Ron was doing a good job so far, but she'd prefer a girl to talk to. One who wouldn't lust after her like all the men she seemed to come into contact with.

'No, those girls have moved on. Just like you will.'

'I haven't even started the job yet!' she said.

'Looks to me like you didn't start from humble beginnings and now you're here, doesn't mean you'll stay.'

'You sound a bit like Mummy Flora.'

'Who?'

'Nothing. Please tell me what I have to do and I will make sure I'm the best worker you have ever had.'

'Glass collecting for now.'

'That's wonderful. Thank you.'

'It's just glass collecting.'

Lily was on a high. So much so, she decided she would break into the stash she kept in her suitcase and buy a bag of fish and chips. Outside and peering intermittently through the window, she waited for the woman behind the front desk at the B&B to disappear out the back and ran upstairs to her room.

She searched for the little drawstring bag, last seen inside the case. Using the strength of rage, she tipped the case upside down and searched through the contents on the floor. It was gone. The little drawstring bag and all the money Mummy Flora had left her in this world was gone. Audrey had taken it. It had to be her. Always in her room, she had probably been pilfering the cash a little each day before taking the lot.

She lay back onto the floor, the contents of her suitcase strewn around her.

'One step forward and two steps back,' she said out loud to nobody, because there was absolutely no one to hear her, no one to place their arms around her shoulders and assure her that everything was going to be okay. Mummy Flora was gone forever. She'd no idea who'd fathered her all those years ago too. Lily was totally alone and even the financial cushion Mummy Flora had provided was now gone. Angry tears sprang into the corner of each eye as she berated herself for yet another moment of sheer naivety.

Collecting glasses was the easy part. Making ends meet for an entire month before payday would not be. Nevertheless, her life quickly fell into a routine of bread and butter sandwiches as she hid in her room during the day to evade 'capture' by the land-lady, grateful for the cold weather so that she could sneak out of her room dressed in a hat with the collar of her coat pulled up to her face. Before her shift began, she enjoyed browsing the second-hand bookstall, trying so hard to ignore the delicious aromas coming from the fruit stalls.

It was three weeks into her stay that she found her suitcase packed and waiting for her at the reception desk.

'What's going on here?'

'I should ask you the same thing, miss,' said the silver-haired landlady.

Lily pulled off her hat.

'Thought you could live here under false pretences did you?'

'I don't know what you mean.'

The landlady's voice was a whisper, yet laced with a rasp that reminded Lily of a fictional witch. 'I run this place, which means I decide what type of people can stay. You understand or do you want someone to translate?'

'I paid for a month, though.'

Two women walked up to the desk and their stares only made her more self-conscious. A whiff of humiliation beckoned.

'Don't worry, I'll refund a week's money. Just leave now.'

'What if I don't?' said Lily in a rare show of defiance. She was tired of being kicked about, humiliated, pushed from pillar to post. She was also tired of being weak and naive.

'If you don't leave, I'll just call the coppers. You can take your chances with them.'

The two women sniggered.

'Now get out!'

Lily could only hope they'd packed everything. As long as she had the blue bootie and the photograph, she didn't care about anything else. The other stuff was just things. Items that had once meant so much, but now meant nothing. She checked the bag and was relieved to find everything she owned in the world, neatly packed.

She dragged the case through the door just as flakes of snow began to fall.

It was easy to sneak her case into the cellar at Flamingos. Just as it wasn't that hard to sneak back in after her shift ended.

The cellar was icy cold and damp, but no worse than Marigold's kitchen floor. She laid her head on a pile of clothes and used her coat as a blanket. Mice and rats no longer bothered her.

She could do this. She could do this.

Mummy Flora had always believed in her and it was time she believed in herself.

Lily's eyes sprang open.

Secrets.

She'd started this world in secret and been taken into a family full of their own secrets! Now, once again, she was hiding out, in secret! But this would be the last time. Like Ron, she was determined to go way beyond what was expected of someone like her and would, one day soon, make her own way in 1960s London. The next few days or a week or months would be a struggle but she would cope. Then she'd be on her way to becoming more than anyone like Marigold or that landlady would have expected of her.

Not that they really mattered.

The only person who mattered, the only person she had left in this world was Lily Baker. And she owed it to herself to build on everything that Mummy Flora had started.

Chapter Twenty-One

Iris

They met wherever they could, usually during her day off. Now, there were no more trips to little teashops, but straight into Robert's room and onto that four-poster bed that was no longer elusive to her.

They would sneak looks during the rest of the week. A kiss and cuddle right after she had overseen the fresh food delivery or had finished peeling a bucket of potatoes. Mrs Taylor knew nothing about their love but Reg had been much more observant.

'Playing with fire,' she said, not for the first time.

'It's my life,' she replied defensively.

'And funeral.'

Iris was confident that Reg's jealousy had a lot to do with the fact that she'd forever be confined to barrow boys while she with her head of curly hair and larger than average lips had snagged the lord of the manor! This buoyed her up so much, she now believed she might not be what her father had sometimes said she was. Every vicious word erased with each kiss and every caress that Robert gave her. When, finally, another day off arrived, she stood in their unofficial meeting place inside the park and when he hadn't turned up at their usual time, she sat on the bench for what turned out to be the next two hours.

A prick of alarm journeyed through her body as each minute ticked by. What if something had happened to Robert, her future husband? Indeed, her future.

Eventually, she ran back to the house, noticing a difference in the atmosphere. When she heard Mrs Taylor's cries from the drawing room, her tummy flipped.

'Is … Is everything all right, Mrs Taylor?'

Mrs Ambers was standing over Mrs Taylor who looked even smaller than usual, sitting in one of the silk-covered single chairs.

Mrs Taylor turned around, her eyes reddened by tears.

'He's gone,' she said weakly. At that moment, Iris saw a vision on her mum lying on the floor; someone placing a sheet over her face; pushing her body on a trolley through the front door she had seen her walk through a day before. It was happening again. She was losing someone and, this time, she wasn't sure if she herself would survive.

'Mrs Taylor … What's happened to Robert?'

'He's gone! On an aeroplane to some forsaken and uncivilised country!'

'What?'

'He could never get the travelling out of his being. Never could. Now I don't know when he'll be back again.'

'Travelling?'

'Yes, now will you please do whatever it is you are supposed to be doing,' chimed in Mrs Ambers. 'Mrs Taylor will require some privacy.'

'It's my day off,' she mumbled, her thoughts elsewhere.

Reg was happy to clear things up.

'He's gone to a place called Borneo or something. Fact is he's gone.'

'He didn't tell me he was leaving.'

'Of course he didn't,' said Reg drily.

*

It was hard to continue as normal, but if she wanted to keep her job and her home, she'd no choice. She had to face the truth: Robert Taylor had jumped on a real-life aeroplane and gone as far away from her as possible because she was indeed everything her father had ever said she was.

Iris cried herself to sleep on many nights, with Reg being a good friend and not once saying 'I told you so'. She found it difficult to visit the park where so many of their meetings had taken place, choosing to work on her day off instead. Besides, working had the power to take her mind away from the reality that she had indeed lost everything. Iris was surprised at how quickly her life snapped back into how it had been before Robert, her day-to-day routine no longer peppered with dreams of a husband and one day being the mistress of this house. Just loneliness once more.

How had she been so stupid? What man in their right mind would want her anyway?

The low mood did not shift, and was matched by a bout of tiredness such as she had never felt before.

'You've been knackered a lot lately,' remarked Reg as Iris doubled over at the sink. 'I heard you puking up yesterday as well.'

'I ate something bad.'

'We had the same things to eat as usual.'

'Maybe my constitution is different than yours.'

'I think you're up the duff,' said Reg.

Of course, Reg wasn't a nurse so her words couldn't be trusted, but something wasn't right. Iris placed her hand onto her stomach. Perhaps if she got word to Robert that he was to be a father, he would come back. It almost didn't matter if she was pregnant or not, at least he'd come back!

It was becoming more uncomfortable to kneel down and scrub the floor and extreme nausea would grip her not only in the morning, but the evenings too. Reg had politely said again that she indeed 'must be up the duff', but still, Iris refused to allow the words to penetrate. When she noticed that her monthlies had stopped altogether, Iris finally allowed for the possibility that her friend was right.

'What am I going do?'

'Up the creek without a paddle, you are.'

'If only Robert knew …'

'He wouldn't do anything.'

'You don't know that. He can take me away from all this.'

'I know, because this ain't the first time he's had it away with one of the girls.'

'What?'

'I tried to tell you he was a wrong 'un. There was a girl … the one before you. Lovely-looking girl. Got her pregnant and Mrs Taylor dealt with it.'

'I don't believe you,' she replied weakly.

'Remember when you first got here and your uniform was too big? That's why!'

'What happened to the girl?'

'Mrs Taylor's not as heartless as you think. Got her a job with one of her posh friends and she's still there now. Learned her lesson and is currently knocking about with one of the barrow boys from the market.'

She placed a hand on her belly. 'Where's the baby?'

'No idea.'

'He loves me.'

'Robert just knows how to sweet talk you lot into bed. Me, I never have ideas above my station. I know who I'm meant for and it ain't some rich, educated gentleman like Robert Taylor, that's for sure. Stick to your own kind I say.'

Reg's words germinated for a moment and then Iris spoke, in a whisper. 'What am I going to do?'

'I know someone who can—'

'No!' said Iris. The forcefulness of her words silenced the usually outspoken Reg.

An hour later, Iris found herself in front of Mrs Taylor. Even with her short stature she was a formidable woman, yet Iris was determined to state her terms – if only she could keep the nausea down long enough to do so.

'What do you want, Iris?'

'I love your son.' She hadn't planned on being so direct, but it was out now and she felt nothing but relief.

Mrs Taylor threw her a wry smile and as if that wasn't unnerving enough, her words were shocking. 'I know.' She walked over to one of the beautifully plumped chairs and sat down. 'The question is, why are you informing me of this?'

'I'm pregnant,' said Iris.

Mrs Taylor's expression did not change. 'I see.'

'I need to get word to Robert.'

'He is overseas.'

'Yes, I know. But I'm sure you can get word to him.'

'I'll need to know you are indeed pregnant first and not trying to extort money from us.'

She hated herself for wanting to cry. 'I would never do that.'

'Indeed,' said Mrs Taylor, perhaps in way of agreement or dismissal – Iris couldn't tell. 'It needs to be confirmed you are at least pregnant before they can—'

'Before they can what?'

'You're not actually thinking of keeping it, surely?'

'Yes ... I—'

'No, my dear. If you want to keep working here and not end up on the streets with a baby, you will do what needs to be done.' She turned her back, effectively telling Iris the conversation was over.

'You won't want to see a grandchild of yours on the street. Not even you.'

Mrs Taylor's shoulders tensed.

'Send word to Robert,' warned Iris.

The bravado she demonstrated in the room with Mrs Taylor softened once she reached her own room. She placed a hand over her tummy and felt an unfamiliar swell of protection. A real-life human being was inside her and although she'd been shocked in the beginning, the thought of it brought a calm she hadn't been expecting to feel. She hoped the baby looked nothing like her and instead took after its handsome father. He or she would have blond hair and gorgeous blue eyes and women would peer into the pram as they walked by. Robert would insist they have help but she would be the one to bring up her own child, with a huge amount of love and caring. This child would get everything Iris had been denied.

When, two weeks later, her underwear was stained with blood and her abdomen screamed with pain, Iris knew what was happening.

'I'll go and get Mrs Taylor!' said Reg.

She grabbed her arm, physical pain finally subsiding, although the emotional pain was just beginning. 'No!'

'She can call a doctor, she'll know what to do!'

'There's nothing she can do now,' said Iris, tears streaming down her face. 'There's nothing anyone can do.'

As my mama said after we lost my little brother, there is no greater pain than losing a child. As a family we weren't always full of words but after that, the silence held our pain. At breakfast, dinner and until the time we laid down to sleep. Just silence. A silence we only wanted penetrated by the sound of his footsteps as he walked back into our lives, saying it had all been a joke.

He never did though.

Slowly, life began to breathe into day-to-day living. The laughter wasn't quick to come, but when it did, it would do so in quick spurts but laced with a guilt that this should not be happening. We should not be laughing without him.

A daughter-in-law has brought a light into my mama's eyes, as has Clyde. But the fresh arrival of a baby, I knew, would bring her the joy I longed to see on her face once again.

When Augustine was with child for all of three months, I was glad we hadn't told Mama. To see the grief in her face again would be too much. Perhaps sending me right into the path of the storm again and I couldn't go back there. Not this time. I needed to be strong for Augustine. And that strength came with an acceptance that I was already a father with my boy Clyde and I was content with such a wonderful son.

And now there is you. Two of you.

I try not to dwell on the confusion. Or the questions. So many questions.

Why wouldn't Rose have written to tell me about you both? I had sent so many letters over the last decade or so, some even with an address. I know things were complicated, but even if she didn't want you, I did.

I would have taken you both!

I would have sold the farm and moved us all to the North. You would have had a good life with me, Augustine, Clyde and Mama. You would not have wanted for anything – I would have made sure of that.

They say there is no greater pain than losing a child – but what about losing two children you have never even met?

Lily

Ron had been true to his word and helped her find lodgings not too far from the club. The house belonged to one of his friends and housed a number of tenants in each of the four bedrooms. The musky room with one window that looked out into a pretty enough courtyard was the best thing Lily had seen in a long time. It was affordable and no one seemed to care about what she looked like. Indeed, not all of the other tenants were white. Unfortunately, because of the night shift hours their paths never seemed to cross.

Working nights at Flamingos meant she had a lot of her days free to do more than just sleep and get ready for her shift. Lily's love of reading had never diminished and she spent the bulk of any surplus cash on second-hand books, mostly educational. She also enjoyed reading books that were autobiographical, keen to learn about the world outside of a club in London. Being confined to one space was never beneficial; her childhood had taught her that. Her time as the sheltered but pampered daughter of Flora Baker had truly come to an end and she felt more and more like the woman she one day hoped to be. A woman of the world. With the countless books she'd read and her interaction with people who had trodden the sands of Egypt or frolicked in the rivers of Italy, she was enjoying her journey. Lily was even persuaded by Ron to try Chinese food for the very first time and could not believe how good it tasted!

Lily never took a day off without being pushed and was always punctual. Ron quickly noticed, offering her extra responsibilities that she grabbed without question, even those that weren't offered.

'What did you do in here?' said Ron, his face a picture of surprise as he stood in the office that was no longer what Lily described as 'looking like a bomb had hit it'.

'I just put the papers in the drawers ... The pens in that mug.'

'Thank you, darling. I don't know what to say. I might cry!'

'Don't do that, Ron, you've got a clean shirt on!' Lily loved to banter with Ron who was fast becoming more than a boss. She wasn't sure she fully trusted him, or any man for that matter, but Ron was also a friend and someone she looked up to.

'I don't recognise the place!' he said, marvelling at his 'new' office. He picked up the newly framed photo of his father and the British West Indies Regiment and kissed it. 'That's just beautiful, that.'

'I'm glad you like it.'

'Take a look at the picture of your girls. At least you can now see your daughter's face. No more dust!'

'Cheeky mare!' he said, with a sniff.

'Glad I could help.'

'I'll pay you of course! For the frames and the labour.'

'No need, Ron. I'd like a promotion though.'

'You've had your eye on being a barmaid. Don't think I haven't noticed you studying the others.'

She smiled.

'Tell you what, I'll give you a trial.'

'I think that's standard after paying my dues for over a year now and I'm never off sick and I've never stolen from you.' Her own confidence surprised her at times, but she knew her worth. Over the past year a succession of staff had come and gone. Some had been caught stealing while others just didn't see the value of turning up for work on time. It had been very easy to stand out.

'I can be of help around here too. I can do your accounts and ordering.'

'Steady on!'

'I've read loads of books on accounting. My mummy was a bookkeeper and she taught me—'

'I don't doubt that, but don't run before you can walk.'

She'd been hasty when what she needed was to be patient. She was no longer a child where everything had been handed to her if she asked; she was now a nineteen-year-old woman.

'We'll get you started at the bar tonight,' Ron said.

'Thanks, Ron.'

'Oh, and I know you think you know it all, but I have a word of advice when it comes to the bar.'

'Stick to serving the Americans, because they tip,' she said.

'How did you know?'

'I hear the barmaids say all the time how the English are a tight bunch of so and so's.'

Ron clutched his rounded belly and guffawed loudly. 'You are something else, you know that?'

June, one of the barwomen, slim and short, eyed her with suspicion as Lily took her place behind the bar for the evening shift.

'No one's off sick today,' she remarked, flicking a strand of blonde hair.

'I know!' Lily replied excitedly.

'Don't tell me you're working behind here.'

'Is there a problem?' Lily couldn't help smiling as she began fulfilling her first order, her mind fixed on how she had seen the barmen pour a whisky many times before.

That night, she wasn't asked to keep the change that many times, but when she did serve a couple of Americans, their behaviour was decidedly different. For a start they would leave the money on the bar, while the English would place it in her hand. The Americans seemed rather brash and sometimes a bit loud, but clearly proud of what they had. She did wonder if her American father had been that way. It was probably what had attracted her mother to him. English men were probably too reserved for her.

Lily would never think to flirt with the customers, but that didn't stop them from propositioning her from time to time. She tried her best to ignore them while making sure they never got close enough to be able to touch her.

'How's it going?' asked Ron. During her first week, he would check her progress almost hourly, but a month into her trial, he seemed more at ease with her transition. As was she.

Lily was also ready to move onto buying new books. She couldn't wait to get her hands on a book that hadn't already been read by someone else. The second-hand bookshop had always been a source of joy but thanks to her wage increase and some generous tips, she could finally afford to buy a new book.

The accompanying ping as she opened the shop door was followed by the man behind the counter looking up from under his spectacles.

'What may I do for you, young lady?'

'Just browsing, thank you.'

'This is a bookshop.'

'I know.'

'We sell educational books ... Science mostly.'

He moved out from behind the counter. 'Are you sure you're in the right place?'

'Yes, I'm sure,' she said, in slow tones to match his.

She pointed to the window display.

'I'd like to start with *Science: Here and Now*, if that's okay?'

'Certainly.' He eyed her with uncertainty before moving to the window display.

'This is our only copy, so if you want it—'

'Yes, I want it.' This wasn't actually what Lily had planned to buy. She'd envisioned browsing the expansive shelves of books until finding a title she felt she could absolutely not live without. But this tiresome man had pushed her into making a quick decision and she was not about to stand for it.

'Actually, sir, I'd like to look around before I make my final decision. As you can appreciate, there's so much choice and I want to make the right one, especially as this is the first step in me becoming a scientist myself.'

'You want to become a scientist?'

'Yes,' she said.

The bookseller reluctantly handed over another book for her appraisal and after the sixth one, Lily realised she did indeed want to purchase the first book.

Brimming with excitement, she headed straight to the park, opened the book on page one and did not look up until page sixty-five. She closed the book and exhaled with a huge smile.

At last, Lily Baker knew exactly what she wanted to do with her life.

Lily flitted between collecting glasses, mixing exotic drinks and looking up purchase orders under Ron's tutorage. How one drink required measured amounts of alcohol and fruit juice fascinated her and further fuelled her determination to one day excel in the field she had chosen for her future. When she had mentioned this to one of the bar staff in passing, he'd laughed in her face – as if to say a woman could never become one of those. Lily was annoyed more at herself than her colleague. How stupid to confide in people she did not care about and who cared nothing for her. Of course they would laugh at her plans. Mummy Flora was the only person who would approve and push her towards such a goal and she would do well to remember that. Unfortunately, someone had let on to Ron and as she wiped a smear from a glass during a particularly quiet time one evening, Ron asked her a question.

'What's this I hear about you wanting to leave here and become a swot?'

'What did you hear?' she said, with a sigh.

'It's not true then?'

'Ron, I work nights here. What I do during the day is surely my own business?' She hoped she hadn't talked out of turn.

'You are right,' he said with a smile. 'I thought you would have confided in me that's all. You've been here a while now and I'm very fond of you.'

Her face softened.

'I'm just interested in everything you do. Like I am with my own daughters.'

She didn't quite know what to say. If this disclosure had been two years ago, she might have replied with a tone of distrust, wondering if Ron's interest was at all unsavoury. Over the years though, she'd felt the relationship morph into one resembling that of father and daughter. And this felt confusing at times, especially as she had never known a father figure before. Apart from Uncle Kenneth.

'I love working here.'

'You even know how to mix a good drink!'

'I have always been interested in science … Ever since I was a little girl. To me, mixing drinks is a science.'

'I s'pose it is. Wow, a girl being interested in science? That's big.'

'The first women in space just happened.'

'Did it? Wow. Didn't know that!'

'Yes, Valentina Tereshkova.'

'How do you know these things?'

'I read!'

She was grateful Ron hadn't mentioned her colour. Perhaps that had more to do with the fact that he himself had still managed to build a thriving business. Indeed, it was clear to Lily that those in society who looked like her and had any sort of financial standing, had usually done so thanks to a connection to the entertainment or sporting industry. But Lily Baker enjoyed mixing things. Lily Baker at the heart of it all wanted to develop medicines that could help people. She may not have been able to save Mummy Flora from a slow death but she'd one day be in a position to save others. She wasn't motivated by money but would make sure she had a comfortable living. Mummy Flora hadn't worked so hard and sacrificed her entire family just for Lily to fail and not fulfil her expectations. Lily was determined to make her proud and, in doing so, become what no one in England in 1963 would ever expect from a 'brown' baby, born to a mother who didn't want her, father 'unknown'. She'd shed the coat associated with that stigma and step into a garment of greatness. As Lily Baker, scientist.

To my Beautiful Twin Daughters,

It's been a few years now since the hurricane of '59. I managed to employ a kindly man by the name of Seth who helps me and Clyde tremendously. He's a good worker but I don't know how long he will last because people have a habit of not wanting to put in the work and time for something that will not ultimately end up being theirs. But I care about this farm. Can you believe that? Me who loathed the thought of tending to it and had to be force-fed the virtues of farm life over city life – I now love the farm! I think it has more to do with Clyde and you two. I started off with no children and now I have three! And I owe it to you all to make this place work. Now, I'm not allowing myself to think that you will ever step foot on these fertile grounds of Savannah, Georgia, but a part of this land will be yours one day, I hope. There I go again, thinking you'll get to ever see this place – or me.

Clyde would be so happy to know he has two sisters. He'd be a wonderful big brother. He is a fiercely protective young man. I see that trait in his mother. When I first came along, he was mistrustful, even at such a young age. But over the years we've built a trust I wouldn't break for the world. We enjoy fishing together and his mother will cook it up. Sometimes we don't catch anything though, but that's okay because we get to talk about so much, like not being segregated from the white folks any more, Dr King being awarded the Nobel Peace Prize, and whether he should ask Hattie Jameson to a dance. Nothing is off limits.

Clyde is my son in more than name only. But now I know about you two, it's like a hunger for a food I didn't even know I desired. I think about you all the time now, what you are doing or what you will become. Yesterday at the store, Mr Carson was complaining about having five daughters and how lucky I am to just have a son. I wanted to tell him about my two beautiful daughters but how could I when I hadn't even told my wife?

When I finally told Augustine about you she was as understanding as I knew she would be and she was the one who encouraged me to seek you out.

'You have to see them, William. It's not right.'

'What if the girls are happy and I go in there, upsetting the apple cart?'

'You won't know until you try.'

'No, I won't do that to them. Me, a six-foot Negro with an American accent turning up and disrupting their perfect lives.'

'That six-foot Negro is their dad!'

I wasn't honest with Augustine. I was scared. Scared of trying to find you again and getting nowhere once more. Scared of the hurricane of '59 paying another visit.

Augustine knows I am not a man to be persuaded, but she applied just enough pressure and over a good amount of time finally managed to make her point sound like the right one.

I told my mama some time later. She cried. A lot. And at first I thought it was because she was disappointed in her little boy, but I was wrong.

'Mama?' I held out my hand to her, but she shrugged it away.

'No, don't,' she said.

'I know I did wrong. I lay with a woman I wasn't married to.'

'That you did.' She wiped at her tears and I hated that I had caused them.

'I didn't know she was married though, Mama. I didn't.' I was desperate to claw back some of my mama's respect.

'I know that, son.' She wiped at her eyes with the back of her sleeve. 'But it has been done and we can't go back. You now have two daughters out there, two Burrell girls and we have no idea where they reside, nothing.'

'The aunt said in that letter that they were adopted out. Rose died. The shame and everything was too much.'

'They will have good opportunities in England. Didn't you say how those British folks were good to you when you went?'

'Yes, ma'am.'

I cleared my throat. I still didn't like to think about wartime, but the darkness which had befallen me during that time was now lightened with the presence of you.

'You have to find them.'

The forcefulness of my mama's words surprised me. Never a meek woman, she had always been softly spoken and calming towards me.

'Mama, I don't know what I should do.'

'You have to fight for my grandbabies. They're out there and they need you!'

'Mama, I haven't got much money to do anything fancy like hire a private investigator.'

'You don't need to do that. Just fly on over there again.'

'Mama, it's not that easy. I've been out the military some time now. And to be honest, they still don't like us Negros flying. The segregated waiting rooms at the airport get on my last nerve.'

'You know that's been over for months now.'

'Mama, you know that doesn't mean anything to some folks.'

'Ignore everything else, you're doing this for your girls.'

'There isn't no overseas travelling version of the green book for Negroes you know.'

'You didn't need it the first two times you went, why would you now? You said it yourself, they better to coloured folk out there.'

'That's right.'

'I don't mean today son. Just promise me that one day ... one day you will make an effort to find those girls.'

'Yes, ma'am. I can save enough money to go back there, see if the aunt can tell me any more.'

'That's it, son. That's how you should be thinking. Get some more money together, the farm's doing good – and then you get yourself back to England and find your girls, you hear me?'

My mama was a determined woman and perhaps I had lost some of that over the years. Perhaps the army had pulled that out of me as did the storms. Of course my mama was right, I had to find you or at least try. I have already let you down once and I'm not about to again. I am coming for you, my beautiful girls. Wait for me. I'll be there. I don't know when, but I will find you.

Chapter Twenty-Two

Iris

She would never have imagined Mrs Taylor ever being more than the sour-faced woman she had always been, but after the miscarriage, she changed. Iris wasn't sure if it was pity or indeed compassion that prompted Mrs Taylor to place her on light duties in the main house, but this promotion placed a noticeable distance between Iris and Reg.

'The only time I get to see you now is when it's time for a kip,' said Reg, lying on the bed and propped up by her elbow.

'We can have a chat now if you want.'

'Unlike you, I've been working hard and need to sleep.'

'I work too, Reg.' She'd tired of this blatant envy, having noticed that even some of the delivery boys weren't talking to her as they used to and she suspected Reg's hand in that.

'Go to sleep, then!' said Iris, pulling the covers up to her chin. She had to admit that working closely with Mrs Taylor was a lot more interesting than mopping floors and cleaning the toilets every day. Mrs Taylor liked to entertain snooty guests and go to fancy places and needed help with what to wear and how she should do her hair. Not that she'd ever ask Iris for fashion advice, but it was fun to go through magazines with her and listen to her bleat on about Lord this and Lady that. Again, it was much better than cleaning a toilet and she wasn't giving it up for anyone.

The only downside for working more closely with Mrs Taylor was that Iris had more time to think. About Robert. The baby. It didn't help that Robert shared the same smile with his mother and on the rare occasion Mrs Taylor decided to crack one, Iris was instantly reminded of him.

Iris stared at the picture on Mrs Taylor's bedside table. Robert tall and proud beside the body of a large animal, an elephant. A gun held between his fingers and his right foot on top of the poor animal's felled head.

Had she really loved this man or been more in love with the thought of living a life of luxury? For a moment, she'd allowed herself to be sold a dream that would see her become more than her mum had been and much more than her father could ever hope to be. Conned into thinking she was on the cusp of a life that really could never be hers. People like her didn't marry men like Robert; they ended up with men like her father!

With Mrs Taylor promoting her, she'd been brought closer to the life she had craved and it wasn't even that wonderful. It was a lonely one filled with nice dresses and an abundance of food but no one around to really share it all with. She thought about her baby again. The void that still existed in her belly. An intense sadness that would wash over her whenever she saw an infant in the street. Some days she was able to bury her thoughts, rationalising that her baby was up in heaven with her mum and they were looking after one another. So many times she had wanted to join them.

At times Mrs Taylor didn't have much for her to do and it wasn't unusual for Iris to take an extended break. One day, sitting on the basement steps, she bit into an apple, listening, as two female members of staff were at the top, smoking.

'Iris Baker. What a sneaky mare that one is.'

'Tell me about it. It looks like sleeping with the boss's son has its perks.'

'I 'eard she was up the duff an' all.'

Iris placed the half-eaten apple to one side and stood abruptly, a shot of anger rising up in her body.

'You better not be talking about me!' she said, moving quickly towards them, her mind unable to conjure up anything but rage.

'What if we were?'

When her hand grabbed at a clump of hair of one of the girls, Iris pulled her so close she could smell her fear.

'Stop it!' screamed the other one. 'Let her go, we didn't mean it!'

She released the pressure off her hair, before realising her other hand was around the girl's neck.

'Stop it! You're hurting her!'

Iris's eyes widened and a space in her mind opened. What was she doing?

She released the girl, who fell into a fit of coughs.

'I'm s ... sorry.'

'I should get the law on you!' said the girl.

'I'm really sorry ...' she said, turning her back on a scene that could have ended so badly. She stepped up her pace, tears filling her eyes as she made her way to the only place where she had ever felt any peace.

The park was thankfully empty and the whole bench free. She put her head into her hands, refusing to cry. Instead, she let out a loud roar.

'Ahhhhhh!' Her fists were clenched, face reddened with the force of it all. She had never shown violence to anyone before, yet had almost choked another human being. This would be funny if it wasn't real life. A life that any minute could end with being thrown in prison. Perhaps that was what she deserved because surely it could only get worse from now on.

Now that she'd been revealed for who she really was.

Perhaps that was why her baby had died. She would have been a terrible mother, unable to control her feelings, destined to take it out on the weakest.

Clearly she was her father's daughter.

To My Beautiful Twin Daughters,

I started thinking about your mother's motivation in not telling me about you both. I got to thinking that maybe she saw what I sometimes did. An inadequate human being fit for nothing.

I know that these thoughts only arrive when the storm is about to hit. But they are powerful and, dare I say it, frightening. I am a six-foot man afraid of some feelings! But I wish I could explain how overwhelming they are. Like a cloak of darkness that covers my entire body and I can't get out of it, can't breathe. I am left feeling like all that is left in my world is pain. Then I feel unworthy. Unworthy to be a husband or a father to my boy and my two beautiful girls. I'm so sorry if this sounds confusing to you. And I can only hope it is not something you have ever experienced. I hope your days are filled with joy and happiness. Blue skies and hope.

1965

Lily

When Lily's landlord announced via a letter pushed under the door that he was selling the house and all the tenants would have to leave, Ron came up with an idea.

'Why not?'

'I can't stay at your place, Ron.'

'It's nothing fancy, just my old bachelor pad I did up and rented out. You'll have the entire flat to yourself. No more sharing stuff and get this ... an inside toilet.'

She looked to the ceiling.

'I'll only charge you the minimum rent because I know you won't mess the place up. Tenants move out next month. Fancy it?'

Of course she agreed. It was a fantastic offer yet she couldn't help feeling uneasy about it all.

A week later, she was standing in the middle of her new home. A modern decorated apartment just five minutes from Flamingos, compact and neat and with everything she needed, along with extras. Like the green wallpaper with large yellow circles decorating the living room wall, a stooped three-bulb lamp allowing the room to look continually bright and in the corner a record player! The inside lavatory was the best part of it all. When she opened the door and caught sight of the white porcelain toilet, tears welled up in her eyes. The memory of having to wait outside in Marigold's cold toilet was still vivid. As was the loneliness of sleeping on a kitchen floor with mice for company and then the cellar at Flamingos. All part of a recent history she would much rather forget but was a part of her whether she liked it or not. Now she would live in her own flat (with an inside toilet), sleep in her own bed and answer to nobody.

She sat on the sofa, which, apart from a few cigarette burns, felt amazingly comfortable. She thought of Ron and their friendship. Although she had long since trusted that his interest in her was platonic, perhaps even fatherly, this did not shake the unease that had only magnified ever since she had agreed to take the flat.

She pulled out the photograph of Mummy Flora and her siblings and everything became clear. Mummy Flora had rescued Lily from a fate that would have seen her languishing in the home for brown babies. Then she had kept her hidden from the wider world with the result that she'd had to learn to navigate life with a naive lens she had finally shed, but not without much heartache. Lily's unease also came with the realisation that Ron had stepped into the role of Mummy Flora in a way; rescuing her by giving her a job and now a home.

She was tired of feeling owned. Marigold had sold her to the Shangri La for an undisclosed price, which meant that even now she was still technically, albeit illegally, owned by them too.

Now at the age of twenty-one, it was time she owned herself.

She moved into the kitchen. The large white refrigerator housed a loaf of bread, tub of butter and a bottle of milk. Ron was even feeding her!

She had to think.

Lily had missed the 'luxury' living of her youth, of having everything she needed at her disposal, and on her wages could never afford a place even close to these standards. She sank back onto the comfortable sofa and let out a puff of breath, deciding that against her own inner wishes, she would stay. For now, she would stay.

When Ron announced he had finally caved into his wife's demands and was taking the family on holiday, Stuart the barman assured him the place would be in good hands.

'I know that because Lily will be looking after things while I'm away.'

'Excuse me?' said both Lily and Stuart.

'You 'eard. I am going to leave this little baby in safe hands while I get to grips with spending each and every day with a bunch of females. I love 'em of course but they can be hard work. Harder than running this place!' He held onto his belly and let out his trademark guffaw. 'So, Lily, it's all yours for a week.'

Stuart flung the dishcloth onto the bar and turned his back on them both.

Lily was unconcerned as excitement began to build inside her as Ron pulled out a set of keys from his pocket. 'You'll be needing these. The place will pretty much run itself for a week. I'll be back before the bills need paying so it shouldn't be a stretch for someone as intelligent as you!'

She felt every eye upon her, Stuart's especially, a barman who had been at Flamingos for many years.

Indeed, she knew how Flamingos operated from behind the scenes. The delivery times, how many barrels needed to be ordered and on what day. The temperament of each member of staff. How to coax a drunken man out of the bar after closing time.

As she walked past the assembled staff, their shoulders slouched, an avoidance of eye contact, she heard Mummy Flora's voice echo in her head, as well as picturing the scene.

'Lily, never think you don't deserve to have something.'

She was perched on Mummy Flora's knee, dried tears on her face.

'But Walter said I couldn't have it!'

'He took it from you because it was his. Though he shouldn't have smacked you, that was wrong but you're older and wiser. You have to learn to rise above it.'

'What's that?'

Mummy Flora just laughed.

'Don't worry, I will be drumming it into you until you realise that anything you get – as long as you've worked for it – you deserve it.'

'Okay.'

'And you don't let anyone tell you otherwise.'

Fifteen minutes after walking out of Ron's office, the bar seemed cloaked in a new atmosphere. She was now being watched, judged and perhaps spoken about. So she walked past the bar, back straight, chin raised haughtily in the air, knowing and fully believing that she deserved this chance to prove herself.

Iris

The law was never called on Iris for her violent outburst. No one would believe a couple of raggedy toilet scrubbers against her word (backed up by Mrs Taylor) anyway? They all knew that. Under Mrs Taylor's protection Iris had almost become a little untouchable, even though their relationship lacked any real warmth – which Iris was comfortable with. She became tired of Reg's incessant jealousy and was happy to take up Mrs Amber's role when she retired. This came with a room of her own and to be on hand for whatever Mrs Taylor required. The difficult part was having to hear so much about Robert first hand and not the idle gossip she'd been used to. Hearing his mother speak of him reminded her just how little he had shared with her. Content to just lie with her in that big bed and give her ideas that were, frankly, well above her station.

So many of his letters would arrive from strange parts of the world, addressed to Mrs Taylor and with Robert's name on the back, which she wished she could read properly. She'd need all day to fathom his handwriting and make out the words as she searched for any mention of her. She may not have been able to read much, but she wasn't stupid. She was certain he no longer thought about her. She certainly thought about him, though, at times with the remnants of love, but at other times with scorn. It was only after true reflection that she was able to see the part she played in the whole sorry situation thanks to her naivety and neediness. But these moments of self-reflection would be short-lived, overpowered by a need to assuage the loss of her baby. Her feelings, as they moved back and forth, were at times confusing and had no real purpose.

In Mrs Taylor's lavish bedroom, Iris sat mending a dress actually worn to Winston Churchill's funeral months before.

'My father bought me that dress,' said Mrs Taylor. Aware that Mrs Taylor hardly ever disclosed such intimacies, she would have to respond with a good enough comment.

'I can tell it's a good-quality fabric. I'll be delicate with it.'

'What of your father, Iris?' The way she asked sounded as if she really wasn't interested, but had asked anyway. Rich people confused Iris on a regular basis.

'He's around. Somewhere.'

'Did you not know your father? Were you a bastard?' Mrs Taylor wrinkled her nose as if the aroma of rotten eggs had entered the room.

'My mum and dad were married and I knew him. We just don't see eye to eye.'

'I see. Well, I will leave you to it. When you have finished, place the dress into my wardrobe.'

I wasn't going to throw it on the floor, Iris wanted to say.

'Yes, Mrs Taylor.'

Iris understood that this exchange must have felt uncomfortable for Mrs Taylor but was confused as to why she'd even bothered. It wasn't as if they were real friends anyway. She held the dress up, as a sadness she hadn't been prepared for hit her along with a memory. A black dress. For a funeral.

Iris blinked back tears, but one escaped and landed prominently on Mrs Taylor's dress. She inhaled sharply. This was not the time or the place. She must not weaken. She closed her eyes and opened them quickly. Just a few more stitches and the dress would be finished.

Reg hardly talked to her these days, unless it was absolutely necessary and was generally work related. Despite it all, she missed her only friend. She missed Reg's colourful stories regarding a boy she had kissed or gone to the pictures with or both. Indeed after Iris's violent outburst the majority of the staff hardly spoke to her and even the delivery boys avoided eye contact, except the bread boy who often said, 'I like a feisty one, me!'

She ignored him.

Iris often felt the pull of loneliness each night as she lay on her bed with only her memories of her mum to keep her company. By now Iris could have had a small infant, a husband and a mother-in-law, however pinched her expression. Instead it was just her, feeling incredibly alone in a big house and with no one who cared if she lived or died.

To My Beautiful Twin Daughters,

I started working the farm again with Seth and Clyde, slipping back into my life but this time with an added purpose. You.

It took some planning, convincing and second-guessing, but here I am in big old London town.

I am in England and I'm coming to find you, my baby girls.

Chapter Twenty-Three

Lily

While bar managing wasn't her calling she had enjoyed the week of being totally in charge. So when Ron offered to make this a permanent fixture on a part-time basis, Lily could not turn it down. She would run the bar Mondays to Wednesdays and although these were less busy slots, it was still her job to make sure Flamingos resembled a well-oiled machine. Even if behind the scenes sometimes there was chaos, with leaky pluming and two warring barmaids accusing each other of seeing the same man.

At first, out of sheer tiredness, Lily was forced to spend the days when Ron took over simply catching up on sleep. But as she began to get used to the grind, she was quickly back to her usual energetic state during the afternoons. Now with a secure wage and a flat to call her own, she once again had space in her mind to plan the next stage of her life.

Lily was now able to buy one book a month. Her joy came from blocking out the rest of the world, sitting on the park bench and leafing through each delicious page and absorbing its rich contents, teaching herself about each subject matter. After hours of poring over science textbooks, one fact stood out to her; the majority of respected scientists seemed to be men.

White elderly men. Women were in the minority and people like her confined to the role of specimen, subjects to be poked and prodded and in many ways told they were oddities, subhuman and less so. At times she wasn't even sure she wanted to enter a profession that held such notions about human beings, but perhaps a part of her thought, hoped, she could one day change the status quo.

It took time for the staff at Flamingos to accept her change in status while Stuart usually refused to engage her in anything more than a sarcastic 'Good morning, boss' each day.

In the days following a local incident, Flamingos was busier than usual and this was the first time that Lily had felt slightly overwhelmed.

'We've got two staff sick and double the customers today,' said Stuart.

'What happened?'

'Don't you read the papers? Freddie Mills got killed the other night, not far from here.'

'Who's Freddie Mills?'

'Only a famous boxer! Where have you been?'

She shook her head. Lily hardly ever watched television, her head either stuck in a book or down one of Flamingos toilets trying to fix a leak.

'Never mind. Anyway, the press need a drink as well as the ghouls who've come to take a look.'

The night was long and all she could think about was bed. As she locked up for the evening, Stuart was wiping down the last of the tables.

'Great job today,' said Lily. 'All hands on deck and we made it.'

'You've already made it, haven't you? Nothing else to prove,' said Stuart.

'If you have something to say, let's do so in my office.'

'Ron's office you mean.'

'Stuart, listen.'

'No, *you* listen. You swan in here shaking that big behind of yours and suddenly you're promoted. It isn't fair. None of this is.'

'You think I got this by doing something with Ron?'

'Of course you did. You're always whispering together and making jokes. We all know you're having it off, so don't deny it. How else would you have got promoted over me? You're nothing but a tart.'

'I won't have you talk to me like that.'

'What are you going to do about it, Miss Manager?'

'You're fired!'

She hadn't actually meant for the words to leave her lips but now they had, she would be sticking by them.

'What?'

She exhaled. 'If you can't respect me as a woman, then you have to go. I'm sorry.'

He turned to face those who had gathered to watch. Their own gazes quickly switching to the side.

'You'll regret this,' he said, barging past her and out the back door.

'Always got your nose in a book!' said Ron one evening just before her shift was about to start.

'I like reading.'

'So does my wife, but she reads stuff like *My Weekly* and romance novels, lovey-dovey stuff.'

'I like science, what can I say?'

'I always said you were different. Not the same as anyone in this place, including me. I won't hang on to you for long. I've always said that.'

'I'm not going anywhere,' she said, trying to sound sincere, but knowing that one day she would be moving on. For now and for the first time in months, the club was running smoothly and efficiently. Ron and many members of staff had commented on this and she knew this was because of her input. She'd even found new suppliers and negotiated cheaper rates with old ones. The club was turning more of a profit and this she felt proved she had earned everything he had 'given' her.

Ron was never off sick until one day, at his wife's insistence, he stayed away due to a chest infection. So, Lily found herself managing Flamingos on one of its busiest nights – a Friday. Her experience and drive did not make this a problem, but when one of the barmaids mentioned that a man was asking for what he was owed, a feeling of foreboding washed over her.

She beckoned the man, smartly dressed in a hat and blue tailored jacket, to follow her into Ron's office. She kept the door open, despite the intrusion of noise coming from the bar.

'I've come for the package,' he said.

'Nothing has been left for you.'

'Ron leaves me a package every Friday.'

'Tell me what it is and I'll see if I can find it.'

'I think you'll find it in the till.'

'You want money?'

The man remained silent, but his eyes told her she had just asked the world's most stupid question. This didn't feel right.

'I can't just give you money ... I'll have to contact Ron.'

'I thought you were in charge.'

'I am.' She wasn't quite sure where to go with this.

The man headed for the door. 'Let Ron know I came around and that I'm not happy. Tell him I'll see him tomorrow.'

She immediately dialled Ron's phone number and his voice, on answering, sounded weak with sickness. 'I'll sort it tomorrow. Don't you worry, love.'

She soon pushed the incident out of her mind. This was about Ron owing money and really had nothing to do with her.

All the staff had gone for the night and as usual she was left to lock up alone. Her mind was already on the remainder of the weekend and a chance to unwind and catch up on some reading.

One of the girls had also invited her to the pictures to watch *Help!* and she was actually considering going. Lily never really had any close girlfriends and perhaps this was the chance to change that.

Once again she checked all the locks were secure, then turned around and immediately felt the chill of the cold night air. She wished it was summer, when early mornings brought light. But working within the buzz of central London meant no one was ever really asleep. There was always a reassuring hum of people around. She could never tire of London.

She turned into the road minutes from where she lived. Much more residential and where everyone seemed to be asleep. She heard footsteps, hurried, urgent, begging her to be fearful. She increased her own steps, her breath becoming heavy. She was almost home. Just one more street. Then a thought: if she was being followed, she didn't want them to know where she lived. What now? Stop or carry on walking? Lily increased her steps, deliberately walking right past her building, wishing she had taken up Ron's offer of having one of the guys walk her home each evening. She didn't need protecting just because she was woman, she'd said, but right now, she needed something. Her heart pounded, her legs were in danger of buckling. She would not dare look behind her. Her walk turned into a run and then relief, when she no longer heard the footsteps.

'What's wrong, love? You're not your usual self,' asked Ron the next day.

'Did you sort out things with that man?'

'Never mind about that.'

'I think he followed me last night.'

'No way. Not his style.'

Ron's response confused her.

'Probably just a punter who took a shine to you. I'll get one of the boys to walk you home from now on.'

The incident at Flamingos forced her to speed up her plans. She no longer wanted to work in fear and at a job where she didn't see a future anyway. She'd become comfortable with the money and had slowed down the process of moving on with her goals. But she was clear on the steps needed to become a bio-chemist and it was time to proceed.

The time was now.

Iris

The bread boy would do. The one who'd said he 'liked them feisty'.

So, when she guided him around the back and hitched up her dress, his eyes lit up with complete surprise and then happiness when she reiterated it was okay and they could 'do it', but to make it quick because she didn't have all day.

Twice a week they would meet and for the five or so minutes they were locked together at the back of the house, where food rotted in drains and rats frequented at night, Iris would lose herself in the sensation of being touched, wanted ... perhaps even loved. Feelings she associated with a much better time in her life. A time when she enjoyed the smell of freshly prepared beef suet wafting in the air; the singsong sound of her mum's voice as she called her name. As the bread boy groaned with delight, she didn't even bother to smile, or to answer him when he said 'Are you all right?' Iris just wanted to stay in the fantasy that did not include the bread boy, but instead contained all the filtered memories of a life she missed with every fibre of her being.

As usual, when it was over, she'd snap back to the present just as the bread boy pulled his trousers up.

'That was lovely,' he said. She smoothed her dress down and turned to leave. Now it was time to get back to being alone again. Her mother was dead. She had no one.

'Wait,' he said, moving beside her. 'Maybe I can take you out.'

'Take me out?'

'Yeah, to the pictures. Maybe we can watch *Help!* I've heard it's a good one.'

'I don't think so.'

'What about something to eat like fish and chips?'

'I don't need feeding,' she said, moving away.

'What would you like to do, then?'

'Leave me alone, okay?' she said and walked back in the direction of the house.

Iris decided to let the bread boy go. His insistent whining interfered with what she longed to feel whenever she was with him – an escape from her reality. His voice was a constant reminder that what she was doing wasn't right and yet … she did not want it to stop. She approached one of the new delivery boys, and then the butcher's son. Iris wasn't concerned with banter or chitchat. She would see a man and within minutes know that she would soon lie with him. It was almost a game; one she hadn't planned on being a part of, but one she had found herself in and was powerless to stop it.

'There's the bitch!'

Iris turned around to see Reg, another worker from the house called Silvia and a girl she didn't recognise move towards her.

'Hands off my fella!' said the girl.

'What are you on about?'

'Just because you're a slag, doesn't mean you can try it on with my man. He isn't interested!'

Iris clenched each of her hands.

'This ain't the way!' said Reg, seeing her fists and knowing what Iris was capable of.

'She tried it on with my bloke too!' added Silvia.

'If you think about it, he didn't exactly say no did he? Have it out with him. Not her!' said Reg.

253

The girl shrugged her shoulders.

'Go home and sort it! I'll talk to her. Go on!'

As the two girls reluctantly walked away, Iris felt the beads of sweat form on her forehead.

'What are you doing?' asked Reg.

'What do you care?'

'You gotta start respecting yourself more. You're getting a reputation.'

'You can talk. You're the biggest slag around here. You taught me everything I know.' She was playing dirty, she knew that. Yet, as Reg shook her head slowly, Iris wished she could take every word back.

'I tried,' said Reg, just before walking away. Iris wanted to call her back, but what was the point? Everyone eventually left her anyway. Reg had already done so once so she couldn't be trusted. Instead she watched her former friend walk away and this time knew they'd never be friends again.

The incident had been the wake-up call she'd needed. Iris certainly didn't want Mrs Taylor finding out about her 'reputation', especially as it could get back to her son. Iris wasn't sure why his opinion still mattered to her anyway, but the day Robert Taylor walked back into the house and into her life, it all made sense.

Gone was the boyish expression and floppy blond hair. He now had a thick moustache that reminded her of her grandad Albert – or what she remembered of him – and he was thinner. He still had an air of snootiness and yet ... and yet there was something that managed to draw him to her.

'Mr Taylor, how was your trip?' she asked formally.

'A long one!'

She suspected he had been back to England over the years, with Mrs Taylor choosing to keep them apart by meeting at their country residence instead.

'Welcome home. I know Mrs Taylor will be thrilled to see you!'

'No doubt she has instructed the cavalry to kill as many cows for my homecoming as possible. A bit like the Nigerians!'

She wasn't about to pretend to know who or what he was talking about.

'It's nice to see you again, Iris.'

He held onto her arm a little longer than was necessary. 'You look wonderful by the way.'

She hoped he didn't see her blush. She hoped he could not read her mind either, and hear what she truly wanted to say. She wanted to start by telling him about the baby they had lost because he was the only person she could truly share that pain with. Surely he wouldn't be as heartless as she had sometimes imagined he would be upon hearing the news. Surely he would take her in his arms and offer the comfort she had craved for such a long time.

Iris was determined to make sure Mrs Taylor got her wish and that her son's homecoming dinner party would be spectacular. So the house danced with the aroma of fresh flowers and a French menu to commemorate the last country he had visited. Apparently, that wasn't actually France but a place in Africa Iris could not pronounce. Mrs Taylor was dressed in a beautiful fuchsia gown, her hair pinned up with sparkling clips and her rouge highlighting a face that simply smiled more now her son was home.

The VIP guests arrived one by one, ignoring Iris or simply offering her their coat, even though she had hired extra staff to do such work.

'Oh, Daphne, it's wonderful to see you!' said Mrs Taylor as a short woman and her gangly escort appeared.

'Where is our boy then?'

'Upstairs and fiddling about with his jacket if I know my son.'

Iris felt a familiar swish in her tummy as Robert appeared at the top of the stairs looking as handsome as always. The guests, each with a drink in their hands, assembled at the bottom of the stairs. Something was about to happen and she'd no idea what that was. She turned to Mrs Taylor who appeared to be beaming from ear to ear. Suddenly, a woman dressed in a long, flowing blue dress and wearing silky white gloves appeared beside Robert.

He spoke. 'Thank you all for coming today and without further ado I would like to introduce you to Maggie who recently agreed to be my wife!'

'Bravo!' came the congratulatory chants as the entire room began to feel as if it was spinning. She felt dizzy, sick.

'Are you all right, dear?' asked a stranger.

Iris made her way downstairs and to the servants' quarters where she belonged. She needed to get away. She needed to be alone.

Lily

'About that business, you know with being followed.'

'I'm sure it was a one-off or they were scared off by the boys walking me home.'

'About that ...' Ron beckoned her into his office and Lily sat on the edge of the table. 'We found out who was following you and it's sorted.'

A rush of relief flooded her. 'Was it that man who wanted money? I knew it!'

'As a matter of fact it was Stuart. Gotta grudge that one and probably blames you for the sacking.'

'To think I felt bad about that.'

'Well, looks like your instincts were right about him He's a nutcase and my boys gave him a proper hiding. You won't hear from him again.'

Despite being relieved that Stuart would be leaving her alone, Lily felt uneasy at the tactics Ron had used. She'd never seen

Ron as a violent man but the way in which he had just brushed off a beating was quite frightening. This wasn't her world. Only hours earlier she was picking up application forms at a local college.

'I was so convinced it was that man …'

'You're just like one of my girls, you. Not going to rest until I tell you the whole story.'

'That would be nice,' she replied with sarcasm.

'I pay him every Friday.'

'Why?'

'He makes sure me and the other establishments in the area are safe.'

'What do you mean safe? We have a police force for that.'

'And sometimes they take backhanders from him too.'

Lily was confused.

'It's called "protection". Come on, Lily, surely you're not that naive. How do you think we all stay safe around here?'

This was all news to Lily and she wanted to hear more. She wanted to hear it all. 'So what happens if you don't pay?'

'Nothing good ever comes out of that.'

Lily closed her eyes and exhaled. In the space of a few hours she had caused a man to be beaten up and discovered Ron was paying gangsters to keep his business afloat. She'd seen the movies, she'd read about the Krays. This was not the life she wanted for herself. It was time to get out.

'Miss …'

'Baker. Lily Baker.'

'Yes …' he muttered, looking down at his desk. The admissions officer had avoided eye contact with her for the majority of the ten-minute meeting so far.

'You have no formal qualifications, Miss Baker. You saying you want to become a biochemist is rather like me saying I would like to become the next James Bond.'

'And why could you not become the next James Bond? Nothing's going to stop me from becoming a scientist. Nothing and no one.' That determined statement had sounded more impressive in her head. Right now it sounded childlike and slightly pathetic in front of a silver-haired man who actually looked nothing like Sean Connery.

'I applaud your determination, Miss Baker, but you have never even been to school.'

'As I said in my application, I was home schooled. Very well in fact. I have looked at the school curriculum in books and, frankly, the work is laughable.'

'I'm glad to see you view our world-class education system as laughable, Miss Baker.'

'Oh … that's not what I meant …' Her words were sounding arrogant in her quest to cover up just how self-conscious she really felt. 'What I'm trying to say is, I have done my research and I know this college could take on exceptional students if they pass an entrance exam, which I am willing to do. Then I must take a foundation course before being allowed to partake in a degree. That I am also willing to do. I also have enough money to pay for any books I will need as I am working.'

'In all honesty, Miss Baker, we'd be happy to enrol you in our programme, but I would prefer you to set realistic goals for yourself. Perhaps take a secretarial class if you do not have an interest in marriage. I would imagine that would be hard anyway.'

'What is?'

'Finding a suitable husband of your …'

Her mouth curled into a smile. 'My …?'

'I mean there can't be many—'

'There are plenty of humans around, if that's the word you're looking for?'

'Right,' he said, nodding his head without conviction.

Minutes later, Lily placed the papers he handed her into her bag.

'Thank you for your time. I look forward to taking the exam and starting in September.' She walked through the door, standing tall, her shoulders erect.

For Lily, the entrance exam felt like something she could have completed as an eleven-year-old! When September arrived, college work was the easy part. The first term covered subjects she had taught herself with all the reading she'd already amassed. The second term was a lot harder and she was glad not to have bothered with making friends, choosing to use her time wisely in the library. When she wasn't studying, she'd be catching up on sleep because she'd have to be at Flamingos until at least half past two the following morning and later during her managerial slots.

Some days Lily felt so tired, she'd 'rest' her eyes as she stood in the bus queue or work through a foggy haze as she battled the need to sleep. She had no time for a social life, even if she desired one. And she didn't. Flamingos was enough of a deterrent anyway. The drunken men patting the bums of waitresses, thick smoke invading her lungs, the loudness of the music that sometimes didn't allow her the luxury of hearing her own thoughts.

She settled into the routine with ease, though. Her determination and need for so much more allowed her to plough through any tiredness or doubt that would sometimes trickle in without warning.

'Good job you're a young 'un,' said Ron. 'I couldn't do what you do.'

'Needs to be done.'

'I've always said there's a job here for you.'

'I know. And I appreciate that, it's just not what I want.'

'Not good enough for yer, is it?'

'You know it isn't that.'

'I know why you're doing all this and I get it. Your mum died, right, and she was sick for a while?'

Having shared a little about herself many years ago, Ron had remembered the important details and she appreciated this.

'That never leaves you. Watching them deteriorate so quickly.' He sat behind the desk. 'Wanna know something I keep to myself?'

He leaned closer.

'I had a son. He got ill. He died.'

'I'm so sorry.'

'I'm not gonna go into it but let's just say, I remember how it left me feeling. As a dad, I felt helpless, so I stuck myself into work to try and forget. It doesn't work ... you always remember. What I'm trying to say is, if there's a way I can prevent another kiddie going through what he did, then I will. That's why I give money to children's homes and that. I hate seeing kids suffer, you know? I think that's why I hit it off with you straight away. I didn't know much about you, but the fact you were by yourself ... I didn't need to know. It was obvious. What I'm trying to say here, Lily, is, I understand. If you learning to make medicines is your way ... then you gotta do it.'

She could admit that, in the beginning, Mummy Flora's death had been an early contributor to her dream. But the more she'd studied and read the books, the more she felt determined to work alongside, and prove wrong, the scientists of the time. The silver-haired white men who said no one like her could amount to anything academic. Lily was on a quest to challenge the beliefs of many.

'I knew you'd get it,' she said.

During the final year of the degree she found the workload much more demanding. She really had to think more, apply herself and force herself to engage with her classmates more, especially when put into groups. Being the only non-white person in the class didn't bother her in the slightest as her goals were clearly defined and she remained focused. When she had to work on projects with other students she would sometimes have to leave early to get to the Flamingos on time and this didn't endear her to the others.

'I'm not failing this module because you're too lazy to contribute,' said Alec, a man she'd been paired up with on a project on the biomedical basis of drug resistance.

She took a sharp intake of breath. 'Lazy? I'm not sure how you've come to that conclusion.' Lily felt the heat rise in her cheeks. 'I suppose I can stay an extra hour ... but I have to make a call first.'

'That would be useful, Miss Baker.'

The thought of spending another hour with this Alec didn't thrill her in the slightest but she could do with the extra hour of study. She hadn't found this particular assignment as easy as she'd hoped.

Inside the phone box, she leaned against the ribbed glass wall. 'I'm sorry, Ron, it won't happen again.'

'I know you said your studying wouldn't affect things, and for the most part it hasn't, but I can't have you making a habit of coming in late when you're supposed to be managing.'

'I know, Ron ...' She attempted to suppress a yawn. The intense study and working nights were taking their toll and she was the last to admit it.

'We're gonna have to have a talk,' said Ron.

The following afternoon, Ron was blunt.

'You're exhausted most of the time and now you're coming in late.'

She stifled another yawn.

'I don't want to lose you, Lily. You're like a daughter to me and I know what this all means to you. So I have a proposition for you. You may not like it, but tough.'

She swallowed.

'Cut your hours down to three days a week with only one day managing and no weekends.'

'Ron, I appreciate it, but the money … I wouldn't be able to afford the flat, even with your discount. Then there's my college books. They are so expensive!'

'Hear me out first.'

She stamped her mouth shut.

'Your pay remains the same.'

'What?'

'I'm the boss and what I say goes.'

Her eyes filled with tears. Happy ones. 'Why would you do that?'

'I'm investing in an incredible human being. Is that a crime?'

She was about to jump into his arms and thank him, but something stopped her. 'I really appreciate the offer, Ron, but I can't. I've had people save me my entire life and it just doesn't sit right with me any more. Therefore, I will have to decline your offer.'

'What will you do then?'

'I'll find a smaller pad, somewhere cheaper. I only have a year left of the degree. I can do this. Let me do this.'

'I can't say I understand, but I accept it.'

'I'll get used to it all. I'll just have to plan my time better.' She hated upsetting him, especially when he'd just made such a kind offer. She tentatively placed her hand on his arm as he quickly pulled her towards him. She tensed automatically, closing her eyes as if to eliminate the image of Uncle Kenneth and the men at the Shangri La from her head. She placed her arms around him, resting her head onto his chest. It didn't feel natural but at least it didn't feel wrong.

'You're such a good man.'

'And you're a good kid. I wish you were one of my daughters. Silly, right?'

'Not at all.'

She heard a sniff.

'I'll go and check on the whisky delivery …' he said, moving away from the embrace.

Chapter Twenty-Four

Iris

Iris wasn't sure how this change in Mrs Taylor had happened, why she felt the need to open up to Iris, but for the sake of her job she would listen.

'It took me a long time to get over the death of Robert's father and now this.'

Mrs Taylor had been supervising the reorganising of her wardrobe and they were surrounded by the aroma of mothballs as they sat among the luxuries of silks, lace and beading.

'With all due respect, Robert isn't dead. He's just gone on honeymoon.' Not for the first time, the sting of that truth struck Iris with its venom.

'My point is that anyone leaving me after that felt like a bereavement. Even dear Mrs Ambers, who had been with me for forty years! Her retirement was necessary, but I found myself grieving her loss just as if she had died.'

Mrs Taylor had never spoken so personally before and Iris understood that it would probably never happen again. At least she hoped it wouldn't because as usual Mrs Taylor made everything about *her* when it was Iris who'd been humiliated by Robert yet again.

'So you're saying that I am grieving?' asked Iris.

'I suspect you have lost much in your life, young Iris,' she said.

When Mrs Taylor turned away, that was the end of that and it would take Iris a while to decipher her words. Indeed her immediate understanding of that 'talk' was the alarming realisation that she just might be stuck with Mrs Taylor for forty years just like Mrs Ambers before her!

Mrs Taylor had more to say.

'He hurt us both, you know. My son. Indeed that boy has continually hurt me since the day he was born. His selfishness knows no bounds. Swanning off around the world to places no man of his stature should be and then marrying a woman I had never met. I had no idea of her family or breeding. He just does what he wants without a thought for anyone, much less me.'

She didn't quite know how to respond when Mrs Taylor took her hand.

'What he did to you was wrong and I'm sorry ... I'm sorry with how things turned out.'

Her voice caught in her throat.

'I'm not so heartless, you know. I'm aware that would have been my grandchild and I'm so very sorry for your loss. It seems my son enjoys hurting people.'

'Thank you.' Perhaps it was from that moment that Iris began to notice a glimmer of life, of hope. Or maybe an accumulation of happenings had led her to finally snap out of darkness and accommodate a real possibility of change. She finally understood why she had received the promotion and why indeed Mrs Taylor might have been drawn to her. They had both poured love into a vessel of a selfish man who had no regard for either of them. For Iris, she could also add her father to that list.

Iris now allowed herself to enjoy her job more. She found it easier to handle the responsibility and the temperament of Mrs

Taylor as they now seemed to have a silent understanding of one another.

Like Mrs Ambers before her, Iris mainly relegated the tasks of the house to the staff and spent most of her time with Mrs Taylor. Reg had left rather than 'take orders from a slag' and Iris at last felt comfortable being second in line to Mrs Taylor. After all, it was her dream job even though she'd never really had a dream that did not involve Robert or Gary. She'd simply one day hoped to be a wife and a mother but in the absence of a husband, this job would most certainly do. That was not to say she wouldn't allow a man to take her out, but unlike before, she'd be more selective. Up until now, she hadn't met a man she wanted to spend an hour with let alone an evening with, anyway. Until Gareth.

'I gather you are sweet on one of the boys who works at our neighbours, the Cunninghams,' said Mrs Taylor.

'One of the men, yes,' she corrected. 'I have agreed to go out with Gareth next week, that's all.'

'I hope you are referring to your day off because I need you here at all times.'

'Yes, Mrs Taylor. On my day off,' she said.

'You could do much worse than him.'

It was during moments like these that she was reminded of their difference in status. Mrs Taylor would rather die than introduce her to the sons of one of her rich acquaintances and that was okay. Why shouldn't that be the case? Whites and blacks weren't supposed to mix, just as toffs and the likes of her. It's what made the world work. Her dad used to tell her that.

Losing Robert had confirmed it.

Of course, Iris had no trouble finding men more in keeping with who she was. With her filled-out bosoms and full lips she was an attractive woman apparently and she was still turning men away. But after her countless liaisons of the past, she was keen to attract a man who would want to settle down with her because her yearning for a family had never gone away. Working for Mrs Taylor would never be enough and she longed to be a part of someone's life.

Indeed, Iris needed to see her dad.

'I will be travelling away on my day off.'

'With Gareth again?' replied Mrs Taylor.

'No.'

'Oh well ... Whatever it is you are doing, make sure it doesn't affect you the following day.' Mrs Taylor stood there, always stoic, her hair stiffly styled in a fashion more reminiscent of a woman of the 1950s, not 1967.

'I will be back in time. But you won't be able to get hold of me on the day as I won't be in the area.'

'You make it sound as if I expect you to work on your day off, Iris.'

Mrs Taylor's attempts to brush this off were not convincing. On many occasions she'd been called away from her once-a-month trip to the park or a much-needed sleep-in. She wouldn't have minded as much if the calls were for emergencies, but usually it was just to plump a few pillows or tend to a suddenly 'sick' Mrs Taylor as she lay in her silk-draped four-poster bed, when only hours earlier she had been fine.

Iris didn't care for or own any fancy clothes. Didn't see the need in buying such things when she hardly left the house. A simple blue dress with long lapels and a white waistband that Mrs Taylor had given her during the annual 'throw away perfectly good stuff' day, made her wonder if the war had affected people like Mrs Taylor as it had affected her mum and everyone in her street. The Blitz spirit her mother used to call it. Or maybe she had heard that somewhere else. It was harder and harder these days to remember the conversations she used to have with her mum.

*

Seven years had passed since their last fraught meeting outside Sal's house and Iris had no idea what to expect. She did not welcome the floods of memories as she walked the long road that would lead to that familiar front door. She knocked and waited a moment before peeping through the window. The net curtains looked dusty and she could make out the sideboard besides which she had once seen her mother lying motionless.

'What?' said a voice coming from inside. The footsteps were slow and laboured and she wondered if this was because of drink or age. Or both.

He slowly opened the door.

'Dad?' she said. He hadn't aged as much as she'd imagined. Specks of grey peppered a full beard, his hair was dishevelled, eyes narrowed in suspicion.

He stared at her for a number of seconds. 'Iris,' he said finally.

'How are you, Dad?'

'You'd better come in.'

She'd been in her former home for a full fifteen minutes and her father hadn't said much, just left her in the living room while he made a cup of tea. The decor had remained the same; the pictures on the sideboard and wall untouched, including the one of the young Baker family, much to her relief. She wondered who cleaned for him and kept the place habitable. Her silent questions were answered when she saw a lace scarf strewn across one of the chairs when she walked into the kitchen.

'What's taking so long with the tea? Did you go all the way to China to get it?'

'Learning about tea and China and all that fancy stuff?'

'It's a joke, Dad.'

'You even talk different. And you're dressed up like a dog's dinner!'

They sat in the living room, two cups of tea on the small table that separated them. A new addition.

'How have you been, Dad?'

'Surviving, considering my own kid left me to rot.'

She ignored the comment and placed the hot tea to her lips, her eyes fixed on him.

He spoke. 'What you been up to all these years then? Married, got any kids?'

'Not married and no children.' She swallowed. 'I work in London now. In a posh house.'

'Oh yeah? I suppose that's the modern thing these days. Doing what?'

'I assist a lady with running the house.'

He scrunched his eyebrows. 'What, like a skivvy?'

'I'm not a skivvy.'

'That's exactly what you are. You're a skivvy for some toffee-nosed cow. I ask yer. A kid of mine, a skivvy. That's why you left me!'

'It's better I get paid for being a skivvy than do it here for free.'

He stood up abruptly. 'You what?'

'Dad, I didn't come here to argue.'

'Why are you here then?'

He was stood over her and yet she refused to give into her fear.

She slowly stood up and smoothed down her dress. 'I came here to see if you've changed, but you haven't. Not really.'

'Get out of 'ere then and don't come back!'

'I will. But before I go, I'm taking a few things.'

'You steal from me, and I'll 'ave yer.'

'Yes, I know what you're capable of, Dad.'

The corner of his mouth twitched.

'I'm taking the photo album and that picture of Mum and her family. That's all and then I'll go and, I promise you, you will never see me again.'

Without waiting for an answer she made her way to the side-board and knelt down as she opened the door. Luckily it was still there, the photo album. She scooped the family photo off the sideboard, clutching the precious cargo under her arm.

'These are all I want. Goodbye Dad,' she said. His mouth opened as if he wanted to say something, but she wouldn't be waiting around to hear what that was.

She hadn't planned on leaving with just a few pictures. She had wanted something more from her dad. An apology … or simply to see that he had changed. In the absence of what she had wanted, she accepted what she had got; a handful of photographs and absolutely no family.

Back in her room her eyes blurred with tears as she once again stared at the photo. It was a grainy shot of her grandmother Lillian, standing behind the entire brood with Grandad as a younger man standing proudly beside her. Aunty Marigold was the most obvious to recognise as she was slightly bigger than the others, her hand resting protectively on the shoulder of the youngest, a little boy named Donald, with Flora and her mum holding hands. She envied the closeness they shared, not for the first time wondering what it would have been like to have a sister of her own. Between them, perhaps they could have protected Mum from the onslaughts of their father. Perhaps they could have formed an alliance. Or what if she'd had a brother? Perhaps her father wouldn't have laid a finger on any of them.

She wiped away another tear as she gazed at another page in the photo album. There was Iris dressed in a knitted bonnet, a pretty little thing. Then she turned the page again and noticed the remaining plastic pouches were empty except for a sky-blue knitted bootie lodged inside. She hadn't noticed this before, and was pleased with the knowledge her mother had kept one of her booties. This was the nicest surprise Iris had ever received. She pulled it out of the pouch, holding it close. It was a moment of happiness before she realised with sadness that almost everyone in that picture was gone. She suspected Marigold would live to old age and didn't care if she never saw her again. Then there was Donald who had languished in a home for the feeble- minded or something like that and had been left to fend for himself. She gazed at his army photograph. Uncle Donald was dressed in his uniform and staring forlornly at the camera, unaware of what horrors awaited him. On the back of the photo her mother had written the name of the asylum where he lived.

She took each photo out of its pouch and spread them on her bed, clear as to what her next move was about to be. Donald was the only family she had left and, whether or not he even cared, she needed him. She needed him.

To My Beautiful Twin Daughters,

I am simply a father looking for his girls.

It was on my second day in England that I travelled to see your aunt at an address she had written on the only letter she had ever sent to me.

The letter that changed my life.

I went from feeling an instant relief that she still lived at the same address, to huge disappointment when she said she'd no idea what had become of you both, or who had adopted you. Something in me said she was lying. I told her I hadn't trav-elled thousands of miles for nothing and I needed something. Anything!

'Please, Miss Marigold, please tell me where they are.'

'I said I don't know!'

'They're your nieces, surely you would have wanted to know they went to a good home after Rose passed?'

It didn't take a genius to work out that her interest in you both may have been limited because of who you looked like.

I had to lower my voice and simmer down my emotion. It finally appeared to work because she turned her gaze to the side and spoke.

'*One told me what had happened to her mum that's all. She was being looked after by friends. The other one ... the darker one ...*'

'*Hold on? They visited you?*'

'*That's what I said. It was ages ago now. Back in 1959 and just after I sent you the letter. Funny that.*'

I exhaled. 'Why didn't you give them my address?'

'*What for?*'

I couldn't believe what I was hearing. Still, I kept my voice low. 'What happened to their adoptive parents?'

'*What?' said Marigold.*

'*You said something happened to the mom?*'

'*Oh, yeah, she died! I don't know!*'

Something wasn't adding up.

'*You don't know?*'

'*They're probably in London now,' she said quickly.*

'*My girls came here and you don't know what happened to them?*'

The woman actually looked at her watch. 'They're probably up the West End I suppose. It's always best to try the centre, isn't that where all the youngsters go to make it?'

What I really couldn't work out was why she hadn't told me you'd been in touch with her when you were both fifteen years old. She'd always had my address in the States because I'd sent all those letters and she was quick enough to send me one telling me to back off! Your aunt is truly a hateful woman. I could see it in that kitchen where we stood because she didn't invite me into the main area of the house. I could see it in the way she looked at me, just like the folks at home who passed me by on the white side of town did. I'd seen the same look in the army and during my entire life. I didn't want to think of how she might have looked at you, treated you. I was only grateful that she had not become your caregiver.

But she's my only link with you both. So I waited patiently as she reeled off the little information she had.

I had so many questions that day, like how was the birth? How did Rose die? What was the name of the family who adopted my babies? Marigold was vague with every answer. She had no names for the family who took you in, nor an address.

According to Marigold, you were probably both runaways, because you'd turned up looking for a bed, having lost your adoptive mom. Having turned you away, she said you could be anywhere. Her explanation for this abominable behaviour was 'I didn't have the room'.

Where would I start in my search? England is a big place ... not as big as the States ... but big enough for you both to get lost in. I don't even have any pictures.

'What do they look like?'

'Lily ... Well, she looks a lot like you. She was the second child.'

That was the first time I had heard your name.

'Lily? That's beautiful ...' I wasn't going to shed any tears in front of this woman. I would most certainly store them for later.

I sat down on a wooden chair, wondering if either of you had ever sat down on it before. Wondering how your voices sounded as you pleaded with your selfish aunt for a place to stay. 'And the other one. What's her name?'

'Iris. She looks less like you.'

I knew what she meant. Where I'm from, you're either light or dark. I knew what life would mean for a lighter child and I hoped you, my little Iris, were taking full advantage of that and helping to take good care of your sister Lily. I hope you take care of each other.

She looked relieved as I headed to the door.

'Mr Burrell, I don't need to tell you that what happened to those babies was for the best ... you know ... they're now twenty-one years old, adults. What's the point in dragging up stuff? If you were really interested you could have come earlier, like when I first sent you that letter way back in '59.'

'*I know ...*'

'*I haven't got a clue where they are now. Just be thankful they were taken in. It wasn't easy you know, during wartime and considering ...*'

I knew what she meant and I had to accept that. What I couldn't accept was what she told me next.

'*They ended up with two decent families, as far as I know.*'

'*What? They ... they were separated?*'

Trafalgar Square, Victoria, Paddington ... the list was endless. But I felt charged with a new determination as I raced around to find you. One first and then the other. One would surely lead to the other anyway. I asked around, where do the coloured folks typically live? I was told Brixton or Notting Hill. I went along, but without a picture to show they just thought I was a crazy American wasting their time. Perhaps I was. I had absolutely nothing to go on, just names. And I was exhausted with nothing to show for it.

I went back to Marigold's because I wanted the full names and addresses of the people who took you in. I had taken the 'moved away' explanation without question, because I'd felt overwhelmed with everything. I don't know. But I wanted more now. I needed more to go on. This time, though, Marigold was flanked by two burly guys with blank glares. 'She doesn't have anything more to tell ya,' said one of the goons. I could take them on, I knew that. But I was in another country, a Negro man at that. I couldn't risk being thrown in jail because I couldn't be sure my own country of America would even defend me.

I sat on the bed in a fancy hotel having realised this had to be it. I owed it to Augustine and my son to give them the best of me, not the rest of me. I'd been half a man for too long. I needed to feel who I was again and that would only happen if I closed the door on ever finding you both. This wasn't an easy decision to come to, believe me. If I had to write down my true feelings,

273

*it might summon a storm and I couldn't risk that here in London
and away from my family and those who love me.*

*My last day in London, I headed to a place called Soho. The
lady at the hotel told me it was where all the bars sit. I'd heard a
lot about this place called Ronnie Scott's where the great James
Brown had played. I also wanted to drown out the thought of
never finding you both. I wasn't a drinking man, but I needed
that to change tonight.*

*I walked the crowded streets of Soho with its amazing colours
and watering holes, Union Jack flags hanging out of windows,
the Beatles blasted loud enough for it to be considered a nuisance but just adding to an exotic ambiance. This area made me
wonder if New York was like this. I must have walked around for
hours, ending up at a backstreet bar named after a bird. It was
quieter than I'd imagined. But I guess it was still early. I just
wanted a drink. Or two. I needed to escape my thoughts for a
minute.*

*The beer felt cool in my mouth. It tasted good. 'I'd like
another,' I said to the server. I can't remember how many I had
before I started to feel the hostility building up inside me.*

*It must have been loud because the bar was filling up and
people began looking at me.*

*'Sir, would you like some help getting outside?' said a man.
A black man with a big stomach. I thought that was a strange
question until I realised he was effectively telling me to get out.*

'I'm good, thanks.'

'I'm sorry, we can't serve you any more.'

*As far as I could tell, I wasn't falling all over the place or
being violent. I just didn't understand why I was getting thrown
out.*

'Sir, I would prefer it if you left.'

*'I want to speak to your manager.' My slurred words weak-
ened the importance of my statement.*

'I am the manager.'

'You? Of this place?'

'Yeah, I actually own the place, so if you don't mind,' he said, pointing to the door. Even when they were being rude, the British were so polite.

A coloured owner of a bar named after a pink bird If such crazy things could happen in the world, why couldn't I find my daughters? WHY?

My feet unsteady, I made my way to the door, but not before kicking one of the chairs under a table and it making a racket that sounded worse than it was. Then I stopped. I looked around me, at all those faces blurring into one large and imposing shape. I let out the loudest howl I could manage. Oh what a release! I didn't care that everyone was watching me. I didn't care that the music was low enough for everyone to hear my pain. I needed that release, I needed the pain to be out of my body. I needed to be free of it all. Of everything.

Chapter Twenty-Five

1968

Lily

All around her, dads, mums, siblings, aunties and uncles milled around people dressed in long gowns and oddly shaped hats. She could clearly hear the endless congratulatory words and see the embraces and even tears of joy. For Lily, though, her happiness came with the fact that she was now a graduate. She would special-ise in biochemistry and assist in the development of drugs in the pharmaceutical industry. Yet, sitting on one of the plastic chairs, Lily had never felt more alone. Elated at her achievement but con-fused at its validity because she had absolutely no one to share this moment with. No extended family and with less than a handful of acquaintances who probably hadn't even learned her surname. Joycey had kept in touch via a few scant letters over the years, but Lily would always ignore any invitations to visit because she'd no intention of coming face to face with Uncle Kenneth. Then there was Ron. He would have gladly come along and played the doting 'father', of course, but she had hesitated each time she'd thought of inviting him. Unsure because of her need for independence and worrying whether even just a tiny part of him was like every other man she had met during her twenty-four years of life. Yet, being subjected to the happiness and togetherness of her fellow students gave her a moment of regret. Of course Ron was a good man! Lily had simply allowed her view of men to be shaped by her experiences with Uncle Kenneth, the men at the Shangri La and the countless drunken customers who asked her out at Flamingos. Whatever her suspicions (all unfounded so far), allowing Ron to play the father role for just one day would have been okay. It would have been better than this intense feeling of loneliness.

She spotted a man she'd never seen before. Smartly dressed in his cap and gown, surrounded by family members dressed in elaborate, colourful costumes she suspected were from some part of Africa. Large head wraps and gold-coloured clutch bags twinkling in the light. So different to the outfits she'd been made to wear at the Shangri La, yet there was a connection – Africa. She smiled at the older lady in the group. It wasn't uncommon for her to make eye contact whenever she saw a person with a similar skin tone. It was a silent acknowledgement of their existence in a world where hardly anyone looked like them. An acknowledgement of kinship even though they would never speak to each other.

She couldn't wait for the ceremony to begin and end so that she could leave behind the spectacle of all those happy families. She'd been so preoccupied with study and work, she never allowed herself to be weighed down by the burden of loss. The reality was that she had no family. A GI father who lived who knew where in America. No name, just a figure who had impregnated a woman and left. A nameless mother who at least thought enough of her to leave her in a home yet not enough to face the wrath of her family and society and keep her. Marigold had shown who she was by selling her to a house of ill repute. Sold by her own aunt! Another aunt Rose lay in the ground along with her beloved Mummy Flora and that only left Uncle Donald, who languished in an asylum all alone, just like she was.

It was at that very moment that she knew what she had to do.

Chapter Twenty-Six

Lily

The grounds were well kept and the building looked like a dilapidated stately home. She had gone back and forth with the decision to visit the institution where she had spent her first year, finally deciding that some things were best left in the past. This was where she needed to be, right here and right now.

At a lunatic asylum.

On the reception desk was a telephone and signing-in book. A petite woman in a nurse's uniform approached her.

'May I help you?'

'I'm here to see a resident.'

'Yes of course. Just give me a name and you can sign in the book.'

'My name is Lily Baker.'

'I mean the name of the patient.'

'Donald Baker.'

The nurse scrunched her eyebrows and looked up at her. 'Are you sure?'

Lily nodded her head confidently.

'Oh … I just thought.'

'Is he ...? Is he still alive?' In her haste to reconnect in some way with the only family she had left, Lily hadn't considered the possibility he might have died.

'Donald is Donald,' she said with a smile. 'I'll go and check he's awake.'

With a sense of relief, Lily walked over to the first set of doors, a large window separating her from the room. Inside was a group of patients dressed identically in patterned gowns. Two were engaged in a game of cards; one man was rocking back and forth where he sat. A woman was sat making smiling faces at nobody in particular.

'There you are,' said the nurse with a tap on Lily's shoulder. 'He's awake now and can see you.'

Inside Uncle Donald's ward were rows of beds, some empty. She looked straight ahead, trying her best to ignore the middle-aged woman cradling a dolly in her arms as she hummed, and the elderly lady calling 'Barbara!' every few seconds. She imagined Mummy Flora walking this same route years earlier and this gave her a sense of comfort and belonging, just as she hoped seeing Uncle Donald would. His bed was right at the end of the room and beside a window, which he currently sat facing. She felt oddly grateful he had a window and a view of the grounds. Or perhaps that would just be torture; to be able to see the outside world he had not been a part of for many years.

'Look who we have here, Donald! A visitor. You don't get many of those do you?' said the nurse, drawing the dividing curtains for privacy. There was no reaction from Uncle Donald just as she had expected. Mummy Flora had mentioned his condition on many occasions. The nurse continued anyway. 'A lovely young lady, too.'

Lily made a mental note to ask the nurse about any other visitors later. A long-lost family member could hold the key to more. An extended family that linked straight back to Mummy Flora.

And then she remembered she was not a Baker by blood and that her parents were unknown: a GI soldier and a poor unfortunate woman without the strength to keep her 'brown' baby. Also, according to Mummy Flora, none of the Bakers had approved of the adoption anyway.

'Uncle Donald,' she said. The only part of him to move were his eyelids. The nurse beckoned her to stand in front of him. Uncle Donald was a very slim man, his face elongated by what she suspected was minimal food and not genetics. His eyes remained connected to the window but she noticed they were green just like Mummy Flora's. This warmed her inside, this connection with a man she had never met and judging by his current demeanour had yet to knowledge her presence.

'Donald, there's someone here to see you,' said the nurse in very high-pitched tones. Still, Uncle Donald did not move.

'I'll leave you to it,' said the nurse. 'If you need anything, you let me know. Just ask for Nurse Polly. There's a few of us here but I'm rather fond of Donald and I'm so happy someone has finally come to visit him.'

'Don't you want to know who I am?'

'It doesn't really matter. You're here and that's what counts.'

'The trees are pretty,' said Lily, unsure of what to say to the man who had shared a childhood with Mummy Flora, along with memories he probably could no longer recall. She'd read about siblings having an undeniable bond. Not like twins of course, but a bond nevertheless.

As she went over to sit on the edge of his bed, he suddenly turned his head in her direction.

'Uncle Donald!' she said excitedly and he narrowed his eyes.

'I'm sorry, I didn't mean to startle you!' She wondered what antipsychotic had been given to him. Probably chlorpromazine or the like. Although psychopharmacology was not the area she had wanted to specialise in, Lily was determined to study his notes to gauge a better idea of his treatment plan.

She gently turned his chair around to face her and there was no obvious objection.

'Hello, Uncle Donald. I'm so glad to be here. I'm so happy to see you.' She couldn't help the tear that rolled down her face, the emotion increasing inside of her when he opened his mouth to speak. The words, however, were not quick to materialise.

'Take your time, it's okay,' she said.

'Mmm ...' he said, closing his eyes with concentration. She silently cheered him on; her uncle who possibly didn't speak for days on end was attempting to communicate with her.

'Mmm ...'

'Take your time, Uncle Donald.'

'M ... Marigo-oold,' he said finally.

She closed her eyes with disappointment. 'No, I'm not Marigold. I'm so sorry, Uncle Donald.'

'Mmmm ... Marigo-ooold,' he said again. And then repeatedly as if it were a new word. Later, Lily asked to see his medical chart hoping that by her next visit she'd be able to suggest a better treatment plan. She wanted to feel hopeful that one day she and Uncle Donald would have a conversation because she needed him. She really needed him.

Having another living relative out there in the world whom she visited every month, bought presents for and basically thought about, gave Lily a sense of belonging she hadn't felt since Mummy Flora was alive. This new sense of self armed her as she searched for jobs with the confidence that she would at least get an interview. When she received notification of three interested companies, the nerves began to kick in. The first one, for a lab assistant at a very well-known pharmaceutical company, was just a few miles from where she lived.

Lily walked confidently towards the building dressed in a cream-coloured cotton suit with a bow at the neck and black Mary Jane strappy shoes. Her hair was pulled into a severe bun she hoped was mostly hidden under the pillbox hat, just like the one she had seen on the magnificent Jacqueline Kennedy Onassis in a magazine. She entered through an impressive set of glass doors, her eyes hungrily searching her surroundings, already feeling like she could actually work there. It would be such a change from what she was used to at the bar.

The receptionist smiled as Lily announced she was the two o'clock interview. With fifteen minutes to spare she was told to wait just outside the office where the interview would take place. Two men were already waiting, sitting on chairs, frantically reading the notes they had made. Lily was confident she had swotted enough to get through the interview comfortably. Her paper on determining the structures of biological molecules had received an excellent grade, regardless of whether or not she had seen her lecturer partake in an extramarital meeting at Flamingos one night. They'd never spoken about it but it may or may not have been coincidental when her paper received top marks.

'Lily Baker,' said the receptionist, 'they're ready for you.'

She walked inside where three men sat behind a large table. She opened her mouth to announce her name and leaned in to shake the first set of hands, just as one of the men spoke.

'Sorry, dear, we are conducting interviews in here.'

'Yes, I know, that's why I'm here,' she said.

'The interview for domestic staff is taking place, I believe, on Friday.'

She swallowed. 'I'm here for the—'

'Friday, dear. Now shuffle along.'

'Erm … Okay …' she said, turning on her heel, inside her head screaming with anger and objections, her body wanting to stay put but slowly moving towards the door nevertheless.

'That was quick!' said the receptionist.

'Yes.' She held onto the desk. Mummy Flora's voice in her head. She hadn't heard her voice for so long and maybe if she had done, she wouldn't have run out of the interview like a coward.

'Don't let anyone tell you you're not good enough.'

'Are you all right, miss?'

She moved towards the exit, needing, wanting to get as far away from that building and Mummy Flora's disappointed voice as quickly as possible.

That night on her bed, she pondered the reasons why she had fled. She couldn't really blame the men, but what had been her excuse? Perhaps, deep down, she knew the job would never have been hers, so why waste her time? She gazed at the mirror, her reflection staring back at her.

She had simply wanted to be a biochemist. Yet now, standing on the cusp of realising each and every dream, she'd run.

She would do better next time. She would never give into fear again. She would do better next time.

Unfortunately, Lily failed to perform well enough at the interviews that followed, according to the feedback. Not many jobs came up in the industry and, if they did, she wasn't seeing them. She was grateful when Ron increased her managerial hours at the club, which gave her something to do in the meantime that did not involve drowning in a sea of self-pity. She spent her days looking for work and still visited her uncle once a month. Sometimes she'd bring chocolate for the staff and patients, and at times she would simply read to him. Polly said that while he still never spoke much, he would mention this 'Marigold' from time to time. And this was progress. The bit she enjoyed the most was sitting behind her uncle and running a comb through his thinning hair while Nurse Polly held up a small mirror. Uncle Donald would close his eyes and smile and Lily could only hope his thoughts were good, fun, happy and focused on a time before the war and the shattering of his life. A time where he had three sisters and two parents who loved him. She hoped he was remembering all of that.

'Does he ever say the name "Flora"?'

'I'm not always on shift but it's not something I've heard him say,' said Polly.

As usual, Lily tried to stem her disappointment at Uncle Donald only being able to remember the one person who had probably never visited him. Yet this would never deter her from sticking to the promise to herself to visit her uncle at least once a month. She owed it to him, she owed it to Mummy Flora and she owed it to herself.

Iris

The need to see Uncle Donald intensified each and every day until, finally, she was forced to ask Mrs Taylor for a favour.

'I need to take at least two days off in a row. I wouldn't ask if it wasn't urgent.'

'What could possibly require two days away from the house?'

'I'm travelling out of London.'

'This really isn't appropriate. Who will help me to dress?'

Iris wanted to say, 'How about you pick your own clothes out?' but instead said, 'I can ask one of the girls to help you, Mrs Taylor.'

'Are you visiting with your father again?'

'Sort of.' She didn't feel that comfortable sharing such privacies with Mrs Taylor, but if she had any hope of an early day off, she would have to.

'Actually, I'll be visiting my uncle.'

'Iris, for someone with no family you seem to have acquired a father and uncle overnight.'

'He's very sick and in hospital.'

'Oh, I'm sorry.'

The change in Mrs Taylor's expression was satisfying. There was nothing wrong with extracting some guilt. It wasn't as if she was lying; Uncle Donald was in hospital, just of the mental kind.

'All this reacquainting with your family ... Does this mean you will be leaving me one day soon?'

'This is my home, Mrs Taylor. It has been since I was seventeen years old. I won't be going anywhere. This is probably where I'll die.'

Although the last sentence had been meant as a kind of joke, Mrs Taylor seemed to digest it as a reality she at least was comfortable with.

The large building from the outside looked pleasant enough, flanked as it was by lush greenery and pretty trees. Yet once inside, her nostrils were quickly filled with the smell of bleach and the bleakness that defied the fact it was a sunny day.

'Can I help you?' said the woman behind the front desk.

'I really hope so. I don't even know if he's still here. Donald Baker? Look, I've brought his picture.' She leaned into her bag and brought out the army photograph.

'What a handsome young thing he was in his uniform!'

'So he's here?'

'Yes of course he's here. He doesn't get many visitors so he'll be glad to see you.'

The nurse may have exaggerated how glad Uncle Donald was to see Iris. She had not prepared herself for his complete blankness as he sat in a chair facing the window. Her heart sank; for him and this life and also for herself. She had hoped they could both reminisce about her mum and form some sort of a relationship, but the only word he had spoken since her arrival was 'Marigold'.

'Aren't you lucky? You now have two visitors who come and see you.'

'Who is the other person?' said Iris.

'A young lady, about the same age as you.'

'What's her name?'

'Lily.'

'Another flower! Perhaps we're related. Well, we must be if she comes.'

'Oh, I doubt it.'

285

'Why?'

'Well, she's, you know … a different colour.'

'What? A coloured girl visits my uncle?'

'Yes, do you have a problem with that? She's the only person who has ever bothered with him since I've worked here.'

Iris knew that was a direct dig at her, but that was okay.

'Well, if she comes again, perhaps I'll meet her.'

The nurse moved away in obvious disgust. Iris hadn't meant to sound so abrupt. It had just been a shock. She'd never mixed with anyone who wasn't white before. She had seen a few different coloured people around London but had never spoken to any of them. They were different to her after all. At least in the way they looked. She hadn't a clue of how they talked, ate or even what they thought about, with no interest in finding out. She'd always been taught that people stayed with their own anyway. So to hear that one had been visiting Uncle Donald, well it was just a shock.

'This is Flora and here's Marigold,' she said pointing to the photograph she was so glad to have retrieved from the house. She was also thrilled to notice Uncle Donald's beaming smile as he too pointed to the picture.

'Ma … Ma-arigold,' he said.

'That's right, Marigold. And here's Flora and here's my mum, Rose.'

He turned away, suddenly disinterested. Iris had also exhausted her enthusiasm. She began to wonder just what motivated that girl to come here regularly when there was absolutely no pay-back. She wasn't sure if she herself would even return again.

The day had been a complete disappointment.

Lily

It had been a particularly hard week at Flamingos. A stag party on Friday had left the men's toilet in a state that involved vomit in the sink and a blocked toilet full of turds and a tie! She'd had to facilitate the throwing out of two rather large men on Saturday and, by Sunday, even though things had quietened down, it was still a busy shift. On Monday afternoon she woke up from an uncomfortable sleep, unable to tap into the sense of fresh renewal, which used to grip her at the beginning of every week. Now, after three months of searching for a job and fourteen interviews, she had yet to find a post even though she had the qualifications each one asked for. She'd telephoned a few of the organisations weeks later to find out who had been given the job and, every time, the name was that of a man. A white man, most definitely. It was harder to not blame her sex or the colour of her skin as a factor, unable to decipher which one made the most difference to the interviewers.

Here she was a qualified scientist and still working at Flamingos. It was becoming harder not to just give up on all this 'scientist nonsense' and work at the bar full-time. But on the day she found herself so very close to giving in to Ron's suggestions, she was told she had a call.

The music was loud as usual, even though the bar wasn't open yet. She gestured for the music to be turned down as she headed to the telephone in Ron's office.

'Hello …' she spoke nervously.

'Hello, is this Miss Lily Baker?'

'Yes it is.'

'This is Callahan Pharmaceuticals calling. You recently attended an interview with us.'

Her eyes followed the new barmaid as she balanced two stacks of newly washed glasses in each hand. Lily hoped she wouldn't drop them, as glasses were becoming a huge expense for Flamingos and the profits weren't as good as they once were.

'Hello?' said the voice again.

'Yes, this is she.'

'Good. Well, I'm pleased to say you have passed the interview stage.'

Lily's silence was not intentional; she just had trouble deciphering what this meant.

'Is there a next stage?' she asked.

The laughter from the other end of the line threw her. 'No, Miss Baker. The job is yours if you still want it. An accomplished woman like yourself surely has many options.'

Again, silence, this time because she wasn't used to being referred to as 'accomplished'. Sexy, exotic, yes. Never accomplished and certainly not by someone in an industry she desperately wanted to be a part of.

'No I ... I mean I do ... I certainly want this job.'

'Splendid. We will be sending an offer letter for you to read and sign, and there will also be instructions on what to do next.'

'Okey-dokey.' How she wished she could utter more words, but her mind ... her mind was all jumbled up in disbelief.

'So that leaves me to say, welcome to Callahan Pharmaceuticals!'

When she hung up the phone, she stood staring at it. Ron appeared, a look of concern etched on his face.

'Everything all right?'

'Yes, yes, yes it's amazing, it's brilliant!'

She threw herself into his arms and held onto him tightly, not caring about any fears she'd ever had about him in the past. What she communicated in that hug was a swan song of gratitude and affection. And when she pulled away from him, her smile beamed brightly.

'You're leaving me, aren't ya?' he said.

'I'm sorry, Ron, although I'm not sorry, if you know what I mean.'

'I do. We both knew this day would come.'

After signing and dating the offer letter, she hand delivered it to Callahan Pharmaceuticals. Lily's induction would last a week, after which she would be dispatched into a real-life laboratory shadowing a colleague named Giles.

As she began drafting a letter of resignation for Flamingos, it was hard to write the words due to the excitement fizzing inside her. This new job had come at the right time and Lily felt in every crevice of her body that her life was about to start again.

She was headed in a whole new direction and she was ready. She was ready for it all!

Six months later, Lily was fully ensconced in her role. As her uniform consisted mainly of a white lab coat she didn't have to think about her appearance as much as when she worked at the club. Sometimes, she missed wearing the boots and stylish hats purchased on Portobello Road, but even when writing up her notes outside the lab, she'd often just stick to bland colours and A-line skirts, keen not to stand out in any other way.

When she was approached to contribute on a biochemical research paper, she was both flattered and terrified.

'This would be a real study?'

'I wasn't aware we conducted counterfeit studies, Miss Baker,' said Giles.

She could have kicked herself for saying something so idiotic. The significance of having her name on a study would propel her even further up the ladder than she had anticipated this soon and the respect this would afford her in the pharmaceutical industry would be huge. This was the big break she had been waiting for and it had occurred in less than a year.

'Your work here is not going unnoticed. You will do an excellent job, of that I am sure.'

That night she celebrated with a glass of wine in her flat. She lay back on her bed and thought of Uncle Donald. As promised, she had visited him monthly, but had been unable to do so the previous month. She hated missing visits but the demands of work had taken over. Now with the study, she would be even busier.

During the next visit, Polly was on shift.

'I think he really missed you last month,' she said as they headed to Uncle Donald's room.

A sting of guilt caught her unexpectedly.

'We can see it in his communication or lack of. It's not always about speech. He was a little bit manic last week and he hasn't been that way for a long time. Not since the doctors changed his medication after you made such a big fuss.

'They all think he isn't "all there" but Donald is there somewhere. He knows you come some time towards the end of the month and he was expecting you.'

'I feel really bad about not coming.'

'Never mind. He had another visitor anyway.'

They stopped just as they reached the door. 'Who?'

'No idea. A woman.'

'Did they say who they were?' Her heart was beating faster than usual.

'I can look in the book for you.'

'Please, please do.'

'I have to see to a patient right now but when you're ready to leave, come and find me.'

As Lily headed towards Uncle Donald's chair, as usual set in front of the window, she couldn't contain her excitement. Someone had come to visit him. A possible family member! She could only hope it wasn't Marigold, visiting after an attack of conscience. She hoped instead for a long-lost relative who knew Mummy Flora. Someone who wouldn't reject her like the family had many years ago.

Staring down at Uncle Donald, she had imagined his greeting would be more animated in light of what Polly had said. But, as usual, his eyes merely looked up as she pulled over a chair and sat beside him. She wasn't sure, but she may have glimpsed a hint of smile. It was quick, almost straight, but a distortion of the expression she had become used to.

After the visit, Lily stood by the reception desk as Polly leafed through the signing-in book.

'Here we go. It was a Tuesday because I was on half day.' She pushed the book closer to Lily, pointing at her name.

'Miss I. Baker? A relative? Oh my! Did she leave an address? Does she have a phone number?'

'Nothing.'

'What did she look like?'

'About your height and masses of curly hair. As I said, I was finishing my shift.'

'Can you get more out of her next time?'

'If there is a next time ... and that's not really our policy. You're noted as next of kin now so we don't really ask anything from anyone.'

She had to think fast. 'What if you call me at work as soon as she comes again?'

'If she comes again. She may also come when I'm not on my shift.'

'I don't know what to do, Polly!'

'Best to let it go, Lily. Just be pleased he had another visitor.'

Lily could not let this go, because there was a feeling deep inside that told her this visitor was more than a distant relative. She was significant to her life in some way. This might just be wishful thinking as Mummy Flora liked to say and simply not based on fact. Lily was a scientist after all and she liked to deal in facts. But there was something bigger at play here and she was determined to find out what that was. How, she'd no idea, she just had to find a way.

Iris

The visit with Donald still weighed heavily on Iris's thoughts. The image of this once vibrant young man as seen in the photo was so at odds with what she'd discovered at the asylum. And he was her only living relative, apart from Marigold who she couldn't even describe as a human being. She knew it was wrong to think such a thing about a man, but it was true. He was unable to acknowledge her or even himself. It had been a pointless visit. She thought, not for the first time, about visiting Marigold. Perhaps the years had mellowed her a bit, but she doubted it. Yet her desperation to connect with someone, anyone, from her family, remained.

'You've been preoccupied for weeks now. What's wrong with you?' asked Mrs Taylor, as they went over the menu for next week's dinner party. The Bentons, old friends of the family, were invited and Mrs Taylor was keen to impress.

'I'm fine, Mrs Taylor. Now do you prefer the tomatoes we had at the last dinner? The cherry sized?'

'There is definitely something amiss. Ever since you returned from that trip to your uncle.'

'It didn't go according to plan.'

'You are happy here, aren't you, Iris?'

Now she was irritated because, as usual, Mrs Taylor was unable to be a confidante without turning the subject back to her.

'I don't want you running away to be with some relative that hasn't bothered with you in years!'

'I still need a job,' sighed Iris. She pulled the sheet of paper close, her forehead wrinkling as she put pen to paper.

'You really do have the worst handwriting and spelling. Perhaps, I could pay for a tutor to teach you the basics? You know … If it was something you wanted … We're not talking university here, just an improvement in English perhaps.'

The thought of learning mildly excited her but she knew that accepting Mrs Taylor's offer would come with a price. So, Iris wasn't about to accept it right now.

Indeed, she would love to learn more than the alphabet, maybe even read a book or two. Learn more words than her current vocabulary allowed. She'd already learned a lot just by being around Mrs Taylor and her toffee-nosed friends but she didn't really see the point in education – especially as a woman. She was much more interested in settling down, anyway. Becoming a wife and mother. Perhaps even right the wrongs of her past and do a better job than her own parents. Gareth was a bit dull, but had enough cash at the end of the month to take her to nice places like the pictures and even a restaurant, which had a rose on each table. And at least being with him meant she was that much closer to having what she needed.

As they walked along the embankment that evening, the night air skimming her face, she knew he was about to ask her something.

'I'm really falling for you, Iris. I've never had a girl like you on my arm before.'

'What do you mean by a girl like me?'

'Beautiful, of course!'

She exhaled.

'I'd say I'm falling in love. With you. No actually, I'm already in love.'

They stopped. 'Really?' she said.

'You're the best girl I've ever met.'

It felt better to ignore the 'love' part of the conversation and focus on something else. 'Who said I was your girl?' She smiled.

'Well, you're not knocking about with anyone else … and I'm not.'

'I'm not. No.'

'So …?'

'I'm just teasing you. Of course I'm your girl.' They continued to walk.

'Phew! That's a relief!' he said, mock-wiping the sweat from his forehead. It didn't really matter that Gareth did not set her tummy alight with desire, he was a good man. Quiet and not some Flash Harry like some of the barrow boys she'd met. Gareth was also everything her dad wasn't and would more than likely make a good husband. He earned just enough to get her away from lodging with Mrs Taylor, although she wasn't about to completely give up work any time soon. She needed the financial freedom her mother never had just in case Gareth ever turned into something all men had the potential to be.

Iris would never be like her mum.

Lily

'I'm getting married!' said Polly, wiggling her fingers, the beautiful gold ring shining against her skin.

'Congratulations, Polly!' She knew that was the required response in such circumstances but had never really experienced for herself the pent-up excitement women seemed to feel when confronted with a piece of metal wrapped around someone's finger! At work, the secretaries were forever cooing over some piece of jewellery as she smiled warmly hoping they didn't see the truth in her eyes – that she just wasn't that interested!

'This means I'll finally be leaving this place,' said Polly.

'Why would you leave your job?'

'I'm getting wed, silly!'

Leaving the job because of a marriage still made no sense to Lily.

'Don't be so shocked. I guessed you were one of those radical types, like in America!'

'The civil rights movement as in Dr Martin Luther King?'

'No, the women who are making all that noise about women's rights this, women's rights that!'

'Oh right … Yes of course,' she mumbled. How strange to be thought of as radical just for wanting to work. But however much they differed in their opinions, Lily knew that the asylum was losing the only member of staff who acted as if she cared for the patients and the only one who could help her find out who Uncle Donald's mystery visitor was.

'I am genuinely happy for you, Polly, and I'm going to miss you, that's all.'

'I've always been very fond off you too ... So don't take this the wrong way.'

Lily was aware of what the next sentence would be.

'Get yourself a young man. We weren't meant to be alone, you know. Old Donald here can't be the only friend you have.'

'I do have friends,' she protested, thinking about her work colleagues such as Giles and a handful of secretaries who sometimes said hello in the toilets. Love and marriage had just never been a goal for her, eclipsed by the need to succeed and at least be taken seriously. Hence her energies were tied up elsewhere. But this didn't stop her from wanting someone to confide in other than a mute Uncle Donald or the TV that echoed in her empty flat as soon as she came in from work. She was almost certain she would never marry and had no family apart from Uncle Donald, so this was it for Lily.

Luckily, she also had the fight.

The fight to be taken seriously as a black and female biochemist. The fight to be seen as an equal in a profession she loved.

She needed this fight because, without it, she had nothing.

Lily hadn't realised just how disengaged and uninterested the rest of the staff at the asylum were towards Uncle Donald until Polly left. She had been a smokescreen and her absence merely highlighted everything that was wrong with where and how her uncle spent his days. He was left alone for the majority of the day apart from mealtimes and the medicine round. Even though she was incredibly busy what with the new study, Lily began to visit twice a month because of Polly's absence, and indeed because she hoped to run into the mystery visitor.

On the day of Uncle Donald's birthday, Lily arrived with a birthday cake, a card and a present.

'Happy Birthday, Uncle Donald!' She raised her voice this time and he responded with a raising of his eyebrows. Any response was celebrated and had only been obvious since the reduction in his medication. She was aware that most members of the staff saw her as a meddling nuisance but that was okay. If she could help Uncle Donald in some way, then it was worth it. She just wished she could also help the other residents.

'Soon, you'll be able to wear this when we go out!' she said, carefully unwrapping the woolly scarf from the decorated wrapping paper. She placed the scarf into his hands, and his stare moved away from the window.

'The new nurse, the horrible one, said she'll serve your birthday cake at dinnertime, then everyone gets a piece.'

Lily placed the birthday card onto the window ledge, so at least he would see it every day. It stood proudly under the glare of the sun as an idea hit her.

She ran to reception, returning with a pen.

'I don't know why I didn't think of this before!' she said, gleefully. Inside the card, she scrawled a message.

If you visit Donald, please give me a call on the number below. I would love to hear from you!

She placed the card back onto the window ledge wishing she'd made it sound more urgent – because it was. She only hoped that this mystery visitor called Miss I. Baker would pick up the card and call, and they could visit Uncle Donald together. As much as she loved him, it wasn't as if he gave scintillating conversation! She was confident that whoever was visiting her uncle would pick up the card and call her. All she had to do was be patient.

Almost three months had passed since Uncle Donald's birthday and according to Sharon on the reception desk, no one had called. Lily had become so obsessed with hearing back from this I. Baker that she had almost missed an important piece of information.

'Sorry, can you repeat that?' she said to Thomas, one of the other biochemists she worked with. Thomas had attended Oxford and wore tanned brogues that were always shiny. He also earned almost a third more than she did.

They had simply been standing in the kitchen, taking about the recent pay rises and how in line it was with inflation – or not – when Thomas had inadvertently reeled off his salary. He'd also added gleefully that he didn't 'bloody well need the money anyway, but it's the principle', which only left Lily even more angry.

Twenty minutes later she was sitting in front of the head of personnel.

'You really need to speak to Mr Simmonds, he makes the final salary decisions,' she said, her face red with worry.

'I bet if we looked at the records, we'd see the women earn less than the men here for doing the same job. Oh, hang on … There aren't any other women working in the labs are there? Just me!'

'Miss Baker—'

'I want a meeting with Mr Simmonds now. I demand one.'

'He's in a meeting—'

'Room Three?'

'Why, yes—'

Lily almost leapt off her chair as a worried voice trailed behind her. 'Miss Baker, please.'

Lily burst into Room Three where four identical-looking men sat around the table, two of whom were smoking.

'Miss Baker, can it wait?' said Mr Simmonds.

'No, not really. It is a matter of urgency.'

He reluctantly stood up from his chair and followed her out of the room where an ever apologetic secretary shrugged her shoulders.

In a small side room, Lily leaned over the desk.

'It has come to my attention that I am getting paid less than at least one man here. I suspect there are more.'

'If you are referring to Thomas—'

'I am.'

'He is an Oxford graduate.'

'I have the same degree, regardless of where I studied, which incidentally was also a good university here in London.'

'It doesn't work like that and you know it. You are not stupid. In fact you are very intelligent.'

She ignored his condescending tone. 'I would just like to be paid the same as Thomas. We do almost the same work … I'd even go as far as to say I work harder as I'm never out of the lab before seven o'clock and I'm also working on the study. I do all this because I want to. I am not expecting extra pay for that, I just want the same pay as Thomas.'

He lowered his voice. 'Miss Baker, you are in an incredibly privileged position here.'

'I don't feel very privileged.'

'You work for a prestigious pharmaceutical company.'

'Which I achieved on my own merits. Top of the class in all my subjects—' She stopped as she noticed the blank expression on his face. As usual, she'd no idea whether this situation had to do with being the 'wrong' sex, colour or having gone to the wrong school. Whichever way, each of these traits were a part of her and she'd no choice but to fight the prejudices they caused.

'Miss Baker, you have been given a chance to be a research student on a study after less than a year at this establishment. To jeopardise your position by say … leaving would be foolish and career-altering. It is not something one would advise. It is not easy to find work in this field. As you know.'

She exhaled. He was right. If she could stay a few more years and widen her curriculum vitae, she'd never have to put up with such inequality again.

For the rest of the day, Lily found it hard to look at herself in the mirror. It was hard to stomach that she had not won that particular fight but her silence meant she could at least still win the war.

Chapter Twenty-Seven

Iris

This non-talking was a drag. She smiled to herself at the term she had heard Americans use in films. Iris was back with Donald because, in some small way, she'd missed him. Yet, once again, she quickly felt robbed of such feeling just minutes into their encounter because whichever way she looked at it, visiting him was a waste of her time. Even that nice nurse Polly had gone, and the other members of staff didn't seem to care if anyone but themselves were alive or dead. She was simply stuck with Donald for the rest of the visit.

She went to pull the photo album out of her bag anyway, her eyes immediately catching sight of the birthday card on the window ledge. She hadn't realised it was his birthday. What was the point anyway? She wondered why the staff would even give him a birthday card.

She knelt by his side, suddenly injected with a fresh determination. 'I'm not giving up on you, Donald. I need you, do you hear? I need you.'

She opened up the photo album. 'This is you!'

His face remained locked, gazing out the window. She tugged at the army photo, pulling it out of the security of the album sleeve. 'Look, it's you! Look!'

She was being forceful but she didn't care. Either he would look at the picture or the staff would run in and drag her out of the facility. She was willing to take that risk. She placed the photo to his face, his eyes widening.

'Look!' She placed it on his lap and his eyes followed. 'That's you. In your army uniform. Do you remember?'

He gazed at the picture, 'MMMM ... Marigold,' he said very quietly as if he wasn't even sure any more.

'It's you, Donald, a proud member of the British army. You fought for this country. You're a hero.'

He opened his mouth to speak, but nothing came out. She longed to hear something more from him before realising that the memories of army life might be too upsetting and she might just have set him back years.

He turned his gaze away, mumbling words she could not decipher. She closed her eyes in defeat and opened them to reveal Donald, once again staring towards the window, this time a single tear rolling down his cheek.

Lily

She hadn't planned on visiting Uncle Donald that day, but she needed to tell someone about how badly she'd been treated by Callahan's. Polly would produce a cup of pop and they'd commiserate together. Then she remembered that Polly no longer worked at the asylum. As much as she loved confiding in Uncle Donald, she'd really like a reaction or at least a nod of agreement.

She considered turning back.

Iris

As for Iris, the day had already been a revelation. That tiny hint of emotion was more than she could have hoped for from Donald.

She hadn't wanted to upset him, of course, but that tear …
this had to mean her uncle was 'in there' somewhere. Perhaps
listening, taking in his surroundings or he had simply given up.
She wished that nice nurse Polly was around. The staff needed to
help him more. She knew nothing about medicines or madness,
but she knew that Donald needed more than he was getting. He
was now asleep in his bed, perhaps overwhelmed by the earlier emotion. Iris felt helpless and sad. So incredibly sad. She
absently picked up the birthday card as her mind scrambled over
what to do next to help her uncle.

Lily

Sharon at reception yawned loudly as Lily made the familiar trip
to Uncle Donald's room. She knew what to expect; her uncle
asleep or 'awake' staring at the window. A recent food stain on
his gown or perhaps some on his chin, which she would wipe
away gently. When she opened the door to the ward and walked
to the end of the room, what she saw was a beautiful young
woman with very curly hair standing by the window, with Uncle
Donald's birthday card in her hand.

The woman placed the card to one side as she faced Lily.
'Hello?'

'I'm Lily.'

'The card?'

'Yes, I put my name and number there so you could get in
touch.' She moved closer and noticed Uncle Donald snoring.

'Who are you?' asked this young woman.

Lily waved both of her hands as if in surrender. There was
something explicitly mistrusting, almost angry about this woman
and she wanted her to be at ease. She wanted to be able to protect
her in some way. 'I'm just Lily.'

'Why have you been visiting my uncle?'

'Your uncle?'

'That's what I said.'

'Same reason you have.'

'I doubt it.' The woman moved her eyes up and down Lily's face and body. 'I'm his family.'

'So am I. Sort of.'

'That's impossible.'

Lily's eyes shot to the photo album and alighted on the photo poking out of it. 'Is this yours?'

'Yes.'

She picked up the album, a striking army photo of a young Uncle Donald staring back at her. 'It's a good idea to show him photos; it could stimulate cognitive function.'

'I don't even know what you're on about with your fancy words. I'd just like to know who you are.'

Lily leafed through the album and a larger photo fell out.

She swallowed as she appraised the familiar Baker family photo. 'I have this exact same photograph.'

Lily sat on the edge of the bed, aware that something amazing was just about to happen.

Iris

Iris wasn't sure who this girl thought she was but she hated how familiar she appeared to be around Donald. And now this nonsense about the picture.

'Why would you have a photograph of my family?' asked Iris, feeling and sounding rather irritated.

'Because that little girl holding the hand of Aunty Rose is my Mummy Flora.'

None of this was making any sense to Iris and for a moment she wondered if this woman had simply escaped from one of the other wards. She had never spoken to such a person before ...

one with that skin tone ... and she'd no desire to continue with this particular conversation.

Lily

That afternoon, neither of them could know if Uncle Donald was listening or not, but the words were so revelatory, so outlandish that even Lily couldn't believe any of it.

At first.

'So you're telling me that that Aunty Flora took you in and adopted you.'

'Yes.'

'But why?'

Lily was trying so hard to like this girl and not take offence at her many insinuations and obvious prejudice. Besides, she'd come across worse in her life and it went to prove just what Mummy Flora had been up against by adopting a child from the home for brown babies.

'Why would she adopt me, you mean?'

'Well, you're ...'

'She adopted me because, in her own words, I was the prettiest little girl she had ever seen.'

That seemed to shut this Iris Baker up for a moment as Lily sat on the other end of the bed. A moment of silence that felt like a lifetime.

'So do you speak French?' asked Iris.

'No, why do you ask?'

'I know a bit about the colonies. I have a friend who visited a lot of them.'

'I have never been outside England. I was born in England somewhere and I have a white mum ... somewhere and a black dad in America.'

'So we're not really related. Not really.'

'I said I was adopted.'

Iris grabbed hold of Uncle Donald's hands protectively, startling him awake. 'He is my family. Not you. I don't even know what you hope to get out of all this.'

'Fine.' Lily would be lying if she wasn't disappointed. A long-lost cousin was better than nothing, even a prejudiced one. 'Well, I'm here to visit Uncle Donald as I have done for a while now. So, you can stay or leave, it's really up to you.'

'I'll stay thanks,' spat Iris.

'Fine.'

She was just a frightened little girl, thought Lily. Ordinarily she wouldn't waste her time on trying to befriend someone like her, but she needed to do this and so much more. This was more than just about feeling alone and not having any family … something inside of her felt drawn to this woman, as if their lives were connected in some way. Of course they were, due to the Mummy Flora and Aunty Rose link, but there was something more she just couldn't place.

Something she had never felt before was pulling at her emotions and begging her to draw closer and closer to this girl called Iris Baker.

Iris

If ever there was a time for Donald to break out of this shell shock, now was it. Because sitting in his room in total silence with this girl felt a little too much. One minute Iris felt no real interest in getting to know her, the next her mind began reasoning that she was indeed the only 'family' apart from Donald that she had. She would have preferred a blood relation but maybe some adoption papers would at least help. Yet what did that matter? She and this girl were different in every single way. Too different. Yet, despite these facts, the only person other than Gareth who cared about her was possibly Mrs Taylor, who was in danger of eating her whole if she didn't establish some sort of life for herself. So maybe, just maybe, this Lily could help her do that at least.

'Do you want to flick through the rest of the album?' Iris asked.

'Yes please!' Lily replied, a little too eagerly.

Lily sat beside her on the edge of Donald's bed and together they talked through every single photograph. In the second to last page, when they got to the last picture of a baby Iris, she fell silent.

'Are you okay?' asked Lily, as if reading her thoughts.

'It's sad that's all. That Aunty Flora and my mum stopped speaking round about the time I was born.'

'I wonder what happened.'

'I used to think it was something to do with my father.'

'Mummy Flora said he wasn't a nice man.'

Iris turned away. As much as she disliked her father at that moment, this stranger had no right bad-mouthing him in any way. 'It's for no one to judge what went on. Nobody's business.'

'I didn't mean to offend you.'

Iris snapped the photo album shut, her distrust returning.

She was just about to leave to get some fresh air when Donald opened his mouth to speak. 'MMMM ... Marigold,' he said, louder than she had ever heard him.

The two women looked towards one another, both unsure, questioning.

Chapter Twenty-Eight

Lily

Lily desperately wanted to place her hand on Iris's wrist in a show of support but the girl was as stiff as a board. Her readiness to divulge even the smallest detail about her life was painstakingly minute but both had managed to agree on just how odious Marigold had been to both of them. Yet she was the only link to a path that involved both their mothers and, for that reason, they would have to visit her at least one last time.

Iris was quick to agree and they immediately set off on the journey. The bus ride was mostly spent talking about Lily's work at the pharmaceutical company and academic achievements. It may have sounded like boasting, but really, Lily couldn't think of anything to talk about that wouldn't require Iris to recount painful memories about Aunty Rose, Iris's mother. She knew they had to be painful because she could sense the pain in Iris whenever she mentioned her mum.

There was a flood of unwelcome memories for Lily as they approached the house. The worst of which had to be sleeping on the cold, mouse-infested floor of Marigold's kitchen, or perhaps the fear of living under the shadow of an aunt she could see despised her. Finding out she had been sold to Mickey Roux at the Shangri La had to be one of the worst moments of her life after losing Mummy Flora, but she would have to place that to one side today.

They were here for answers.

'I'm not sure I can do this,' said Lily as they stood yards from Marigold's front door. 'I'm not sure I can go in there!'

'What did she do?'

Iris hadn't been the only one not forthcoming with information.

'You said she'd give us some answers about the past and that we could get her to visit Donald and that she might be the breakthrough he needs. And us ... this is for us too, Lily. You said so!'

This was the first time Iris had referred to them both as an 'us'. It was silly really, she was only her cousin and not even a blood relative at that, but the word 'us' allowed Lily to relax.

'Panic over?' asked Iris.

'Panic over.'

It was Lily who knocked on the door and a short man with greasy hair opened it.

'Yeah?' he said.

'We're here to see Marigold,' said Lily as the man eyed her suspiciously.

'Are you Aunt Marigold's eldest? John, right?' said Iris, stepping forward. 'It's me, Iris! Aunty Rose's kid.'

'Really? Bloody 'ell, It's been a while. Yeah, I'm John.'

As he scooped a rather stiff Iris into his arms, Lily felt a prick of unexplained jealousy. Surely he'd known who she was too, considering he'd stepped over her a number of times as she lay on the kitchen floor. She shouldn't have cared really, considering he was as awful as his mother.

'We've come to see Marigold,' said Iris.

'Oh right. I suppose you 'eard then.' The previous light in his face quickly dimmed.

'Heard what?' asked Lily, yet his face and words remained fixed on Iris.

'Mum's sick.'

'We hadn't heard,' said Iris.

'It's really bad ... I'll let 'er explain.'

He led them into the house and a host of memories came back for Lily, none of them good. Her body tensed and when they walked into the bedroom she was instantly transported back nine years, to her mother gaunt and thin in her own bed and barely able to sit up.

Lily remained opposite the foot of the bed, staring blankly at the woman who had almost destroyed her life. She wanted to unleash the fury she knew was inside, yet all she could feel ... was pity.

'Thank you for coming. I don't deserve it,' Marigold's voice was hoarse and devoid of the strength that had once frightened Lily to the very core.

Lily would have preferred the evil Aunt Marigold and not this weakened version. The once imposingly large woman was now reduced to half her size, wisps of hair on a head once full of a healthy mane. The top half of her frail body propped up against a mountain of pillows made her look not unlike Mummy Flora during her last days. The room was grey with a slight odour of bleach. When John opened the curtains for some much needed light, the clearer sight of Marigold was shocking. This was not the woman she had fantasised about one day confronting.

'Not the way I'd planned to lose all that weight but oh well!' Marigold said.

'Do you remember our names?' asked Iris.

'Yes, I know who you both are. Iris and Lily in that order.'

Both women looked towards one another with confusion. John offered his mother a drink, which she waved away.

'It was always going to happen. Secrets can't stay secrets for ever,' she said.

Iris

Iris felt cheated. She'd wanted to release a tirade of abuse at Marigold for abandoning her mum and thus contributing to her early death on the floor like an animal. She had also abandoned Iris. Not caring about her enough to check if she was all right and then rejecting her years later when she came for help.

Instead she sat on the chair beside the bed, as Lily remained standing at the foot. Marigold was not as they had expected, but this didn't explain Lily's rigidity and the blank look on her face. Iris hoped she was all right, yet didn't have the space in her own heart to really care. What Lily was thinking or did was of no concern to Iris, for she had her own questions. Indeed if Flora was alive Iris would have unleashed her anger onto her too. But all she had was this very sickly woman.

Yes, Iris felt cheated.

'You're so lovely. A lovely young girl. What are you now, twenty-five?' said Marigold, in between coughs Iris felt were exaggerated.

'Twenty-four,' she replied dismissively.

'You still have all that curly hair!'

'Marigold, we haven't spoken in years—'

'That's my fault. I know that. I have done wrong to so many people. Not least of all you two. It's time I put things right before I go. Will you let me?'

'What did you mean by "secrets"?'

Her eyes flickered shut just as her son reappeared. 'Mum, it's time for your kip now. Iris, can you come back later? She's had a really long day,' he said.

She looked towards Lily who didn't appear to have moved since they'd arrived.

'Come back tomorrow or something.'

They moved to the sitting room, Iris's eyes searching for any traces of her mum. She immediately clocked the one family photograph that existed of them all.

'We'll come back tomorrow,' said Iris as Lily followed silently behind. This wasn't the confident scientist she had begun to get to know on the bus over. The bragging little princess who had lived a rather good life from what she heard.

'Or you can stay here if you like?' said John.

'I should stay with Lily.' It was clear the invitation had not extended to her cousin and Iris for some reason felt it only right she stay with her.

Inside the room at the B&B were two beds.

'I think I'm going to travel back to London,' said Lily.

'Why would you leave now?'

'For one, I'm tired of the way I'm looked at … like I'm an animal or something.'

'Don't worry about John, he's an idiot. And Marigold was nice enough to you.'

'So I'm supposed to be grateful?'

'Not what I said.'

Iris could sense her anger was about much more than that.

'The bed's comfy enough and it's only for one night. Marigold's clearly on her way out and she's the only person alive who can tell us what truly went on with our mums. Now I for one want to know even if you don't.'

'Our mums?'

'Flora was your mum, wasn't she?'

Lily's smile told Iris she was winning her over.

'Close your eyes and get some kip!' said Iris.

'I need my things, like my special soap and a wrap for my head.'

'Do you think you're a movie star or something?'

'My hair is different to yours and I need to wrap it up before I can go to sleep.'

Iris began to see red. Who did this girl think she was? 'I knew you had airs and graces but all this fuss you're making ...'

'How dare you tell me I have airs and graces? Just because someone wants to better themselves doesn't mean they are trying to be something they're not. That should just be normal.'

Iris would try to stem the anger forming. She would count to ten, anything. She was not like her dad.

But Lily wasn't about to shut up. 'You don't realise how much easier you have it, Iris. Even the landlady here looked relieved when she realised we'd come together. People either don't want to acknowledge I exist or they're just rude about it. You weren't even sure about me, were you?'

'You don't know what you're talking about. '

'Yes I do, we both do. You're just as racist as the rest of them.'

'I'm not a racialist.'

'Racist, the term is racist!'

'You see, correcting my English now!'

'Yes, I am because it obviously needs correcting!'

Iris should have knocked her lights out at that very moment, and if it had been anyone else, she would have. But there was something stopping her; tiredness or simply a need to have someone in her corner. Because in the morning when Marigold finally revealed whatever 'secrets' she knew about her mum, she would need it. So Iris exhaled a multitude of times, threw herself back onto the bed and closed her eyes. If Lily wanted to argue with herself, then she would leave her to it.

Lily

The following morning, Lily was blurry-eyed and her mind a haze of fog. Sleep had been difficult to come by as her head raced with thoughts. She'd been robbed of the chance to show Marigold what a success she had become despite all she'd done to prevent it. A bedridden, ailing woman wasn't what she'd expected and there would be no joy in showing off about her accomplishments because the woman was clearly dying.

Lily ran her hand through her hair, which overnight had turned into a hard mass of tight coils, and would now be unmanageable until she got home and applied grease and gave it a thorough combing.

Marigold's house seemed less familiar the following day. The curtains were already opened, with Marigold being fed a porridge-like substance, her face lighting up when she saw them.

'Sorry about yesterday I get pretty tired around six-ish,' she said.

'That's okay,' said Iris, sitting on a chair beside the bed. Another chair on the other side had appeared since yesterday and Lily thought it right she sit on it. John greeted Iris and ignored her. She no longer cared.

'That's better. The two of you together again. After all these years,' said Marigold, clearly delirious. It was doubtful they would get much out of her today.

'When you're on your deathbed, it gives you time ... So much time to look at all the shit you've done. And I've done my fair share.'

Iris cleared her throat, the expectation on her face palpable.

'The worst thing I did was keep the secret for twenty-four years. But it ends now.' The fit of coughs could not have come at a worse time. John pulled out a handkerchief, placing it under Marigold's chin.

She cleared her throat loudly.

'She panicked, said her old man would kill her if he found out. Having it off with a coloured man back then wasn't good and if you were married, even worse.' She turned to Iris. 'It wasn't as if your dad was in the war, lazy bastard, but it was still adultery.'

'What are you on about?' asked Iris.

'Your mum got with a black man and conceived a child.'

'What? No way. You're wrong in the head.' She stood up abruptly.

'Her,' said Marigold, pointing to Lily. At first Lily believed someone was standing behind her but in her heart she knew. She knew that Marigold was pointing at her.

'You're lying!' screamed Iris in a way that meant Marigold's next words needed to be louder and more forceful.

'That's enough, Mum,' said John.

'They used to meet every chance they got. In the summer of 1943 the GIs came strutting their stuff. No one could resist really. What a time. Anyway, eight months after he left, boom – Lily was born.'

'We're both twenty-four so that proves you're lying,' said Iris, as Lily's mind went blank, unable to decipher the knowledge that she was Aunty Rose's child. Rose who'd had an affair with an American.

'Both you and Lily are the same age.'

'How is tha—?'

'Check your birth dates. You'll find they are the same.'

Both girls looked at one another.

'You're twins!'

The room fell silent.

'Rose had you both. One white, one black.'

'This is bonkers!' said Iris before launching into a bout of insane-sounding laughter.

'If I hadn't seen it with my own eyes I never would have believed it,' said Marigold.

Iris stood up and began pacing the floor, her body shaking slightly. This wasn't supposed to happen. What was happening?

She looked closely at Lily, unable to get past the darker skin, the slightly broader nose. There was no way they were related in that way because that would make her that name Robert had called her ... Mulatto ... Mixed.

'Isn't this the worst load of old tosh you've ever heard?' said Iris, wanting, needing, some solidarity in this absurd situation.

'Maybe something like this is possible,' said Lily.

'You are off your head if you think that.'

'I'm a scientist. The most impossible things are sometimes ... possible.'

'The blue bootie,' said Marigold. 'The blue bootie, do you still have it?'

Both girls answered. 'Yes.'

'Rose knitted them ... She thought she was expecting only one child. Hoped it was a boy ... I remember Flora took one. I wasn't sure why. I'd all but forgotten about it till I saw it in your stuff, Lily, when you showed up here nine years ago.'

Lily closed her eyes, refusing to remember the circumstances of her stay, overwhelmed by the current news. Trying to digest it all and knowing deep in her heart that it was true. Iris was her twin sister; she had felt it the very first time she had heard about her visits to Uncle Donald. Her feelings growing the more time they had spent together. She had a twin sister. All this time she hadn't been alone.

'I have ... the other, the ... one,' said Iris absently. 'It was in the last page of the photo album.'

Iris's body shook with emotion, as she thought about the bootie safely tucked away in her room. Her stomach swishing violently with the knowledge that this could be true. Her mother had given birth to another child on the very same day as she was born. To Lily. Now she wanted to scream, she wanted to tear someone's hair out, punch the wall, as Marigold continued to reel off the circumstances of her birth and her life. When Marigold spoke of a near miss, a chance meeting when they were both fifteen, she'd had enough. 'I can't deal with this,' she said, heading towards the door. Only when she was outside, was she able to breathe deeply. This was too much, all too much.

She jumped at the sensation of a hand on her shoulder, fighting the instinct to turn around slap her 'assailant'. It was Lily. Her eyes red.

'Are you okay?'

'What do you think?'

'Marigold has been filling me in but I think you need to hear it too, Iris.'

'I can't. I need to go away for a very long time before I can go back in there.'

'She may not have that long, Iris.'

'I have work in the morning. I can't get in late. Mrs Taylor will be expecting me.'

'This is an emergency.'

'What is?' She sounded confused and, maybe, she was.

'It's not every day you find out you have a twin sister, is it?'

Lily

Marigold's eyelids flickered. 'There's one last thing I have to give you. I know you want to go home, but you mustn't leave yet.'

Lily wanted to hate her and display the same range of emotions as Iris. She had a lot to hate her for and she'd forgotten none of it. Perhaps Marigold's cruellest act was to prevent both sisters from meeting one another on that fateful day. To know she had sat in a cold and lonely toilet outside as her twin sister stood inside Marigold's house. To know that Marigold could have reunited them at that moment ... Oh, she should be overcome with feelings of complete and utter rage. And perhaps deep inside these feelings all existed. For now, though, she would continue to be a calm presence as Marigold pieced together the fragments of their lives.

Sometimes it was hard. Especially when Marigold could offer absolutely no explanation apart from plain vindictiveness for not letting each twin know about the other.

'I couldn't tell your father anything when he came looking three years ago because I didn't know where you both were. But not letting you both know about each other when you were fifteen ... No excuses. To this day I don't know why I did that. Maybe I just hated everyone – even myself.'

In that moment, Lily had almost faltered. She'd almost joined Iris – her sister – in letting loose the ball of rage she could see fighting its way throughout her body. The thought of one single human being dictating the directions of their lives almost too much to bear. Marigold was not a human, but an evil, evil person. A witch even and Lily wasn't sure she could stay in the same room as her any more. Her patience ebbing with each microsecond.

As if right on time, another bag had appeared, this time bulging with what looked to be paper. Letters. Lily picked up the bag as the first of many envelopes fell to the floor.

Iris bent to pick some up. 'They're addressed to my mum.'

'At this address. Postmark America.' Lily knew who they were from before Marigold had even finished the sentence.

'They're from your father, Mr William Burrell.'

It had been the most overwhelming of days and revelations.

The startling realisation that Marigold had actually sent a letter to William Burrell just before she and then Iris had appeared on her doorstep brought on a wave of revulsion at the pointlessness of Marigold's evil. Lily did not want to think about what could have been. Not yet. There was just too much to decipher in her cluttered brain; too much to collate for her shattered heart.

Luckily the room at the B&B was again available for the night but both sisters had no intention of sleeping. Each sat in their own pregnant silence as they opened up each letter one by one and absorbed the precious written words from their father. Not even Iris's awkwardly pronounced words as she read out loud could disturb the enormity of this moment. His address was at the top of many of the letters, that much she had noticed after peeping inside a few. Lily actually had an address.

For her father.

Their father. The news that she was not only related by blood to Mummy Flora and Uncle Donald was almost completely over-shadowed by the fact that she would soon find her real father and that just a few inches away from her at that very moment was her twin sister, Iris. She was a twin! All these years of feeling alone when she had spent eight months in a womb with another person.

Iris.

A beautiful, yet angry young woman with long, sprawling curls. Who probably couldn't think of anything worse than hav-ing a twin sister like her. And yet for Lily, it had been the best news of her entire life.

'This doesn't make any sense,' said Iris, her shoulders slumped over as she sat on the edge of the bed. She looked small and vulnerable.

'Is that because you can't imagine your … mum being unfaithful to your dad?'

Iris shrugged her shoulders. 'I couldn't blame her. My father was a brute and treated her like she was nothing. I just couldn't imagine her with a—'

'A coloured man?'

Iris placed her hands onto her cheeks and exhaled. 'This is so confusing. I don't know what to feel, how to think.'

'According to these letters he really loved her, our dad. Here, take a look at this if you don't believe me!'

'No, I don't want to read it.'

'You will one day though, right?'

She shrugged her shoulders again and Lily had to remind her-self that Iris probably couldn't read very well.

'I still can't believe this is happening. Nothing in my life makes any bloody sense any more!' screamed Iris, throwing herself on the bed and turning her back to Lily. 'I didn't ask for this. I didn't ask for any of this. How can you be so calm?'

That's okay, Lily thought, she needs time. They all just needed time.

The thing about time is, it's the one thing we're all running out of. The minute we are born we are already dying. I know that doesn't sound very light-hearted, but I'm actually in a good mood as I write this. There is something about being free from restraint because, girls, I have felt like a trapped man my entire life. The constraints of society and what it thought I should be versus what I wanted to be. Even my own father made me feel that way because he did not allow me to be the man I always imagined I should be. So, for once I am making the decision for my life and my own self. I have decided to accept that I will never see you and in doing that have also decided to stop writing to you.

It's taken me a while to come to this decision and wasn't something which came to me overnight. But today as the sun shines over the porch on the farm that now has my name on the deeds, I know it's what I have to do. Clyde, my son, is about to be married. He will embark on his own family and maybe one day give me grandkids. Me and Augustine are going into our late middle age and we enjoy the simple things in life like tending to the trees, trimming the bushes and marvelling at just how pretty the Georgian sun can be. I'm not inhuman enough to not think about you every day, but in my heart you'll have to stay. I can't put my life on hold by thinking that I have to find you but I'm going to have to trust that the lives you have lived are the best lives you could ever have. I have to believe that the fact you don't know anything about me means that you can never miss what you have never had.

So this is the last letter I will be writing to you, my darlings, and like the rest I'm going to keep this letter hidden away somewhere in this house, so that when I am plagued by second thoughts, I will simply read it and reread it.

Goodbye, my twin babies.

Chapter Twenty-Nine

It was like she'd been waiting for this moment her entire life, another section of the puzzle that represented her person, finally coming together piece by glorious piece. Just like the set of sky-blue booties that were reunited after many painful years apart.

She understood that for Iris, it wouldn't be a smooth ride.

Even though many weeks had passed, she was still taking Marigold's revelations hard. Although Lily was the younger of the two, she had vowed to protect Iris as much as possible, as well as be there for her whenever she felt ready to fully accept Lily into her life.

For Lily, she had to sometimes pinch herself to believe she actually had a twin sister. Someone who looked nothing much like her yet shared some similar characteristics, like the way she looked up to the ceiling when deep in thought; those almond-shaped eyes that everyone used to comment about. Apart from their first eight months spent in the same womb they had spent a good few weeks together in the same bed as they lay in the arms of their mother, Rose. She in no way blamed Mummy Flora for the part she played in this deception. Indeed she could not have loved her more for what she had done. Even now in the late 1960s, times were difficult for many black people and she could only imagine what it must have been like for them in the 1940s.

Mummy Flora had made a huge sacrifice and for that she would always love her.

Lily's days off from Callahan's were now spent getting to know her sister. Sometimes they would visit Uncle Donald and take it in turns to push him about in the new wheelchair they had both bought him as a gift. He still didn't say much, but the nurses had commented on catching a smile or two on his face. As Lily's expertise in the field of pharmaceuticals grew, so would her knowledge of whatever was out there that could possibly help her uncle. She would stay abreast of cutting-edge research and perhaps one day be a part of it, determined that Uncle Donald would one day be cured.

Trips to the park were no longer spent alone. Lily was now regularly joined by her sister, who also loved sitting in the park. They would talk about anything, with Lily careful to leave out anything academic as she'd learned that Iris wasn't keen on 'all that science lark'. One day though, she couldn't resist surprising Iris with a thrilling discovery.

'There's actually a flower called the Twinflower!'

'Really?'

Lily couldn't be sure if Iris's tone was of indifference or boredom.

'Yes, a biologist called Carl Linnaeus he—' Her sister began to stifle a yawn. 'Well, it's a flower called a Twinflower and I thought that as our dad is called William ... that's a flower too! We can be a family of plants, just like Mummy Flora and Aunty Rose were!' The mention of Rose's name allowed a rare smile to appear on Iris's face and this filled Lily with absolute joy. It was as if a void had been waiting to be filled by her; as if Lily had been waiting for Iris her entire life.

For Iris, she knew that, eventually, she'd be where Lily was emotionally.

She just needed time.

Now whenever they met up, whether it be in the park or a pub, Lily would bring along one of William Burrell's letters written to their mother.

After painfully admitting she wasn't 'that good' at reading, Lily now read them to Iris. Pronouncing each word clearly and slowly and never making her feel stupid. Listening to Lily read, it was easy to imagine how in love they must have been and this made her feel a little bit better. Grateful that her mother had experienced true love before she died. She even sometimes thought of Gareth when Lily read, knowing that he too was the one for her, and the man she would one day marry.

Lily insisted on telephoning Iris at least once a day, much to Mrs Taylor's annoyance. If anything, her boss's seemingly unin-terested reaction to the whole life-changing event had further convinced Iris it would be better to move out of the big house. Mrs Taylor was distraught of course and insisted her headaches had increased, but Iris needed the freedom of living away from where she worked.

Lily had asked her to move in with her, but she'd refused. Not because she wasn't tempted, but because she needed to find out who she was before she could live with her sister. She needed to truly know who Iris Baker was supposed to be and she was still learning, as bit by bit the puzzles from the past were pieced together – and the biggest piece so far was in the shape of a pretty black girl who wore beads in her hair. She would soon realise that a twin like Lily was the greatest gift her mother had ever given her. But before she could fully acknowledge that, she would continue to stand stiffly beside her when all she wanted to do was hold her hand and sink into her embrace. She would also avoid some of her phone calls just to put some 'space' between them, when really she loved the sound of her sister's voice.

She would eventually get better at this twin thing though, she was confident of that.

For now she had to grapple with the knowledge that everything she had been brought up to believe about herself, her parentage and even her colour, had been questioned and then shattered.

She just needed time.

Now that her time of the month was late, she felt most certainly that she was pregnant for the second time in her life. Yet, Iris couldn't be certain what colour the child would turn out. What if it came out like Lily? Over the past few weeks, Lily had done some research at work and found out that such occurrences were not an impossibility. Of course, as Gareth was white, it was unlikely to happen with this baby she was expecting. Either way, she would never do what her mother had because Iris had longed for a baby ever since she had lost the first one and she would make sure it felt loved and cared for, whatever its colour. She was certain Aunty Lily would make sure of that!

Even though Iris woke up most days confused as to who she actually was, three possibilities hung in the air; she would soon become a wife, hopefully a mother and she was Lily Baker's twin sister. One half of a Twinflower and they would always be part of one another. These facts alone caused her to feel a hint of the happiness she had not felt in a very long time.

Six years later – 1974

She placed her hand inside her sister's palm, glad she'd worn a summer dress and sandals as the heat felt stifling and greater than she could ever have imagined. Her hair was plaited into thin strands, which framed her face, red and white beads at the end of each one. The large trees hanging with Spanish moss were just as beautiful as she'd imagined. Her father, the man who had sired her, William, had described the land perfectly through the letters he had written. She smiled at Iris, herself locked in her own thoughts, her face painted with a thoughtful smile, her curly mane pushed into a high bun to beat the heat.

'You all right?'

'Not really … Missing my little one. I've never been this far away from her before.'

'Rosie will be fine. Gareth's wonderful with her.'

'It's not really a man's place, is it?'

'Who says?' Once again, Lily was reminded of how different they were and not just in looks.

'Are you ready?' asked Lily as they approached the house.

'As ready as I'll ever be. And don't act as if you're not nervous, this is big, this is huge!'

Her sister knew her too well. The façade that often allowed her to play tough at work just to get through the day with a bunch of men was not fooling Iris. At times she was still that little girl brought up by a loving mother who thought it best to protect her from all the world's ills. Even travelling all the way to America, to Savannah, Georgia, would have been frightening enough were it not for the company of her twin sister. As long as she had her, Lily would forever feel safe.

They moved closer to the house, walking by the multicoloured sets of flowers in full bloom, wondering what exotic names they possessed, marvelling at the huge trees. She wondered what it would have been like to dance around these trees and play in this huge yard. Would there have been siblings? Of course, of what she knew about this area back then, perhaps even now, their life would have been far from idyllic. How would their mother have fitted into such a life? Indeed, would Rose and William been able to live like man and wife if their love was deemed illegal?

The three of them had a lot to talk about.

Lily and Iris reached the strangely shaped wooden house with an old rocking chair outside. Iris sat on it, her body swinging back and forth playfully.

'So are you going to ring the bell or just stand there?' she said.

Lily needed a little more time because inside that house was their father. Not Sidney Poitier, as she'd once thought, but her father, an American GI who had stolen the heart of their mother and had loved her so much, he had written a number of beautifully detailed love letters that never swayed from the love he had felt for her. That was real love. They had been conceived in love.

Her hand hovered over the doorbell just as the door squeaked open.

Iris stopped swinging. There he was, standing there like an aberration. Tall and proud, wisps of grey around a thick beard and almond-shaped eyes that reminded Lily of the handsomeness that must have captivated their mother all those years ago. When he placed the walking stick to one side, he opened his arms out to her and she no longer felt like a thirty-year-old woman, but a little girl who had longed to feel this her entire life. To feel a part of something, anything that would fill the void that had been growing for longer than she could remember.

'My baby girls!' he said as Lily sank into his embrace. His arms were strong and firm around her. Iris stood from the rocking chair and William Burrell instantly opened his arms to receive her too. She slowly walked into the fold, sinking her face into his chest; twin daughters finally in the arms of their dad. Their closed eyelids clouded into black and the only sound they could hear was that of the trees, their leaves scrambling for freedom in the sight of a midday breeze.

For Lily, this felt like a dream. Instead of walking, she was gliding into the house with Iris following behind her.

'This is Clyde, your big brother,' said William. The man stepped forward, bashful. 'He's not used to so many woman in one room!'

'Stop that, Dad!' he said playfully. 'It's so nice to meet you.' He proffered his hand and Lily felt the roughness of his skin. He worked the land, she could tell.

As if Lily were the first twin to be born, Iris followed her in everything she did and remained speechless for the most part.

A short and slightly plump lady appeared.

'This here is Augustine—'

'Augustine Jewson from the letters! Hello!' said Lily. She'd always imagined her stepmother as taller somehow – as William had written of her as someone with so much strength.

Lily put out her hand and Augustine shrugged it away, instead launching herself into Lily's startled embrace and then Iris's stiff effort.

'I am so pleased to have some daughters around here. My, am I pleased!'

Even Iris managed to laugh at that.

'When we bring Rosie, there'll be even more!'

'I can't wait to meet her. Those pictures you sent ... Beautiful!'

William stood beside his wife, his eyes surveying each twin as if they were the most beautiful of masterpieces.

'The letters were lovely ... the ones you sent to our mother,' said Lily. 'We've read every single one.'

'That's good to know because I have a lot more for you to read. The ones I wrote when I found out about my two beautiful twin daughters.'

'Really?' asked Iris.

'We have a lot to talk about. Thirty years' worth of life to catch up on. For now, though, we must eat. You can't come to a southern home and not eat!'

'Wait till you taste my ham hock!' said Augustine.

'My wife's cooking is the best, but don't ever tell my mama!'

Lily swallowed. 'Is your mum here, too?'

'Yes, my mama is right here, still living and don't let her hear you say otherwise. She's been waiting on you. Come through.'

William led his daughters through another door and there she was sitting on a chair and looking up to the ceiling. She reminded Lily of what someone with royal blood would look like. Her hair was plaited into two rows, her light brown skin barely lined and looking like that of a woman much younger.

'Come, girls, come here so I can look at you,' she said.

The regal air made sense once Lily was up close. This woman, according to William's letters, was of good standing and class and these traits still lingered in her being. At well over ninety years old, she sat in her old, weathered chair as if it were a throne.

'My grandbabies ...' she said, as a tear slid down her cheek. Lily bent to her knees and held onto her grandmother's hand.

'Never thought I would live to see the day. Oh thank you, Lord.'

Lily didn't actually know what to say and if she did speak would have found it hard as a lump rested in her throat.

'And you, little lady, oh my ...' She looked up to Iris, standing over them both.

'You look so much like her.'

'Who? Who do I look like?' asked Iris.

'You look so much like my mother's mother, it's uncanny. She looked just like you.'

'But I'm—'

'Almost white, yes I know. Let's just say we got a lot of educating for you. You probably don't know much about what the slave masters did to the women they owned.'

'I don't ...'

'You don't need to right now, baby. Just let me take a better look at you.'

Iris knelt down on the other side and their grandmother's face lifted even further. 'You sure are Anna Mae, oh you are.' As the older woman began to weep with tears of joy, so did Iris, but for different reasons. To be told she looked like any part of this family would not have made sense without the grandmother's admission. As if sensing this shift, Lily, with her remaining hand, held onto Iris as the three women, united in blood, cried for three very different reasons.

Epilogue

My Dearest Rose,

You were the love of my life.

When we met that summer in Alderberry I had no idea you would also give me two more loves that would change and shape me as a man, our two little flower girls Lily and Iris.

Our two daughters are exceptional human beings. They have been through so much hardship and loss and yet both have come out in a way that would make you proud. They have added so much to my life as well as those around me, like Mama who even in her old age never thought she would see such a thing in her lifetime. My son Clyde loves his new sisters and Augustine accepts them like they are her own, if that sweet potato pie she made them is anything to go by!

They may live in England but we talk every week on the telephone and my letters are frequent. Rose, you know what I'm like with writing letters and I make sure I write one once a week to my girls whether they like it or not! Lily is very good at writing me back but Iris, not so much. I think she takes after her mom that way!

I never thought that life had the possibility to get better, but it does every single day and I owe it all to that chance meeting in 1943, when I saw that beautiful girl in a beautiful flowered dress look my way. That one glance changed my heart and my life forever.

I Will Always Love You, Rose Baker.

Until we meet again,

William

Acknowledgements

I'd like to thank God for everything; Judith Murdoch and Gillian Green for always adding that extra sparkle to the manuscript; Aunty Florence W. Makanjuola and my dad Mr Olawanle O. Fasehun – beloved elders of the family who continue to impart such wisdom; and Theo Olusegun Dare for being my beloved a beautiful light during the early writing process.

I must also thank – Mrs Sheila Graham, no longer here, but a huge part of this book – from the colloquial 1940s language to the wartime dishes she continued to prepare during my childhood (with better ingredients!). This book is partly inspired by a very moving story she told me many years ago. And one I promised to tell. It is my sincere wish that she and all who pick up this book enjoy my take on this particular slice of a very important history.